****

Advance to Contact:
1980

Soviet Endgame—Book One
****

By Alex Aaronson and James Rosone

****

Published in conjunction with Front Line Publishing, Inc.

Copyright Notice

Disclaimer: Although the story is based on events that could have happened in the world, the story is entirely fictional and should be treated as such.

ISBN: 978-1-957634-61-6
Sun City Center, Florida, United States of America
Library of Congress Control Number: 2022917764

Table of Contents

Dedication

To Lacey, whose tolerance of me, like the grace of God, is unearned and a total mystery.

Special thanks to Commander George "Bud" Biery (USN Ret), CWO4 Dave "Caveman" Murray (USMC Ret) and Brian Lasagna.

Chapter 1

4 November 1979
US Embassy
Tehran, Iran

The worst day of Howard Chandler's life started out pleasantly enough. The young Foreign Service Officer, or FSO, got into the office early and read yesterday's *Washington Post*. He then took his coffee over to Eddie Cain's office. Cain was a Miami Dolphins fan, and Chandler needed to make sure he understood how badly his Oilers were going to beat them this coming Monday.

"Knock, knock," said Chandler as he peeked into Cain's office.

"Hey, Howard, come on in," replied Cain.

"You looking forward to reading all about the Dolphins' inevitable implosion?"

"No way, pal. Our defense is stacked. It's the second coming of the no-name defense."

"Bah, whatever," replied Chandler. "I'll see your immovable object and raise you the irresistible force that is the Oilers' run game." There were few things in life that Howard Chandler believed in as much as he believed in running back Earl Campbell. The two had crossed paths at the University of Texas, where Chandler was getting his master's degree in international relations and Campbell was playing halfback for the Longhorns.

"How're you settling in? Tehran can be a bit of a culture shock as an initial assignment," said Cain.

"It's not bad," replied Chandler. "It's a lot cooler here than I expected."

"Don't get used to it," laughed Cain. "You'll have plenty to complain about when it's a hundred and one out come July."

"On the upside," said Chandler, "it can't be as swampy as a Houston summer."

"Amen to that, and there's no chance of a hurricane."

Chandler looked over to a bookcase next to Cain's desk and saw a framed photo of the man with his wife and son, who looked about three.

“I’ve been meaning to ask you,” said Chandler, “how do you and Irene make it work? I mean, I always assumed that if I started a family, I’d bring them with me.”

“For most postings, Irene and Danny would be right here with me. But with things as crazy as they are with this Islamic Revolution, we’re just playing it safe. I’m not going to lie to you, though. It’s been a rough go. She’s with her parents in Virginia, and Danny loves spending so much time with his grandparents. But it’s lonely. You never notice how much you depend on someone until they’re no longer around.”

“Man, that sounds pretty rough,” agreed Chandler. “I guess I don’t have anything to worry about for a while. I don’t even have a girl back home. I’m a total free agent.”

“Hah, I’ve seen this movie before,” said Cain. “You’re about two months from meeting the woman of your dreams out there.” He gestured towards the city outside his window. “This town is full of smart and beautiful women.”

“Hey, pal, you’re a married man,” joked Chandler.

“Yeah, I’m married, I’m not blind,” replied Cain. “Anyhow, what does Henderson have you doing today?”

“Just monkey work,” said Chandler. “Mostly entering visa applications into the new computer system.”

“Ah, yes. Just what you were hoping for when you signed up, I’m sure.”

“Eh, someone’s gotta do it," said Chandler, "might as well be me. And, hey, at least I can’t really screw it up.”

“That’s a good attitude, keep it up.”

Chandler left the office and headed off to his post at the computer. The embassy had recently installed a new computer system, which would streamline the application process and help the State Department flag suspicious or rejected applications. There was a considerable backlog, so he really needed to get a start on the day. On his way up to the computer room on the second floor of the Chancery building, he looked out a window and could see protestors milling about along the fence line.

On his way upstairs, he ran into Paul Myers, the station’s regional security officer, or RSO.

“Hey, Paul, looks like the protests are starting out early today,” said Chandler.

"Yeah," replied Myers, "the Ayatollah has declared today National Students' Day to commemorate some kids that were killed by the Shah's secret police last year."

"Are we doing anything special about it?" asked Chandler.

"There was some talk about closing the embassy, but Mr. Laingen decided against it." Bruce Laingen was the chargé d'affaires—the officer in charge of the embassy in the absence of an ambassador. "Don't sweat it, but stay alert. You never know when things can get sticky around here."

"They don't call it a 'hardship posting' for nothing," said Chandler with a grin. It was unsettling to have so many people so angry at you. It didn't help that they were just outside the walls of the compound. Chandler wasn't too concerned, though. The embassy had been "captured" just nine months earlier, on Valentine's Day. It had taken about three hours for the regional government to get control over the crowds. It was a frightening event, but in the end, there was only one man taken hostage and the affair was more or less over within a week's time.

Chandler spent the next few hours peacefully entering data into the computer. Around ten o'clock, he decided it was time for a break. He headed down to the break room on the first floor to grab some coffee. As he stood there watching the cream swirl in the blackness, he heard a shout.

"Hey, they're coming over the walls!"

Chandler looked out the window, but he couldn't see anything from here. To get a better look, he crossed to the other side of the building, the south-facing side where the main entrance was, and looked out the office window.

"Holy shit," he said. There were at least half a dozen men wearing face coverings in various stages of climbing the wrought-iron barriers that surrounded the embassy grounds. He walked down the hallway to the main entrance. There he again ran into Paul Myers, who raised his radio.

"This is a recall," said Myers. "I need all Marines to the primary post."

"Paul," said Chandler, "what do I do?"

"Get up to the second floor and wait for instructions." Both men started up the stairs.

"Is there anything I can help with?" asked Chandler.

"How's your Farsi?" asked Myers.

"Passible—I spent my junior year at Ferdowsi University in Mashhad as part of the Georgetown exchange in seventy-five."

"All right, stick with me and translate," said Myers. "But try to stay out of the way. The Marines and I will handle any action." After a second, he added, "Oh, and stay away from the windows." The two men headed to the communication vault, where they were met by several of Myers's Marines.

"Listen up, Marines. We've been through this before. We're going to get through to the authorities and we'll get them to settle these students down. Remember the rules of engagement. We can't shoot anybody, but they don't know that. So we're going to arm up to convince them that we mean business. And no tear gas on the campus, but if anyone gets in the building, we'll gas 'em."

Myers was interrupted by a shout. "They're coming in through the basement windows!"

Without hesitating, Myers said, "Quinn, round everyone up and get them to the vault. Roberts and Murphy, get down to the basement and put a lid on this thing." With his orders given, Myers picked up the phone and started dialing.

His first call was to Bruce Laingen. Laingen was over at the Iranian Foreign Ministry and not on the embassy grounds. Chandler listened as Myers filled him in on the situation, and could hear Laingen reiterating that there would be no shooting of the protestors.

Myers hung up the phone and made a second call. From the sound of it, this call was to local law enforcement. Myers was trying to explain the urgency of the situation, but it sounded to Chandler like he wasn't getting anywhere. After a few minutes, Myers slammed the receiver down.

"Dammit, this is bullshit," said Myers. "Let's get to the basement before this gets any more out of hand."

They quickly descended the stairs two at a time, getting to the basement within a minute. Once there, Chandler could sense that the scene was about to turn south.

There were several Marines holding shotguns and shouting at the intruders. One of the Marines racked his shotgun, and there was a gasp among the students.

"Hold it!" said Myers. "Let's get everyone calmed down a notch." He scanned the crowd, trying to find someone who looked like they were running things. "Chandler, find out who's in charge here."

"Who is responsible here?" asked Chandler in Farsi.

"I am," replied a young, bearded man, also in Farsi. "We do not want to harm you. We simply want to make a declaration."

Chandler turned to Myers. "He says they just want to make a statement and that they don't want to hurt us."

"I see," replied Myers. "Tell him that they can't do that here. We need them to clear out of here. We are prepared to defend this area. Everyone needs to go back out through the windows."

Chandler translated. The men looked at the Marine guards and the shotguns they held. With an air of resignation, they departed through the windows they had originally broken and climbed through.

Myers's radio crackled to life. "Boss, we've got more trouble," said one of the Marines.

"What is it?" asked the RSO.

"They're on the roof. You'd better get up here."

"Look," said Myers, "we need to fall back to the second floor. We're going to cede the low ground to these creeps."

"Roger that, sir," replied one of the sergeants. Both Marines followed Myers and Chandler up the two flights of stairs to the second floor. Once they made it there, they could hear the students stomping on the roof. A Marine guard approached Myers.

"I just chucked a canister of CS gas in each of the heads and secured the doors with rope. But they're going to get in for sure if we don't get some relief soon." The sounds of windows breaking filled the corridor.

"OK," said Myers, "let's fall back to the vault."

"Paul," said Liz Swift, the Chief of the Political Section and the senior official on site, "we need to destroy these guns." She pointed at the shotguns the two Marines from the basement were carrying. Myers hesitated. "If we're going to be overrun, the guns are going to cause more harm than good. Mr. Laingen was clear that there was to be no shooting."

"You heard the lady," replied Myers, "break 'em down." The Marines hurriedly broke down the shotguns and set the component parts aside. "I need everyone in the vault, and keep the shredders and incinerator going. We need to clear as much of this material as we can." As the staff kept up the document destruction, Chandler heard the unmistakable sounds of the crowd bursting into the lower floor of the building.

"I'm going to go calm them down," said Myers. "Mike, I could really use your help," he continued, looking at Michael Metrinko, one of the best Farsi speakers on the staff. "No offense, kid," he told Chandler, "but I want the big guns for this." The two men left and closed the door behind them.

****

Howard Chandler had never been so afraid in his life. Eddie Cain came over to Chandler. "You know," said Cain, "we get paid the same rate during times of international crisis." Chandler recognized the use of humor under stress. It was a tactic he often used.

"The real crisis for you," replied Chandler, "is going to be when Earl Campbell runs for a buck fifty on your fish tomorrow."

"Keep thinking that, buddy," said Cain. "Campbell's good, but that defensive line is going to bottle him up and sell him." Before they could continue, they heard shouting from the other side of the door.

"That doesn't sound like it's going well," said one of the Marines. Then there was the sound of a single gunshot, followed by silence. After what seemed like an eternity, there was a pounding on the door. From the other side of the door came the call.

"It's me, Mike," said Metrinko. "They've killed Paul. They're going to kill me next, and they're threatening to burn down the building. I guess they know our playbook too well." All eyes in the vault shifted to Chief Swift.

"Open the door," she said without flinching. The Marine nearest the door unlatched the lock and turned the handle. The door flew open as the Iranians on the other side pushed it in. One of the Iranians yelled at them in Farsi. Metrinko translated for him.

"He says for everyone to get on your knees." The man pointed at the Marine nearest him and said something to Metrinko. "OK… if he points at one of you, you need to come out into the hall." The Marine went first, followed by another. The man was working his way through from the front of the vault to the back. Chandler lost count of how many had been brought out before it was his turn. When pointed at, he dutifully went out into the hall.

He was surrounded by armed and angry men. They pointed their guns at him and shoved him to his knees. Once he was on the ground, they bound his hands behind his back with a strip of fabric, then took a second piece of fabric and wrapped it around his eyes, blinding him. Now helpless, he was kicked in the back and fell over on his side. There was shouting and laughter. Someone yanked him to his feet and roughly dragged him down the hall. He was disoriented from the ordeal, but he was fairly sure that they took him to the room in the southeast corner of the building. He couldn't remember whose office this was. His handler shoved him into a chair and bound him to it. He then heard the chilling sound of a semiautomatic pistol being charged. He felt the barrel against his head.

"*Marg bar Amrika!*" shouted a voice. Chandler's heart stopped as he waited for death.

Click. The laughter of several men told Chandler that he wasn't going to die just yet.

Chapter 2

4 November 1979
Situation Room, White House
Washington, D.C.

"How exactly did this come to pass?"

President Jimmy Carter's question was reasonable enough, and it was a question that everyone in the room knew was coming. But knowing that a question was inevitable and having a satisfactory answer are two very different things. There was a lengthy pause as the President looked around the Situation Room. Before him had gathered his national security team. Opposite Carter was Harold Brown, the Defense Secretary. To Brown's left was CIA chief Stansfield Turner. To his right sat General David C. Jones, the Chairman of the Joint Chiefs of Staff. Sitting next to Carter were Secretary of State Cyrus Vance to his left, and National Security Advisor Zbigniew Brzezinski to his right.

It had been two hours since the first reports of students storming the US embassy in Tehran had come in, and so far all the incoming news was bad.

"Mr. President," said Secretary Vance, "as you know, the situation in Iran has been tenuous for the past several years. Right now they are on the verge of civil war. We have been working to intervene. However, we're in a very precarious position here. The Ayatollah and his allies have rallied their people by blaming Western greed and anti-Islamic influence for all the suffering of the Persian people. Our attempts to mediate as we did between Egypt and Israel at Camp David last year have stalled because of the perception that we're biased in favor of the Shah. Frankly, it's by the grace of God that things haven't devolved into open fighting in the streets. The refusal of the Shah to relent is pushing this to the breaking point. His Prime Minister, Shapour Bakhtiar, is pushing to break up the SAVAK—"

"Excuse me," interrupted the President, "the what?"

"Sorry, sir, the Shah's secret police. They're the force that has been persecuting the revolutionary movement. The Shah refuses to rein them in. In fact, the Shah seems in denial about what's happening in the streets outside his palace."

President Carter thought back to January, ten months before. The Shah had been ready to flee Iran and let Bakhtiar take over the government. However, his agents had told him of the Ayatollah Ruhollah Khomeini's plans to make a triumphant return to Tehran as soon as the Shah had fled. The thought of not only losing the country but losing it to Khomeini had been too much for him. Instead, the Shah had barricaded himself in his central palace and commanded the government and military from an increasingly isolated position.

"To be honest, Mr. President," continued Vance, "given the situation on the ground, we should be thankful that things haven't collapsed into total civil war. I think that our diplomatic restraint is all that has kept this from—"

Dr. Brzezinski broke in: "Are you suggesting that this is somehow a foreign policy victory… something we should be proud of?" As much as everyone had known Carter's opening question was obvious, so too did everyone understand that Brzezinski and Vance would have a fight about it. President Carter knew better than anyone, and though he knew he couldn't prevent it (in fact, he relied upon the conflict between their two philosophies to provide him with the right path forward for his administration), he sought to at least delay the fight.

"Gentlemen, we need to cut through the nonsense. To do that, I need to understand what happened. Once I'm satisfied that we have that, I'll leave you to work on the solution."

"As you say, Mr. President. Mr. Vance, please... continue." Brzezinski may as well have told Vance to roll over and beg. It was clear that he was exerting his control over the room. There was a power struggle within the administration over foreign policy. These past few months had shifted the balance of power in favor of the National Security Advisor and away from the Secretary of State.

"Right… so… as I was saying, the Ayatollah has done a fair job of boxing us out of talks by labeling us a biased negotiator. This has been effective at preventing us from supporting the Shah as robustly as we would like. Our overt support of the Shah and specifically our sending in a team of doctors to treat the Shah's leukemia and gallstones last month is being cited as evidence against us."

Carter sighed. "We never should have sent those doctors. If Kissinger hadn't held SALT hostage, we wouldn't be here now."

Earlier in the year, the former Secretary of State to Presidents Nixon and Ford had withheld his support for the second Strategic Arms Limitation Treaty (SALT II), unless the Carter administration would send a team of doctors to save the dying Shah. Carter and Vance saw SALT II as one of the pillars of the Carter legacy, along with the Camp David Accords. Keeping SALT II on track was paramount for the administration. Even though Carter himself had wanted to keep his distance from the Shah and give Prime Minister Bakhtiar time to settle the populace down, he had acquiesced.

"I wouldn't bet on that, Mr. President," said Vance. "It's true the students are using this as a trigger, but if we hadn't saved the Shah, they would have pointed to our history of arms sales, or even the CIA's involvement in the coup of 1953. These students are supporters of the Khomeini faction and we believe that they're trying to push the situation to the breaking point. They're actively pushing for a revolution."

"That's all good and well, Cyrus, but you haven't answered the question," said Carter. "How the hell did this happen? Why didn't we see this coming? We're the United States of America, for God's sake!"

"Mr. President, there have been peaceful demonstrations for the past year. Student groups have protested near our embassy frequently. There were no immediate indications that this was anything other than another peaceful protest."

"Until it was no longer peaceful?" said Brzezinski.

"That's right. Until it wasn't. And when the protest turned into an occupation, our Marines were operating under State Department orders to deescalate the situation, and they disarmed as to avoid civilian casualties." At this, Brzezinski shook his head in obvious contempt. "As a direct answer to your question, Mr. President, this happened because we're trying to keep the peace between two sides in a potential civil war that could have a drastic effect on the entire region. I need not remind anyone in this room of the effects of the OPEC embargo of seventy-three. If we have war in the region, it could get out of our control in an instant. It is imperative that we maintain a peaceful transition of power to fill in the vacuum left by the isolation of the Shah."

"Thank you, Secretary Vance. I appreciate your candor. I think we all agree that peace in the region is preferable to the alternative and that we need to work to ensure that this situation doesn't spiral out of control. What are we looking at here? What are our options?"

"I think we really can't define that until we understand what the students want. What are their demands?" said Vance.

"Nonsense," said Dr. Brzezinski. "Mr. President, these are American citizens we're talking about. Members of our foreign service and our military. It hardly matters what the demands of these terrorists are. If we're to seriously engage with them, and give them anything in exchange for the hostages, all we will have done is to encourage every other angry group in the region to take hostages of their own."

"Now, Zbig, it's not black and white," said Vance.

Brzezinski cut him short. "Cy, we've heard your position. Your thinking is that we need to negotiate with the terrorists and find out what they want so we can understand what we can give them. I reject this outright for the obvious reason I've already stated: capitulating to their demands will encourage further hostage-taking or even bolder attacks on our interests in the region. It's clear that we must take firm and decisive action. And any firm diplomatic action *must* be accompanied by a military option, and the will to use force. The old saying is as true as it ever has been: 'how they see you is how they perceive you.'" This last was met with furrowed brows, but everyone at the table had heard enough old Polish wisdom to allow Brzezinski to continue unabated.

"Mr. President, by all means, we must engage in a dialogue with these pirates. However, the result should not be some deal *for* them, but rather a plan on how to deal *with* them. My recommendation would be to work with State to find out as much as we can about these students. Let Mr. Turner work with his people in the Agency to get as much information as we can on the ground, and Dr. Brown and I will work together with the Joint Chiefs to get a real workable solution to this problem."

"I see," said the President. "Harry, Stan? Where do you stand on this?"

"From the Agency's perspective, Dr. Brzezinski is right," said Director Stansfield Turner. "Our mission is to support *any* executive response, be it diplomatic or military. I've already been in touch with our section leads for Iran, and we have assets in play. We'll be working with Defense and the Joint Chiefs regarding the military situation on the ground, and we will funnel anything we can garner regarding the political situation to State. At the end of the day, Mr. President, we're here to gather intelligence, and that's precisely what we're doing."

When Turner finished, Secretary Brown spoke up. "As Director Turner mentioned, right now we don't have the intelligence needed to create a plan of action. My recommendation is to move a carrier battle group to the area and start warming up our air bases in Southern Europe so that once we have some intel, we'll be able to act quickly. We have *Nimitz* in the Mediterranean and we can transition her to the coast of Iran.

"We could pull in the USS *Coral Sea* as well. They're in the western Pacific. We could deploy either or both battle groups to the area without drawing much attention," said Secretary Brown.

"Any attention will be bad at this stage," said Secretary Vance. "State will need all the maneuvering room we can get, and sailing thousands of sailors and hundreds of aircraft off the coast of Iran could destroy any hope we have of establishing our peaceful intentions."

Dr. Brzezinski interjected, "Cy, our intentions are to protect our people and our interests in the region—"

Vance didn't let him finish. "Zbig, we can't do that if we don't have any diplomatic options because we've spooked these rebels into a corner. You've laid out how you want military options in case diplomacy doesn't work, and you're already looking at military actions that will *ensure* that it doesn't. Mr. President, we have got to keep this under control, and we cannot escalate the situation by antagonizing our adversaries at this early stage."

"Enough." The President shut down the discussion. "I have a sense of where things are. I understand that there are many forces at work here, and that we will have to take great care in how we move forward. At this point we're keeping all options on the table, but we will not be making any overt moves that may interfere with our ability to handle this situation diplomatically. Cy, we will proceed with talks to understand what options State can come up with. Zbig, I need to be ready for the possibility that we cannot resolve this through talks. I need you to work with Harry and the Joint Chiefs to put together some military options. Thank you, gentlemen, that will be all."

And with that, the men at the table rose and left the room, each saying, "Thank you, Mr. President."

****

20 November 1979

White House
Washington, D.C.

Despite the competition between the offices of the National Security Advisor and the Secretary of State, a direct meeting between the heads of those two departments was a rarity. Today was one of those rare instances, and Secretary Vance had walked over from the Truman Building to the White House to meet with Dr. Brzezinski.

"How are the talks with the terrorists going, Cy?" asked Brzezinski.

"As well as can be expected, I suppose."

"That's neither confident nor diffident. Don't be coy, Cy. We need to be open about this situation if we're going to move forward with a solution."

"I'm not being evasive, Zbig, we're just at the beginning of a lengthy process. It would be difficult enough if we were dealing with a state actor or even a state-sponsored organization. In this instance, we're dealing with a radical group with no state backers, but rather the support of a dissident group within the government of one of our allies. This requires precision and a delicate hand. I don't think I'm exaggerating to say that this is akin to brain surgery," said Vance.

"We've been working on freezing assets of Iranian nationals here in the US, but it's slow going. Because we're only dealing with a faction of the Iranian people, we can't just cut off oil imports, or freeze all financial dealings with the entire country. Once we've lost that option, it becomes a nightmare to figure out who and what we can freeze. Even when we clamp down on assets, there are many ways to work around our efforts. I imagine Harold is having similar problems with the military aspect. You can't just bomb everyone."

Brzezinski was well aware of the communications and logistic issues that Vance was encountering. He had sources in the State Department that had kept him up to speed. He hoped to ensure that Vance understood the relative importance of the Iranian situation in the bigger picture of geopolitics. From Brzezinski's perspective, this Iranian issue was a hiccup in a global trend of democratization. An important hiccup to be sure, but still just a momentary blip on the radar of global trends.

"I think we need to keep this situation in the correct perspective," said Brzezinski. "Right now we are on the verge of something great. The communist regimes in Eastern Europe are feeling the pressure of falling behind. Despite the Soviets' best efforts to prevent the populace from seeing the economic and cultural development of the West, they simply can't hide it. We're updating the infrastructure for Voice of America, and we believe that we can step up our pressure to bring human rights reforms to these regions. This situation in the Middle East could undermine some of those efforts. The longer it takes to quell this uprising, the more momentum we lose on our global efforts."

"I'm not blind to the global perspective, Zbig. We're working towards the same goals here. But as we agreed during the Camp David meetings, stability in this region is instrumental to advancing global human rights, and slowing down Soviet expansion."

"No doubt, I don't dispute it," said Brzezinski. "But Iran has never attacked or invaded their neighbors—unless you're still holding a grudge against them for the Greco-Persian Wars."

"Zbig—"

Brzezinski cut him off. "No, you're right, Cy, I apologize for the hyperbole. Yet it is true that Iran hasn't joined the Arab nations in the wars against Israel."

"That's true, but we have no idea whether a Khomeini-led Iran would join in the next Israeli war. Even if Egypt honors its commitment, Iran could more than make up for their absence," said Vance.

"I think we both know that there won't be another Arab-Israeli war. The end of the Yom Kippur War should have resolved any doubt about that. Any successful invasion of Israel will be pyrrhic at best."

"Yes, the nuclear threat. That changes things a bit. But you and I know that—who's to say that Hussein or Khomeini does?" said Vance, referring to the leader of Iraq and the leader of the Iranian faction. During the Yom Kippor War between Israel and her Arab neighbors, the Israeli military had placed their nuclear forces on combat alert for the first time. In effect, the last time the Arab forces had attacked Israel, the world had come close to witnessing nuclear weapons fired in anger for only the second time in history. It was a frightening thought that had sobered everyone who was aware of the fact.

"I have every confidence that the moment Prime Minister Begin feels any imminent threat, there will be an open announcement of those weapons and Israel's willingness to use them," said Brzezinski. "I'm not as concerned with a new war between Israel and her enemies as you seem to be, and certainly not when weighed against the bigger picture.

Communism doesn't offer the world anything appealing in the social or economic context. The entrenched regimes in Eastern Europe are weakening. I have full faith that the Asian experiments will fail. This will assist us in Africa and the Americas. We are at a moment when the only compelling aspect of the Soviet Union is its military power. This will no doubt appeal to many of the despots of the world, but even Soviet military power will soon suffer from the inability of their economic systems to keep up with the West."

"I'm not suggesting anything that contradicts your grand vision of the world, Zbig. I'm just saying that it will take time to come to terms with these radicals, and we can't just rush through it. The entire history of the world will not turn on whether this takes one month or six."

"It's a distraction, and if we can't take care of it quickly, it will lead to greater consequences than you realize, Cy. Of that I'm certain," said Brzezinski.

Realizing that they were at an impasse, Vance politely excused himself and headed out to return to his office.

Chapter 3

24 December 1979
Tajbeg Palace
Kabul, Afghanistan

Sergeant Misha Kozyrev looked at his squad. The men of First Squad, Second Platoon, 9th Company, 345th Independent Guards Airborne Regiment were eager to start the mission. With the infantry compartment of their BMD infantry fighting vehicle open, the men lounged in the winter evening. This lull in the action did nothing but take the edge off their appetite for war.

As the minutes counted down towards 1930 hours, the men of First Squad initiated a predeployment ritual. They each picked a tread on the BMD and began urinating on it.

"Valya! Get out here, you need to piss on the tank!" said Private Koshelev.

"Go to hell!" was Valya's response from inside the BMD. "There's no way I'm going to take a chance that the lieutenant sees me out there. Besides, I don't have to piss."

"Come on, Valya, it's for luck!" said Private Dudin.

"Leave him alone. If he doesn't have to piss, he doesn't have to piss," said Junior Sergeant Taras Knyazev, the squad's driver, as he buttoned up his pants. Valya was already in trouble with the lieutenant, and Misha couldn't blame him for wanting to steer clear of the man.

"All right, men, mount up. We will move out soon," said Misha. "Taras, over here," he called as he gestured for his driver to join him. "OK, we've got our orders. There are a pair of guard posts flanking the road heading towards the palace. The lieutenant will engage one with his headquarters BMD. Second Squad will engage the other. Our job will be to run in between the two once they are engaged." Taras raised an eyebrow at that. "What? Have you no faith that Aleksenko can take out one of those guard posts?"

"I'd rather not bet my life on it," replied Taras, "but orders are orders."

"Once we're through," continued Misha, "we engage the last of the perimeter guard shacks. It's about two hundred yards past the first two, on the north side. Third Squad will cross behind us and engage anything that remains between us and the palace. Once we neutralize all the guards, the platoon will then re-form and we will assault the palace in force."

"What could possibly go wrong?" asked Taras as he climbed up the BMD.

"Once we make it to the palace for the assault, you and Tisha will need to head back to the northwest rally point and pick up more troops." Tisha Dezhnyov was the BMD's gunner. "We must get as many men as we can in that building."

"Understood, Sergeant. You can count on us. And don't worry, Tisha will keep the big gun on you to cover your advance," said Taras with a wink. What good was having a 73mm cannon if you couldn't count on it for some cover fire?

"Just keep you and the vehicle safe. I don't want to have to walk home after all this is over," said Misha as they dropped into their positions and Taras started the big diesel engine. None of the other Desantniks in the BMD needed to know the plan. Soviet doctrine didn't waste time confusing the men with too many details. Once they were ready to disembark, they knew they would assault the palace. Until then, all they could do was sit tight and wait as they sat idle, ready for their baptism.

The call came over the radio: "Storm Three-Three-Three." Before the transmission ended, the platoon started their lumbering advance towards the palace. The Headquarters Squad was in the lead, with Second Squad following, then Misha and First Squad, with Third Squad bringing up the rear. Misha was concerned with his assignment. On the one hand, running the gauntlet between the two guard posts was certainly the most dangerous and important aspect of the assault. Therefore, by rights, First Squad should have the assignment. All the same, he couldn't help but think Aleksenko had used his political standing to ensure that while First Squad was taking the most risk, he himself would engage the enemy at long range from relative safety.

Misha stared through the small commander's viewport as they advanced towards the palace. If there was one blessing on this mission, it was that he didn't need his peripheral vision. His focus was on a straight line between where he was and the third guard post, past the other two. Anything going on to the left or right of him wasn't his concern. As he peered through the port, he watched the lieutenant's vehicle make a gradual left turn until it was out of sight, and then Aleksenko's BMD made a sharp turn to the right. From where Misha sat, the mission was progressing like clockwork.

****

Outside of Misha's view, however, the plan started to unravel quickly. Aleksenko watched through his command port as the lieutenant engaged the first guard post with his 73mm cannon. On that cue, he ordered his driver, Private Bespalov, to execute a ninety-degree right turn. As they started the turn, Aleksenko could hear the sounds of small-arms fire bouncing off the armed skin of the BMD. It sounded like hail on a tin roof, he thought. It was the same thought that had occurred to nearly every tanker since the First World War.

During the turn, Aleksenko lost sight of the target. Just like Misha's, his view was fixed to the twenty degrees on either side of the centerline of his BMD. Aleksenko had ordered the turn to create space between his vehicle and the two BMDs that were to blitz past the guards. This would draw fire from the enemy, helping ensure the safe passage of the blitzers. Unfortunately, the turn also took his main gun off target. The gun had been aligned forward, and the turn had put the gun pointing over ninety degrees to the right of the target. Before the gunner, Corporal Zaytsev, could get the turret back on target, there was a horrendous explosion and the entire rear of the BMD was lifted into the air and shoved sideways several meters.

"Report!" roared Aleksenko as the sound of the explosion rang in everyone's ears.

"Driver here! The vehicle is not responding to steering or throttle commands!"

"Gunner here, the turret is not responding!"

"Meatbox here! All soldiers accounted for, we're all alive!" said Corporal Nezhdanov, the senior Desantnik in the infantry compartment.

"Everyone out of the tank!" yelled Aleksenko as it occurred to him that they had all survived whatever had hit them. As he scrambled out of the command hatch, he could see what had happened. Something, probably a rocket-propelled grenade, had hit the left rear tread, ripping two entire hub assemblies from their axles. His BMD was as good as dead, and he was thankful to still have all of his men. Just then, in addition to the high-pitched sounds of bullets ricocheting off the armor, he heard the sickening thud as metal found meat. The screams of his men scrambling out of the infantry compartment let him know that as fortunate as they had been with the RPG hit, that luck had run out.

"Take cover behind the tank!" he screamed to the remaining men. Three of the four men in the meatbox, including Corporal Nezhdanov, never made it to the protective cover of the BMD. Then, just as quickly as they had started, the sounds of incoming fire stopped. The sounds of the battle drifted away from what was left of Second Squad as the rest of the platoon closed on the guard posts.

****

From the command perch of First Squad's BMD, Misha could hear the violence as Aleksenko's BMD was mortally wounded, but it was all out of his view. As First Squad approached the guardhouses, they started taking enemy fire.

"Full speed, Taras! Give it all the power you've got!" shouted Misha. He could hear Tisha opening up with the 7.62mm coaxial machine gun on the turret, while the two forward-mounted machine guns started spitting fire at enemy soldiers. He knew that as they crossed, more guns would open up from the small firing holes in the infantry compartment. But all of these, except for Tisha's turret-mounted gun, were of very limited accuracy. They were really just throwing lead in the general direction of the enemy to keep that enemy from taking the time to aim concentrated fire at the BMD.

As they approached, the firing never stopped, but it never picked up either. Just a smattering of small arms, nothing at all like Misha had feared. As best he could tell from his position, the plan was working. The enemy was preoccupied with the first two BMDs, and First Squad was blitzing through the gap.

The enemy may have taken out Second Squad's BMD, but in the time it had taken to hit the vehicle with the RPG, then attack the dismounting soldiers, First Squad crossed behind the enemy before they could bring another RPG online. In fact, both First and Third Squads' BMDs had blown through the two guard posts and were heading away before the enemy could ready a second rocket. Had Second Squad's BMD still had their gun in the fight, they could have kept the heat on the enemy and the blitzing squads would have made it through unscathed. Without that BMD, they weren't so lucky.

After clearing the two forward guard posts, Misha broke left to engage the third. He knew that behind him, Third Squad would break right to advance on the final barricade before they made it to the palace.

"Tisha, fire the main gun on that building at our eleven o'clock!" commanded Misha. When you had a big gun spitting HE rounds, there was no point in waiting to see the actual enemy soldiers. Better to just batter the building and see if you couldn't bring the entire thing down on top of them.

Over the radio, Sergeant Shishov called out, "We've taken an RPG to the engine. It's destroyed. We're right behind you, Saber Two-One. We're evacuating the vehicle!"

"Son of a bitch!" exclaimed Misha, frustrated at his inability to see what was going on. He popped the command hatch and peered around. The turret blocked his view of Shishov's BMD, but he could clearly see the thick black smoke and the streaking tracer fire coming in from that first guard post. "Taras! Reverse, fifty meters!" yelled Misha. "Tisha, target the guard building, two hundred and ten degrees!" Misha ducked as the big gun traversed counterclockwise until the building was in the crosshairs, and Tisha pulled the trigger.

The gun exploded with a 73mm punch that rattled the building. The enemy immediately shifted fire from the dismounted Third Squad men to Misha's BMD. As the tracers came his way, Misha ducked back down into the command seat and slammed the hatch shut. Every seven and a half seconds, the big gun landed another haymaker on the building until it ultimately collapsed. Between Tisha's pulverizing the building with the main gun and Aleksenko's men taking revenge on the survivors as they scrambled out, the guard post was finally neutralized.

As the surviving members of Third Squad low-crawled to a wooded area just south of the third guard post, Tisha went back to work on his original target. By this point, a BMP, the larger cousin of the BMD, lumbered into view. It was one of the BMPs from Alpha Group. As Misha watched the vehicle approach, it suddenly spat machine-gun fire into the wooded area north of the guard post. It didn't take long to realize that the guards in that building weren't interested in guarding any longer and had tried to flee the combat area. Unfortunately, all they accomplished in fleeing was exposing their position to another enemy fighting vehicle. The BMP slaughtered them en masse.

As the guards were being massacred in the trees, the radio crackled to life.

"Sergeant Kozyrev! Advance on the objective and engage the last guard post!" ordered Lieutenant Kadtsyn. Misha didn't know what was going on over the command channel, but his best guess was that the Alpha Group BMP was tasked with finishing off whatever was left at the current objective.

"Taras, turn one hundred and eighty degrees and advance on the road!" he ordered. "Tisha, target the building at the top of the hill on the left side." Both Desantniks acknowledged the orders, and the tank and turret each turned to comply.

****

Aleksenko and his men knew that there was no point hiding behind their dead BMD any longer. They needed to get under some real cover before something else came onto the battlefield. Infantry in the open was always the worst-case scenario for ground pounders like them. He looked at what was left of his squad. He had Lav Bespalov, his driver, Yuliy Zaytsev, the main gunner, and rifleman Alyosha Protasov. As they huddled next to the BMD, Aleksenko addressed his men.

"We need to get out of here. We don't know if or when the enemy will counterattack to support the palace defenders. If that happens while we're out here, we'll be lined up like lambs to the slaughter." The men nodded their understanding but said nothing. "We will occupy that building over there." He pointed to what was left of the guard post that until a few minutes prior had been their target. "Once we're there, we'll see if we can get in contact with command and find out how to get back into the fight."

The shock of the attack and the slaughter of their friends was giving way to a blend of hot anger and cold hate. The emotional mix left the men uneasy, but with a deep-seated need for action. Controlling this energy and channeling it towards accomplishing the mission was the role of a good NCO. Aleksenko was determined to see them through this.

****

As First Squad's BMD rumbled towards the final guard post, Misha could hear Tisha's big gun open up on the target. From his position in the command seat, he couldn't see the damage being done. There wasn't much incoming enemy fire either. Just the odd round pinging the BMD every now and again. With that in mind, Misha again popped the hatch and peered out at the battlefield. He shifted his gaze to the left and saw the objective. The building was much like the other three they had passed, and from where he was sitting he couldn't see any occupants. He could also see that they were approaching a turn in the road.

"Taras, turn left at the intersection," ordered Misha.

Taras grunted in reply.

As the BMD turned and started up the last hill between First Squad and the palace, the rate of incoming fire picked up. Again, Misha slammed the hatch shut.

"Tisha, concentrate fire on the palace!" he ordered. Tisha grunted an acknowledgment, and Misha could hear the big gun traversing to the right as the vehicle continued to climb the hill. Again, the machine guns in the vehicle's bow opened up on the enemy. The BMD continued climbing the hill. The intensity of the firing grew with each meter the squad advanced.

When it reached a point where Misha didn't think it could grow any stronger, Taras called out to him. "I'm going to see if I can use the building for cover!"

With that, the BMD made a sharp turn to the left. The sounds of the rounds pinging off the vehicle shifted from the front to the right side. Then, after a few more seconds, the hits abruptly stopped. Taras had positioned the BMD behind the guard post, giving them shelter from the onslaught.

"Let's go, you dogs! Everyone out!" screamed Misha as he popped his hatch. This time, he swiftly scrambled out through the hatch and hit the ground running to get into the guard post. As he ran, he fired bursts from his AKS-74 rifle. At the same time as Misha was assaulting the building, the rest of his riflemen had popped the rear hatch in front of the engine and scrambled out. They too made for the guard post at a run. As they were doing this, the sound of an outgoing round from Tisha's 37mm gun emphasized the chaos of the situation. As the rifle squad ran into the building, Taras slammed the BMD in reverse and left his squad behind as he headed to bring more troops to the fight. All the while, Tisha continued to pour cannon rounds into the palace to keep the defenders' heads down.

Inside the building, Misha took stock of his team. He had four Desantniks with him. Three were armed with AKS-74 rifles. The fourth Desantnik, Private Andrei "Andrusha" Koshelev, the squad's machine gunner, was armed with an RPKS-74 light machine gun. This weapon looked very much like a larger version of the AKS-74. It had been designed to be more stable in sustained fire, to give the Desantniks an effective squad automatic weapon. With this, Misha was preparing to storm the palace.

"Koshelev, lay down some covering fire at the entrance. Fenenko, keep an eye out for any other shooters, and push them back if they show their faces," said Misha. Valya nodded. "Dudin, Shuldeshov, you two are with me. Once Andrusha starts to give them hell, we will make for the entrance. We're going to rush it in force. Once we're over, you two will follow." Misha pointed at Valya and Koshelev.

"Understood, Comrade Sergeant," said Andrei Koshelev.

"Strength and honor!" shouted Misha, quoting the regimental motto.

"None but us!" shouted the Desantniks in reply.

Koshelev stood with his back to the wall next to the rear door of the guard shack. Valya stood to his left, next to a window facing the palace. Misha watched as Koshelev steeled his nerves for a second, then turned toward the palace entrance, firing a steady stream of 5.45mm rounds. As the machine gun began destroying every window and chipping away at the wood and concrete, Valya kept his eyes on the upper floors of the building, searching for anyone who might take a shot at the squad.

"Go! Go! Go!" shouted Misha after a few seconds of gunfire. He and his team spilled out of the building and across the short courtyard. They crossed in mere seconds, running at a full sprint. A palace guard on the fourth floor above the entrance seemed to notice the movement and raised his rifle. Valya had him in his sights before the enemy soldier could get a shot off. He squeezed the trigger of his AK, and the soldier disappeared from view.

"Clear the entry!" shouted Misha as his men took cover in the palace building. He needed Dudin and Shuldeshov to keep the enemy at bay while Koshelev and Valya crossed over from the guard post. He turned back towards them and motioned for them to make the move.

Misha looked back at the men in the guard post and motioned for them to cross. The two of them burst out of the door and made their run for it. Valya slipped on several of Koshelev's spent shell casings and fell back with a thud and a scream. At first, it looked to Misha as though Valya had been shot. He had been running, then his feet had come out from under him and he'd crashed backward. Misha rose from his squat and started for Valya. When Koshelev saw Misha rise, he knew something was wrong, but he was in a full sprint for the entry. As Misha cleared the building on his way to Valya, a burst of fire opened up from above.

"No!" screamed Misha as he watched the rounds tear into his squadmate. He turned on the run and fired indiscriminately in the general direction of the incoming fire. He made it to Valya's position and grabbed the Desantnik by the legs, dragging him back to the relative safety of the palace entrance. Koshelev had pulled back into the clearing to add more suppressing fire to cover the sergeant's return trip. As Misha pulled Valya into the entry, Koshelev followed and the entire assault team of First Squad took up the position.

"Oh, shit," groaned Valya once everything had slowed down. "I'm dying, Sergeant."

"Shut up, Valya," replied Misha. He didn't know if the young trooper would make it or not, but he knew that Valya would be lost for sure if he thought he was dying. "I've seen you get worse than this on the football pitch," he quipped. Valya was sheet-white. As Misha pulled his uniform shirt open to assess the wounds, it was apparent why. There were three large holes in his chest. Valya was right. He was dying.

"I should have pissed on the tank," whispered Valya, the last thing he ever said.

Just then, more shots rang out from inside the building.

"Here they come," shouted Private Dudin as he fired down the hallway.

"Stand fast, men!" yelled Misha, knowing that they would have to hold this position until the rest of the platoon had caught up with them. He knew that it was aggressive to take the entry with just his squad, but he was caught up in the chaos. Now he and his men might die, and for what? The twenty yards between the guard post and the entry? It was too late for that now, though. Now he just had to keep everyone else alive until the rest of the platoon could get there.

****

While the rest of First Squad was battling in the palace's entryway, Taras had pulled the BMD down the hill. He was heading back toward their original objective, the third guard post. Once he was at the bottom of the hill, he would move on to the northwest rally point to collect up some more men for the assault. On his way down the hill, he saw the lieutenant's BMD climbing up.

"It's about damn time," he said to nobody in particular. As he reached the bottom of the hill, he made a right-hand turn and continued to where the smoking hulk of Third Squad's BMD had come to rest. That was when he heard Tisha yelling down to him.

"Sergeant Knyazev, there's Sergeant Shishov to our right in the tree line." It was true—there on the side of the road were the five remaining members of Third Squad. They were waving down the BMD as it passed by. Taras stopped the vehicle, and Tisha popped up through the gunner's hatch and yelled down to the men.

"Climb in, we'll get you up there before all the fun is over!"

Shishov and his men climbed up the rear of the vehicle and into the crew compartment. As he slid into the commander's chair, Shishov scolded Tisha. "There's no fun here today, Dezhnyov, just killing to be done."

****

Misha could see that Lieutenant Kadtsyn and the HQ Squad were dismounting from their BMD to occupy the guardhouse across from the entrance. Kadtsyn had arrived with his squad intact, and after the five men poured out of the BMD, the vehicle reversed to leave them and collect up additional men for the assault.

Inside the building, Misha and First Squad were in a fight for their lives. The men Dudin had seen approaching had taken up positions in the corridors that branched off from the primary hallway. From the relative cover of those halls, they began pouring rifle fire into the general area that First Squad had claimed as their own. In response, Dudin and Shuldeshov returned fire as best they could. With so many rifles firing in the tight confines of the building, visibility was rapidly dropping.

Every shot seemed to knock off some stone or tile and create more dust. That dust would hang in the air, creating a fog that added to the chaos. *If there is a bright side to all of this*, Misha thought, *it's that we haven't heard the dreaded sound of a PK machine gun*. The sustained automatic fire could be a difference maker in this situation. With that in mind, he called out to Koshelev, his machine gunner with the RPKS.

"Andrusha! I need you to go lay down some fire in the corridor by Dudin. Push them back or we will have to fall back to the guardhouse!"

"Understood," replied the gunner. As Koshelev moved into firing position, Dudin dropped the long magazine out of his rifle and reached to his vest for a fresh one. During that brief moment before Koshelev had made it into position, Dudin was struck in the head by an enemy round. His helmet came loose and flew backward against the wall on the far side of the room. Dudin fell back, dead, and Koshelev quickly began laying down a steady stream of fire from his forty-round magazine. Misha, seeing that they would not hold the entrance at this rate, decided it was time to escalate things.

"Rodya! Toss a grenade down the corridor!" he called out to Shuldeshov. As he gave the order, he pulled a grenade of his own and removed the safety pin. Both men threw the small explosives, with Misha waiting just long enough to see where Rodya's grenade would land before throwing his. This maximized the destructive force they were unleashing. As the explosions detonated within seconds of each other, the unit was granted a respite from the sound of incoming fire. Visibility was still terrible, but they knew that they'd bought themselves some time.

"We can't stay here," Misha told his two remaining troops.

"Comrade Sergeant, I don't see how we can advance without more men. If we get deeper into the building, we'll risk getting cut off from one of the alternate routes," replied Corporal Shuldeshov, the only other remaining NCO. He was right. This entryway opened up in several directions. Straight ahead, down the corridor they had been fighting in, there were multiple corridors splitting off. Between that and the fact that there were stairwells on either side of that corridor, there was no way that they could advance without risking getting shot from behind.

"Shit, we're going to have to fall back to the guard post if we don't get help soon," concluded Misha.

During this lull, Lieutenant Kadtsyn brought his squad in from the guard post. "Sergeant! Move your men forward and secure that corridor!" he shouted.

For a moment, Misha considered telling the lieutenant to go fuck his mother. As far as Misha could tell, the man had sat behind them in the safety of the guard post. He hadn't advanced until Misha's men had done the fighting and paid the price. But Misha was a sergeant in the Soviet Red Army. He would follow the lieutenant's orders.

"Understood!" was his only reply. "Koshelev, give us cover fire straight down the corridor. Rodya, take the left side, I'll go right."

With no hesitation, Koshelev opened up the RPKS, sending ten rounds a second down the hall to ensure that nobody would be foolhardy enough to poke their heads out. Moving quickly at a low crouch, Misha and Rodya each moved to the first intersecting corridor and cleared the opening. On the right side of the hall, Misha found two dead Afghan soldiers. He didn't have the time or interest to check them to see if they had fallen to the rifles or the grenades. He simply ensured they were dead and called out, "Clear!" At the end of the hallway was an open landing for a stairwell. The dust wasn't so opaque in these side halls, and Misha could see the stairs on the far side.

As soon as Misha had cleared his side, he checked with Rodya, who was already looking back at him. Rodya had his rifle pointed down the corridor in the direction they had just advanced. Once the two made eye contact, they began firing bursts from their AKS-74s, returning the favor for Koshelev as he advanced behind them, taking a position on the right side with the sergeant. They were now exposed in three directions. The enemy could approach them down the main corridor, as they had in the first attack that had killed Dudin, or they could attack from the stairwells on either side.

"Secured!" Misha called out to let Lieutenant Kadtsyn know that it was safe to advance. As Misha looked over his shoulder, he could see that instead of the lieutenant, it was Sergeant Shishov advancing with Third Squad. Shishov and his men crossed to the opposite side of the hall from Misha and Koshelev. Only when the first two squads had advanced and ensured the security of the area did Kadtsyn lead his men forward. Once they had assembled, Kadtsyn laid out the plan.

"Shishov," said the lieutenant, "take your men to the fourth floor and secure the hallway there. Kozyrev, take your squad and secure the third floor. I'll cover the second floor." Each of the men nodded in understanding, if not agreement, with the assignment.

"Oh, Kozyrev," continued the lieutenant, "leave a man here to cover the stairs. We can't have anyone coming up behind us."

As he heard the order, he knew how absurd it was. His was the smallest squad at this point. It would make more sense for the lieutenant to peel off a man from his own squad to hold down the ground floor. But he knew there was no point in mentioning this.

"Understood!"

As the men of Third and Headquarters Squads departed to fight their way up the stairs, Misha called out to Koshelev. "Andrusha, I need you to hold down this floor. You have a better chance with that thing"—he pointed to the man's machine gun—"than Rodya and I would. Once we've cleared the third floor, we should link up with Alpha. As soon as we do, we'll send some relief your way. Do *not* shoot us when we come down, understood?"

"Understood, Comrade Sergeant," said Koshelev as Misha and Rodya followed the other squads and started up the stairs.

****

As soon as they were up the stairs and out of sight, Andrusha was suddenly aware of just how alone he was. The sounds of battle still raged through the building, but here in his tiny piece of the palace, it was still. Or was it? Andrei's mind was racing. He considered that perhaps it wasn't that there was very little sound and motion in this corridor. Rather, the calm of the scene was only by comparison. Compared to when people were shooting at him and he was watching his friend die, this was peaceful and calm. It probably helped that his hearing was still hazy from the sound of rifles and explosives. He couldn't be sure if the bursts of fire he heard were just on the other side of the wall or if they were hundreds of meters away.

He couldn't dwell on it. He was now in a tough tactical situation. He had two stairwells he was responsible for, one on each end of this hallway. And there was still the main corridor that they had advanced down to secure these hallways. If there should be another attack, it would probably be from that direction. So he positioned himself with his back to the entry, facing the most likely enemy approach. This allowed him to monitor all three positions without putting himself in the direct line of fire from the main corridor.

Andrusha found himself tightly wound. He knew that anyone coming into his line of sight could be there with murderous intent. He also remembered Misha's final admonition not to shoot his own men. He had to balance the fear of getting shot against the fear of shooting the wrong person. It wasn't a comfortable feeling. *It's so much easier when you can just point at the enemy and shoot. When everything is moving fast amid the chaos of battle, you make split-second decisions and then you move on or you die.* Sitting here in the relative quiet waiting for something, anything, to happen was wearing him down.

After what seemed like a week of sitting and shifting his eyes from threat to threat, Andrusha heard the unmistakable sounds of footsteps hurrying down the stairwell to his left. He couldn't make out anything but the clatter of boots on the stairs. He backed away from the stairs and placed himself in the main passageway without realizing that he'd just exposed his right flank to that approach. He crouched against the wall and aimed his RPKS at the bottom of the stairwell. He knew that he would only have a split second to decide as the boots continued their descent. He was so fixated on the target in front of him that he hadn't noticed the movement down the main corridor to his right.

At last, the men in the stairwell came into view. Andrusha was still trying to make out their uniforms when suddenly a burst of fire exploded from the stairs. Koshelev instinctively pulled back. As he did, he saw men approaching from his right. But he was committed. He didn't have time to consider whether this split-second decision he was making was better than waiting in the quiet. Instead, he remained committed to the action he'd decided on: to spray down the stairwell and kill anything trying to get out.

He squeezed the trigger, and the sound of automatic fire filled the corridor. In the moment's violence, he never heard the Alpha sergeant telling him to seal off the exit. As his forty-round magazine ran dry, the Alpha sergeant took aim and peered into the kill zone, looking for additional targets. There were none.

"Damn, Private, I think you massacred them all," said the sergeant as Andrusha swapped out his empty magazine for his last fresh one. Not knowing who the sergeant was or what the full situation was, Andrusha kept his mouth shut and charged his rifle. “You do know that you just assassinated the President of Afghanistan, don’t you?”

Andrusha stared at the sergeant in disbelief as the two walked towards the stairs to secure the scene.

Chapter 4

24 December 1979
Kremlin
Moscow, USSR

KGB Chief Yuri Andropov looked out over the desk at his counterparts, Minister of Defense Dmitriy Ustinov and Minister of Foreign Affairs Andrei Gromyko. With General Secretary Leonid Brezhnev's failing health, these men found themselves more and more in control of the country. With stagnation crushing the Soviet economy, they were on borrowed time. There was no way that they could keep up with the West. They had a very narrow window of opportunity to act. Like all good Soviets, they had a plan. Now, that plan was bearing fruit.

"Do we have reports from the front?" asked Andropov, looking to Ustinov.

"Yes, Comrade Director," replied Ustinov. "Our forces have successfully occupied the palace. President Amin was unfortunately killed during the operation." Ustinov's grin showed that he didn't find the death unfortunate in the least. "Once we pacify the local population, we'll have enough presence in the region to prompt an American response. The situation in Afghanistan will come to a quick and decisive resolution in the coming weeks. I can assure you of that."

"And what of the next phases of the operation? How are our preparations in Iraq?" asked Andropov.

"President Hussein is a bull-headed idiot, but I believe that he will remain a useful idiot. If left to his own devices, he would most likely throw everything he has at the Iranians, with no regard for tactics and no clear understanding of his strategic objectives," said Ustinov. "But I believe that General Lapunov can contain him. If Hussein will take the counsel of our military advisors, we will be ready to make a push into Iran by spring. The key to this will be avoiding responsibility for the mess we are about to create."

"That will be my concern, Dmitriy," replied Andropov. "We have plans in place to ensure that the world understands that our only desire is for a peaceful resolution to this unfortunate conflict." Andropov then turned to Gromyko: "And what of the Americas? How are the preparations in Managua proceeding?"

“In principle, everything is proceeding according to plan. The new government is, of course, interested in our economic and material support. The locals aren’t exactly keen on stepping up a military conflict with their neighbors, but there are still counterrevolutionary rebels moving across their borders with El Salvador and Honduras. We will be able to move in support to help put down those rebel movements. Much like in Iraq, our principal challenge will be getting as much force on the ground as we can without triggering an outright war,” said Gromyko.

“Again, we have a plan in place that will give us the cover we need. What challenges are you expecting at this point?” asked Andropov.

“The Cubans are getting nervous about providing the airstrips for our patrol aircraft. They are less confident in our ability to avoid repercussions than you are, Yuri,” replied Gromyko.

“In that case,” said Andropov, “we will have to make sure the repercussions for not working with us are even more terrifying than the threats of the Americans.”

Chapter 5

24 December 1979
Situation Room, White House
Washington, D.C.

"Why are we just learning about this after the fact?!" demanded President Carter, his voice slightly distorted through the speakerphone. For the second time in as many months, Carter's national security team was struggling to catch up to events in the Middle East. Last time it was the Iranian hostage situation. Tonight, it was the Soviet invasion of Afghanistan. The administration couldn't keep up with the rapidly unfolding situation, and Carter had had enough. "Cy, what have the Soviets had to say about this? Why have they occupied Afghanistan?"

"Mr. President, Ambassador Dobrynin has announced that the instability in the region caused by local warlords has forced his nation into military intervention. These warlords have threatened to destabilize the duly constituted Afghan government and to destroy the will of the proletariat in the region."

"Horseshit," said the President. Like anyone who had been in the White House since the establishment of the Soviet Union, Carter had read enough *Pravda* to know when the USSR was dressing up their offensive actions in the language of the global communist revolution. He reflected on how the US did much the same, but he admired when a president like FDR would break through the nonsense, like when he'd declared that Nicaraguan strongman Anastasio Somoza "may be a son of a bitch, but he's our son of a bitch." Carter had been working hard to reinvent American foreign policy to get away from propping up dictators. He and Brzezinski had been working to put humanitarianism at the forefront of foreign policy. To hold even "our sons of bitches" to higher human rights standards.

"Director Turner, what does the CIA have on this?" Carter asked.

"Mr. President, we've been tracking down some unusual logistical activity in the Soviet Near East, but we had nothing on our radar regarding the mass deployment of Red Army units into the Afghan countryside. We've seen the buildup on the Soviet side of the border, but none of our sources in Moscow gave us any indication that an invasion was imminent. Given that degree of secrecy, I can't believe that this is simply to quash an uprising. We'll need to confer with the NSA and DIA to see if any of the real-time intercepts can fill in the blanks, but right now, Mr. President, we've been caught with our pants down," said Turner.

The sheer obviousness of the statement exacerbated Carter's already swelling anger. "Clearly," replied the President. The icy reply cut short the conversation at the table, with nobody willing to speak up next. Concern over the Afghanistan situation had been growing for months. The conventional wisdom maintained that the Soviets would continue to treat Afghanistan as a semistable buffer state. They had been sending advisors to the Afghan Army for months now, and they had sent in some military forces to help quell the rural uprisings. But a full-on invasion came as a shock. Afghanistan's location wasn't of particular strategic value, other than as a counter to the US presence in Iran, with which it shared a border. As far as the geopolitical balance of power in the region, most observers considered the Soviet client state of Iraq to be a suitable counterweight to Iran. Perhaps the Soviets didn't find Iraq so suitable. It was with that thought that Dr. Brzezinski spoke up.

"Mr. President, if I may…"

"Of course, Zbig. What do you have for us?"

"I believe that we have to look at this Soviet incursion with a view to the grander stage. With the SALT talks bogged down, and the whole flap over their army brigade in Cuba, not to mention our increased defense budget and our turn towards China, I believe the Soviets are taking this action in Afghanistan as an opportunity to reestablish the initiative in our relationship. Surely they understand that whatever actions we take in Iran will have to consider the presence of a considerable military force right next door. To that end, we need to ensure that there is a powerful response to this near provocation. At the least, we need Ambassador McHenry to address the UN General Assembly and condemn this action in the strongest terms. I would suggest we also put into force the grain embargo that we've been contemplating."

"I think," said Vance, "we need to consider the possibility that the Soviets aren't looking at such grand designs and instead are countering what they see as a direct security threat on their southern flank. This business with the Islamists in Iran has been seeping out into the surrounding Muslim countries. The Saudis have been dealing with the

Wahhabi unrest in Mecca, which can be considered a direct response to the Islamic revolution in Iran. It's too early to tell what the long-term impact in Pakistan will be. In any case, we can rest assured that the Soviets believe that regardless of the outcome, it will be better for them to be in complete control of Afghanistan than to have a rogue province along their Central Asian border."

"Thank you, Cy," said President Carter. "What is your initial thought on our response?"

"I agree with Zbig. We need to make a powerful statement of condemnation, and we need some kind of economic sanctions against the USSR. We should also consider increasing our military assistance to Pakistan. That should ensure that Moscow understands that invading their neighbors will have a price."

As Secretary Vance concluded, President Carter moved the agenda forward.

"OK, it looks like we're in agreement as to an outline for a direct response. Cy, I want you to take the lead in putting together the nuts and bolts of this. Work with Harry on the military details regarding Pakistan, and maybe look at China as well. We might as well leverage what we've been working on out there."

"Understood, sir," replied Vance.

"Now, what, if any, impact will this Soviet action have on our situation in Iran?" asked the President. "It doesn't matter if the Soviets are working on a grand strategy or just responding to a regional dustup—only a fool would believe that these situations are unrelated."

"Mr. President," replied Dr. Brzezinski, "by taking such direct and provocative military action in the region, the Soviets may have done us a favor."

"How so?" asked Carter.

"The only hesitation that I've had on the use of military force, and I believe that Secretary Brown agrees with me on this point, is that such force may embolden the Soviets in Afghanistan. With those concerns now overtaken by recent events, I believe our path to Tehran is now open."

"Now just a minute, Zbig," said Vance. "The fact that the Soviets are now in force in Afghanistan is in no way clearance for us to inject our own forces into Iran. If anything, this should make us more cautious, not less. If we put troops in Iran while we make these strong condemnations against the Soviets for Afghanistan, we will undermine our own position, not to mention needlessly increase tensions in the region."

"Cy, I'm not suggesting that we invade the country, or even send in a major military presence," said Brzezinski. "I'm only suggesting that this shift in the regional situation will allow us to execute a rescue mission using military force. The Russians won't be able to mount a complaint in the United Nations without looking foolish. And Brezhnev will not risk looking like a fool. This Soviet action removes one impediment to our rescue mission. It's my belief that without having to worry about the risk of a Soviet response in Afghanistan, we no longer have sufficient concerns to stop us from acting."

"Thank you, gentlemen," said Carter, stopping the debate. "I have a lot to consider here, and I think we've taken this as far as we can today."

Chapter 6

1 January 1980
US Embassy
Tehran, Iran

Howard Chandler had spent almost two months living the same day over and over. Since the embassy takeover in November, he and the other ten hostages in his room were woken up each morning by a guard kicking their mattresses. He would then be hefted up and transferred from the mattress to a wooden chair. The chairs were tied back to back to give the hostages one more obstacle to overcome if they wanted to escape. If one hostage managed to get their feet untied, they would have to carry the second. Once tied to the chair, he would begin his day. He would remain tied to the chair until he was allowed to eat a meal.

The Iranians would bring in food from local cafés or fast-food joints and the Americans were required to eat in silence. The Iranian captors had drummed silence into the hostages from the first days of the crisis. Any attempt to communicate between the hostages was swiftly punished. The beatings weren't too severe, but they were instant. In fact, the only time Chandler had held a conversation since November 4 was early on, during the "interrogations."

From what Chandler could tell, the assumption by the students was that everyone in the embassy was a CIA spy. To that end, they brought each of the hostages to the "bubble room" for interrogation. The bubble room was a conference room that was surrounded by a clear plastic cube. Under US control, this room had been used for classified conversations. Under Iranian control, this was where they conducted their most serious meetings. The interrogations certainly qualified as that.

On the third day of the crisis, a guard untied Chandler and took him to the bubble room. The guard remained behind Chandler as he was shoved into a chair at the conference table. On the other side sat a bearded man Chandler hadn't seen before. The bearded man sat ramrod straight in his chair and held a rattan stick in one hand. At the instruction of the guard behind him, he placed his hands on the table. The bearded man spoke with a British accent. He asked Chandler what his code name was. Chandler had no idea how to react to that. The question was so absurd, he almost laughed out loud. The stern look on his interrogator's face kept him quiet.

He was grilled about his contacts in Iran. When he protested that he'd only been on station for a week, the rattan stick struck his hands with lightning speed. The searing pain shot through Chandler's body. Apparently, "I've only been on station for a week" was a popular answer. Through the course of three of these meetings, and reading the extensive personnel files on site, the Iranians finally decided that he wasn't worth pursuing any longer.

Chandler knew that today was New Year's Day, 1980. A week prior, the Iranian students had held a small Christmas celebration for the hostages. It was very out of character for the Iranians, and Chandler was sure they were using it as propaganda to show the world how reasonable they were.

As his guard hauled him from his mattress to his chair, Chandler nervously held his thumb to the palm of his hand. If his thumb slipped, he knew he'd be in for a beating. More than that, he'd lose the one communications channel he had.

The day before, while he and Eddie Cain were being tied back-to-back on the chairs, Eddie had slipped a piece of paper into his hand. Chandler had held that paper in his hand until he was finally allowed up for breakfast. He'd then slid the paper into his pocket. Excitement had run through his body as he'd considered the possibilities. What could be on that paper? It was everything he could do to wait until he had a modicum of privacy in the toilet before reading the note.

Sitting in the bathroom stall, Chandler had unfolded the note.

H—

There is a pencil under your mattress. I put it there last night. Keep the pencil with you at all times. Write at night. Trade in the morning.

—E

It was the most amazing thing Chandler had ever read. In those five sentences, Eddie had given Chandler hope. He'd spent all of that day wondering how to best use this new line of communication. With the process being new, he didn't want to risk sending anything sensitive until he had more faith that they wouldn't get caught. So that night, he had written a simple note back to Eddie recalling the Dolphins vs. Oilers game they'd been looking forward to when this had all started.

Each day, during the transfer from the mattress to the chairs, the two men would exchange notes. They'd quickly established a code, based on football, that they would use to plan their escape.

This had lasted all of a week. A fumbled exchange during the transfer left a note on the floor with no way to retrieve it. A passing guard noticed the scrap of paper and picked it up. After glancing at it for a few seconds, he began screaming at the men in Farsi. Though Chandler didn't speak the language, it was clear he was in trouble. Chandler watched the man storm off. *He probably needs to find someone who can read English*, he thought.

Within five minutes, the guard was back, but this time he brought someone Chandler hadn't seen in two months: his bearded interrogator.

"What is this?" he demanded, shoving the note in Chandler's face.

"It's just a note to Eddie about the Dolphins," replied Chandler.

"What does it mean? What Dolphins? And what is meant by 'end-around'?" The note was suggesting that the escape plan they were working on would require misdirection.

"It's a football thing. The Dolphins are a team, and an—"

"Nonsense!" shouted the interrogator. "There are no 'wide receivers' in football. This is a code of some kind. What are you planning?"

"What? No, the wideout is—"

The interrogator slapped him hard across the face.

"I am not an idiot." The man turned to the guard and said something in Farsi. The guard motioned to another guard and they untied the two hostages and forced them out of the room and down the hallway. It took Chandler a minute to figure out that they were headed to the basement. On the way down the stairs, Eddie lost his balance and fell to the bottom of the stairwell.

"Shit, slow down, man," said Chandler, slipping. When they reached the basement, they passed the custodian's closet and made a right-hand turn into the laundry room. To his horror, Chandler could see what appeared to be dried blood around the main drain hole in the middle of the floor. "Hey, wait. This is—"

"Get on your knees, Yankee!" The guards pushed the two men onto the floor. "Now, what is going on here? What is this note?" Chandler heard one of the guards charge a handgun, then felt the metal cylinder of the barrel against the back of his head.

“Oh shit, man,” stuttered Chandler. “It’s just American football. Ask around. That one woman, the one from Philadelphia, she’ll know. She can clear all of this up!” Chandler was panicked. He could hear an exchange in Farsi, but he didn’t dare turn his head. He heard someone leave the room.

“When Masoumeh gets here, we will know the truth. She will see through your lies, and you will die here. We’ll wash your blood down the drain, like we did to your friends before you.” With that said, a silence fell on the hostages as they waited for their fate to be resolved.

“What is this?” Chandler recognized the grating Yankee accent of “that woman from Philadelphia.” “You expect me to believe that you have one opportunity to communicate, and you waste it talking about sports?”

“Ma’am,” replied Chandler, “I’m from Texas. Football is an important part of our culture. Hell, it’s nearly religion to us. Besides, we knew that we couldn’t talk about anything serious or you’d kill us. You gotta believe me, lady.”

“These two idiots almost died for their obsession with sports. And they wonder why we reject their pathetic Western ‘culture.’ I say you put them in with the other troublemakers and leave it at that.”

“I agree,” replied the interrogator. Then, after he conferred with the guards in Farsi, the two men were hauled back upstairs, then on to the second floor. They were taken through a conference room, then into an adjacent office. There were two armed guards standing in front of half a dozen Marines.

“The easy part of your confinement is over. You will not leave this office until we have the Shah in our hands.” With that, the interrogator left, and Chandler’s heart sank.

Chapter 7

15 January 1980
Camp David
Frederick County, Maryland

The President's national security team had assembled at the presidential retreat to come to a final agreement on how to resolve the hostage crisis. The men sat in the main entertaining room of the Aspen Lodge wearing polo shirts and blue jeans, with only Vice President Walter Mondale opting for a button-up shirt with a sport coat. Their casual dress belied the serious demeanor of the occasion.

General Jones, the Chairman of the Joint Chiefs of Staff, started the meeting.

"Gentlemen, thank you for coming out. I know that you've been eager to see the plan we've put together. That's why we put together this presentation." Jones then laid out the plan for Operation Eagle Claw. The Army, Navy, Air Force and Marine Corps would coordinate to get a commando team into the US embassy. The Air Force would fly the commandos into Iran on C-130 transports from bases off the coast of Africa while the Marine Corps flew a separate assault team via helicopter from the USS *Nimitz* in the Gulf of Oman. The helicopters would be refueled by the Air Force in the middle of the desert at a spot creatively dubbed Desert One. While the Army was assaulting the embassy, the Marine Corps would capture Manzariyeh Airfield. This would allow the Air Force to land additional transport planes that would then fly both the hostages and the rescue team to safety.

There were some eyebrows raised at the rather dramatic step of establishing a refueling point in the middle of the desert, and the complexity of grabbing the airfield and extracting the hostages via the soccer stadium, yet everyone in the room maintained a hyperfocus on the general. Once he explained that the Marines would leave the helicopters in place for later retrieval—or for destruction, depending on the political situation in Iran—and it was clear that the presentation had concluded, all eyes were on the President.

"That's one hell of a plan, General Jones," said Carter. "I have no doubt that you've worked with all the services on the details of the execution. What happens if we need to abort the mission?" was the only question the President had.

"Mr. President, if we need to abort at any point prior to the hostage rescue team breaching the embassy, the teams will board the C-130s at Desert One and depart for Masirah Island off the coast of Oman. Once we have committed to the assault on the embassy, the only way out for our people will be on board those transports at Manzariyeh Air Base." Replied the general. President Carter considered this but did not ask for any additional clarification.

"General Jones," said Dr. Brzezinski, the NSA, "this operation appears to rely on a very complex organization and coordination of forces. Is this truly necessary?"

"Thank you, Dr. Brzezinski. Yes, it is the consensus of all the Joint Chiefs that this operation requires the cooperation and utilization of all the forces described herein. A previous version of the plan had included Army Airborne Infantry in order to eliminate the need to use Marines. However, that would have introduced additional complexity and even more aircraft into an already crowded operation."

"I see," replied Brzezinski.

"To be frank," continued the general, "organization and logistics are truly what set our military capabilities above and beyond those of any other nation on earth. Our boys are strong and they'll fight as hard as anyone. Our technology is first-rate. But at the end of the day, we can get things done and move things around that nobody else would even think of. This operation is a showcase of that prowess and reputation, and I assure you that reputation is well deserved."

"I have no doubt of that, General Jones. When can we implement this?"

"We've already identified the units that will be used, and training will commence as soon as we have the approval. In some cases, the training is already underway under the general operational training programs. For example, the coordinated helicopter operations, the air support from the Air Force and Navy pilots, and the general infantry assault of the Marines are all missions within the general purview of those units to be assigned. Once we have the authorization, we'll move everyone out to California and begin rehearsals in the Mojave, between Fort Irwin, Edwards Air Force Base, Twentynine Palms, and Naval

Weapons Center, China Lake. With training and transit time, the soonest we'll be ready to implement would be the beginning of February."

"Gentlemen," said the President. "As I see it, we have only three possible choices at this point. First, we continue with the status quo. Cy continues the negotiations, and at best we agree to a terrible compromise that gives undue power to the Ayatollah. At worst, the negotiations continue with no resolution." At this statement, Secretary of State Cyrus Vance furrowed his brow.

"Second," continued Carter, "we could launch a major military operation against every last stronghold of this 'Islamic Revolution' and completely destroy the organization, thus convincing this Khomeini that we mean business." The audience was taken aback. Nobody had expected that, and it took a few seconds for each of the men to understand that this wasn't a serious option. Carter was simply framing what he had concluded was his preferred option.

"Third, we move forward with the hostage rescue as presented by General Jones," the President concluded. "Cyrus, your people have been on the ground out there. You've been in these negotiations for two months. What can you give us to support the first option, that paints a less grim picture than what I'm seeing?"

"Mr. President, this situation is fluid—" began Vance.

"Cyrus, cut the bull. It's time for the hard choices. We aren't leaving this room until we have a decision, and we don't have time for excuses or hurt feelings," chided the President.

"Yes, Mr. President," said Vance, "of course. We are not having success in negotiations. To be frank, I believe the Islamic Revolution will not negotiate in good faith until they have secured some degree of power and stability in the region. So long as the nation teeters on the brink of a civil war, they will merely string us along with promises and plans. They will not agree to a deal," said Secretary Vance.

"I think these 'revolutionaries' overplayed their hand, Mr. President," said Dr. Brzezinski. "When the Ayatollah first returned, they thought there would be a swift ushering in of their Islamic fervor. When that failed to materialize, they took these hostages in an attempt to force the issue. With the Bakhtiar regime's easing of restrictions against the press, and the dissolution of the secret police, the populace has cooled off. I believe that the Revolution sees these hostages as the only guarantee of their safety, and the only possibility of their successfully seizing power," concluded Brzezinski. Vance knew that if there was any chance that the State Department was going to keep control of this crisis, he needed to make that case right now. Otherwise, the hotter heads in the room would prevail.

"You're making an awful lot of assumptions," said Vance. "We need to be careful with assigning the level of despair among these revolutionaries and the level of contentment of the Iranian populace. The rise of this Islamic Revolution didn't happen in a vacuum; there are a lot of disaffected people living there. Anything that we do militarily right now could very well plunge the entire country into a war. If Iran devolves into a shooting war, we're going to have one hell of a problem in the region, especially with the Soviets on the doorstep. That doesn't even address the economic crisis we'll have here at home."

There it is, thought Carter. *This is the best case Vance could lay out for nonintervention and the continuation of negotiations. He's betting on my risk aversion so close to the election.*

"You may be right, Cy," admitted Brzezinski. "We will have to make a calculation based on the probability of outcomes. If we believe that the outcome of a successful rescue will be war in Iran, we must continue negotiations. If we believe that the outcome of a successful rescue will be peace, we must move forward with the operation."

"And if the mission is unsuccessful?" asked Vance.

"Failure is a matter for contingency planning. If you plan for failure, you will fail," replied Brzezinski.

"Dammit, Zbig—" started Vance.

Brzezinski cut him off. "Let me finish, Cy. I believe that we're all in agreement that a successful operation will result in our best possible outcome. Is that correct?" Brzezinski was met with nods from most of the men present. Only Vance remained unmoving. "I believe that makes our path clear. Before we can fully commit, though, Cy is one hundred percent correct: we must deal with contingency planning to ensure an acceptable outcome if our operation is not a success," concluded Brzezinski. Vance was visibly furious. It was clear that he had lost the room, and that the best he could hope for was to go on record in opposition to the plan. But there was nothing he could do now: Eagle Claw was a go.

Chapter 8

18 February 1980
0300 Hours
USS *Nimitz*
Arabian Sea

"It's go time, jackass." The hoarse whisper jolted Sergeant Rodriguez from his light sleep. The flashlight pointed at his chest made sure that there was no confusion and that he knew this was, in fact, go time.

"Dammit, Page, why do you always have to bring the damn flashlight?" whispered Rodriguez into the darkness of the berthing compartment.

"Because I know you're going to try and go all Sleeping Beauty on me if I don't bring some insurance," replied the shadow that was Staff Sergeant Dominic Page. "Anyhow, we're meeting on the hangar deck in fifteen, so get your guys and get moving, formation in thirty. I'm grabbing Third Squad."

With that, Page was gone, and Rodriguez was alone with his thoughts. By now, autopilot had kicked in. Muscle memory pushed him through the process of putting on his shirt and boots (he'd long since taken to sleeping in his utility pants). This was the sixth time he and Page had had a similar conversation in the past two weeks.

Sergeant Rodriguez and his fellow Marines from Kilo Company of the Third Marine Battalion, Sixth Marine Regiment (3/6) had been plucked from the rest of their unit in the 38th Marine Amphibious Unit (MAU) at the end of December and dropped into the desert at Twentynine Palms in California. 3/6 had originally been slated for a three-month deployment, but the float had been cut short with the US discovery of the Soviet battalion in Cuba. They'd been rerouted to move reinforcements to the Marine detachment at Guantanamo Bay. All told, they'd spent five weeks out. In order to get their money's worth out of 3/6, they'd pulled Kilo Company to support a special project they were calling "Eagle Claw."

Rodriguez grabbed his cover and crept along the narrow space between bunks stacked three high on either side. Rodriguez considered the previous "go times." Each one had held the potential for his first actual combat experience. Each time had excited him. Each represented the culmination of his young life to this point and was the ultimate goal of the peacetime Marines in his unit. In moments of self-reflection, he could admit that each time had also scared the hell out of him. That fine line between excitement and panic was the razor's edge that was wearing him down. Each middle-of-the-night wake-up call was a little less exciting than the last. There was still that twinge... that "oh damn, here we go!" feeling, but it was a bit less each time.

As he moved from rack to rack, waking the rest of Second Squad, he considered the drill. His men would assemble on the hangar deck. They would check out their gear, suit up with their All-Purpose Lightweight Individual Carrying Equipment or ALICE packs, take on live ammo, and line up in formation. There, they would get a brief on the operation, at which time Captain Goodwin or Lieutenant Beck would tell them that the operation was on hold, and they would load up on the CH-53 Sea Stallions and fly around the Arabian Sea, pretending to look for mines, or whales or whatever the hell was out there. Nothing to it.

He was thinking about that as he made it to the head, where he ran a razor over his face and looked in the mirror. Like most of the Marines, he wore his hair in a "high and tight," closely shaved along the ears with a short tuft of hair on the top of his scalp. This was the haircut that had earned the US Marines the nickname "Jarhead" (though whether this last bit was fact or mere legend was a topic of heated drunken debates in seaside bars all across the globe). His black hair, angular features and tan skin showed his Aztec heritage. His family had lived for two generations in San Diego. That time might have given his Spanish a Yankee accent and had certainly given him a deep sense of being "American," but he was definitely a *Mexican* American, as his friends would constantly remind him.

Once the twelve men of his squad were all moving, he headed up to the hangar to see what intel he could squeeze out of Staff Sergeant Page. As he walked along the cramped passageway that would lead him up to the main hangar, it amazed him how normal life at sea had become. The USS *Nimitz* was no longer the newest or biggest carrier in the fleet (that honor belonged to the USS *Eisenhower*), yet *Nimitz* remained the ultimate symbol of American military power. There were no supercarriers in any other fleet, and no carrier was more "super" than the USS *Nimitz*. Named after Fleet Admiral Chester Nimitz, who had overseen the Pacific theater during World War II, *Nimitz* was the lead ship in a class that would define force projection for the next thirty years. As Rodriguez was considering the ship he was living in, he came to the ladder well that would take him up to the hangar.

Once he cleared the hatch and entered the vast open hangar, he quickly crossed the deck to where he could see the Marines assembling near a map of the Arabian Peninsula and Iran. He could already see Sergeant Mason with Staff Sergeant Page and hoped that he wasn't too late to get a sneak preview of the day's action. Sergeant Jimmie Mason was the squad leader for First Squad. He and Rodriguez had come up through the ranks together and had a sporting rivalry going. Each sergeant was looking to outperform the other in all aspects of Marine life, from physical fitness tests to marksmanship to the efficient management of their respective squads. Everything was fair game between them.

"Hey, Rodriguez, you just wake up from your siesta, you lazy wetback?" asked Mason.

"Piss off, Jimmie. I heard Queen Elizabeth was up on the 04 deck lookin' for a date, ya limey." As the two came within arm's reach, they exchanged shoulder punches and a brief chuckle at their now-familiar greeting.

"Can it, you two," admonished Staff Sergeant Page. "We've got things to go over. Looks like today's the day, meatheads."

"No kidding, Page? We're going to the show?" asked Rodriguez.

"That's right, the big leagues. Nothing's final until we hear it from the boss, but it looks like we're going today," replied Page.

Rodriguez spoke up. "It's not the fight that I'm concerned with—it's getting there. If anything goes wrong, man… that's a long walk home."

"Amen, brother," said Mason. "There's going to be plenty of pucker time once we cross that point of no return."

"Attention on deck!" bellowed Lieutenant Beck, drawing every Marine's attention as Captain Thomas Goodwin strode over to the group.

"All right, gather around, Marines," Goodwin called out to his men. "Let's hit the high points before formation." With that, the leadership of Second and Fourth Platoons, Kilo Company, 3/6 Marines, formed a semicircle around their company commander.

"Gentlemen, the powers that be have passed down that today is the day we've been training for." Without hesitation, the no-nonsense captain continued, "We will depart from *Nimitz* at 1800 hours, just after sunset. The platoons and supporting personnel will be dispersed in eight CH-53s, code-named Bluebeard One through Bluebeard Eight. We will be flying into Iranian airspace here, to the west of Chabahar Bay." He pointed to a spot on the southern Iranian coastline. "Once we're feet dry, we'll have some time on our hands. It's a solid four hundred miles to our first rally point here."

He pointed to a patch of desert in the middle of the map. "We will refer to this point as Desert One. Keep in mind that this is on the edge of the operational range of the CH-53. This is an extreme mission and we're taking extreme measures to accomplish it. This is why Second Platoon is taking this mission solo. We can't afford to take on any more weight in those birds if we want to make it to our rally point. We will arrive at Desert One around midnight and will disembark while the aircrews conduct refueling operations. At Desert One, we'll rendezvous with a new Army unit that's supposed to specialize in hostage rescue. Staff Sergeant Page, what were they calling that unit again? Delta Rangers?" asked Captain Goodwin.

"Delta Force, sir," replied Page.

"Sure… Delta Force… whatever," said Captain Goodwin. "First and Second Squad, along with supporting personnel from the Weapons Platoon, will load onto two of the CH-53s. Third Squad will load onto another two choppers along with an Air Force combat control team, with the Army taking the remaining choppers. This force will then deploy to our second staging area here," said Goodwin, pointing to an X on the map to the southeast of Tehran.

"This is our second rally point, Desert Two. Once on the deck, we will be responsible for obscuring the choppers. We'll hold at Desert Two until sundown the following day. That's a lot of sitting on our asses, so get cozy. Once we have cover of darkness, we'll strip off the camo netting and say a fond farewell to the Army. We will perform a helo assault here"—he pointed to a red circle on the map—"at Manzariyeh Air Base."

Rodriguez was struck by how remote the area was. Desert surrounded it for miles on all sides. There was no apparent reason for it to be there.

“Wow, that makes Twentynine Palms look like Manhattan,” said Sergeant Burton, the squad leader for Third Squad.

“Shut it, Burton,” said Staff Sergeant Page. With that, Captain Goodwin flipped the map over to reveal a detailed map of the airfield.

The airfield was oriented from the northwest running to the southeast, with a wide runway and a narrower taxiway running parallel. In between the two, on the southeastern side near the midpoint of the field, was a single building labeled “Control Tower.” Further down the line to the east, there was a small cluster of buildings labeled “Fuel and Maintenance.” Within those few buildings rested the tiny pulse of whatever passed for civilization in this wasteland.

“The assault is straightforward. Two landing zones, four helos. First, Lieutenant Woods will land with the bulk of Weapons Platoon and our Air Force tagalongs here in this elevated terrain.” Captain Goodwin pointed at a small patch of hills to the southeast of the airfield. “From there, the mortar squads will set up and prepare for supporting fire on the airfield. Daryl”—Captain Goodwin nodded towards the Weapons Platoon commander—“you need to hustle on this. We have the second set of helos coming in on your heels ten minutes after you hit dirt, and we need those tubes ready to get hot.” Lieutenant Woods nodded back, affirming the order and instruction. “Sergeant Burton, you need to detach a fire team to support Lieutenant Woods’s Weapons Platoon.”

“Roger that, sir,” came Sergeant Burton’s reply.

“Lieutenant Beck, you’ll take the rest of your platoon, plus a squad of M60s from Fourth Platoon along with Doc Watts and Rodgers, and land them here.” He indicated a spot about one mile due south of the control tower. “From there, you’ll advance in a line towards the objective. By then, Fourth Platoon will have dropped smoke and some HE on the objective. Daryl, take it easy on the high-explosive rounds. We just want chaos out there, not carnage. We need to capture the field intact with all of its fun parts operational.” Lieutenant Woods nodded.

“Once you’re upon the objective, Lieutenant Beck will take two fire teams along with the remaining two M60s and set up a fire position on the southeastern edge of this taxiway. You should have a clean line of sight along both objectives. From there you’ll split your assault team into two forces, one for each objective. Mason, your men will secure the maintenance facility. Rodriguez, you get the control tower. Mason, I know I don’t need to remind you, but there are a lot of things that will go boom in your objective. Take out any bad guys in the area, but do not destroy the facility. According to assets on the ground in Iran, we should encounter light resistance. We're looking at a squad-size unit at most. The latest imagery shows little to no activity. But we will not be caught by surprise. For this operation, the rules of engagement are straightforward. If it's in uniform, capture it. If it's holding a gun, kill it. We need to keep civilian casualties to a minimum." Goodwin emphasized his next point with an extended index finger directed at each of his NCOs. "We can't have civilian casualties, but do not unnecessarily endanger your men. Once the buildings are clear, we will set up defensive positions and turn control of the tower over to the Air Force combat controllers. Any questions?" There were none. "All right, fall in by squad, and let's get this passed down to the men."

The officers and NCOs all pivoted and strode in the direction of their charges. As Rodriguez took his place at the far right of his squad, he considered what he had just heard. He would be leading men into combat. OK, so it wouldn't be the Inchon landing, but still… combat. Men, his men, might die out there. The thought was there, but it wasn't fear. It wasn't trepidation. It just was. The fact registered, and his psyche filed it away as something to be dealt with later as it raced through the hundreds of things that had to be overseen and tended to between now and contact with the enemy.

The formation was as routine as expected. The captain repeated the broad view of the mission, knowing that the platoon and squad leaders would fill in the blanks with the individual Marines as to their responsibilities during the operation. As Captain Goodwin worked through the plan, Sergeant Rodriguez imagined that every man in the platoon was working through the same anxiety to some degree or another. Their fathers and uncles had fought in the Second World War, or Korea. Many had brothers who had fought in Vietnam. So far, it didn't look like his generation would see combat. This could be their only opportunity to see how they stacked up to the generations of Marines who had gone before them.

Once the formation broke up, the squad leaders huddled up with their men to go over the squad-level details of the operation. Rodriguez looked over his squad. Corporal Lionel Mack was the team leader for the second fire team in Second Squad.

"Hey, Mack," called Rodriguez, "what's the word with your apes? They in good order?"

"Sergeant, it's like Christmas morning here in this hangar," replied Mack. Rodriguez looked over to Lance Corporal Estrada, Private First Class Oliver, and Private Yates. It was apparent from their animated conversation that the Marines were excited by the prospect of action. Or maybe it was just the excitement of getting off the ship and out of the monotonous routine of life at sea. Either way, the prospect of the operation to come had everyone on full blast right now. It was up to Rodriguez to channel that energy into preparation and readiness.

"All right, Marines, let's go over this," called Rodriguez as his squad gathered around him. He noticed that Petty Officer Third Class Watts, one of the platoon's corpsmen, had joined up with this squad. Hopefully, they wouldn't need him out there, but it was always good to have Doc around. "This is straightforward. I will not repeat what the captain has already gone over. You've all ridden in the CH-53s more than enough by now. We will be doing a whole lot of nothing before we get to our objective. You need to stay sharp, you need to stay focused. And we will need to keep each other on task and motivated. When we hit the objective, we will be the most prepared, most put-together unit in the field."

The squad broke out with grunts of "Yut!" with a "Rah" or two thrown in for good measure.

Rodriguez continued, "At the objective, our task is to capture the control tower at the airfield. We'll be approaching on foot from about one point five clicks out. First and Third Squad will move to the east to secure other facilities, so we'll be on our own here in the west. If necessary, First Squad can redeploy towards the tower and give us some added firepower, but that'll be determined by the situation on the ground. For all we know, the tower will be empty and we'll be supporting First Squad.

"As for the assault itself, we will advance to contact as a squad. We'll have Strickland and Adams from Fourth Squad with an M60 for some rock and roll." There were a few chuckles at the Vietnam-era reference to the fully automatic light machine gun being deployed. "When we make contact, we'll envelop the objective. I'll take team one to the west, and Corporal Mack will take team two to the east. Team three will support the machine gun to help cover our advance."

Rodriguez let everyone take in the plan. None of this was an actual surprise to anyone. Their training would be actualized in combat for the first time. Hopefully, two hundred years of tactical evolution within the Marine Corps wasn't all a bunch of BS.

"OK, any questions?" asked Rodriguez.

"Yeah, Sergeant, why the hell did they wake us up at 0300 to tell us about a mission that won't happen for another eighteen hours?" asked PFC Oliver.

"Fifteen hours, dumbass," corrected Lance Corporal Estrada.

"Piss off, Estrada," replied Oliver. "But seriously, Rodriguez, what gives?"

Deep inside, Rodriguez smiled. Once upon a time, he had been a dumbass PFC asking the deep questions about the wisdom of Marine Corps leadership. Out loud, he deadpanned, "I'm not sure, Oliver, but I saw General Barrow over in the chow hall looking for you. I think he was going to explain it all to you in detail."

There were assorted laughs from several members of the squad while Oliver protested, "Yeah, Sergeant, you're always seeing people…"

Chapter 9

18 February 1980
1900 Hours
Bluebeard Five
Arabian Sea

Major Jason "Ripsaw" Thomas and his copilot, Philip "Snow" White, were flying Bluebeard Five in the middle of the eight-ship formation. They had left *Nimitz* and flown to the northwest, over the Gulf of Oman and right into what was neither friendly nor enemy territory. Today, Iran was a no-man's-land. It was caught between the United States and the Soviet Union in the Cold War battle of influence. Less than six months ago, this had been allied airspace, and they could fly in and over with no concern about detection, or any hostile action. Now, though, it was anyone's guess. To half the population, they might be heroes. To the other half, they were emissaries of an evil force that represented everything that had gone wrong with their nation for the past sixty years.

Having taken off at sundown, each pilot was fully focused on maintaining formation. Keeping station was imperative for keeping visual contact. This was especially important as they were operating under strict radio silence. They had lifted off and formed up into two line astern columns. This formed two straight lines of four helicopters each, with the odd choppers to the left and the even to the right. They maintained this formation until they were twenty-five miles from the Iranian coast. As they approached the coastline, they maneuvered into an echelon right formation. This put the lead chopper, Bluebeard One, in the front-left position of the formation, with each trailing helicopter to the aft and right of the one before it. The pilots adjusted the formation to reduce the chances of detection and, if detected, make it more difficult to identify the composition of the flight.

Once they had cleared the coastal settlements around Chabahar Bay, there wasn't a soul around for a hundred miles, and they re-formed into the dual-column formation. Once they had cleared the settlements, Lieutenant Colonel Richard Higgins in Bluebeard One turned on his navigation lights. Each of the birds in the formation followed suit. This was the extent of their communications from this point all the way into

Desert One. The sense of isolation was powerful. Each chopper flew towards Desert One in a group, but also alone.

"Dear Lord! What the hell is that?" exclaimed Ripsaw, pointing off to the right, forward of the chopper.

"I don't know what to make of that, Rip," replied Snow. "It looks like some kind of fogbank."

Ripsaw grunted. "A fogbank, over a hundred miles inland. This is just fantastic. I think it's one of those haboobs they warned us about. A sandstorm." Both pilots looked to their forward left, to Bluebeard Four. Bluebeard Four continued on. There was no way of knowing for sure, but both Ripsaw and Snow knew that on up the line, every aircrew was having the same conversation. The only question was whether anyone had any idea what the hell they were looking at. More importantly, did anyone know what the hell to do about it?

After a minute with no apparent changes in course, Major Thomas noted, "I guess we'll find out whether or not that thing is friendly." As they hit the cloud, everyone on board Bluebeard Five could feel the wind buffet the helicopter.

"Damn, Rip, this is crazy," said Snow. As they moved deeper into the cloud, they watched as each of the navigation lights of the preceding choppers blinked out of existence as visibility continued to drop rapidly.

"I've lost visual on everyone except Ozzy in Bluebeard Four," said Snow.

"Roger that. As long as everyone can see the guy in front of him, we're golden," replied Ripsaw.

"Yeah, as long as Colonel Higgins doesn't get us all lost."

"Aw, cheer up, Phil, at least we won't die alone."

Snow couldn't help but chuckle to himself at the morbid observation. Sometimes in the service, the only thing that could keep a crew together was the gallows humor brought on by a certain fatalism common among those who served. The next twenty minutes proved one of those times. The intense gut-wrenching feeling of attacking the unknown didn't let up.

****

In the rear of the CH-53, Corporal Lionel Mack was riding with the rest of his squad. He was pretty sure his ass had grown into the nylon seat on the helicopter. That thought was compounded when he realized that he had only been sitting there for around an hour. He still had two hours before they arrived at Desert One. With this thought, he resigned to go back to his newfound favorite pastime: staring at Private Yates, who was sitting directly across from him.

He thought about his older brother Harold, who was back in Stockton. Harold had gone into the tractor factory like the other men of his family. He had a good job with the union, he'd married a girl he'd met not long after high school graduation, and they were expecting their first child in June. That life, that "American Dream," could have been his. But from where he was sitting on this chopper, that life was twelve thousand miles away. That life might as well have been on Mars.

Sometimes Mack had wondered if he'd made the wrong choice. If that life would have been a better fit for him. Today, though, with his team riding with him into battle on this stallion, he knew there was no way he'd ever trade with Harold. There'd be time for a real life and a family once he was through kicking ass.

As Mack sat in his nylon seat staring at Private Yates, he accepted that he had absolutely no control over what might happen to him. It occurred to him that the closest feeling he'd encountered to this was during his junior year of high school. He had been riding with a friend during a flood (just a heavy rain, really, nothing like the flood of '55) when his friend had hit some water and hydroplaned. Then, as now, he knew that things weren't going the way they'd planned, and there was nothing he could do. The chaos had terrified him for about fifteen seconds while the car had angled to the right, then caught traction again, only for his buddy to overcorrect coming out of the slide, whipping the car in a hard left spin. The car had come to a stop safe and sound, but those fifteen seconds of helplessness had shaken him deeply. Today, those fifteen seconds had stretched into fifteen minutes, with no sign of abating.

"Hey, Yates, I bet your recruiter never mentioned this part to you when you signed the contract, did he?" yelled Mack over the sound of the helicopter. He'd noticed that Yates had gone from pale white to a lighter shade of green and thought getting his attention off whatever dark thoughts he was having might do some good.

"He sure as hell didn't, Corporal," replied Yates meekly.

“Oh yeah, just remember how he told you you’d be swimmin’ in poontang wearing those dress blues, Private. Keep livin’ the dream.”

At that, Yates couldn’t help but smile. It was a near-universal truth that Marine Corps recruiters could always sell the “women love a man in uniform, and the Marines have the best uniform” line to an interested young man.

Private Simon Palmer was sitting in the middle of the ship, right across from PFC Oliver. Palmer looked horrified as an oily black ooze dripped from the ceiling down onto the deck in front of him.

“Aw, damn! We’re leaking oil or something!” exclaimed Palmer.

“Oh, damn!” yelled Oliver. “We’re going down!”

Palmer turned as white as a sheet. He was clearly on the verge of panicking. Mack looked over and noticed that Oliver was grinning. As soon as Oliver saw the look of recognition on Palmer’s face, he burst out laughing.

“That ain’t funny, jackass!” said Palmer.

Just then, Estrada chimed in. “Take it easy, Palmer. Do you know what they call a CH-53 that doesn’t leak hydraulic fluid?” There was a pause as Palmer stared blankly back at Estrada.

“Empty!” yelled several of the surrounding Marines who had witnessed the interaction. It was widely known in the Corps that the CH-53 was a bleeder. Finding one without some kind of hydraulic leak was like finding a unicorn. Even Palmer knew that. But in the bumps and bruises of the storm, he wasn’t able to connect the facts that he should have known to what he was seeing with his own eyes.

Then, as suddenly as it had begun, the wind and sand just quit. Bluebeard Five burst out of the haboob and into the cloudless Persian night. As visibility returned, they realized that the flight had made it through the trial with no apparent casualties.

As the tension in the air of the cargo compartment lightened, Yates called out to Mack, “All in a day’s work, right, Corporal?”

Now it was Mack’s turn to smile. Yates was all right. He was the youngest member of the fire team, but he was a quick study and he did what he was told. That was something he could work with. He felt that Yates was a good Marine, and he had the potential to be a great Marine.

As they flew on, Mack could faintly hear Estrada and Oliver belting out their personal rendition of AC/DC’s “Highway to Hell.” It had become a common occurrence on the many chopper rides they had taken over the vast and empty sea. It was always kind of fun and silly at the start of a flight but quickly became tedious. Normally, Mack or one of the other NCOs would have told them to knock it off, but after the tension of the past hour, everyone was content to let it go.

****

In the cockpit, Ripsaw was trying to get his bearings after the haboob.

"What the hell?" asked Snow.

"Aw, damn," replied Ripsaw. As visibility had returned, so had the familiar navigation lights of Bluebeards Three and Four. What had caused the alarm was the absence of any sign of Bluebeards One and Two. "I need your head on a swivel, Phil. Call out if you find any sign of them." With that, Ripsaw looked over his left shoulder into the night sky, hoping for any indication that the flight leads were in the area. Much to his consternation, there was none. The haboob had reduced their flight by at least two helos.

Even without the two lead choppers, Ripsaw knew the mission was still a go and that they needed to get their birds and the Marines in them to Desert One to complete the objective. And so they flew on, maintaining their position in the formation as the Sea Stallions continued northwest for their rendezvous with the C-130s and the Army's Delta Force. Ripsaw noticed a warning lamp on the instrument panel.

"Hey, Phil, check out that reading on the nav system. Run a diagnostic and see if you can sort it out."

"Roger that, Rip, let me take a look." Snow ran through the diagnostic procedures to trace the fault indicated by the warning. The sincere hope was that this was a computer glitch. Just some kind of bug that choked up the system now and then. As the minutes ticked off with no reply from Snow, Ripsaw had a sinking feeling. *This will not be simple.*

"Bad news, boss," said Snow. "I've got nothing showing this is just a computer issue, and I can't get navigation back online."

"That doesn't leave us a lot of options," replied Ripsaw. "We could try to fly back on a reciprocal bearing and pick up *Nimitz* at sea, or we can try to stick with Captain Osborne and head on to Desert One. Either way is a crap sandwich. Heading back might mean going back through those storms we just got out of, but if we get separated from Bluebeard Four, we won't know where the hell we are. We might as well be in the middle of the ocean for all the landmarks out here. We'll be done for if we have to put down." There was no argument from the right seat. "I guess we'll take our chances with Bluebeard Four. I promised you we wouldn't die alone after all."

This time there was no chuckle in response. At this point, even gallows humor was wearing thin.

****

19 February 1980
0115 Hours
Desert One
Iran

As Bluebeard Five neared the rally point, Sergeant Rodriguez looked over his shoulder out the side door of the helicopter.

What the hell is that? he wondered. On the ground he could see the smoldering heap of what looked like a truck. Within minutes, he felt the slight bump of the helicopter touching down.

As he cleared the ramp, Sergeant Rodriguez immediately headed to the established rally point to the southwest of the helos. As he trotted over to the area, he could see Fire Team Three already falling in. They had flown in on Bluebeard Six and had a bit of a head start. Fire Teams One and Two were falling in behind him and sprinted ahead to get formed up. Rodriguez took the report from each of the team leaders showing that Second Squad was all present. Rodriguez addressed his men.

"All right, Marines, that was a hell of a ride, and now we've got some time to stretch our legs. We'll only be here long enough to refuel the choppers, so don't drift off. Any questions?"

"Yeah, Sergeant, where's the rest of the platoon?" asked Lance Corporal Kevin McKinney.

"You worry about your assignment and your teammates," replied Sergeant Rodriguez. "If and when I get any information on First Squad, I'll let you know."

As he'd approached their assigned rally point, Rodriguez had noticed that the rest of the platoon had assembled, or was in the process of assembling, but there was no sign of First Squad. He did some quick operational math in his head and wondered what this meant for his squad. His best guess was that they would take a fire team from his squad and some of the Weapons Platoon to augment the Headquarters Squad to take the fuel and maintenance facilities. That would best allocate resources to where they were needed without radical changes to existing assignments. *Then again, I'm just a dumbass E-5, what do I know?* he thought. *I'm here to follow orders and accomplish missions.*

"Ours is but to do and die," Rodriguez muttered as he set out to find Staff Sergeant Page or Lieutenant Beck.

He found both back near the helos. Lieutenant Beck was talking to one of the pilots that Rodriguez didn't recognize, and Page was standing with Sergeant Strickland from the Weapons Platoon. "Hey, Dom, what's the word?" asked Rodriguez.

"Looks like we lost Jimmie and his boys somewhere en route," replied Page.

"Damn, man, that sounds pretty bad," said Rodriguez.

"Don't wet your pants just yet, Rodriguez. LT's talking to the pilots, and so far nobody saw any of the choppers go down. They just lost them in the sandstorms. From the sound of things, that transit wasn't exactly by the book, and the entire operation is running late, but still within the window."

"Any word on new orders?" asked Rodriguez.

"Nothing yet," replied Page. "I'm guessing we'll shift Marines from protecting the mortars to the assault team, but who knows? Right now it's just hurry up and wait. Once we get the choppers refueled and the Army pukes ready to load, we'll get with the captain. Until then, we will wait for First Squad to show up." Rodriguez noticed the LT heading their way.

"It's a fine night for a firefight!" called out Lieutenant Beck as he approached them. He seemed almost giddy at the prospect of action.

"Any word on First Squad?" Asked Page.

"Nothing solid. From what we can tell, one of the pilots thought he saw lights off to the west as they were coming through the storm, but he couldn't be sure since they were locked onto the ship in front of 'em," replied the LT.

"What's the story with the fire off to the southeast? It looked like something got blown up out there."

"No clue, Rodriguez. I've only talked to the pilots and they don't know any more than you do. Listen, I need you guys to keep your Marines corralled for now. I'll get with the captain and see about any updated orders. Staff Sergeant Page, why don't you see if you can track down someone from that Army unit and get the skinny on the local situation?"

"Roger that, sir!" said Page as he turned and headed out into the darkness towards what looked like the center of the operation.

"We'll need to be ready to bounce. I don't want the operation to be sitting here on hold because your apes can't form up and load into the choppers on time. Just be ready to fall in when I get back with any updates. Now get the hell out of here," ordered Lieutenant Beck.

"Sir!" replied the remaining two sergeants, who turned and headed back to their Marines.

"Rodriguez, you're with me," said Beck.

Rodriguez followed Lieutenant Beck as he headed off in the same direction as Staff Sergeant Page. They found a makeshift command post set up to the north just ahead of two of the C-130 tankers. He could see Captain Goodwin talking with a couple of the Marine pilots and an Army colonel.

"What do you think, Ripsaw?" asked Captain Goodwin. "Is your bird fit to fly?"

"She'll fly, Captain. We might not get where we want to go, but she'll fly," replied Major Thomas.

"Be that as it may, Major, flying blind could put this mission in jeopardy," interjected the colonel.

"With all due respect, Colonel, I'm confident in my skills and those of my copilot. If we can navigate across the vast ocean, I assure you we can fly over this desert without getting lost," Major Thomas responded.

"Well, son, we're flying under wartime conditions. Here's my ultimate word on this: You can take that bird up, but you're only on the Manzariyeh operation, and you're only hauling Marines. No real people. Got it? We can't have you flying to your death in the middle of the desert with a hold full of civilians," said the colonel.

"Understood, sir, just grunts, no humans."

With that, the pilots headed back towards the helicopters.

"Captain Goodwin," called Lieutenant Beck as he neared the other officers. "Good morning, Colonel."

"How was the ride in, Omar?" asked Captain Goodwin.

"Shitty, sir, but not worth complaining about," replied Beck.

"At least you made it in, Lieutenant," said Colonel Willis, frowning.

"We still don't have any word on First Squad. None of the sky jockeys saw them go down, but they aren't here either," said Captain Goodwin.

"There's a rumor going around that one of the rear chopper pilots might have seen them break formation during the storm," added Lieutenant Beck.

"Nothing to be done about it now," said Captain Goodwin. "Colonel, if you'll excuse us, we've got some operational adjustments to make." The three Marines then returned to the rally point.

Platoon leadership huddled up for orders. Rodriguez listened as the captain and Lieutenants Beck and Woods went over the situation. In the end, they decided the fire team that had originally been attached to support the mortar teams was going to rejoin Third Squad on the Assault. This would leave the assault force short two fire teams but would still give them a full squad to take the fuel and maintenance facilities. It wasn't optimal, but it was what they had.

"Semper Gumby, sir," said Lieutenant Beck as they concluded their planning.

"Semper Gumby indeed, Omar," replied Captain Goodwin, repeating the popular spin on the Marine Corps motto of "Semper Fidelis." As the thinking went, if Semper Fidelis was Latin for "Always Faithful," the secondary motto for the Corps must be Semper Gumby: "Always Flexible." They broke up their ad hoc meeting and took their place at the head of the formation.

"All right, assholes, fall in!" yelled Lieutenant Beck. The assorted Marines of Second and Fourth Platoons quickly found their spots in the formation and awaited orders.

Captain Goodwin addressed the men. "Marines, our mission has not changed. We will continue on tonight to our second rally point, and tomorrow we will assault the airfield at Manzariyeh. For most of you, your orders have not changed. Sergeant Burton will update Third Squad on any assignment changes for his men, and Lieutenant Woods will brief Fourth Platoon. I know there are a lot of questions out there about First

Squad. Right now we don't have any answers, and right now there's nothing we can do about it. Whatever has happened has happened, and we still have a mission to accomplish. Staff Sergeant Page, can you enlighten us on the fire to the south?"

"Sir, the Army lit up a gas tanker truck that was barreling towards the LZ. Word around the NCOs is that the driver survived the blast and took off in a second vehicle, so all the world probably knows we're here. Oh, and a bus full of Iranians is being detained on the other side of the refueling area. So, yeah, it couldn't be better," reported Page.

"OK, mystery solved. I want all you meatheads ready to board the choppers as soon as we get the green light. It won't be long now," concluded Captain Goodwin.

Chapter 10

2240 Hours
South of Manzariyeh Air Base, Iran

Rodriguez could hear his heartbeat as though it were in his helmet. Every bump of the ride had his blood pumping harder. Just when he thought he would explode, he felt the helo flare and set down on the ground as the ramp came down, unleashing the raging hounds inside. Lieutenant Beck hit the ground first and immediately headed to his left, north of the helo, to establish the assembly area for the assault force. Rodriguez was right behind him. However, he stopped just past the ramp to ensure that the rest of his squad dismounted without trouble. If anyone were to get hung up or fall down, Sergeant Carlos Rodriguez would be there to ensure they got out of the chopper and were ready for the assault.

"Third Squad, on me!" Lieutenant Beck bellowed as the Marines funneled out of the helo and into the Iranian desert. Rodriguez could hear the *whump...whump* sound of outgoing mortar rounds. The downforce of the rotors created a thick blanket of sand and debris that blasted the Marines. The platoon was pelted harder as the engines screamed louder and the Sea Stallion lifted off and returned to the sky. Rodriguez looked up as Bluebeard Five wheeled around to dash away to the south. He couldn't make out the pilots. A wall of sand obscured visibility skyward. Besides, he had more pressing issues to tend to.

"Second Squad, let's go!" shouted Rodriguez as he ran to his designated position at the head of the formation. He could taste the grit of the desert as he spoke. Cobb and Fire Team One fell in to his left, with Mack and Fire Team Two on his right. Fire Team Three and the machine-gun team were directly behind him as they began their advance towards the airfield. From this distance, they couldn't make out the objective, but they could see flashes from the mortar rounds exploding on target.

Rodriguez reached back and pulled out the handset on the PRC-77 radio on his back. He keyed the radio.

"Playboy, this is Hustler Two-Two. Coms check, over."

"Hustler Two-Two, this is Playboy. We read you," came the affirming reply.

"Hustler Two-Two is assembled and moving out to our objective."

As they pushed forward towards the objective, the distance between Rodriguez's and Beck's forces increased. Third Squad veered to the east to close with any forces in the fuel and maintenance facilities while Second Squad was shifting to the west to advance on the control tower. Increasingly, Rodriguez felt isolated. He could feel the weight of command as he lost sight of the LT. It wasn't a conscious worry. It was more of a tugging at the back reaches of his mind.

Ever since the ramp had dropped, his training had kicked in, and he was focused solely on the mission. He had spent years preparing for this opportunity. His team had spent weeks rehearsing helicopter assaults. He had spent days considering everything he could think of on this specific mission and objective. As he jogged at the front of his squad, he was hyperfocused on one thing.

Advance to contact.

As his squad closed on the objective, Rodriguez could make out the form of the control tower in the distance. The five-story building was the only shape on the flat horizon. His team was moving at a slow jog and was meant to keep the pace for the squad. As they closed on the tower, a cloud of sand exploded in front of him, followed by the terrifyingly familiar sound of a machine-gun burst. His first thought was that Strickland had had a negligent discharge. But that thought was immediately erased by the sound of Strickland firing a very intentional burst just off to the left of Fire Team One. The original burst had come from the control tower. Rodriguez remembered the dozens of briefings he'd been through explaining that the US government had armed the Iranians with US equipment. These soldiers had been, until a few months ago, allies. This was it. Contact. The enemy had caught Second Squad with their pants down, but there was still a mission to accomplish.

The opening burst of fire was a good bit short of the assault team, but it sufficed to get everyone's attention. Just as they had rehearsed, Sergeant Strickland dropped to a knee and unloaded his 7.62mm reply. The muzzle flash of his M60 lit up the fire team, who, because they had stopped and taken a knee, were now receding behind Rodriguez and Mack's teams. The squad was about four hundred and fifty meters from the tower. Strickland's assault wasn't meant to kill (though nobody would argue if an Iranian or two stepped in front of a bullet). His mission was to spray that tower with enough lead to ensure that none of the occupants would hazard another volley at the Marines.

Rodriguez picked up his pace. Now that the enemy had detected them, he knew that the longer they were in the line of fire, the greater the chance of taking casualties. As Fire Team One moved forward, he caught sight of Corporal Mack. Rodriguez signaled for him to take his team and flank the left side of the tower. This would effectively swap the roles of Teams One and Two. *And to think I spent all this time practicing shooting to the left*, Rodriguez thought wryly as he veered to the right to gain some separation between the suppressing fire from Team Three and his team.

Once Rodriguez was sure that Mack had received his tasking, he took off at a sprint to the right flank of the tower. The squad was presenting too wide of a target for the enemy to concentrate fire on the whole. In fact, since Strickland had opened up on them, they hadn't seen any return fire. Once they had closed to about two hundred meters, he ordered his men to drop and open fire on the tower. This gave him an opportunity to report on his situation.

"Playboy, this is Hustler Two-Two. We're taking light machine-gun fire from the control tower. Estimate that there's a single machine gun, probably an M60. We are engaging the enemy. Out," reported Rodriguez.

The angle created by Fire Team One's maneuver to the right had exposed the east side of the building to the assault team's field of fire. They concentrated their shots on the windows they could make out. Firing in three-round bursts, each Marine could put ten salvos on the building before they needed to reload. From their position, it was almost like being on the range back in Lejeune. Rodriguez was confident that Mack was working on the left side of the building at the same time.

****

Mack was a few seconds behind Rodriguez in giving the order to fire. In those seconds, his team was taking fire from somewhere on the fourth or fifth floor of the building. The moment the first rounds hit, Fire Team Two went prone and returned fire with their M16A1s. As they punched through the windows of the tower, they were still receiving sporadic fire from different locations in the building.

"Oliver! Put some forty-millimeter just under the top floor!" shouted Mack. PFC Oliver was the team's grenadier and had an M203 40mm grenade launcher attached under the barrel of his M16. At this range, it wasn't a sure shot to get the round into the relatively small window, but much like Strickland's M60, Mack hoped that the noise and violence of the round would convince the attackers to stop shooting at him. He was ordering up some chaos for the enemy.

Oliver obliged. He'd had a round chambered and immediately took aim as best he could and fired at the building. The round sailed on towards the tower, and for a moment, Mack thought it would sail through the centermost window of the fourth floor… a perfect shot! But as the round continued towards the target, it dropped and struck just below the window. Gravity had denied Oliver's dream shot. But the round had the desired effect. Without knowing what had hit them, the defenders instinctively pulled back from their firing positions, trying to sort out their own safety before going back to trying to kill the Marines.

By this point, Fire Team Three had advanced under the suppressive fire of Teams One and Two. Once they were inside three hundred yards of the tower, they resumed firing the machine gun. The difference in the weight of fire between the two teams armed only with M16s and the team with the fully automatic M60 was palpable. For the teams in the assault's front, the increase in noise was undeniable. For Fire Team Three, they could feel the difference when the gun opened up. But most importantly, in the dark recesses of the control tower, the fear felt by the enemy shot up in intensity to debilitating levels.

Fire Team Two closed the distance to the primary entrance to the building. *Damn*, thought Mack. He knew that this was the most likely scenario for the mission. That Second Squad would have to take the tower one floor at a time. But there was a part of him that had hoped these guys would just throw down their weapons once they saw what they were up against. Not today.

As they neared the building, he called out, "Estrada, make us a door!"

Estrada took a knee and reached to his back to retrieve his M72 light anti-armor weapon (LAW). Just as he had trained countless times, he pulled the pin out and flipped the front cover off the angry end of the tube. While holding the front of the weapon, he pulled the two sections apart until he could feel them lock, then quickly double-checked by pushing them back together. Once he was sure he had locked the unit, he put it to his shoulder and took aim at the wall of the tower. Estrada needed to ensure that there wasn't anyone standing behind him before he unleashed the LAW.

"Backblast area—" Estrada never finished the sentence as he depressed the firing lever on the top of the tube. With the adrenaline rush of combat, he'd cut short the last word: "clear." Fortunately, the backblast area was, in fact, clear as a burst of explosive gases erupted from the rear of the weapon. The rocket-propelled grenade leaped from the launcher and shot across the open terrain to the tower. Estrada had hardly pressed the trigger before the wall exploded out with the force of HE from the rocket's warhead. As the dust cleared, they could make out the new "door" Estrada had created.

Fire Team Two filed into the control tower. As each Marine cleared their zone, they called out, "Clear." The ground floor was empty, which made sense. There wasn't much point in occupying the high ground if you wouldn't take advantage of the elevation. As Mack considered this, he found the stairwell that led to the second floor. It was in Yates's zone, and Yates was looking to his left as he neared the base of the stairs.

Mack could see from where he stood that Yates was oblivious to the danger he was walking into. He yelled out, "Yates! Get down!"

Yates stopped short, just as a burst of rifle fire sprayed the stairwell. In a panic, he fired at the wall of the stairwell as he fell back. Mack ran over to the landing and sent a three-round burst up the stairs. *No sense in letting the bad guys get comfortable*, he thought.

Estrada squatted just outside the threshold of the stairwell while Mack stood over him. On Mack's signal, Estrada fired two bursts up the stairwell while Mack followed them up with a grenade. As the explosive detonated, Estrada took off up the stairs, followed by Mack, with Yates and Oliver bringing up the rear. Visibility on the second floor was considerably worse, with the debris in the air from Mack's grenade. He and Estrada had just begun to fan out when there was a burst of fire from across the room. They heard a Marine cry out and the sound of someone falling back down the stairs behind them.

Mack and Estrada returned fire in the direction of the muzzle flashes and were rewarded with an anguished scream and broken glass. They cleared the room and found an Iranian soldier slumped next to a window at the base of the next stairwell leading up. The tower had stairs on the opposite side of the room for each floor. Mack thought that this could be a long night if they had to fight it out for each floor of the tower. But that was the operation, and that was why they were there. Mack was getting ahead of himself. He turned around and headed to the stairwell, where he saw a thick trail of blood leading back to the ground floor. There was no other sign of either Oliver or Yates.

****

While Mack and Fire Team Two were engaged in the stairwell, Rodriguez led Fire Team One behind the building, along the northern wall. After Rodriguez and Cobb had moved past the center point of the building, there was a burst of gunfire and Rodriguez turned to watch Lance Corporal Kevin McKinney drop to the ground and cry out, "Oh, shit!" while grabbing at his left shoulder.

Before Rodriguez turned back, he heard Palmer call out, "Corpsman! Watts!" But there was no point—Watts was already running forward to McKinney. Cobb and PFC Boone sprayed fire up at a window on the second floor, pushing their assailant back into the building while Doc Watts and Palmer pulled McKinney out of the field of fire and to the east-facing wall of the tower.

"I got this, Palmer," said Watts as he treated the cursing lance corporal. "Get back to the team."

Palmer ran back to his position, where he could hear Rodriguez yelling to Cobb, "We've got to get in there now! We can't afford to sit around here playing whack-a-mole with these assholes."

As Rodriguez and Fire Team One were entering through the door that Fire Team Two had created just minutes beforehand, they could hear the burst of fire from the second floor. Before he could react, he saw two bodies tumbling down the stairs and sprawling out on the landing. As they raised their weapons toward the stairs, they could hear PFC Oliver yelling.

"Motherfucker!" said Oliver as he scrambled to his feet. Without a second of hesitation, he grabbed Yates by the harness and pulled him clear of the stairway. "Corpsman! I need a corpsman here!"

Doc Watts hadn't made it back to the team yet. He was still with McKinney on the east wall, but Palmer immediately moved in to see what aid he could render.

"Oh, damn," whispered Palmer when he saw what was left of Yates. He'd taken a shot to the chest, and one to the head. He was dead before he crashed into Oliver on his way down the stairs. Rodriguez could tell that Oliver had no idea how bad the situation was. He was still hollering for the corpsman. Palmer grabbed Oliver by the shoulder and repeated the words that Doc had told him outside the tower: "I've got this, Oliver, get back to your team." That seemed to yank Oliver back into this world. He looked at Palmer for a fraction of a second, then turned and started back up the stairs.

"Mack, you guys still up there? We're coming up!" said Rodriguez to the Marines on the second floor. He turned to Palmer and said, "Wait here with Yates until Doc gets here," then turned and headed up the stairs, followed by Cobb and Boone. As they rumbled up the stairs, each Marine unconsciously avoided the thick streaks of blood that marked the end of Private Yates. At the top of the stairs, Rodriguez saw Estrada covering the next stairwell while Oliver huddled up with Mack, undoubtedly updating him on the situation downstairs with Yates.

"All right, we've got six of us here. Palmer and Watts are with Yates. McKinney is down too," said Rodriguez. "Estrada, take point on the next staircase." Without a word, Estrada moved toward the stairwell. Rodriguez held his breath, watching as Estrada edged around the corner with his M16 at the ready. The only surprise waiting for him was the lack of gunfire. Rodriguez let out his breath.

Estrada stepped over the dead Iranian and continued to creep up the stairs. Rodriguez followed. He could hear the muffled sounds of someone groaning on the floor above him. In fact, he couldn't be certain that it wasn't more than one person. Behind him, Mack had entered the stairwell, trying to ride the edge between "too far away to support" and "so close you both get killed."

Besides the wounded man upstairs, they could hear noises in the distance. Within the stairwell, the silence was near complete. Rodriguez could hear his own breathing. He could feel his heart pounding. The sweat that was beading on his forehead threatened to drop into his eyes. He continued up the stairs. As he neared the top, the room above took shape. At first, all he could see was the ceiling above and in front of him. Each step exposed more of the room. The ceiling gave way to walls. As he climbed the stairs and more of the room came into view, he was exposed to a scene of absolute carnage.

The Marines had blown in every window in the room as they'd fired from outside the tower. There were three bodies on the floor, one of which was the source of the groaning Estrada had heard. That was the only body that was moving. The only one showing any signs of life. Estrada moved quickly now, covering his assigned zone and ensuring that there were no more enemy soldiers. Behind him, Mack and Rodriguez fanned out. The rest of the squad stood by with Cobb on the stairs and Oliver remaining on the second floor. The one thing that they didn't see on this floor was the M60 machine gun that had opened up on them in the field. That was bad news.

Because the threat level was still high, the squad was trying to go about the business of securing the floor as quietly as possible. Rodriguez signaled to Estrada to check on the wounded man. In this case, Rodriguez wasn't particularly interested in the man's wounds or in rendering aid. He was simply checking him for weapons and ensuring that he wasn't a threat. If he lived long enough for them to secure the entire objective, they'd see if Doc could take some time to treat him. Until then, it was his hard luck. Though truth be told, he was the lucky one on this floor. He still had a chance of surviving the night.

When they had first entered the room, the crushing tension had abated. Discovering that the room was devoid of any threat was a relief. It was a very temporary relief, however. Once the moment had passed, Rodriguez had realized that by clearing this room, they had dramatically increased the odds that they would find the machine gun waiting for them in the next room. It was a toss-up now. Fifty-fifty. That gun and its operator were waiting on either the fourth or fifth floor. That knowledge compounded the dread and the foreboding that he'd experienced in the stairs just minutes earlier.

Estrada looked back at Rodriguez, who signaled for him to continue on to the next stairwell. As he silently approached, he suddenly heard a cry from above. It was a guttural yell. If that yell had any distinct meaning, it was totally lost on the Marines. All they knew was that it meant someone was up there, and as the yell grew louder, they knew that he was heading right for them.

As soon as they heard the man cry out, Estrada backed away from the stairwell, and everyone in the room ducked back to get out of the firing arc from the opening of the stairs. A sustained burst of automatic weapon fire opened up, and the wall at the end of the stairs exploded as the rounds tore into it. Cement fragments were flying everywhere, but there were no exposed targets for them to hit.

Suddenly, as the enemy soldier made it to the bottom of the stairs, he turned and brought the room into his field of fire. Rodriguez had ducked back down the stairs on the opposite side of the room, while Mack had taken cover under a desk in the opposite corner. As the attacker entered the room, still yelling and spraying rounds—*spraying and praying*, thought Rodriguez—Estrada ended him with a three-round burst from his M16. And then another for good measure. Just in case.

As soon as the noise from the brief firefight subsided, Rodriguez could hear another man calling out from the floor above. This time, though, the meaning was clear. The man called out with a thick Persian accent, "I am surrender! I am surrender!"

The rest of the squad had entered the room once Estrada had neutralized the M60.

"What the hell is he saying?" asked Cobb. "His English sucks."

"It's a lot better than my Arabic," said Oliver.

"Iranians speak Farsi, dumbass," corrected Estrada.

"Piss off, Estrada," said Oliver as the possibility that they had secured the objective sank in.

Chapter 11

19 February 1980
USS *Coral Sea*
Arabian Sea

The USS *Coral Sea* had been around the block. She had been laid down during the Second World War and was still sailing today. The modernization of her flight deck allowed her to field the latest in US Navy attack aircraft, which had made her an effective fighting force for over three decades. This had earned her the nickname "Ageless Warrior."

Lieutenant Junior Grade Samuel "Pharaoh" Bell wasn't so convinced of the "ageless" part of that moniker. He'd only been on board for three months, but he was pretty sure he could hear the ship creaking. He'd asked around about whether the ship had won any honors during the War of 1812, but nobody found that amusing. In fact, the only satisfying response he'd gotten from his joke was when Lieutenant Barber had replied, "Yeah, but at least she's paid for."

Pharaoh was a member of the Royal Maces of Attack Squadron 27. The Maces had been an A-7 Corsair II unit since their commissioning in 1967. They had flown five combat tours in Vietnam from the USS *Constellation* and USS *Enterprise* and were pioneers in fielding the Navy's premier light-attack aircraft. Named after the medieval weapon that specialized in punching holes in an enemy's armor, the modern-day Maces punched holes in the enemy's air defenses with their AGM-45 Shrike antiradiation missiles. Besides the AGM-45, the A-7 could mount an assortment of guided and unguided weapons, from the latest AGM-65 Maverick to the Mark 82 general-purpose bomb. Together with the VA-97 Warhawks, they made up *Coral Sea*'s "jab" while the larger A-6E Intruders of VA-196 represented the "haymaker."

Tonight, Pharaoh sat in his designated chair in the squadron's ready room. This was it. Pharaoh was about to get his first combat mission. Lieutenant Nathan "Scooter" Hayes stood at the front of the cramped room, going over the details of the plan. The Maces, along with the rest of Carrier Air Wing Fourteen's attack squadrons, were providing close-air support for ground forces in northern Iran. During the next eight hours, the flight deck of *Coral Sea* would be in a constant state of controlled chaos. Aircraft were being readied, launched, recovered, refueled, and rearmed in a constant cycle. This was necessary to provide complete coverage of the patrol area for the expected duration of the mission.

"We do not have a detailed picture of enemy forces," said Lieutenant Hayes. "In fact, we have no actual picture of enemy forces at all. We could expect anything from zero opposition to a major deployment of armored forces from here in the south of Tehran. Our primary area of responsibility will be on the avenues of approach to this air base here"—Hayes pointed to Manzariyeh—"with an emphasis on Route 71 between Tehran and the city of Qom to the south of the air base. Given the unknown character of our targets, each aircraft will carry four Mk-20 antitank cluster bombs."

The Mk-20, known as the "Rockeye II," was an unguided bomb that had been introduced in the late 1960s. When dropped, it would fall to a predetermined height (which depended on the fuse installed in the bomb) before splitting in half and spreading almost two hundred and fifty individual bomblets along the target area. Each bomblet on its own would be bad news; when taken as a whole, they were catastrophic. The principle was very much the same as a shotgun: a shot pattern significantly increases the odds of scoring a hit.

"We will coordinate with the Main Battery on this mission," said Scooter. The "Main Battery" was the nickname for VA-196, the A-6 Intruder squadron on the Ageless Warrior. A mission like tonight's would combine the flexibility of the Corsair with the specialized capabilities of the Intruder.

"Each section will be flying with an Intruder for radar support. As we make our road reconnaissance passes from north to south, you will coordinate with an A-6 and the E-2C Hawkeye. Once the Tadpole locates a target," said Scooter, using the nickname for the A-6, "they'll light it up and mark the target with flares." Scooter walked through the rest of the briefing, and the aviators cleared the room.

After the aviators checked out their aircraft with maintenance control, they headed for the locker room to get suited up for the mission. As Pharaoh was pulling his harness over his G-suit, his section leader, Lieutenant "Buzz" Barber, walked over to him.

"Hey, Sam, try to relax, okay?" said Buzz. "You've been through the training. You've done everything you can to prove that you can complete this mission. You belong with us up there, so just relax and let it come to you. I don't need you wound too tight and second-guessing everything out there tonight."

"Roger, Lieutenant, thanks for that," said Pharaoh.

"What he means to say is 'don't screw up or we're both dead,'" said Lieutenant McGuire with a smile. There were several philosophies on how to deal with nerves on a night like this, and everyone had their own opinion about which philosophy was best. It seemed that Buzz believed a boost of confidence should fix Pharaoh up for the mission. For the eternally confident "Heaver" McGuire, only gallows humor would do the trick. At the end of the day, there was only one cure for the nerves, and that was experience. Good or bad, they were all going to get that tonight.

As Pharaoh pulled on his flotation vest and grabbed his gloves and helmet, he considered what Buzz had said. It was true, he'd been through all the training. He knew how to operate his Corsair. As the thousands of bits and pieces of training came together, he instinctively knew that he was the right man for the job. As soon as he'd come to that conclusion, he tripped over the watertight hatch leading out of the locker room. He struggled to catch his balance, and when he did, he was rewarded with cheers of "Nice dancing, Grace!" and "Oh, hey, I just put that there." It seemed as though that was exactly the reminder he needed not to get carried away in his own brilliance.

Pharaoh made his way to the hangar deck, where he found the plane he'd be flying that night. This Corsair was Bureau Number (BuNo) 157502 and could easily be identified by the squadron ID number 410 painted on the front of the fuselage on the large air intake just under the cockpit. He was greeted by Seaman Richard Carr as he walked up to the aircraft. Carr was one of the squadron's aviation machinist's mates and the plane captain for 410. Though one of the younger men in the squadron, Carr was responsible for ensuring that the aircraft was mission ready before every operation. Once 410 returned from the mission, Carr would be responsible for the postflight checks that were necessary to turn her around for the next mission.

"Evening, Lieutenant," said Carr as Pharaoh approached.

"Evening, Seaman Carr, everything in order?"

He knew the answer before asking the question. If something hadn't been in order, they'd have known about it when they'd checked with maintenance control right after the mission briefing. The two men performed a final walk-around preflight check, verifying that the plane was in good order and that the weapons load-out was as advertised. Once they had completed this, Pharaoh climbed the ladder and performed a quick visual inspection to ensure there were no loose foreign objects in the cockpit. *The last thing I need is a screwdriver bouncing around in here with me*, thought Pharaoh. Once he was sure it was clear, he lowered himself into the aircraft.

Carr had followed Pharaoh up the ladder. "Good luck, Lieutenant," he said as he helped Pharaoh strap in and secure himself to his seat. Once he was secured, Pharaoh began the process of readying the aircraft for engine start-up. As he was working on the aircraft in the cockpit, Carr was on the deck getting the engine itself ready to go. Once both sides had completed their tasks, the Allison TF41 engine roared to life. Carr began his final checks, ensuring that the engine was running optimally, while Pharaoh checked for any anomalous readings in the cockpit.

Pharaoh then turned his attention to the yellow-shirted aircraft handler in front of 410. Following the Yellow Shirt's directions, he waited for his turn to move his plane up the flight deck, closer to the catapults at the bow of the ship. As he started the progression, he could see other Corsairs being readied for launch. The thick jet blast deflector protruding like a short wall behind the Corsair in front of him obscured his view of the plane. Pharaoh knew that on the other side of that wall, there were "little green men" working to fix the catapult to the nose gear to prepare for launch.

Suddenly, the Corsair in front of him shot forward, racing down the flight deck before dropping off the forward edge, then climbing out away from the ship. As the blast deflector came down, another aircraft handler led Bell forward to the catapult. Once there, those same little green men set the catapult for 410. As the catapult built up pressure, Pharaoh pushed his throttle forward to full. The aircraft was held in place by a holdback bar as Pharaoh made one last prelaunch check. He reached for his instrument panel, thinking, *The last thing I need to do is turn on the navigation ligh—*

Before he could finish the thought, the catapult released, and Lieutenant JG Bell and his Corsair shot down the deck like a bullet.

Chapter 12

19 February 1980
US Embassy
Tehran, Iran

Captain Kyle Ball felt the lightness of the pistol he held in his hand. The suppressed Ruger MK I Target .22 pistol wasn't standard-issue for the Army, but then, nothing was standard-issue for Delta Force. This mission certainly wasn't standard. He silently crept up to the guardhouse and shot the guard stationed there in the side of his head before he had a chance to react. The tiny subsonic round rattled around in the man's brain, killing him instantly. No, this wasn't standard at all.

Captain Ball was leading a three-man "kill team" that was charged with silently eliminating the external guards so that other operators could blow the doors. Once the building was breached, the entire seventy-seven-man unit would surprise the Iranian students who were holding fifty-two Americans hostage within the embassy compound. They had flown for seven hundred miles in special MC-130E transports, then for another four hundred and fifty miles on board US Marine Corps CH-53D helicopters, and finally the last hundred miles crammed in the back of miscellaneous cargo trucks.

Ball looked back towards Roosevelt Avenue and could see the other members of the Blue Element. This was Ball's element, and it was responsible for securing the eastern side of the compound. Blue Element was scrambling up ladders and over the walls protecting the embassy grounds. Ball followed them over, making contact with Master Sergeant Tony Rivera, his teammate, for the assault. The two of them would clear rooms in the main embassy building. He could also see Red Element taking up station on the western side. Once they were in position, for a fraction of a second, Delta Force was a tightly coiled spring waiting for the signal to explode.

A demolition team gave them that signal when they blew an enormous hole in the wall that they had just climbed over. At the exact moment that they destroyed the wall, men on both sides of the building were breaching and entering. As he approached the main embassy building, he could see flashes of gunfire as the boys lit up terrorists inside the compound with their CAR-15 carbines. Even with the suddenness and violence of the action, they carried it out with methodical efficiency. The team had been working on this exercise for the past month, and everyone knew their assignments.

The building Ball and Rivera were assaulting had three stories, two above ground and one basement. They entered through the doorway on the eastern side and followed the team in front of them up the stairwell directly inside the entry. Once they made it to the second floor, they broke right and started down the hall. They passed several other two-man teams that had come in ahead of them and were in the process of clearing other offices. They could hear the explosions of stun grenades, and the air was filled with a residual haze. Their objective was in the third office on the left side of the hall.

Ball passed the door and took up station on the far side, ready to enter. Because the doorway opened towards the team, Rivera, who was armed with a Model 37 shotgun, reached across the door and tried the knob. It was unlocked, which meant he wouldn't have to use his shotgun to pick the lock. He pulled the door towards himself, allowing Ball to throw a flash-bang into the room. As soon as the grenade detonated, the two men entered the room with their weapons at the ready. They were greeted by a burst of gunfire and a man yelling, "*Marg bar Amrika!*" The two soldiers returned fire and ducked back into the hallway.

****

"*Marg bar Amrika!*" The shout shook Foreign Service Officer Howard Chandler. But what scared him more than anything else was the sound of the machine gun opening up. They had woken up when the first explosions had ripped through the night. In the minutes since then, their guard had been constantly shouting at them in Farsi. The guards rounded up hostages and pushed them into a corner of the office.

Chandler was crushed between bodies as the hostages tried to put distance between themselves and their irate guard. This room housed the "troublemakers," and Chandler was increasingly worried that whatever was happening at the embassy was putting him in danger. He could hear Eddie Cain trying to calm the crowd. Everyone was just about settled when they heard an explosion in the office next door.

The gunfire that followed was a constant string of rounds. Chandler felt a sharp bite as he was shoved forward. Then it happened again. He put his hand on his chest and it was soaking through with warm blood. He coughed and felt warm liquid on his hand. He fell to his knees, knowing he'd been shot. It occurred to him that he was dying as he fell to the floor.

****

"The target is in the second conference room," said Rivera. Ball knew that once they cleared the first room in this office, there was a doorway to an adjacent conference room. They needed to get into that conference room.

"Frag out!" shouted Ball as he tossed a grenade into the room. Their brief entry into the office gave him enough time to see that there were no hostages, just the terrorist in the doorway. Once the grenade detonated, the two reentered the room, covering the conference room door with their weapons. The door was now closed. On the other side, they heard automatic gunfire and screams.

Oh, damn! He's executing them, thought Ball. He could tell that Rivera had reached the same conclusion as he lowered the shotgun and blasted the lock assembly. With the door compromised, Ball kicked the hell out of it, and it flew open. As soon as it was open, Rivera was in the room with his "Delta Special" M1911, shooting the Iranian madman to death. It all happened over the course of two seconds.

"Clear," said Rivera.

Ball entered the carnage and began going from hostage to hostage, looking to render aid. By the time the counting was done, he found ten dead hostages and five living. There was nothing to be done for the dead, and Rivera and Ball went about removing the bindings that held the captives' wrists together.

They hustled out of the conference room, back through the office, and into the main hallway. The smoke in the hallway made it difficult to see, and the shell casings on the floor presented a slipping hazard. Other teams were also clearing hostages, and the combination of Delta Operators and terrorized civilians were streaming out of doors in the center of the building. As they exited the building, a pair of sergeants guided the civilians to the gaping hole in the wall that had signaled the start of the operation.

Having handed off their charges, Rivera and Ball sprinted ahead to rally with a Delta squad that was providing perimeter security for Amjadiyeh Stadium, where massive CH-53D helicopters would fly the hostages out.

Chapter 13

2320 Hours
Manzariyeh Air Base, Iran

Fred Poole looked out at the airfield as he rode shotgun in a commandeered JetRanger helicopter. Earlier in the evening, the chopper had belonged to British Petroleum, but right now it was the temporary property of the CIA. Poole considered the paperwork that would result from this, but then he immediately stopped considering it. That wouldn't be his problem. His problem was that he needed to get from Tehran to Manzariyeh in a hurry, and he'd solved that problem.

Poole had been with the Agency since 1959. As an academic with a master's degree in Slavic languages, he quickly found a home in the Soviet–East European Division of the Agency. After this initial assignment at CIA headquarters in Washington, D.C., he'd found his way to Ankara, Turkey, where he worked out of the US embassy. His assignment was to monitor Soviet activity in Bulgaria and the Caucasus republics of Georgia, Armenia, and Azerbaijan. For the bulk of his career, he had bounced between Ankara and D.C., building his contacts, forming relationships with CIA assets that were working in Turkey, and monitoring Soviet assets operating against the US interests in the region.

Poole had fallen in love with Turkey from the moment his 707 had touched down. The exotic nature of this crossroads of the world had pulled him in. The passenger manifest of the airliner read like the guest list at a United Nations mixer. East meets West, Asia, Africa, and Europe collide, and within the chaos of that collision there was unbounded room for intrigue. Fred Poole wanted to understand it all. He needed to unravel the mystery and create order out of that chaos.

He'd been in Sinop, Turkey, when the call had come in for his temporary assignment to Iran. Sinop was located in the northern tip of the country, along the Black Sea coast. He'd been working with the signals intelligence collection facility in Turkey, trying to make sense out of a tip he'd received from a source in Baku, Azerbaijan. This source reported a dramatic increase in JP-4 jet fuel shipments from the refineries in Baku to the Soviet town of Kaspiysk. What stood out as alarming was that Kaspiysk had only a small regional airport nearby, some ten miles away in Makhachkala, and no apparent need for a massive dump of jet fuel. Before Poole could dig into the analysis of the problem, the Agency had whisked him away to Tehran.

Poole's role in the operation was to help coordinate between the existing Agency assets on the ground and all the various commanders in charge of the participating military units. This liaison role was of incredible importance considering the complexity of the operation, and he'd been running around like a madman ever since the mission had kicked off. He'd been in touch with Captain Goodwin and headed out from Tehran the moment the Marines had secured the airfield at Manzariyeh. He was also in touch with the Air Force combat control team to ensure that they were expecting him. Having notified both teams on the ground, he now just had to pray that nobody on the ground had an itchy trigger finger tonight. It would be just his luck for some asshole with an M2 to light up his chopper as they came into town.

Fortunately, everyone had been briefed on his arrival, and he and his pilot made it down without incident. The JetRanger set down on the southeast side of the airfield, between the taxiway and runway, just past the maintenance facilities. Captain Goodwin had set up his command post in the empty hangar that Lieutenant Beck had secured during the initial assault. Poole entered the hangar through the enormous aircraft door on the north side.

"Captain Goodwin. It's nice to meet you face-to-face," said Poole as he approached the folding table where Goodwin sat with Lieutenant Beck and a staff sergeant from the Air Force combat control team.

Captain Goodwin rose and put out a hand to greet Poole.

"Mr. Poole, I presume?"

The men shook hands, and both took a seat at the table.

"It looks like you boys have had a good night of it so far," said Poole. "As soon as I knew that the Delta boys were engaged at the embassy and that this airfield was in safe hands, I came out to help coordinate the extraction."

"We've taken the field intact," said Captain Goodwin. "The Air Force has everything they need up and running in the control tower, and other than a lot of broken windows, this place is no worse for the wear."

"How'd the assault go? I take it they didn't put up too much resistance?" asked Poole.

"To be honest, I think we caught a lucky break there. We captured one of the guards after the assault, and he filled us in on how the night went from his point of view." Poole raised an eyebrow to encourage Goodwin to continue. "Apparently, as soon as our mortar teams dropped HE on the airfield, the entire contingent of guards hauled ass to the control tower because their *ostavar*—I guess that's their NCO or junior officer—was holed up in there. They had no idea what the hell was going on and weren't ready to commit to action without direct guidance. Anyhow, they abandoned this facility and made a stand at the control tower.

"Once the Iranians saw our Marines approaching from the south, they opened up on them with an M60. I don't know if it was the low visibility, a lack of training, or just nerves, but their wild-man machine gunner didn't accomplish anything but tell my guys where they were. From there it was a textbook assault. My guys stormed the tower, took out the remaining bad guys, and captured the last man standing. Apparently he'd been pleading with his ostavar to give up, but this osty went all John Wayne, grabbed the M60, and tried to go out in a blaze of glory."

"And did he?" asked Poole.

"From what my team tells me, there was a lot of blaze, not so much glory."

"Any casualties?"

Captain Goodwin stopped short. This reminder of the grim price of the work they did was still new to him.

"We lost one killed, one wounded," replied Goodwin.

"I'm sorry to hear that, Captain. The good news is, that should be the end of the fighting for your team."

"We've got a defensive perimeter set up, in case you're wrong," said Goodwin.

With that, Poole took his leave and headed for the control tower to touch base with the combat control team. There were two points in the mission where the coordination between forces created significant points of failure. The first was at Desert One for the refueling. At that point, the Army, Air Force, and Marine Corps were all moving parts in a complex shuffle to get each of the C-130s on the ground, get Delta Force offloaded, the tankers set up, the Marine choppers on the ground, Second Platoon offloaded, the helicopters reloaded and everyone out of the area. It was a logistical nightmare, and other than the loss of two Sea Stallions, it had gone off without a hitch.

This next phase of the mission was even more complicated. Once the hostages were rescued from the embassy grounds, Delta needed to herd them to a stadium a few blocks away. At the stadium, the Marine CH-53s would pick up the hostages and Delta Force and transport them to Manzariyeh. At the same time, two Air Force C-141 transport planes would land at the air base. All the personnel would be loaded into the transports and taken to Incirlik Air Base in Turkey with follow-on flights to Aviano Air Base in Italy. There were a lot of moving parts, and the mission could go to shit if any of them failed to move in unison. Fred Poole was not going to let that happen.

Chapter 14

2320 Hours
Amjadiyeh Soccer Stadium
Tehran, Iran

Major Jason "Ripsaw" Thomas was approaching the stadium at around one thousand feet altitude. The US Army's Delta Force had rescued the American hostages, and now the Bluebeards were going to extract everyone from Tehran and get them to the C-141s that would be waiting for them at Manzariyeh.

"I still think this is a terrible idea," said Captain Philip "Snow" White. "The colonel was very clear that he didn't want us moving any of the hostages."

"Ahhh, young Captain," replied Ripsaw. "With years comes wisdom, and today's wisdom is that it's far easier to get forgiveness than permission. Once we've got everyone on the ground in Manzariyeh, nobody's going to care about the specifics of that one conversation in the middle of the desert."

The haboobs were a test of their flying abilities. Flying without their computer had tested their air navigation skills, and now it looked like this part of the extraction would be a pure test of their grit. In order to get the hostages and the Delta Force out of Tehran, they needed to set down on the soccer field, load up, and get back to Manzariyeh. No problem. Except they were landing three at a time on the field. Captain White was correct, there was plenty of room down there for all the choppers. But without detailed markings, this was more of a challenge. They had to dead reckon based on the out-of-bounds markers on the field. One CH-53 would land on the northeast corner, another CH-53 on the southeast corner, and a third would land on the west side at midfield.

Once each of the helicopters had taken on a load of passengers, they would lift off again and head southwest towards Manzariyeh. While the first three were on their way out, the second three would land to take their place and retrieve the last of the rescue team and any remaining hostages. Other than the stadium surrounding the extraction zone, this was a fairly straightforward mission for them. It was a tight fit, but no worse than they would find on a beachhead somewhere in North Korea or Estonia. Their big break on this mission was that nobody was shooting at them.

"Damn! Did you see that?" called out Captain White.

"Whatcha got, Snow?" asked Major Thomas.

"There was some kind of blast out there to the northeast, over by the airport. It looked like a fireball erupting over the airfield."

"That, my friend, was probably the Spectre," replied Thomas. He looked over his right shoulder, past his copilot, just in time to see another flash of orange. Two miles off to the east, an AC-130H gunship was orbiting around Doshan Tappeh Air Base to ensure that no Iranian air assets took off to complicate the extraction. The S2 guys couldn't say who in the Iranian military might be sympathetic to the student "revolutionaries." To ensure that the Americans ruled the air, the Navy had F-4 Phantom and F-14 Tomcat fighters flying combat air patrol over the region. Closer to the action, though, the Air Force had placed this AC-130H Spectre right over Tehran to provide an instant reaction to any attempts to get airborne. Bluebeard Five was witnessing that reaction.

The AC-130H was a monster. Flying in a slow orbit around the targeted airfield, the aircraft could bring an incredible weight of fire to bear against any enemy ground targets. In fire support missions, they would deliver what the pilots called a "full broadside." This comprised two 20mm Vulcan cannons, one 40mm Bofors cannon, and an absurd 105mm howitzer. It was enough lead to ruin anyone's day. Tonight they were ruining the night for some unlucky pilots who tried to take up a Bell UH-1 Iroquois helicopter. They had missed the crew running out to the chopper, but as soon as the rotors started turning, it had caught their attention. Within an instant, one of the Vulcan cannons opened up. The Huey disappeared as the 20mm high-explosive rounds tore through the body of the helicopter. The explosion sent the rotors spinning across the tarmac.

Thomas had to turn his attention back to the stadium. They were approaching quickly and needed to get on the ground as soon as they safely could. As they dropped onto the field, Captain White could see a couple of dozen people huddled in the stands just off the field. *Good*, he thought to himself. *I don't want to be sitting on the ground any longer than we need to.* In the back of the helo, the crew chief waited at the ramp and prepared to take on their cargo.

As soon as Bluebeard Five had hit the pitch and the ramp was down, soldiers from Delta Force guided civilian hostages to the loading ramp. The hostages scrambled up the ramp as the crew chief sorted them out, ensuring that each hostage was secured and as safe as they could be given the circumstances. It took longer than it would have if these had been trained Marines, but they were on the ground for less than five minutes. As soon as they had stowed the last hostage, the crew chief signaled ready, and Major Thomas lifted off. As they gained separation from the field, Thomas began a rapid turn to his right for his egress to the south. That was when he almost pissed himself.

"Dear Lord!" yelled Captain White. As Bluebeard Five was pulling out of the stadium, the oncoming form of another behemoth helicopter filled his view. Bluebeard Eight was coming right at them! The approaching chopper was on its way to replace Bluebeard Five on the soccer field. Rip couldn't afford to give up altitude and was forced to crank his chopper in a hard left turn while the incoming chopper grabbed altitude to hop over the lower helicopter. It was a simple mistake in the direction of approach. The incoming CH-53 thought Bluebeard Five would lift off and continue to the north instead of wheeling back to the south. It was a very tense moment, but they had managed to just dodge catastrophe. Once Thomas had them out of harm's way, he began looking around for Bluebeard Four, whom they were to follow to Manzariyeh.

"I lost Wizard in that shuffle," said Thomas, referring to Captain Barry "Wizard" Osborne, the pilot of Bluebeard Four.

"Roger, Rip, that's them at about three o'clock," replied White. Thomas's evasive maneuver had sent his helicopter off to the east, while Wizard had kept heading south. Thomas banked back to his right and had just acquired his escort when there was a sudden streak of red flashes right in front of the cockpit.

"Oh, for cryin' out loud!" yelled Rip as he again jerked at the flight controls, trying to make his position unpredictable to whatever was shooting at them from the ground. They could hear rounds hitting the helicopter as they made a mad dash to rooftop level, hoping to cut off the angle of the attackers' line of sight. They ran to the east, jinking north to keep the enemy guessing as to their new position before Rip gave the helo a little altitude. As soon as they got some air under them, red tracers cut through the air, surrounding their forward view. Rip ducked back down and continued racing to the east. After several more minutes of running and dodging, he popped up again. This time there were no more incoming rounds. They were safe again, and again, they were separated from the rest of their flight.

The radio came to life. "All Bluebeard units, this is Eagle Two. Flight operations at the stadium are shut down. Delta units are prosecuting anti-aircraft units in the area. Orbit to the east of town. Will advise once it's safe to resume operations."

"Looks like we got in there just in time," said Rip.

"Well, damn, Rip. I've lost 'em this time," said Snow.

"We'll head south and see if we can pick them up," replied Rip as he turned the chopper to his right and headed south, along the outskirts of Tehran. They had known that getting separated from the formation was a major risk given that their navigation system was on the fritz. This was exactly why they weren't supposed to be flying with civilians.

To ensure that they could make it back to the air base, their plan was to get to the far eastern side of Tehran, then head south, following the city's perimeter. As they came around to the west on this clockwise circle, they would find Route 71, the Tehran-Qom Road. Once they found the intersection of Route 71 and the perimeter road, it was a straight shot of 221 degrees for seventy-five kilometers, and they'd be landing at Manzariyeh.

"Might as well put on the spooky glasses," said Rip. With that, Captain White reached down the right side of his chair and found his AN/PVS-5 night vision goggles. While it was technically permissible to fly while wearing a pair, Rip hated the thought. The lack of peripheral vision gave him a real "periscope" view, and the two-dimensional readout was disorienting. If given a choice between the goggles or instruments, he'd rather fly on instruments alone. Captain White, on the other hand, had nothing better to do than put on the goggles and start looking for their road and the route to Manzariyeh.

When he donned the AN/PVS-5, Captain White's world went from muted color to a million shades of green. The goggles took whatever ambient light was available and amplified it, creating an eerie green world of shadows and light. As they flew just outside the city, White could see the outline of downtown Tehran. The glow of the city provided enough light to give the city a strong glow when compared to the empty outskirts. In between those two extremes there was a lot of ground. Out there somewhere was Route 71.

"I think this is what the Land of Oz would look like if you were tripping on acid," said White.

"Just call out when you find the road. I hate flying blind like this," replied Thomas.

White guided Thomas to the west as they crossed the southern edge of town. He'd spent the better part of their downtime at Desert Two studying the map of the Tehran roadways for just this contingency. Looking at the tangle of roads on the map was one thing. Seeing them from the air at a hundred miles an hour was another. Seeing it live at a hundred miles an hour in this green-and-black terror-vision was just about too much. The disorienting nature of the night vision was nauseating. In some ways, White would rather be flying when he wore them. At least then he'd have control and could anticipate any movement, and nothing would surprise him. He shook off the thought. He knew the grass was always greener in the other chair.

"Okay, we're in business now," said White as he located what he believed to be Route 71. "We're coming up on it now, get ready to turn left to two-two-one in three… two… one… mark." As Snow counted down, Thomas turned the chopper to the left and headed to the southwest. It wouldn't take long and they'd be able to unload the hostages and fly out with them on the cargo planes. It would be a shame to leave the Sea Stallions behind, but there was no way they could get them back to an allied airfield without refueling again, and there just wasn't time. White was just about to take off the AN/PVS-5 when he noticed something on the highway to the south.

"Hang on, Rip, there's something going on down there," said White. He couldn't make out details, but from up here in the dark it sure looked like something was heading south on Route 71, toward Manzariyeh. As they got closer, White could make out more and more detail. It was clear that there were several vehicles traveling as a group. "I think we've got a column of some kind down there. We'd better call it in." As White was just about to key his mic, another burst of tracers came hurtling towards them.

"Dammit!" yelled Rip as he tore the controls to the right and began an evasive climb-and-dive routine to evade the incoming fire.

"Eagle Base, this is Bluebeard Five. We have a column of ten to fifteen hostile vehicles headed to your position from the northeast on Route 71," Snow called out above the cursing of his pilot. "Composition unknown, but at least one vehicle has an anti-aircraft capability. We are observing fire."

Unbeknownst to the Marines, a column of armored vehicles belonging to the newly formed "Revolutionary Guard" had assembled at Ghale Morghi Air Base in southern Tehran and set out to relieve the beleaguered defenders at Manzariyeh.

****

19 February 1980
Tehran, Iran

Captain Ball and his team were providing security near Amjadiyeh Stadium. The two men kept their heads on a swivel, ensuring that they detected no movement in their zone of responsibility. Out of the darkness, they could hear the *whoomp whoomp whoomp* of the approaching Sea Stallions.

"Here they come, boss," said Rivera. "If anything's going to go wrong, this is probably the time." Both men otherwise ignored the arrival of the Marines. Whatever happened behind them wasn't their concern. They could hear the helos land and take off again. Flashes of orange caught their attention. They were rising from an area within their zone. Ball's radio came to life.

"Falcon Two-One, this is Eagle. We have an unidentified anti-aircraft vehicle in your sector, approximately three blocks to your north. We think it's a VADS. Kyle, I need you to eliminate that threat. This is our number one priority."

"Eagle, Falcon Two-One, understood," replied Ball. Before he had even signed off, Rivera had signaled to bring the team together for a briefing.

"Listen, men. There's an anti-air threat a few blocks north of here. We need to remove that threat before we can get the LZ open again. That means that we're not leaving this city until we can take out that threat. We nearly lost one helo already, and we can't risk it. I don't know about you, but I can think of a thousand ways I'd rather die than getting shot down while holding my dick in a chopper." As the men took in the information, the captain continued, "We believe the objective is an M163 located in the Argentine Square, about a quarter mile north of here along Roosevelt Ave."

"Captain, why don't they take it out from the air?" asked one of the Staff Sergeant Cord Wheeler.

"Because it's in the middle of town, and we can't afford collateral damage. That area has a densely packed civilian population, so we can't take any shortcuts here. We need to work our way to the objective along Roosevelt. Before we get to the square, we'll split into two teams and take up positions east and west of the square. Sergeant Rivera will take his men west, and my guys will stick to the east. We'll advance simultaneously and engage the objective. It's unknown if the vehicle has a supporting ground force, or if it's just a lone wolf out there. Benson, Luna, you two are on the LAWs. Remember, the sooner we get this done, the sooner we can get the hell out of here." With that, the ten operators moved out along Roosevelt Avenue.

As they approached the last block before the square, Sergeant Rivera took his team to the left while Ball turned to the right. Each team moved cautiously through the quiet streets, looking for any signs of resistance. Ball could hear the rumble of the diesel engine as he neared the edge of a shop that would lead to the square. As his team positioned themselves for the assault, Rivera called in that he had eyes on the target. It was indeed an M163 air-defense unit. On the ground there were four riflemen keeping a loose watch around the vehicle.

Ball peered around the building to his left. He could see the M163, and two of the guards. He ducked back around the corner and gave his team their orders. "Wheeler, you're with me. There are two guards in our sector. I'll take the one on the left. Yours is the one on the right." Benson was already deploying the M72 launcher, pulling the two ends of it apart. "Reed, Porter, you two provide security and watch in these areas of approach." He motioned towards the alleys that were branching off the main road, then got back on the radio and let Rivera know they were ready to move. Once Rivera confirmed his team's readiness, Ball ordered the team forward.

It happened in an instant. The team slipped out of the shadows and shot all four of the guards. With the attack coming from both east and west, the VADS wasn't able to decide on which way to shoot. The poor ground-level visibility was ruining any chance the Iranians had to defend, so the driver did the only thing he could think of doing. He ran to the east, right into Benson, who fired the LAW into the side of the vehicle as it passed.

The explosion punched a hole into the side of the M163 but didn't disable it. The turret spun towards Benson and unloaded a burst of 20mm rounds. The blast was high and hit the wall well above Benson, raining chips of concrete on the soldier. From the west side of the ambush, Staff Sergeant Luna fired the second LAW, which blew the left track off, causing the vehicle to slow, then stop. Just as the Delta Operators took aim to shoot any retreating enemies, Ball could hear the popping of the 20mm rounds cooking off. Benson's original shot had finally managed to kill the vehicle.

With the threat neutralized and the area secured, Ball's team withdrew. Now they just needed to get back to the stadium, get on one of the transports and get the hell out of here before an organized response complicated things even more. They ran the quarter mile back to the stadium.

Ball retrieved his radio handset and called in, "Eagle, this is Falcon Two-Two. The threat has been eliminated and we're back in position. Do we have an ETA on our extraction?"

"Falcon Two-Two, Eagle. Negative. Something's gone wrong at the secondary extraction point. Sit tight, and we'll let you know when we have more news."

It was going to be a long night.

Chapter 15

2330 Hours
Manzariyeh Air Base
Iran

Fred Poole approached the Marine sentry on duty in front of the control tower. Captain Goodwin had radioed ahead, and Lance Corporal Nelson was expecting Mr. Poole.

"Evening, Mr. Poole," greeted Nelson. "Lieutenant Beck is up on the top floor. He's expecting you."

"Thank you, Marine," replied Poole as he passed by. Poole opted to enter the control tower through the original door instead of using the giant hole in the wall. The destruction of the evening was evident throughout the first-floor room. Debris from the hole was strewn all over the floor. Bloodstains leading from the stairs to the floor had been hastily cleaned up but were still visible. Poole had seen battlefield scenes like this before, but not since Vietnam had the destruction been caused or the blood spilled by US Marines. He shook off the thought and continued up the stairs to the main operations floor at the very top of the tower.

"Mr. Poole?" asked Lieutenant Beck when he caught sight of Poole coming up the stairs and entering the room.

"Evening, Lieutenant Beck, what's the word on our traffic?" asked Poole, wanting to get a handle on the situation before any of the perfunctory chitchat might start in. It wasn't that he was opposed to small talk, or that he wasn't curious about getting more details from the Marines on the operation that night. It was just that he had to make sure that the communications between the airfield, the Delta Force, and the Marine choppers were all flowing as designed.

"Everyone's talking and everyone else is answering. It looks like this is the one part of the operation that's working like it's supposed to. But don't take my word for it, Master Sergeant Hurst here is the genius who got all this operational." Beck gestured towards an airman sitting at a console in front of the large windows overlooking the runway. "Hey, Lane, here's a bona fide spook who'd like to have a word with you."

Master Sergeant Lane Hurst turned his attention away from the radio he was monitoring and took off his headphones. As he stood up, he extended a hand towards Poole and said, "Good to meet you, Mr...."

"Poole," answered Fred. "Lieutenant Beck tells me you're the man of the hour up here. How're coms coming along?"

"Everything is operational, and we've established contact with all elements of the operation here. When the Marines took this tower, they were kind enough to leave this floor and all the equipment intact, so it didn't take long to get everything up and running. In fact, from where I'm sitting, the entire Manzariyeh operation has gone off as smoothly as we could hope for. It doesn't sound like we could say the same for the embassy assault."

"The last I heard before leaving Tehran was that Delta had made contact and the rescue was underway. What have you heard since then?" asked Poole.

"We're only getting bits and pieces, but it sounds like they're taking serious casualties on the ground," replied Hurst.

"That's bad news," said Poole, stating the obvious. "These Delta guys were specially trained for hostage situations like this."

"Obviously, I don't have the full picture here, Poole, but from what we can piece together, it sounds like the hostages are the ones taking losses," said Beck.

"I suppose that makes sense," said Poole. "I don't know much about these Iranian 'students,' but from what I can tell, they aren't exactly professionals. We could never be one hundred percent sure of how they would react in this situation. If some of them panic, things could get messy."

"Surely the Army accounted for that in their planning," replied Beck.

"It's one thing to imagine something can go wrong; it's a totally different thing to get ahead of it in real time," said Poole.

"I guess it's true—even the best battle plan won't survive first contact with the enemy," mused Beck, citing the old battlefield cliché. Poole knew they wouldn't solve the mystery of the embassy and moved the conversation back to their side of the operation.

"What's the ETA on our transports and the hostages?" he asked.

"The C-141s are ten minutes out," replied Master Sergeant Hurst. "The first choppers from the embassy are heading out from the stadium as we speak. We've got thirty-five hostages, along with the medical team from Delta Force and an additional squad. But they've shut down the LZ, so we're not sure how long it's going to take to get the rest of Delta out of there."

"That's a bit out of order, isn't it?" asked Poole.

"It is. We'd hoped to get the Starlifters on the ground and ready for takeoff before the hostages arrived, but the window between taking the airfield and getting the hostages out was just too tight. It looks like we'll be on the ground a little longer than we'd hoped, but it won't be too bad," explained Hurst. Just then, fate paid them a visit.

"Sergeant Hurst, you and the lieutenant will need to hear this," interrupted an airman at one of the control tower radios as he handed Hurst a set of bulky headphones. Hurst shifted the headphones to his other hand. With both of the square earpieces flipped outward, both Hurst and Beck could place one over an ear. They listened as the radioman continued an exchange with one of the inbound helicopters.

"... Five, can you repeat your last? Over."

"Eagle Base, repeat, we have eyes on a column of ten to fifteen hostile vehicles heading your way southbound on Route 71," came the reply over the radio.

"Bluebeard Five, can you verify hostile intent?" asked the radioman.

"Son, they just got done shooting at my ass, so I'm pretty sure they aren't out here collecting for the Red Cross!" said Bluebeard Five. Poole recognized the line from the Clint Eastwood movie *Dirty Harry*, but it seemed fitting.

"Well, damn, looks like I've got some work to do. I've got to report to Captain Goodwin for orders." With that, Lieutenant Beck headed for the stairs.

"Thanks for the update, Sergeant Hurst," said Poole. "I'm going to head down to the command post and see what I can do to help."

Both men headed out of the building and down to the hangar, where Captain Goodwin was coordinating the defense of the airfield.

Lieutenant Beck made it down the stairs and across the open area between the buildings in quick time. Mr. Poole lagged behind at a trot. Beck wasted no time in relaying the news.

"Bad news, boss, we've got company headed this way," said Beck.

"I'm aware, Lieutenant. You're fast, but you're not faster than the radio," replied Goodwin, holding up the handset of his field radio.

"What's the plan, Captain?" asked Lieutenant Beck.

“I need you to head down to Rodriguez’s position on the south side. Have him detach a fire team to augment Burton’s squad on the north side. You’ll take command of the defense to the south, and I’ll take command of the northern approach.”

“Roger that, sir!”

“Omar…,” said Goodwin, his rare use of Beck’s given name emphasizing the importance of what he was about to say. “We have no idea what the composition of this force is, just that they’re mobile and they have enough firepower to scare off our helos. I need you ready to reinforce our position if this gets hairy. If this column breaks through, this entire operation will be compromised, and if we’re lucky, we’ll be dead and won’t have to read about it in the Iranian newspapers.” There was no hint of hyperbole in Goodwin’s proclamation. Just cold, hard fact.

“I understand, sir. We will hold this airfield, and we will protect those civilians,” responded Beck. As he turned to leave, he strode past Mr. Poole, who had been standing behind him.

“Captain Goodwin, what can I do to help?” asked Poole.

“I don’t know, Mr. Poole, what can you do to help? Can you handle a rifle?” asked Goodwin.

“I’ve had familiarization training on the M16,” said Poole.

“Lieutenant Beck!” called Goodwin, just catching Beck before he’d made it out of the hangar. “Get Mr. Poole a weapon and take him with you.” He turned his head back to Poole and said, “Don’t get fancy out there, Poole. Just point the dangerous end downrange and don’t shoot any of my guys.”

“Understood,” was all Poole said in return as he turned and fell in with Beck, heading out to the perimeter.

Chapter 16

2330 Hours
Qom, Iran

"What do you mean we can't find them?!" demanded Major Saeed Nouzari, the commander of the 1st Battalion of the 17th Division, Iranian Revolutionary Guard. Nouzari had been working to round up his division for the past ninety minutes, but a general lack of organization and practice was thwarting his efforts. So far, he had gathered one hundred and eighty-seven of his three-hundred-and-twelve-man force, but he was critically short on drivers. He was now struggling to round up crews to serve his APCs and trucks so he could get them to Manzariyeh Air Base in force. He didn't know what was out there, but he knew that one of his counterparts in Tehran was already on the move. If Colonel Vahdat and his men from Tehran rescued the beleaguered air base before his forces in Qom did, he would never live it down.

Major Nouzari knew Colonel Vahdat. While he respected the man's office and authority, he felt that Vahdat's commitment to the revolution was perfunctory at best and self-serving at worst. Men like Vahdat didn't join up with the cause because they truly believed in the divine inspiration of the Ayatollah. They joined because they hated the Shah. Or worse, they joined because they felt that the Islamic Republic was inevitable and they knew that getting in on the ground floor of the new Persian Army would mean a greater chance for leadership and promotion. He didn't know Vahdat well enough to tell which camp he fell into, but he was confident that he was not a man of sufficient faith to lead Allah's forces to victory. With that thought in mind, Nouzari knew that he couldn't delay any longer.

"Lieutenant Abdi! Get the men loaded. We will deal with the malingerers and deserters when we return!"

Nouzari had never been in combat before. Nor had any of his men, so far as he knew. Sure, they had all gone through training, and he had a decent mix of veterans and fresh faces. But none of them had been tested. Tonight would be a significant test for all of them. From what Nouzari could make out from the garbled fragments of radio transmission he'd been able to pull in, the evening's chaos had begun in Tehran, with Manzariyeh quickly coming under attack. His first thought was that the civil war had finally broken out and that he was about to engage the remaining lackeys of the Shah. A quick, decisive victory would go a long way to kicking off the war and would put him in a position to prove himself as a worthy soldier for the Ayatollah.

Once they assembled the men, he had his doubts. The reports he was receiving didn't amount to any major ground movement. Instead, there were isolated firefights, emphasized with major air support. Once the force structure revealed itself, Nouzari concluded that they were facing an external threat. But who? Iraq had been making noises of late, but it made no sense for Saddam's forces to strike this far north. If the Iraqis were to attack, it would be along their shared border in the south. The Soviets appeared to have their hands full in Afghanistan, but it was possible that they were performing some sort of limited strike. That left the United States and Israel. Of the two, Nouzari would have bet everything he had that it was the Americans. Yes, tonight would be a test, and he would prove himself.

As his column advanced to the northeast, Nouzari picked up transmissions from Vahdat's 1st Special Company. The original reports were spectacular. The column had successfully fought off a helicopter attack and was continuing on toward the objective. It looked as though both forces would converge on the enemy at approximately the same time and point. They would have more than enough firepower to overcome what resistance there was and secure the airfield.

Chapter 17

2330 Hours
25 Miles Southeast of Tehran, Iran

Lieutenant JG Samuel "Pharaoh" Bell guided his A-7 Corsair II through the blackness of the night sky. It had been just over an hour and ten minutes since his launch from *Coral Sea*. He was orbiting south of Tehran at fourteen thousand feet. A thousand feet below, lost in the darkness, was his section leader, Carroll "Buzz" Barber. The two Corsairs were standing by to engage any enemy targets on the road between Tehran and Qom.

"Milestone Three, this is Eagle Two, over." The call coming over the radio startled Pharaoh. Eagle Two was the E-2C Hawkeye orbiting about three hundred miles to his south—the quarterback for this operation. He was directing the action in this well-orchestrated game plan. Milestone Three was the A-6E from the Main Battery that was searching out the targets. The Corsair was effectively blind at night. It lacked the airborne moving target indicator (AMTI) that the Intruder would use to locate the enemy. Eagle Two was responsible for coordinating the A-6 as it made a low pass along the road, searching for the enemy, and the A-7s who were waiting for the call to come in and engage any identified targets. With so many planes flying lights out in the night, it was imperative that the Hawkeye keep everyone in place.

Eagle Two directed Milestone Three to begin his road recon pass. The Tadpole dropped to five hundred feet and flew along the road from north to south. As the pilot kept the aircraft on course, the bombardier/navigator kept a vigil on the AMTI, searching out the enemy. As the Intruder searched for targets, the Corsairs held steady watch to the north, waiting to pounce on anything that came up. Eight minutes after Milestone Three reported the beginning of their run, another transmission came across the strike channel on the radio.

"Eagle Two, this is Milestone Three. We have a contact bearing two-nine-zero degrees. It looks like it's on a side road parallel to the primary route, but to the west. Engaging."

With that, the A-6 grabbed a bit of altitude and prepared to drop its Mk-20 cluster bombs and parachute flares to illuminate the target. While this was happening, Eagle Two came over the radio again.

"Charger Four, this is Eagle Two. We have located the enemy force bearing two-two-zero degrees, range twenty-four point five miles from your current position. Engage."

"Eagle Two, this is Charger Four, roger. Engaging."

With that, Buzz and Pharaoh broke out of their orbit and began flying southwest towards the newly identified target. As they did, Buzz shed altitude, dropping to a height of five thousand feet to make his attack pass. As he neared the reported location of the enemy, he could see the explosions as the A-6 completed the initial run. Besides the orange fireballs rising from the vehicles on the road, Buzz could see the white flares burning as they descended on their parachutes. The Navy had caught the column in a valley, which was now completely illuminated.

Buzz could see that Milestone Three had destroyed the lead vehicles in the column. This had stopped the rest of them on the road, making them ideal targets. As he approached the column, red tracers reached out into the sky. The fire was disparate and uncoordinated. It seemed to Buzz that the enemy had no idea what they were shooting at, just that they were shooting. He lined up on the center of the remaining column and pickled his four Mk-20s from five thousand feet of altitude. The Mk-20s dropped from the aircraft, then split open, pouring out nearly a thousand Mk 118 bomblets that blanketed the vehicles in the column. As he completed his pass, Buzz got on the radio to let Pharaoh know that he was breaking off to the right to ensure there was no chance of a collision.

Pharaoh came in after Buzz and repeated the maneuver, adding another thousand bomblets to the blanket of death covering the enemy column. The results of the attack were devastating. The column had tried to disperse, but the coverage from the Mk-20s was simply too wide. There was no place for them to go. As the bomblets hit the armored exteriors of the M113 APCs, the shaped-charge warhead would explode, punching a hole in the vehicle and filling it with flames and explosive gas. When the bomblet hit the canvas top of one of the trucks, it would tear right through, not exploding until the inertial fuze ran down. Trucks that weren't directly hit by the attack ran into trucks that had been. Other trucks swerved off the road and became bogged down in the sand. It would take time for the survivors to dig out and form up to continue their assault.

As Pharaoh was flying over the target area, he caught something out of the corner of his eye, mixed in with the various tracers. It was a streak of orange following Buzz. Before he had a chance to warn his section leader, Buzz dropped a line of flares and banked hard to his left. The missile chased the flares into the distance. Once it had overflown its intended target, there was no way for the missile to reacquire. Pharaoh concluded that the missile must have been a MANPAD, or man-portable air-defense missile, fired from some dismounted infantry.

As he pulled out of his attack run, turning to the left, Pharaoh wondered if they'd make another pass on the target. He'd dropped his main ordnance, but each A-7E was armed with an M61 Vulcan 20mm cannon.

"Buzz, this is Pharaoh, are we going in for a guns pass?"

"Negative, Pharaoh, there's no reason for us to get up close to that triple-A, not to mention that MANPAD fired off at me. Eagle will vector in the next strike if it's needed, but from where I'm sitting, there's nothing left of that force down there. We're Winchester and RTB," said Buzz, referring to the fact that they were out of relevant weapons and needed to return to base.

Pharaoh followed Buzz as they banked left and headed south, towards the Persian Gulf, and their home on *Coral Sea*.

Chapter 18

20 February 1980
0010 Hours
Manzariyeh Air Base, Iran

Sergeant Rodriguez was surveying his area of responsibility to the southeast of the airfield. He had stationed Second Squad along the raised dirt perimeter of the airfield. He kept the Marines in close intervals to ensure interlocking fields of fire, with the M60 deployed in the corner at the midpoint of his position. As he peered out over the berm, he could see nothing but desert sand in the surrounding miles. Just as when they had landed at Desert Two, he found the stress and anxiety of leadership catching up to him. Now he had set his men to digging in. There wasn't anything left to do but watch… and wait. It was a welcome relief when Private Boone tapped him on the shoulder to let him know that Lieutenant Beck and "some dude" were approaching from the hangar.

"Sergeant, how're the Marines?" asked Beck as he approached Rodriguez.

"Everyone's where they need to be, sir," said Rodriguez. As the lieutenant introduced Mr. Poole, Sergeant Burton of Third Squad interrupted them.

"I've got movement to the northeast. About two hundred meters altitude, heading right for the airfield."

There was a moment of tension as Rodriguez unwittingly held his breath. Before he even realized he wasn't breathing, he heard Master Sergeant Hurst announce over the radio, "That should be the first of our choppers coming in from the stadium." Rodriguez let out his breath.

Lieutenant Beck introduced Mr. Poole to the men, and to ensure the safety of his Marines, Sergeant Rodriguez suggested that Poole stick with him to "augment the leadership team." Everyone knew it was just a code for "keep the civilian where you can see him" and everyone was okay with that. Rodriguez took Poole to the section of the rise to the east of Strickland's machine-gun position. This gave them the best vantage point to survey the field, without crowding out the machine-gun team.

"I suppose you're wondering why I called this meeting," quipped Poole. Rodriguez knew that they had a long watch ahead of them and that small talk was the best way to pass the time without losing focus.

"I assume it has something to do with all this sand," replied Rodriguez, gesturing to the wide-open landscape in front of them as the helicopter flew over their left side and landed at the airfield.

Rodriguez and Poole spent the better part of the following half an hour going over the casual details of life that might move people from being strangers to acquaintances. Rodriguez told Poole about his wife, Nancy, and his daughter, Jennifer.

He and Nancy had had a whirlwind of a courtship. Back before he was an NCO, he had sworn that he'd never marry so long as he was in the Corps. He and his brothers had drunk many sacred beers in manly toasts to eternal bachelorhood. But then there was Nancy. He'd met her on a Saturday at a townie bar while out with his friends. He wasn't sure about love at first sight, but there was certainly something at first sight. She was objectively beautiful. He knew this because when she'd first walked into the bar, Mason had said, "Damn, Rodriguez, she's hot enough to be a stripper!" From Mason, that was high praise indeed.

In fact, she was not a stripper. She worked as a bank teller at the credit union right outside the base. It had taken Rodriguez more courage to talk to Nancy than anything he'd faced in the Corps up to that point. He had absolute courage in the field and in his element, and he had never felt intimidated by women. But at that moment, there was something that said, "You will mess this up, Marine!" He couldn't get that feeling to subside and it was maddening to him.

As he was reflecting on it now, thousands of miles away in the Iranian desert, maybe that was love at first sight. There was something in the back of his mind that put paramount importance on making sure that this woman was a part of his life.

Perhaps, had things gone in another direction, he would have forgotten that feeling. If they had not connected that night, or if after a few dates she'd turned out to be just another townie party girl, maybe that moment when he had first seen her would have faded into the background. But that wasn't the way things had worked out. Instead, he'd walked across the bar from the table his friends were at to where she was standing next to the cigarette machine and asked her, "Did anyone ever tell you you're once… twice… three times a lady?" He smiled as he remembered it, but he'd been internally horrified as he'd heard himself speak the words. It was quite probably the stupidest thing he'd ever said to anyone.

Apparently Nancy found something charming in Rodriguez's Hail Mary pickup line. She was a fan of the Commodores, and he had this great embarrassed smile as he realized how truly terrible the line was. She was taken by his awkwardness at that moment. Here before her was a brawny and fearsome warrior. One who could put the fear of God into most of the boys she'd ever dated. A man she could depend on to fight and die for his country. But right then he was putty in her hands.

Poole talked about being in Dallas on the day that JFK was killed. He'd said, "Before you ask, no, I was not on the grassy knoll, and I wasn't there in an official capacity. It was just coincidence." He'd also talked about how he had been read in on MK Ultra, but he wouldn't confirm anything about that beyond what had been declassified.

The spook intrigued Rodriguez. It was hard not to be intrigued when you could tell that the person you were talking to was holding back on the details of his past and present. And there was always the nagging suspicion that Poole was overplaying the mystery of his position for dramatic effect.

The infuriating thing was that there was no way that Rodriguez would ever know just how much of the evasiveness was necessary and how much was just set out to make for an enjoyable story. It really didn't matter—Poole was a standup guy as far as Rodriguez was concerned. He could be sitting in the tower with the Air Force, but he was down here with the grunts, putting himself in harm's way. That on its own was enough to earn the man the benefit of the doubt.

Rodriguez and Poole kept watch as each of the CH-53s came roaring overhead and landed at the airfield. As they counted off the choppers, they knew each one represented another step in getting this mission completed and getting the hell out of here. If it hadn't been for the column that Bluebeard Five had reported, they might already be loading themselves onto the C-141 Starlifters and heading back to safety.

When the radio reported VA-27's successful attack on the column, Rodriguez breathed a brief sigh of relief. The Air Force had given clearance for the Starlifters to land and to begin the extraction operation. Rodriguez wasn't sure what to make of the entire operation and his first taste of combat.

They'd secured the airfield. That was his role. But he'd lost a man and had another wounded. That would always be with him. Still, all things considered, for the Marine Corps this was an absolute win. Poole had filled him in on the scuttlebutt about problems with the hostage rescue, but Rodriguez knew that there wasn't anything he could do about that. Maybe the world would consider tonight an abject failure, but as far as he was concerned, Second Platoon of Kilo Company, 3/6 Marines, had heard the call and answered.

Captain Goodwin interrupted Rodriguez's internal drafting of his after-action report as his voice came through the radio.

"All units, this is Playboy Actual. We've got movement on the perimeter. It looks like a Jeep moving in slowly, at seven hundred yards, my twelve o'clock." From his position, Rodriguez couldn't see a thing. The action, such as it was, was all happening over his left shoulder, on the far side of their defensive positions. "Hang on, we've got trucks inbound as well," said Goodwin. The crack of rifle fire split the night as Third Squad engaged the threat. The sound of those M16s opening up seemed to release all the tension in two tightly coiled springs. This Iranian attacking force was about to unload that tension on Captain Goodwin's defenders.

With the action taking place outside of their area of responsibility, Rodriguez reminded his charges of some basic rules. Everyone knew these, but in the heat of the moment, this was the time they'd be forgotten.

"Keep your eyes on your sectors! We can't get distracted by Third Squad over there. Find targets in your target arcs and take your time with your shots. Strickland, remember, short, controlled bursts." He felt silly saying it, but with all the action happening to their left, he didn't want anyone sneaking up on them.

That was when he heard Lieutenant Beck call out over the noise, "We've got trucks inbound! Mack, Cobb, light 'em up!" With that, the sound of gunfire got a lot closer. The trucks had crossed over from Third Squad's zone into Second Squad's. Rodriguez still couldn't see anything, but he knew that they hadn't made it too close to his zone because he hadn't heard the M60 to his left open up. It was a little impulsive, but Rodriguez thought to take a chance.

"Strickland! Adjust your target zone to the left, and engage the nearest truck! We'll cover your right flank." This would allow the unit to bring the bulk of their firepower to bear on the incoming threat. If someone tried to flank them, Rodriguez figured he'd just readjust the M60 back onto his side of the fight. After all, this was why they'd placed the M60 on the corner of the position: to allow Strickland to engage targets to the front of the defense, or to the right.

****

Corporal Mack was firing his M16 as quickly as targets appeared. At first, his entire fire team had opened up on the truck itself, which was quickly rendered inoperable. Yet even before the truck had come to a halt, infantrymen began spilling out. During this initial point of chaos, the Marines held nearly every advantage. By destroying the truck, they had taken the initiative away from the enemy, and by virtue of their dug-in positions and high ground, they were able to pick off soldiers as they desperately tried to find cover in the open desert.

Mack watched as four two-and-a-half-ton trucks advanced on Second Squad's zone. The enemy had stopped the remaining trucks (or perhaps they were stuck, Mack couldn't be sure, and it didn't really matter) and were taking cover behind them. The Marines began taking fire, but it was still sporadic and disorganized. As the Marines continued to fire at the Iranians, they watched as a truck broke free from the attacking line and made a dash for the southeast corner of the defensive line. The sudden movement and threat of a breach brought every gun available onto that single target, including Strickland's M60. Once the burning shell of the truck came to a stop, however, there was no mad scramble to get out. The truck was already empty, but for the dead driver, who was about to cook off behind the steering wheel. That momentary shift of attention was exactly what the attackers had needed to get their assault coordinated. They were still taking cover behind the trucks; however, now their fire had become more concentrated and organized.

****

While Mack and Beck were fighting off the attack on the front of the position, Rodriguez caught sight of movement coming into his zone to the right of the position on the southeastern side of the airfield.

"We've got more trucks coming in!" called out Rodriguez. "Joseph! Engage those Deuces!" Corporal Joseph had been the furthest away from the action up to this point, and he had his fire team ready to contribute. They opened up on the incoming trucks, but they kept coming.

Rodriguez called out to Strickland, trying to get the M60 over to the right to engage the new threat, but in the pandemonium of battle, he wasn't able to get through to him. The M60 team was desperately beating back the enemy's frontal attack. The Iranians had identified the M60 position and had concentrated fire in their direction.

As the trucks continued to advance to the west of Rodriguez's position, he could see that if he didn't stop them, they would turn the corner and roll up the right flank of the defensive position. Rodriguez grabbed at his radio.

"Playboy Actual, this is Hustler Two-Two. We have enemy trucks moving to flank us on the right, to the south-southeast of the airfield. We need additional support!"

Captain Goodwin replied immediately. "Understood, Two-Two. Gallery Three-One, move to BP Five. We've got trucks moving in on the right flank—I need you to stop them."

Rodriguez knew that Burton would need every gun he could get if those trucks were fully loaded. As he cradled the transmitter, he turned to Poole.

"Grab yer ass, Freddy, we've got to reposition."

"Roger, Sergeant," was all Poole could think to say as the two of them pulled up and out of their firing positions and moved along the defensive berm, with Rodriguez ensuring that they were low enough to keep from being silhouetted along the ridgeline. As they crossed to where Corporal Joseph set up his team, Rodriguez saw PFC Burgess lying on the ground surrounded by blood while Lance Corporal Montgomery attempted to render aid.

When the firing started, he just stood there like an asshole. "Sergeant!" said the lance corporal. Rodriguez knew that the Marine wasn't angry with his dying friend, but in the heat of battle, anger was the only emotion that Monty had.

"I've got him, Monty. Get back on the line. I'll get him to Doc." Rodriguez knew it was a lie, but it was a lie with a purpose. He needed every gun on the line, and it was too late for Burgess. "Grab his legs, Poole," he said to Fred. The two of them carried Burgess to the flat terrain behind the defenses. As he left his comrade on the battlefield, he whispered "*Santa María, Madre de Dios, ruega por nosotros pecadores ahora y en la hora de nuestra muerte*." He wasn't a devout Catholic, but the line had been rolling around in his head ever since Yates had been killed. As he and Poole continued down the line, he thought of the age-old observation that there were no atheists in a foxhole.

****

As the Iranian forces pressed the assault, Corporal Mack could see that Sergeant Strickland and his assistant gunner, Lance Corporal David Adams, were in a serious situation. The attackers had quickly identified the M60 as the biggest threat on the wall and had concentrated all of their fire on that position. Adams rose to load a new belt of ammo into the gun when a round hit him in the shoulder, which caused him to flinch and stand up to keep from losing his balance. As soon as he stabilized himself, another several rounds wracked his body, and he collapsed and rolled down the berm. Strickland went after him.

As Mack was firing another three-round burst at the infantrymen positioned behind one of the trucks, he heard PFC Oliver cry out in pain. He looked over to see Oliver's M16 tumbling down the berm while the Marine grabbed at his shoulder and slid down after his rifle. Whatever Oliver's problem was, he wasn't dying, and there wasn't much that Mack could do right now even if he was. So Mack continued picking targets and firing. As he stopped to reload his rifle, he suddenly realized that he could no longer hear the M60. As he seated the magazine and charged the weapon, he realized that with Strickland's machine gun out, his job had just gotten considerably harder. As if the enemy had been reading his thoughts, he noticed an uptick in the volume of fire directed at his position.

Mack went back to work with his newly charged M16 and called out, "Oliver, get your damn rifle and get your ass back up here!"

****

Rodriguez and Poole had made it to the edge of the line, past Joseph's position, and kept moving down, looking for Burton. As Rodriguez was looking around, trying to get a position on Burton, he heard Poole whisper, "Uh-oh."

Rodriguez's head snapped back in time to see the black form of a two-and-a-half-ton truck moving into position in front of them. They both dropped to the deck, praying that they hadn't been spotted. Poole was on the ground with his rifle in front of him and his hands over his head, as if he could create a safe shell to protect him from the fight. The bullets kicked up the sand around him.

"Shoot back! For cryin' out loud, Poole, you have to shoot back!" Rodriguez screamed as he sent three-round bursts in the enemy's direction. "We don't have time to stay here!" he continued. "There's a rise about twenty yards behind us. We need to lay down more fire and get the hell outta Dodge before they get organized!" Poole retrieved his rifle and shouldered it.

As soon as he had sent his third three-round burst at the shadowy attackers in front of him, Rodriguez shouted, "Get up! Let's go!" Before Poole could react, Rodriguez yanked him to his feet. The two of them retreated back the way they had come. Rodriguez ran past Poole when he heard the CIA man scream. He turned to see Poole go down with a crash and turned back towards the enemy, firing two bursts as he ran to Poole's body.

"Come on, pal, you can't stay here," said Rodriguez as he helped Poole to his feet.

"It's my leg. The bastards shot me in the leg," said Poole. They stumbled to the rise, where they were able to take cover behind the uneven ground. Rodriguez looked at Poole's leg to assess the damage.

"Looks like no Hail Mary for you tonight," said Rodriguez as he pulled out his first aid kit and handed it to Poole. "It looks like it went through the muscle on your thigh. Wrap that up with a bandage and gauze and don't mess around. It won't take them too long to figure out what happened to us. Two guns are a lot better than one, amigo." On cue, there was a smattering of rifle fire off to their right side. *Good*, thought Rodriguez. *They don't know where we are—they're just hoping to get lucky.* With that, he got on his radio.

"Lieutenant, this is Rodriguez. Poole and I are pinned down on the extreme right flank. We never hooked up with Burton's squad. We've made contact with approximately twenty to twenty-five hostiles coming up behind us—they're about to roll us up!" Rodriguez had forgotten all sense of COMSEC for the moment. He just had to get the situation out there before this whole operation went to hell.

"Hustler Two-One, this is Playboy Actual. I'm sending Gallery Three-Two to your position." *That has to be the last uncommitted reserve*, thought Rodriguez.

****

As Rodriguez and Poole were running into the flanking attack, Corporal Mack continued fending off the frontal assault. He and Estrada had dropped countless Iranian attackers, yet no matter how many they shot, there were always more coming. The longer the enemy could concentrate on their position, the more dangerous it got. Once the M60 had gone off-line, the enemy had quickly found the general location of Mack's fire team. In the two minutes since then, the enemy was getting closer to picking out the individual firing positions. Yet this was a static defense. There was no place to fall back to. Any maneuvering along the line would open a hole that the enemy could pounce on and pour through. They had to hold. Mack noticed that Oliver was back on the line. That was a good sign. Oliver was a good Marine. That was Mack's last thought as a bullet caught him in the face and the defense of the air base was no longer his problem.

****

Poole and Rodriguez sat still as stones as the enemy approached. After Rodriguez had made the call to the lieutenant, he advised Poole that they would have to lie in wait, and once the enemy was in close, they were going to kill as many as they could. They were most likely going to die there tonight. The plan was to wait until Poole had a "can't miss" target. Once he opened fire, Rodriguez would join in, and they would shoot their way out of this mess.

The bark of Poole's rifle set off a killing frenzy. Poole's round sank into the chest of his target, dropping the soldier to the ground. An avalanche of lead came in return. It felt like every Iranian weapon in the field was firing at the two men in their tiny hiding place. Then, when Rodriguez returned fire, he was joined by a cascade of bullets coming down upon the enemy from above and behind Rodriguez. Burton's fire team had joined the fight. It was still terrible odds, but they were improving by the minute.

The enemy fell back a few paces, looking for cover, and trying to acquire the new targets that were shooting at them. The change in the balance of power was short-lived, however. The enemy apparently understood that their best chance at surviving the night was to continue the attack. Knowing this, they pressed on. They couldn't stop, they couldn't falter. They would take this base.

Rodriguez could just barely make out Third Squad's Fire Team Two, the last reserve unit, as it neared the tarmac on the north side to engage the enemy's flanking attack. As they steadied to fire, Lance Corporal Joey Owen was shot in the chest and fell without a cry. The rest of the fire team dove for cover. The attackers had detected the team's approach and dedicated a fire team of their own to ambush them. The defensive plan was coming apart. Rodriguez and Beck had let the enemy flank them, and now the platoon would get hacked to pieces.

Rodriguez felt the shame of failure as he continued to fire at the advancing enemy. He stood up from behind the rise. He was going to die, but at least he could take as many of these bastards with him as possible, and he wouldn't have to live with the shame of his failure. He methodically shot a running Iranian and searched for his next target. This was the exact John Wayne stuff that he was constantly reminding people not to do. Much to his surprise, it seemed to work! The enemy ran before him! As he raised his rifle to resume shooting them, he heard the roar of a dragon and felt the wind kick up around him. As the Iranians fled toward their remaining trucks, he saw the belly of Bluebeard One as it raced overhead, flared, and landed on the far side of the enemy.

He fell to his knees as he watched what could only be First Squad disembarking from the Sea Stallion, rifles ready and firing at the enemy.

Chapter 19

29 February 1980
39th Medical Group Hospital
Incirlik Air Base, Turkey

Corporal Franklin Cobb was still putting all the pieces together. He had been on the defensive perimeter of the air base when the Iranians had made a push. He'd had PFC Boone and Private Palmer with him, and they'd been giving the enemy hell. As he recalled, they had stopped the enemy cold. The attack had faltered, and he'd believed the remaining attackers were about to break and run. And then nothing. Just a blank spot in his mind until he'd woken up here this morning. The doctors had told him he had been out for the past nine days, and he had no reason to doubt them. Still, he couldn't get his head around those missing days.

Cobb thought back to this one time on liberty in the Philippines. He'd lost a few hours that night. He was sitting in a shady bar in Olongapo City, drinking one of the many San Miguel beers he'd had that night. He was talking to this amazing LBFM, and he was pretty sure he was doing all right. And then he woke up in a cheap hotel room with a zero percent recollection of whatever had happened the night before. He'd counted himself lucky that he'd still had his (now-empty) wallet, and he'd prayed that he wouldn't have to visit Doc in the coming weeks when he got back to the ship.

But this was on a whole different scale. In the PI, he'd been embarrassed and lost a few hours. Now he wasn't sure how to feel, and it had been days. He had no word about the battle, about his friends, about the mission. He was just stuck here on a lonely island, surrounded by the sterile white walls of his hospital room. His meditation was interrupted by a knock on the door. He asked who was there, but his visitors didn't bother to wait as they barged into the room.

"Check it out! He lives!" exclaimed Corporal Joseph as he, PFC Oliver, and Sergeants Rodriguez and Mason spilled in.

"Damn, Cobb, the way the command made it sound, I thought you'd look like hamburger, but you're looking ready for action, Marine," said Rodriguez. Cobb knew he meant it to be reassuring, but it fell flat on him, as he knew all the damage was hidden by his bedding.

“No can do, Sergeant, I think I’ll have to sit out the next few innings,” replied Cobb. There was something off about the scene, but he couldn’t put his finger on it. He looked over and noticed Oliver with his arm in a sling. “What happened to you, Oliver? You forget which end of the rifle was the dangerous one?” he asked.

“Oh, man, I’m about the luckiest bastard on the field! During the firefight I caught a ricochet off the stock of my M16. The rifle was pretty ate up, and so was my shoulder, but damn, I’m lucky that it wasn’t just a few inches to the left, man.”

“No kidding, dumbass. I’m what happens when it *is* a few inches to the left,” replied Cobb, trying to keep some semblance of good humor. He could see that Oliver felt bad about the situation. He didn’t want the private to dwell on it, so he moved the conversation along. “Rodriguez, what the hell happened out there? I haven’t heard anything in here. The docs either don’t know or don’t care to tell me anything.”

Sergeant Rodriguez gave Cobb the full after-action report. He gave his version of the battle, most of which Cobb had experienced firsthand, but it was helpful to his hazy memory. When he got to the part about Private Burgess getting killed, Cobb added, “Damn, I liked that kid,” but otherwise, he let Rodriguez tell the story.

“It looks like they shot you when the enemy maneuvered past our right flank. We were fighting them off with Burton’s team, but there were just too many of them. I thought for sure we would be overrun,” continued Rodriguez. It was at that moment that Cobb suddenly put together what had struck him as “off.”

“Wait! Jimmie?! Where the hell have you been?” Cobb hadn’t seen Sergeant Mason since the evening of the eighteenth, when they’d left the USS *Nimitz* en route to Desert One.

“Hey, First Squad had to get their beauty sleep while y’all were sweatin’ it out at that air base. But don’t worry, once we figured you couldn’t handle it on your own, we came to the rescue,” replied Mason with a wink.

“It’s true,” said Rodriguez. “I honestly thought I was about to die when Jimmie and First Squad came flying in and caused the attack to falter and break. They saved us all.”

“Damn, man. I guess I owe you a beer, Mason. But what the hell happened to you guys?” asked Cobb.

"We were flying into Desert One when we hit some kind of sandstorm."

"We were all there, dumbass," chimed in Oliver.

Ignoring him, Mason continued, "It was loud and crazy in there, and with all the bumpin' and jumpin' we thought for sure we were going to get shaken out of the sky. The pilot put us in a rapid turn and descent. When we were on the ground, the colonel told us that the flight was going to hold there and wait out the storm. At the time, we had no idea that it was just our two birds. We figured everyone was lined up out there in the desert. It wasn't like anyone was about to just head out and have a look. Even on the ground, those storms were vicious."

Mason continued to go through the harrowing events of his two days. After the two birds had sat down during the storm, they'd waited it out, just like the colonel had ordered. "It took about an hour for that damn sandstorm to pass, and even inside the birds we were getting covered in sand and grit. That stuff was getting in your nose and your eyes… everywhere," said Mason.

"Once everything had settled down, the zoomies spun the birds up again for takeoff, and that's when the wheels fell off the wagon. When the aircrew of Bluebeard Two had started their preflight check, they were showing a main rotor failure. Our chopper was showing a fault in the secondary flight controls. I guess the sand and wind had done a number on the electronics. There was no way those guys were lifting off in Bluebeard Two, and the colonel figured they had the best chance of getting Bluebeard One flight-ready. That was a whole lot of nothing to do for us. We couldn't break radio silence for fear of tipping off the enemy, and we couldn't help with the repairs."

"So you just jerked off for a few days while we were in the middle of the fight?" Asked Cobb.

"Yes, sir, Corporal, sir," said Mason with a laugh. "Seriously, though. By the time we got up and running, we barely got to Desert One before the Air Force had pulled out. By that time, we figured that if we could get to Manzariyeh in a hurry, we could catch a ride out of here. Our only other option was to wait out the mission and try to call for an extraction after the dust had settled. None of us wanted to try that."

"You'd be lost in the desert forever. Some sheik would come wandering by on a camel in a hundred years and find your dirty old bones," said Oliver.

"Piss off, Oliver," replied Mason.

"We really could have used you on the line out there. But, man, I'm glad to see that you and all those assholes of yours didn't buy it out in the middle of that sandbox," said Cobb.

"Yeah, that's true enough," replied Rodriguez. "Frankie, Mack's dead. He caught it on the same front line as you. In fact, his team took the brunt of the attack. All told, between taking the airfield and the defense, Fire Team Two took one hundred percent casualties, Mack and Yates were killed, and Estrada and this idiot"—he pointed at Oliver—"were wounded."

"Damn… that's a real shame. Mack was a hell of a Marine," said Cobb quietly.

"The best of us," agreed Oliver, in a rare serious moment. "If Strickland hadn't come off the line like a pussy, I bet Mack and Benny would still be here," he added.

"Knock it off, Oliver, this ain't the time," said Rodriguez, ending the controversy before it began. "There are rumors working around the unit about Strickland, but don't worry about it, it's just talk."

"What about the overall mission?" asked Cobb. "Did they get the hostages out?"

"They got most of them out. It sounds like things went to hell when the Army got into the embassy compound," replied Rodriguez.

"Yeah, one terrorist went all psycho on the hostages. He just started executing them," chimed in Joseph.

Rodriguez continued, "They lost seventeen of the hostages during the mission. The brass is calling this a victory. After all, the Delta guys didn't take any losses and we saved most of the hostages. It's all ticker tape and celebration on the news. Dan Rather even called it 'the rebirth of American military resolve' when it was first reported."

"So, we did good?" asked Cobb.

"We did outstanding, Marine. Don't forget that," assured Rodriguez.

The men of Second Platoon continued to reminisce. Cobb let his comrades know that he would be transferred to Germany as soon as he could travel and that he was due for surgery as soon as it could be arranged. The rest of the platoon was heading back to the States. They'd be in North Carolina before the end of March if leadership didn't change their minds. As the visitors took their leave, Rodriguez excused himself from the group.

"I've got another stop to make," he announced and left the rest of the team to head back to their temporary lodging in the barracks.

****

Rodriguez walked down the hall to room 203, where he found Fred Poole sitting up in bed, listening to Warren Zevon on a small radio while flipping through a copy of *Newsweek*.

"Where the hell'd you get the radio?" asked Rodriguez.

"I told you, I practically live here in Turkey these days. I had a friend mail it down along with some of my other personal effects from Sinop," replied Poole.

"Well, old man, how's the leg?" asked Rodriguez.

"I'm not going to say that it doesn't hurt, and there's no way I'm winning any footraces anytime soon, but all things considered, it's doing all right. How are you holding up?"

Rodriguez thought about that for a second, not quite sure what Poole was asking. "Nothing to worry about on my end. The only blood I got on me was yours," he said with a grin.

"Oh, I'm well aware of your ability to dodge bullets, Rodriguez. I was thinking more about how you were dealing with everything that happened that night. You know, it wasn't your fault." During the immediate aftermath of the battle, while Rodriguez and Poole had been waiting for Doc Watts to check out Poole's leg before they boarded the transport, Rodriguez had explained to Poole how he'd jacked it all up, and how his shifting the M60 had nearly allowed the enemy to overrun the position.

"Oh, I know that, Fred. The captain went over all of this, and how you and I are heroes for sealing off the flank, and how we need to focus on the success of the overall mission. I've been through the wringer on these after-action reports," replied Rodriguez.

"That's not really what I'm getting at. In our line of work, sometimes you have to make a tough decision. The results of that decision are life and death. When it's over, there's no point in second-guessing what you've done. I know that you feel responsible for Mack's death. I know that you think that your leadership of the squad got your friend killed. But that's not right at all. You have no way of knowing what would have happened had you acted differently. It's a counterfactual argument. Let's say you hadn't shifted the machine gun. Who's to say that the entire front line doesn't get overrun because you didn't have enough firepower? You don't know, and you can't know."

"But I do know what I did, and I do know what hap—" Rodriguez started, but Poole cut him off.

"You're not listening to me, Rodriguez. You made a decision that most men will never have to make in their lives. And people died. But people also lived. I truly believe that I'm alive because you made that decision. I think you're alive too. In fact, I think that thirty-five American hostages are alive because an E-5 sergeant decided to engage the nearest threat with his only machine gun.

"Look, I've been at this game for a long time," continued Poole. "I know I'm not a grunt, but listen to me. You are a leader. You're a smart man, and you are cool under fire. The only thing that could ever hold you back in anything that you do is this constant doubting that you have. Don't get me wrong, that doubt is an important part of who you are. It makes you human. But you have to overcome that doubt. It's not about the lives that you've lost yesterday. It's about the lives that you will save tomorrow. Never forget that."

Rodriguez didn't have a reply to that. He just nodded as he considered what Poole had been saying. Poole reached down the side of his hospital bed and grabbed a duffle bag. He hoisted it over the side rail and rummaged through it.

As he was searching in the bag, he told Rodriguez, "I should get out of the hospital in a week or so. Then I'll be in Turkey for a while longer—it shouldn't be more than a month. Then I'll be back in D.C. We have a project coming up, and I think it might interest you." He had found the card he was looking for in between the pages of a notebook. He pulled the card out and handed it to Rodriguez. "Take this and call me in April."

Rodriguez looked at the card. On it was printed nothing more than Poole's name and a phone number with a 202 area code. Rodriguez put the card in his pocket.

"I'll do that, Fred. You take care of yourself, okay? And try not to get shot again. I'm not going to be around to save your ass." They both laughed at that as Rodriguez turned and headed back to the barracks.

Chapter 20

29 February 1980
Oval Office, White House
Washington, D.C.

President Jimmy Carter sat with his back to his guests, looking out the window overlooking the south lawn in front of the West Wing. He thought about how very little the view had probably changed since 1961, when John Kennedy had first moved into the office. Now, here he was, fighting to keep that drunken bum Ted Kennedy from seeing the same view. Sitting in chairs on either side of the couch facing the President's desk sat his Chief of Staff, Hamilton Jordan, and his campaign manager, Timothy Kraft. They were both there to help Carter ensure that Kennedy would wait his turn—1984 would be a fine year for the Kennedy clan to regain their throne.

"Well, Tim, what are we looking at for next Tuesday?" asked the President. The campaign was looking forward to the Vermont and Massachusetts primaries on March 4. So far in the campaign, Carter had withstood Kennedy's push in Iowa, Maine, and New Hampshire. The only close call had occurred in Maine, where Carter had edged Kennedy by three percentage points.

"Mr. President, we're likely going to have to concede Massachusetts," answered Kraft. "But we've known that since Kennedy announced his run. You know how much Boston loves the Kennedys—there's not much we can do about that." It was true. There really wasn't. As a general rule, any politician who had the nerve to make a run to be the leader of the free world would be guaranteed to carry their home state, and the Kennedys would never have a problem with that. "As for Vermont, all the polling shows we'll take that easily. While we've always maintained a lead in Vermont, the latest polling is off the charts. In fact, all of our numbers have been through the roof since last week."

"We caught a bump back in November when the hostage crisis began," said Jordan, "and we've been riding that through the new year. News of the rescue has really boosted your overall approval rating to over seventy percent. So long as we keep this up and we don't have any surprises in the economy, I think Kennedy will drop out. His campaign was counting on bad news, and so far we've avoided that."

When Ted Kennedy had thrown his hat in the ring back in the summer of 1979, there had been a genuine concern that the situation in Iran would spiral out of control and that President Carter could not contain it. As the world had learned during the 1973 OPEC oil embargo, a foreign policy disaster in the Middle East would quickly become a domestic crisis at the gas pumps. The economic impact of another oil shock and the perceived blow to American global power would cripple the current administration. Ted Kennedy would be there to take the reins of government and save the republic.

However, that crisis hadn't materialized. Iran was still a mess, but through Bakhtiar's calm leadership and the presence of US forces in the region, they had kept a lid on it. As the oil kept flowing from Iran, the US economy continued its recovery from the recession of 1973–1975. As of today, it seemed, there was nothing in Iran that would derail the Carter reelection campaign.

"What about the Republicans?" asked Carter. "I know Bush has the early lead, but what are we looking at there?"

"Sir, the Republican field is still wide open. They have a lot of candidates out there, which makes this a bit harder to read," replied Kraft. "It looks like it will come down to Bush or Reagan, but John Anderson is polling well in Massachusetts and Vermont. Obviously we'll know more come next Tuesday, but I think we need to work on the premise that we will be facing Bush or Reagan in the general election."

"Very well," replied the President. "Once we've whipped Kennedy, we'll move on to whoever the Republicans put out there." The meeting continued through the mundane details of running a national campaign. The stage was set: the Carter machine had its orders, and even now—eight months before the general election in November—they were marching towards victory.

Chapter 21

8 March 1980
Abadan, Iran

Saeed Nouzari considered the month that had passed since the American hostage rescue. The remnants of the Revolutionary Guard were dispersed. Some were allowed to rejoin the Iranian Army (though usually with a loss of rank), while others walked away from military life altogether. For a few zealots, however, there was a third path. This was the path that Saeed had taken. He and his friends had formed the "Sword of the Revolution" to continue the fight.

The last month had been all about organization. It was all about collecting the people and equipment they would need to reignite the revolution. Saeed and his childhood friend Naser Entezami had met with another veteran of the Battle of Manzariyeh, Shahab Yazdani. Together, Shahab was able to procure all manner of explosives and weapons, while Saeed and Naser focused on recruiting more like-minded revolutionaries. Now it was time to make it count. Tonight the Sword would strike its first blow.

The Iranian town of Abadan was just downriver from Basra on the Shatt al-Arab River. From here, they were about to move men and explosives across the border and into Iraq. The target tonight was the fertilizer plant south of Basra. Run by the Iraqi "State Company of Fertilizers," it was one of the biggest nonpetroleum chemical plants in Iraq. Many in the Iranian military, Saeed included, believed that it was also a front for manufacturing chemical weapons. Tonight's raid would be historic. And it would just be the beginning.

"Do you have everything ready?" asked Naser. As the hours ticked down, the excitement in the room was building to a boiling point.

"Yes, the truck and the explosives are already in Iraq near the town of Safi. Tonight I'll drive north of Safi and cross the river there," said Saeed. Once across the river, Saeed would make contact with Halia Sayed, one of the Arab Shiites that Shahab had contacted in Iraq. As brothers in the faith, the Sword knew they could count on these men to strike at the Iraqi infrastructure. At least, that was what Shahab had argued. The Hussein regime had been brutal in their oppression of the Shiite population, and men like Halia had endured enough of the humiliation. Saeed had to admit that their ability to move in and out of the target area was invaluable.

"Excellent," replied Naser, bringing Saeed back into the moment. "And what of your return?"

"That will be more difficult," replied Saeed. "We have supporters in the hamlet of Badra. It's hundreds of kilometers to the north and far enough out of the way that it should be safe. Halia and I will hide out there for a few weeks, and once it is safe, we will cross back over into Iran."

"I have to admit, I'm jealous of your assignment on this mission. I wish I could go with you, my friend," said Naser wistfully.

"Your time will come, Naser, and soon," replied Saeed.

The drive up to Shafi was uneventful. He didn't know his driver by name. The two of them had never met prior to tonight. That anonymity would create a layer of security should something go wrong on either side of the river. To ensure that security, there was no small talk. The two men shared the car in silence as they moved north down the river road. After what seemed like days of silence, the driver made a left turn off the main road onto a small gravel path. They followed this path to the riverbank.

Saeed climbed out of the passenger seat and headed for the trunk. He was met there by the driver, who used the key to open it. From within the trunk, they removed a small black inflatable raft. Saeed connected a compressor to the valve stem on the raft and started the small electric compressor that was connected to the car battery. He closed the trunk as much as he could to muffle the noise. Again, the men were engulfed in silence as the raft inflated. The stars were sprayed across the sky on a moonless night. The two of them might have been the only people on the planet in that lonely moment.

Once Saeed had inflated the raft, he opened the trunk, turned off the compressor, and retrieved the small paddle he would use to pull himself across the river. The driver waited in silence as Saeed pushed the raft into the river and paddled with brisk, controlled strokes. He would wait there for another fifteen minutes before pulling the blacked-out car back to the main road and heading north, away from anything connected with the attack.

As soon as Saeed had the boat in the river, the current pulled him south. He had expected this. His point of entry was far enough upriver that he could paddle all the way across, then drift downriver for a while to reach his exit point. If he wasn't able to make his landing exactly where they'd planned, he could still deflate and hide the raft, then hike to his extraction point, where he would meet up with Halia. But he knew that it would be best and easiest if he allowed the river to take him right to the spot, so he pulled harder and faster on his paddle.

As his arms felt the strain, Saeed looked downriver at the west bank. In the dark it was difficult to make out the opening in the foliage that would mark his rendezvous point with Halia. Once he'd made it to the far side of the water, he paddled backwards against the current to slow his progress and give him more time to find his partner in the dark.

Suddenly, as he was passing by, he saw the break in the trees. Saeed pulled like mad to get to the shoreline before the current took him past. His arms, already tired from the trip across the river, were crying out for mercy. Saeed knew he needed to make it to that bank. Just as he was about to slip past, Halia, who had been hidden by the shadows, tossed him a rope. In a bit of good fortune, Saeed grabbed the rope just before it slid off the edge of the raft. He made the grab. Unfortunately, he lost his paddle in the effort, but there was nothing he could do about that now. By the time anyone went looking for them, that paddle would be floating in the Persian Gulf.

As Halia pulled him to shore, the two greeted each other with a firm embrace.

"It is good to see you tonight, my brother," said Halia.

"Tonight has been long in coming," replied Saeed.

The two men walked back to the truck, each dragging a side of the raft. Once they had made it to the truck, Halia deflated the raft and stowed it out of sight in the back of the truck. As Halia was doing this, Saeed changed into a uniform from the Iraqi State Company of Fertilizers. Once he had secured the raft, it was time for Saeed to be stowed out of sight. The cargo bed of the truck was filled with large drums of zinc oxide. Hidden amongst them were two empty drums, each with one side cut out. By sitting with his back pressed against one and pulling the second in towards his knees, Saeed was easily lost in the cargo.

Halia was scheduled to haul the zinc oxide to the plant, where it would be used in the production of ammonia. Neither Halia nor Saeed had any clue how it would be used, and it didn't really matter to them.

All they knew was that this white powder was their ticket into the industrial plant where they would wreak havoc. As he had for so much of the night, Saeed found himself alone with his thoughts.

It took the pair just under an hour and a half to make the journey from Shafi to the fertilizer plant. As they moved through the security checkpoint, Saeed held his breath. This was his first covert mission. Up to this point, his military career had been traditional and overt. He had spent no time training in the arts of sneaking around and avoiding detection. From that perspective, this would be the most terrifying mission he had executed. On the other hand, he thought, the enemy wasn't expecting anything. They'd be as relaxed as they ever would be. Every mission that came after this one would face much tougher scrutiny. And so would begin the cat-and-mouse game where the enemy would learn to better secure the objective and the Sword would learn to overcome those defenses.

Saeed could hear Halia stop the truck as he sat within the cocoon of his empty canisters. He couldn't hear the exchange between the gate guards and the driver, but he could imagine how it was playing out. Half of his mind was playing through the routine ID check, while the other half was projecting his worst fears. In the blackness of his nest, Saeed couldn't keep his mind from focusing on the impending doom that awaited him upon his discovery. Those fears were validated as he heard the driver's-side door slam shut. He held his breath as he waited for any clue as to what was happening on the outside. Saeed was helpless to do anything. As he tried to calm himself, he was sure that the guards would hear his heart beating as it tried to burst out of his chest. He had to focus on his breathing to keep from hyperventilating when he heard the rear cargo doors of the truck clink loudly as the latch was released.

Now he could hear the conversation between the Guard and Halia. Just having that connection to the outside world was enough to bring Saeed down a notch. He remembered now that this was routine. Halia had told him that the guards would stop the truck and give it a cursory inspection when they arrived. The guard was verifying the cargo on the manifest against what was on the security team's inventory. He could feel the truck bounce when the guard or guards boarded. He could hear the guard counting out loud. He was just six feet away from the man, but Saeed now felt perfectly at ease as he conquered his subconscious fears. His breathing returned to normal as he heard the cargo doors slam shut.

When the truck began moving again, Saeed extricated himself from his hiding place. He pushed out with his legs, straightening his knees for the first time in over an hour. The stretch felt wonderful, and the rush of air was refreshing. The stale air of the truck was a notch fresher than what he'd been breathing in his tiny lair. As Saeed separated the two canisters containing him, he pushed additional contents in the truck out of the way. This made enough room for him to stand. It was a challenge to keep his footing while the truck maneuvered through the chemical processing complex, but with the support of several canisters of zinc oxide, Saeed made his way to the rear door of the truck.

Once Halia made his final stop, Saeed unhooked the hand truck that was stored in the cargo area. As soon as Halia opened the rear doors, Saeed was sliding canisters onto the hand truck for offloading. The offloading crew on the early-morning shift was notoriously lazy and none were on hand to witness Saeed's miraculous appearance. While Saeed loaded the canisters, Halia attached a ramp to the rear of the truck and Saeed offloaded the zinc oxide. When he did so, he was careful to note the four canisters in the corner on the passenger side. He had marked them with a small blue triangle. Above all else, he had to make sure he kept track of those canisters.

The unloading of the cargo went off as planned. Halia moved the truck from the loading dock to a parking lot outside. It was common for him to leave the truck while he rested for a while after his delivery. This morning, however, he wasn't resting. Instead, Halia and Saeed were heading into the factory, pulling the hand truck with four canisters. Security on the inside of the plant was mostly lax. There were some restricted areas, but those were centrally located and not a direct part of the plant's operations. This helped confirm Saeed's suspicions that this was a chemical weapons research facility.

As they made their way deeper into the factory, the operations staff largely ignored them. There really wasn't anything too unusual about two uniformed men transporting canisters. They made their way to a nondescript supply closet, where Saeed unloaded the canisters and began opening them. There was nothing out of the ordinary about the closet. On the other side of the wall, however, were the primary compressors for the last stage of ammonia production. Behind that wall, hydrogen gases were being pumped through the system at over two hundred times the pressure of the earth's atmosphere.

Saeed ensured the timer was functioning properly, then inserted the detonators into the plastic explosives Shahab had provided. The Sword was fortunate to have found the explosives. Shahab had a man on the inside of the Iraqi Army who could secure the Soviet PVV-5A plastic explosives, and several cases of antipersonnel mines. Shahab had been light on the details, but if this man was as reliable as Halia, the Sword could maintain operations for months. When the device was placed and activated, the two men left the hand truck in the closet with the bomb and began walking back to the truck.

The decision as to how long to allow for this aspect of the mission had been agonizing. They needed to ensure that the men had enough time to get out of the plant. However, each second that was added to the timer increased the risk that the bomb would be detected before it detonated.

There is nothing to be done about it now, thought Saeed as he tried to force his body to keep a regular walking pace when he desperately wanted to run away from the danger that he knew was just minutes away.

As they drove away from the plant, Saeed considered how easy it had all been. Sure, there had been harrowing moments in the back of the truck, but once they were in… there had been nothi—

The explosion startled Saeed as the truck sped away from the fertilizer plant. Just as he processed that the mission had succeeded, the shock wave shook the truck and nearly caused them to veer off the road. The Soviet explosives had ruptured the high-pressure hydrogen lines, causing a massive explosion. After the initial fireball, secondary explosions went off as hydrogen and natural gas tanks ruptured and added their fuel to the hellscape. Halia didn't pause; he simply corrected his course and hurried the truck east along the access road before turning north on their run to Badra.

****

8 March 1980
Baghdad, Iraq

"The Sword of what?!" Iraqi President Saddam Hussein was enraged. His staff had woken him up in the early-morning hours with news that there had been a tragic accident at one of his chemical weapons research facilities. As the emergency fire teams battled the blaze and the

Iraqi Chemical Corps assessed the damage, news came out over the AP wire that a group calling themselves the Sword of the Revolution had claimed responsibility for the explosion. "This was no accident. This was a deliberate attack!"

"Yes, Mr. President, it was an attack," replied General Georgiy Lapunov. He'd been watching Hussein rage for the past five minutes. Ever since he'd left Moscow for this dry, godforsaken pit he had been looking forward to this day. He'd rehearsed this as best he could, and now he would maximize the effectiveness of the situation. "This is exactly why Moscow sent me here: to help ensure the security of the Iraqi Republic in the face of their unstable neighbor to the east." Internally, Lapunov knew that his actual job was to convince Saddam that the security of the Iraqi Republic hinged on doing exactly what the Politburo in Moscow wanted. Today, what they wanted was an Iraqi invasion of Iran.

Moscow knew that it wouldn't take much to push Saddam into war. The man was already predisposed to war against Iran. It was a miracle that hostilities hadn't already erupted during the chaos that was the Iranian political landscape over the past eighteen months. To be sure, Saddam was willing. But was he capable? Like so many strongman dictators in the world, Saddam fancied himself a military leader. The rationale being that if a man could rise through the ruthless politics of the Ba'ath Party power struggles, then he knew how to win a fight. Sure, Hussein understood power dynamics. Maybe he understood general strategy to a degree. Yet with that, the man did not understand military strategy or tactics at all. He had confused political power with military savvy, and unless General Georgiy Lapunov could intervene, it would be his undoing.

"These damned *ajam* must be dealt with forcefully!" said Saddam, using the Arabic slur for their Persian neighbors. "We cannot allow such attacks to weaken our nation and kill our people!"

"I agree, and we will deal with them together," said Lapunov. "First, we must marshal our forces. We cannot attack blindly. The only way for this to work is to hit the Iranians so hard that they will not recover."

"Yes," said Saddam. "We will smash the Persians across the entire border. We will drive them out of the valleys and across the desert plains and into the sea!"

This type of diatribe was exactly what Lapunov expected… and resented. It summed up in two sentences exactly what was wrong with Hussein as a military leader. That might well have been the best solution, but there was no way he could possibly accomplish it with the military he had. It was time for General Lapunov to go to work.

"Mr. President, I have no doubt that we can defeat the Persians in a military campaign. I am here to help ensure that comes to pass." Saddam looked at him warily. "But we must focus our efforts on what we can best attain, and then once we have secured that, we can move forward. You are correct, we can push them back unto the ends of the earth, but it all starts with a first step." Having placated Hussein's sense of national superiority, Lapunov sharpened the focus of the Iraqi leader. Together, they planned the start of total war between the two nations.

Chapter 22

9 March 1980
Camp Lejeune
Jacksonville, North Carolina

Sergeant Carlos Rodriguez had been back in the States for an entire day. And what a miserable day it had been. As he sat in the NCO club, he thought back on the whole miserable return home. Charlie Company had pulled stakes out of Turkey two days ago. They'd caught a C-130 out to Germany, where they'd paused for a day while there was some mix-up with the Military Airlift Command. Once the MAC guys had sorted out the supply chain, there were no "Cadillacs" available. These were the C-141 Starlifter aircraft configured like a civilian airliner. Instead, the Marines were slammed into another C-130 troop carrier from the 435th Operations Group, which was rotating back to Georgia for an overhaul. They were then bused from Marietta, Georgia, back to Lejeune. That damn bus ride took almost as long as the trip from Germany to Georgia.

The trip home was just the start of his problems. In fact, as he stared at the bottle of Budweiser on the table in front of him, he realized the trip home was just standard BOHICA crap from the Marine Corps. It was coming home to his empty, mostly unfurnished house that made every goddamned thing unbearably unjust. It wasn't like he'd expected a ticker-tape parade or even a grand homecoming like they'd get when the entire fleet returned from a deployment. He would have been more than happy to just come home and go to sleep in his own bed with his wife next to him and their baby down the hall.

"Freakin' Jody. This is some real BS, Rodriguez," said Staff Sergeant Dominic Page, Rodriguez's platoon sergeant, who had walked up to the table while Rodriguez was lost in thought. Like so many of the phrases and terms in the military, Rodriguez had no idea where the term "Jody" came from. He'd heard it countless times since he'd joined the Corps. Jody was the guy who was stealing your girl while you were deployed. He'd take advantage of your absence to get some action, usually to a ruinous effect. Here, Jody had been one Duane Hamilton, a townie who worked at a local Chevy dealership. At some point in the past four months, he'd had some kind of love connection with Nancy, and just like that, everything Rodriguez had thought he knew about the world was gone. "Stupid chicks, man," added Page for emphasis as he took a pull on his beer.

"Come on now, Page, I don't need any grief from you," replied Rodriguez defensively. It didn't matter that she'd broken his heart. Rodriguez wasn't ready to let people insult his wife. Besides, he still wasn't sure that the situation was a total loss. The way he figured, now that he was back, he could fix what they'd broken, and with enough work, things would be like they were.

"Hey, man, I'm just here for support," replied Page. "There ain't nothin' you can do right now, so let's get you good and drunk, and maybe tomorrow you'll be so hungover that none of this seems all that bad."

"That's a terrible idea, Page," said Rodriguez.

"But you don't have a better one, do you?" asked Page. "Right now you haven't gotten past the 'cry in my beer' phase, and let me tell you, buddy, that phase is a waste of time."

The two Marines sat in silence for a few minutes while the music played and they sorted out their thoughts. Page broke the silence. "Listen, Rodriguez, I wanted to talk through something before everything falls back to normal around here." Rodriguez looked at his friend with interest, hoping that this conversation would have nothing to do with his personal life.

"You and the other sergeants have been on my ass about 'Nam and what we'd learned about that experience. I've never once gotten into it with you guys. To be honest, the Marine Corps dumped anything of tactical value into training manuals. And anything of personal value wouldn't make any sense until you've been through the grinder. Truth is, this operation was practically a rerun for me. I've been through it before, and going back in was a totally different experience." Rodriguez was confused. He had no idea where Page was going with this.

"Prior to Manzariyeh, my only combat experience wasn't in Vietnam. It was on Koh Tang Island, off Cambodia." Try as he might, Rodriguez couldn't quite put a finger on the name. "I was a lance corporal with 1st Battalion, 4th Marines. We went to the Tang to rescue the crew of a merchant ship the Cambodians had captured. There were a lot of common elements with what we did in Iran. We flew to the rescue site on older models of the Stallion, and our plan was to hit the beach, engage the enemy and, once they were subdued, rescue the crew of the SS *Mayaguez*," said Page.

"Unlike what we did in Iran, this entire thing went to hell from the jump," declared Page. "Damn near every chopper that came in was taking automatic weapons and RPG fire. I watched our lead chopper take two RPGs and go down in the drink. We were the second bird in line, and we took an RPG to the tail rotor. Those were the longest seconds of my life, watching the ground spin around in circles while reaching up to grab us. I don't know how he managed it, but the pilot got us down on the beach in one piece. That's around the time they decided that our beach was too hot for landing operations."

"Seriously?" replied Rodriguez.

"Seriously. We were stuck there under intense fire for a solid twenty-four hours. We'd taken cover in the bush, and thank God for the Air Force. We used close-air support to keep those bastards off us, but the entire thing was a total goat rodeo, Rodriguez."

"So what's the point, Dom? Am I not supposed to worry about what happened in Iran because you saw some shit in Vietnam?"

"No, man, that's not the point at all. And it was Cambodia. Anyhow, the point is that in this line of work, things go wrong. There's nothing to be done about it after the fact. You can't bring them back, and you don't get a do-over. But you now have something that's more valuable than all the training the Corps has dumped on your worthless ass. You have combat experience. You need to learn from that, and you need to apply those lessons to running your squad, and one day your platoon." Page was emphatic.

"If you can't learn those lessons," he continued, "that's the only way that Mack and the boys will have died for nothing. Look, five years ago, I thought that was probably the beginning and the end of my combat experience. Last month proved me wrong. Manzariyeh probably won't be your only ride either."

Rodriguez thought it through. Page had a point. There was some wisdom to be found in the chaos of that firefight. And if he were to find himself in another battle, that experience could be the difference between life and death. Not only his life but those of his men as well. Page hadn't explicitly said that the experience in Cambodia had shaped the operation in Iran, but it was hard to reach any other conclusion. As Rodriguez turned it over in his mind, his thoughts were interrupted when he heard his name come across the PA system in the club.

"Ladies and gentlemen, we have a special dedication tonight for Sergeant Carlos Rodriguez."

Rodriguez looked up from the table and scanned the room. He caught sight of Mason and Burton heading towards the table that he and Page were sharing. As the next song began with a piano flourish, both Burton and Mason burst into song. As the two sergeants belted out a warbling rendition of Gloria Gaynor's "I Will Survive," Page and Rodriguez burst into laughter.

"What the hell is wrong with you idiots?" asked Rodriguez once he decided the joke had run its course.

"Aw, come on, Rodriguez. You needed a laugh," replied Mason. "There's too much to celebrate to let you keep moping around here."

The four NCOs made a night of it. They drank at the NCO club and relived the best parts of their relationships with the men they'd lost. They recalled the time that Yates had come to PT so drunk that he'd shit his silkies on the pull-up bar. Page did a spot-on impression of Corporal Mack yelling at his team to unfuck themselves. There were snippets of the lives these men had shared and the reminder that in death, all sins were forgiven. Nobody had an unpleasant word to say about any of them. Tonight, they were heroes.

After they'd toasted the dead, and the survivors had sufficiently bragged about their bad-assery, the Marines stumbled home. Mason and Burton headed back to the barracks while Page and Rodriguez headed to Page's orange 1974 Dodge Charger for the short drive back to Midway Park, and their homes in the married enlisted men's housing area.

"Try not to knock over any telephone poles!" advised Burton as Page pulled out of the parking lot.

The drive was short and uneventful. As they pulled up in front of Rodriguez's house, Page said, "You going to be okay here, man? You could always crash on my couch if you want."

"No, man, I'm good. Besides, Tiffany would kick your ass if you dragged me home and we woke up the kids," replied Rodriguez.

"All right, Rodriguez. Take it easy and try to get some sleep. I'll see you tomorrow," said Page.

With that, Rodriguez got out of the car and watched as Page rolled slowly down the road toward his place. Alone, Rodriguez looked at his house. It was a two-bedroom "cracker box." Much like everything in the military, it was a utilitarian structure. It wasn't meant to be pretty. Nonetheless, Rodriguez had always thought it was beautiful. It wasn't so much the house itself, he admitted to himself. Rather, it was what the house represented. It was his home. The home he had built with his own labor, by being a Marine. He was a man, and he had done what he was supposed to. He'd built a life that provided for his wife and child. They had this house because of the work he'd done. He was proud of that work and proud of that family. And now it was gone. Everything was gone.

Or was it? As his rambling drunken thoughts continued, he remembered that there was one thing that he'd bought for himself. One thing that he loved almost as much as the whole concept of his perfect life. He walked around the right side of the house to the backyard. He'd always thought it strange that they didn't have fenced yards here. That could be a problem when Jennifer got older. *Who cares about that now?* thought Rodriguez. Before he could dwell on it, he saw what he'd come for, and it brought a wide, stupid grin to his face. It was Bernice. His blue-and-white 1970 Pontiac Firebird Formula 400.

He reached into his pocket and pulled out the keys as he approached the driver's-side door. It took him a few stabs before he could get the key in the door, but once it was open he easily spilled into the driver's seat. He'd always loved those cars. When they were first introduced ten years prior, he'd vowed that one day he would have one. And he'd made that dream come true. He knew that he should have sold it when he got married and was supposed to settle down, but he just couldn't bring himself to. So instead, Bernice just sat under a shade tree and graced the driveway behind the house with her presence.

He slid the key into the ignition and turned the engine over. The starter kicked the motor and after a couple of rotations, the engine caught and rumbled to life. As he felt the satisfying shake of the 350-horsepower engine, the stereo kicked on and filled the car with the sounds of the Commodores' song "Sail On." The song slapped Rodriguez back into the reality that he'd come here to avoid for a while longer. After having spent the day pretending not to be hurt by it, then spending the night pretending to have fun with his friends, Rodriguez finally gave up and broke down. He sat in his beloved car, crying over how fake everything was and how none of this really mattered. Not the car, not his family, not the house. Whatever he'd thought he was working towards… none of it mattered. It was all just so much BS.

Chapter 23

9 March 1980
White House
Washington, D.C.

"You can't be serious, Zbig," said President Carter, genuinely shocked.

"I'm quite serious, Mr. President," replied Dr. Brzezinski. "I think this would be a shrewd move on your part." It had been a week since Cyrus Vance had resigned as Secretary of State, and Carter had assembled his foreign policy team to elicit names for a replacement. Up to this point, Edmund Muskie, the senior senator from Maine, had been the frontrunner. The meeting had been moving along slowly until Brzezinski had dropped a name that might as well have been a basket of snakes: Jeane Kirkpatrick.

"I think she made her point very clear that we're all incompetent, Zbig," said Dr. Brown.

"Sure, Harry, she writes with vitriol, but her criticisms weren't baseless. I think our recent successes in Iran could temper that criticism, but her point is well made: we cannot let the Soviet success in Nicaragua bleed into neighboring states, and her thoughts on a Marxist Mexico are chilling enough."

"I thought we dispensed with domino theory after Vietnam? How are we still even talking about this?" asked Hamilton Jordan, Carter's Chief of Staff.

"Just because we choose to ignore it doesn't mean it stopped being true," replied Brzezinski. "The People's Republic of Cambodia and the Lao People's Democratic Republic should be a testament to that." It was true—while America had washed its hands of the affair, the communist influence in Vietnam had spread to the neighboring countries. The United States had just chosen to ignore that aspect of the defeat, as it was a lasting reminder of their failure in Vietnam. Nixon had gotten them "Peace with Honor," and that was the end.

"Gentlemen," interrupted the President, "if we're going to consider this, let's take it from the top. Dr. Brzezinski, why do you feel that this is a good idea?"

"Mr. President, Dr. Kirkpatrick represents a dissenting voice, for sure. But it is dissenting in the right direction. I believe that her criticisms of my role in our policy are fair. I have neglected some of what's going on in the third world, especially in Latin America, to pursue what I see as issues of greater importance in Eastern Europe. Her position in her essay 'Dictatorships and Double Standards' has merit. When we let the communists run Somoza out of Nicaragua, there was no telling how the new Sandinista government would act. There are already signs that the Ortega wing of the Sandinistas is consolidating power, and if there's one thing we can be sure of, it's that once the revolution gives way to a totalitarian state, the human rights of the people will suffer."

"And what of her criticism of Iran?" asked CIA Director Stansfield Turner.

"I think that is where we can really bring this whole marriage to consummation," replied Brzezinski. "I propose that we offer to meet her halfway. We can accept that her general criticism of our policies on the third world is valid, and she can walk back her objections to our handling of Iran. I think she will agree that the situation in Iran has vastly changed in the months since she wrote her dissenting position. If we can show her that Iran is on the verge of transforming into the modern representative government that we have envisioned, I believe that she would be amenable to coming on board."

Carter turned to his Chief of Staff. "Hamilton, what do you make of this?"

"Mr. President," responded Jordan. "I'm not against the idea per se. I think we'll want to vet Dr. Kirkpatrick, but I can't imagine anything coming up that would preclude her from consideration. I'd defer to Tim for anything more than that at this point." He looked over to Tim Kraft, Carter's campaign manager.

"How about it, Tim?" asked Carter.

"From the broad strokes, I think this will be a big hit. She's been a powerful Democrat force in academia. With the current swell of support for a more aggressive foreign policy, especially with the Soviets, I think she will be well received by the public. Right now the Republicans are a mess. With Connally winning the South Carolina primary, it's a free-for-all. Either way, though, regardless of who the Republicans choose, having Kirkpatrick on the team will keep them from being able to call us soft on communism."

Kraft was referring to the knife fight that had come out of the Republican primary race. A week ago, it had been thought that the race would come down to Reagan or Bush. Since then, however, the former Texas governor, John Connally, had poured massive amounts of money into South Carolina with the goal of showing that he had the support of the South. Connally had been betting that if a Republican could win sufficient support in the South, that Republican could challenge Carter on his home turf in the general election.

As it was, George Bush had won Iowa and Massachusetts while Reagan had New Hampshire and Vermont, with Connally picking up South Carolina. It was a wide-open field. No matter which candidate won the nomination, though, the GOP would want to make defense an issue. The Carter administration's decision to cancel the B-1 bomber had come under scrutiny, and despite the increases to the military budget, the perception that he was weak on defense had dogged Carter.

"In fact," continued Kraft, "the only issue I can see from an election perspective is the elephant in the room… there's never been a woman as the Secretary of State."

"I've thought about that, Tim," said Hamilton Jordan. "We may really have an opportunity to make some history here. With the Equal Rights Amendment stalled in the state legislatures, it may look like we could lose some votes by putting a woman in the position. The opposition will accuse us of naming Dr. Kirkpatrick to subtly push for the ratification of the ERA. But we can't forget that women make up half of the voting population. Even Mrs. Schlafly would have to agree that there's no reason a woman can't do this job."

Jordan was referring to the lead dissenting voice against the ERA, Phyllis Schlafly. Mrs. Schlafly's position was that the ERA would hurt women's position in American society. She based her argument on what she perceived as important protections that women would lose. These included the exemption from Selective Service in the event of a new military draft, and a preferred place in family court. In the ERA's absence, there was a presumption that a woman would receive financial support from an estranged husband and that she would be the default primary guardian of any children from a dissolved marriage. If it were constitutionally forbidden to make these distinctions on the basis of sex, she argued, women would be at a considerable disadvantage.

Jordan continued, "To minimize any damage this could cause in more conservative wings of the party, I would recommend that we float the idea that Dr. Kirkpatrick's appointment is in an 'acting' capacity. She'll complete Vance's term, and when we win reelection, the entire cabinet will be reevaluated for the term starting in January 1981. I believe that this will secure us the votes we need, and then in January of next year, you can just fire Stan here"—he used his thumb to indicate Director Turner—"to let everyone know that you were serious."

There was a slight pause as everyone tried to understand why the President would want to fire his CIA Director. It wasn't until, after a few seconds, Jordan broke into a wide grin that the room realized he wasn't serious. The tension dissipated as laughter broke out around the table. It looked like they had a plan to move forward with this nomination.

As the meeting broke up, Harold Brown quipped, "The only person who would object to this was Cy."

Chapter 24

19 March 1980
Jacksonville, North Carolina

One of the benefits of working at the First Federal Credit Union was working banker's hours. Nancy Rodriguez considered herself lucky for that. She could get over to her mother's house to pick up Jennifer and be back at her apartment in time to get dinner going before Duane stopped by. It was a comfortable routine that she had fallen into over the past month, and as she grew more comfortable, she felt more confident in her decision to flip the table on her life.

Her mother couldn't understand it. As far as Janice McNamara could tell, Nancy had taken a perfectly good family and thrown it all away for no good reason. Most of Nancy's friends felt the same way, even though most were polite enough not to mention it. The only person she felt was one hundred percent on her side (well, besides Duane, obviously) was her friend Rebecca. Thinking of her friend, Nancy pulled her 1978 beige Ford Fairmont wagon out of the parking lot.

Rebecca had been a steady rock over the past few days. Nancy knew that Carlos's homecoming would be the most difficult time in her life. She had loved the man. Even though she was the one who wanted out of the marriage, leaving him was still the hardest thing she'd ever done. She knew that she couldn't be there when he came home. She couldn't face that. Instead, she'd left him a note telling him she and Jennifer were staying with Rebecca and to call her there.

Carlos had made the call, and Rebecca answered. Carlos had always liked Becca, and she made a great ambassador between the two. She broke the news to Carlos, letting him know that Nancy was with her, and that she had moved out of their house. The marriage was over. No, she wouldn't see him today. Yes, she was sure. She and Jennifer were doing well and were splitting time between Rebecca's apartment and the McNamaras' while she moved into her new apartment. Once she had calmed Carlos down and gotten him off the phone, she turned and consoled her best friend.

As Nancy played it out in her mind, she remembered commenting that she had no doubt that Carlos had hit the NCO club with Dom and the boys. Where else would he go? Hell, that was probably where he'd have been had she not moved out. She stopped her mind from racing away with that thread. Yes, Carlos spent more time with his friends at the bar than she'd have liked. But she tried not to make him the bad guy when she thought about him. He was a decent man—they just didn't see eye to eye on some fundamental aspects of their relationship.

Nancy had concluded that Carlos had been raised on too many episodes of *Leave It to Beaver*. It seemed to Nancy that for Carlos, creating that ideal 1950s nuclear family was an obsession. He'd be the breadwinner, and she'd be the perfect housewife. That vision had never worked for Nancy. She'd tried over the past few years to let him know that. She wanted to go back to work. She really enjoyed her job as a bank teller. Carlos wouldn't hear of it. "I'm not out there risking my life and working all these hours so my wife has to go out and work too," he would say. From what Nancy could tell, Carlos believed that her desire to work called his manhood into question. She'd repeatedly told him it wasn't about needing the money. She found some meaning in that work. Some value that she hadn't found anywhere else.

Once the arguments made it that far, they would move on to fighting about whether or not she was a good parent. Wasn't that enough value in her life? Being a mother and taking care of their baby girl? Carlos never came out and said she was a terrible mother, but it didn't take much to read between the lines. The idea that these two aspects of Nancy's identity could be different, and each with their own value, was something that she could never bring Carlos to understand.

She noticed her father's car in the driveway as she pulled up. *Damn, what's he doing home early?* she wondered. It wasn't that she didn't love her dad, or that she didn't want to see him. She just knew that he would badger her about getting back together with the father of her child. She dreaded that conversation. Telling her father he was wrong was only slightly less difficult than telling her husband she was leaving him. She'd spent twenty-two years learning right from wrong from this man, and now he was wrong.

"Hi, Mom, I'm back," she said as she came in through the front door into the sitting room.

"Hey, princess, it's good to see you," said Brad McNamara, her father.

"Oh, hi, Daddy. You're home early."

"I just wanted to sneak out and spend some time with my best girl," he said, pecking Janice on the cheek. This wasn't a show for Nancy's benefit. This was just how they acted. When Nancy thought about it, she realized that they had given her quite an unrealistic expectation of love and family life. Though she imagined both of them thought it was realistic, and the faults in her married life rested with her.

"You two," she said, smiling. "Where's Jennifer?" Her two-year-old was usually waiting for her when she got there.

"She's still sleeping. We had a late day at the park," said Janice. "Poor thing wouldn't let me take her out of the swing. I think she just wore herself out."

"Say, sweetheart," said Brad. Nancy knew where this was going, and she knew that her best bet was to intervene before he got started.

"Daddy, please. I know that you want me to work things out with Carlos. I know that. But we're working through this as best we can right now. I really don't want to have this argument—"

"We're not having an argument," protested her father. "We're having a conversation."

"I don't want to have this conversation every time we get together, Daddy. I know how you feel. I love you very much, but I need to sort this out on my own." Much to Nancy's relief, her father let it go with that. She chatted with her parents and caught up on the day's events. She took in her mom's report of Jennifer's daily activity, feedings, naps, and one spectacular diaper catastrophe. Once she collected up her daughter and spent enough time to be considered polite, she loaded everything up in the station wagon and headed out for her new apartment.

She lived a few miles down from her parents. It was a clean one-bedroom in a safe complex. She was thankful that she lived on the first floor. Carrying Jennifer and all of her necessary supplies was enough of a juggling act. She couldn't imagine having to deal with stairs. She fumbled for her keys and managed to get the door open without dropping the baby or bag. Sometimes it was the minor victories in life.

She entered her sparsely decorated apartment and set the "baby bag" down by the front door. She hadn't had the time she needed to get fully moved in. The prominent feature of her current living room decor was a square aluminum frame supporting white mesh with a padded rail on top. She and every other mom she knew called it a playpen. Carlos called it the "Baby Jail." That comment had always annoyed her. Casting the playpen in a negative light made her feel like she was doing something wrong by using it.

Nancy shared the one-bedroom with Jennifer, who could still be contained in her crib on a good day. She'd have to figure out something else soon, as the child learned how to climb in and out at will. She'd get to that in time. *Time*, she thought. *I'm running out of time.* She set Jennifer in the playpen and headed to the compact kitchen. She pulled a frozen lasagna out of the freezer and set the oven to three hundred and seventy-five degrees. If she timed it right, she'd have dinner ready by six. Perfect. *Thank goodness for banker's hours*, she thought.

Having finally made it from the office to her parents' house to the apartment and gotten dinner started, she went back and lifted Jennifer out of the playpen. She could finally spend some time with the most important thing in her life.

Chapter 25

20 March 1980
Situation Room, White House
Washington, D.C.

The National Security Team, with Secretary Kirkpatrick filling the chair once occupied by Cyrus Vance, looked up at the image projected on the wall across from the conference table.

"What exactly are we looking at, General?" asked Dr. Brzezinski.

General Edward Meyer used a pointer to pinpoint exactly what he was talking about.

"These shapes here along the southwestern border with Iran show the massing of the Iraqi 5th Mechanized Division outside Basra. This would not be too alarming on its own. The 5th MD is based out of Basra, but they aren't normally kept in such a state of readiness. What is more alarming are these images here." He clicked a button on the handheld controller and the slide projected changed to an airfield to the southwest of the city. "These are Iraqi Su-20 Fitters. This is bad news. The Iraqis use them for close-air support, and they call it the 'bomb truck.' When combined with the 5th MD mobilization, and these images showing the mobilization of the 9th and 10th Armoured Divisions"—he clicked again to bring up yet another grainy photo—"they provide the Iraqis with the ability to cross the border and disrupt Iranian interests in the area, or even to occupy large swaths of Khuzestan Province."

At first blush, the news was grim. "Are we certain that this isn't simply a reaction to the recent cross-border hostilities with Shiite terrorist organizations?" asked Brzezinski.

"No, sir. If they had only mobilized their infantry, they could realistically make that argument. The strike aircraft, however, don't have a place in that scenario. They're utterly useless against the small teams of assailants that have been pulling off these attacks."

"Could they be bluffing?" asked Kirkpatrick.

"That's a possibility, ma'am, but I must defer to Director Turner on that."

All eyes looked to the Director of the CIA.

"It's absolutely a possibility. In fact, based on what we know, we think it's a probability. We can't rule out the use of force by the Iraqis, but we think right now Iraq is trying to push for concessions from Iran. They know that the Shah is still reeling from the revolutionary movement and they're taking advantage of that fact. We're hearing similar noises out of Afghanistan and even the Soviet Union. Attacks have sprung up in most of Iran's neighbors."

"What about Iran? What are they doing to contain the violence? What are they doing to counter the threat from Iraq?" asked Brzezinski.

General Meyer, who was still at the front of the room, took the question. "Right now Iran has made no overt military moves to counter the Iraqi deployments. We've been coordinating with them and supplying them with our intel on the situation, but we have also advised them to stand down while we try to get the situation under control. As for the internal situation…" He looked to Turner.

"This is a difficult situation to be sure. Without care it could turn catastrophic," said the Director. "It combines the challenges of a traditional criminal investigation with the added difficulty of a tense international border and the threat of military force. Right now, to the best of our knowledge, this 'Sword of the Revolution' is comprised of former soldiers in the militia forces of Khomeini. Most of them have experience in the Iranian military, and the collapse of the revolution has upset all of them. Worse than that, they also appear to have support across the borders in Iraq and Afghanistan. That's not too surprising given the fairly arbitrary nature of the borders out there, but it is alarming."

"I can agree that this is a difficult situation," said Brzezinski. "But you haven't answered my question: what are they doing about this 'Sword of the Revolution'?"

Turner shifted in his chair, looking uncomfortable. "Right now, the Iranian Army is conducting what we might call a purge of their ranks. When the revolution fizzled out, the army was originally open to reintegrating the militia members. Since these attacks began, however, there's the belief in the top levels of government that this new threat has infiltrated their military. They're identifying militia members and jailing them." There was a brief silence as the room considered Turner's words.

"As you can imagine, this is causing a real shakeup in the command and control of the Iranian armed forces. Worse than that, we don't know how effective this purge will be. I can't speak for all of Iranian leadership, but there are definitely some cases where the purge is being used as a political maneuver to gain advancement or settle grudges."

"What is the effect of this purge on Iranian military readiness?" asked Secretary of Defense Harold Brown.

"I'll stop short of calling it disastrous, but it's certainly not good," replied Turner. "We have no way to quantify their readiness, but there are gaps in the chain of command where officers are being removed, and their replacements are often inexperienced and sometimes may not even fully understand their new responsibilities."

"And this is why we're here today," said Brzezinski. "We need to support the Iranian government as best we can during this transition. With Iraq threatening war, I believe that we should deploy elements of the new Rapid Deployment Joint Task Force. The question is, which elements and to where?"

"Sending troops to Tehran is out of the question," said Secretary Kirkpatrick. "I've been in talks with my people on the ground and they are adamant that the Bakhtiar regime will not allow a major US force on the ground. The regime has, in my opinion, a well-founded fear of rekindling the revolution if they're seen bringing in Western forces. They don't want to risk a flare-up when they're so close to finally getting the nation back on track."

"What about Turkey?" asked General Meyer.

"That's a tricky one," said Turner. "There's a lot of unrest brewing in Ankara between the warring factions of their government and the military. We have intelligence that indicates there may be a major shift in power soon, and from what we can see, that will not bode well for the US presence in the area."

"Pakistan," said Secretary Kirkpatrick. "We can use Pakistan to stage our military presence."

"It's not ideal," said Brzezinski. "We must relax our stance against their nuclear program if we hope to have them agree."

"I understand that, and we will have to address that. But right now this gives us the chance to signal our dedication to keeping peace in the region, and to deter the Iraqis from any aggression while our allies in Tehran get organized. We shouldn't need more than a year to get Iran back on its feet."

"That's still about a thousand miles away from Iraq," said General Meyer. "I don't know how much force projection we can achieve with that kind of distance."

"We have carriers we can leave on station," said Admiral Hayward, the Chief of Naval Operations. Hayward had been brought into this meeting specifically to handle the question of carrier availability. "If we can utilize the port facilities in Karachi, we can keep two carrier battle groups in the Gulf of Oman or Persian Gulf for the duration of the crisis." For the past year, the Navy had increased their presence in the Indian Ocean in response to the tensions in Iran. This subtle shift in logistics might make that a permanent fixture of naval posture.

"That would keep the Iraqis honest," said Brzezinski. "Admiral, what exactly are we talking about by bringing in two aircraft carriers? How much would that change the balance of power in the region?"

"Our intel indicates that the Iraqis are operating five fighter and twelve attack squadrons. That gives them a combat fleet of around three hundred aircraft. The Iranians are more or less even with them in that regard, but they most likely have an edge technologically. During Operation Eagle Claw, the Navy had about one hundred and forty combat aircraft in theater. If used without limitation, that's enough to make a decisive impact."

"Naval air power alone may not be sufficient to deter Iraq," said General Meyer. "They could very well accept an exchange where they concede the air after gaining initial ground objectives. We're going to need a land threat to go along with the Navy."

"What about sending Marines in with the Navy?" asked Director Turner.

"Let's hold off on that, Stan," said Admiral Hayward. "We've got some additional tasking for the Corps in our next agenda item."

"We can move elements of the 82nd Airborne Division. This is what we envisioned when we included them in the RDJTF," said General Meyer, refering to the Rapid Deployment Joint Task Force that Carter had created for just this sort of emergency. "It's just a matter of understanding from where we will stage them."

"State will work on both Egypt and Pakistan. I know that in either case they'll be a thousand miles from the Iran-Iraq border, but they'll be closer than anything else we can put together," said Dr. Kirkpatrick.

"Okay. Harry, can you get this written up and I'll take it to the President?" asked Brzezinski. Secretary of Defense Harold Brown nodded but said nothing. "With that, I will turn the meeting over to Secretary Kirkpatrick to update us on the situation in Latin America."

"Thank you, Dr. Brzezinski," said Kirkpatrick as she rose from her chair and moved to the front of the room. "It's no secret that one reason I was brought into this administration was to bring greater insight into the influence of the Soviet Union in the Western Hemisphere. This is an area that I feel has been underserved by our government, and as my first initiative I have instructed State Department resources to investigate the depths of Soviet collusion with the leftist governments in the region. Nowhere is this more significant than in Nicaragua." The room was passive, giving no overt response to the proposition.

"Further, I have worked with Director Turner and the heads of the NSA and DIA to verify what we're learning from the official dispatches between Cuba, Nicaragua and the USSR. It has become apparent that the Ortega wing of the Sandinista government is working closely with the Soviets, including direct military support." She clicked the projector controller and an image of the port facility at Bluefields, Nicaragua, appeared on the screen. "These images show the delivery of T-55 tanks from Cuba. We believe that the Soviets have orchestrated the transfer of at least fifty of these older tanks, and at least thirty of the smaller PT-76 light tanks, shown here." *Click*—the projector displayed another image of the Bluefields port. "Possibly the most alarming of all are the new Mi-24 attack helicopters being delivered here." *Click.*

As the briefing continued, it became obvious to many in attendance that what Dr. Kirkpatrick might have lacked in brevity, she made up for in detail. She scrutinized all the intelligence she could show them and explained in depth the ramifications of each piece. As she concluded her presentation, Brzezinski addressed the room.

"Gentlemen, I believe that Secretary Kirkpatrick has laid out a very valid issue that we must address immediately. I understand that Harry and the Joint Chiefs have put something together for a response?"

"That's right," said Dr. Brown. "We have a two-pronged approach here. We will focus our efforts on supporting Honduras. We will bring some of their military officers up to the School of the Americas in Fort Benning. After a brief orientation training period, we will send Army Special Forces units down to Panama to conduct live-fire and situational training before sending the entire group back to Honduras. Then we'll start the process over with another class." On the face of it, there was nothing controversial about this plan. It was standard to train up Latin American militaries through the School of the Americas. There was some controversy about some of what they had been taught. President Carter had banned the use of training materials that advocated the use of assassination and torture as tools for counterinsurgency. This would be the first major push for the school without the prohibited materials.

"Okay, that's a start," said Brzezinski. "You said two prongs. What's the second prong?"

"One disadvantage of this training program is that it lacks the visibility that we're looking for. It will no doubt pay dividends. This is especially true if, God forbid, we end up with a shooting war down there. But we're looking for something more brash to get the Soviets' attention and to let them know that we will not sit back and let them take over Central America while we're distracted in the Middle East." The anticipation was building in the room as Brown let that settle.

"This current crisis presents us with an opportunity to test one of the fundamental assumptions of our current war-planning strategy with the Soviets. In the event of a full-scale conventional conflict between NATO and the Warsaw Pact countries, we will need to secure the naval supply routes and the sea lines of communication through the Caribbean so that supplies can transit on the southern route to Europe. To do this, we will need to neutralize Cuba. However, we don't currently have any resources dedicated to that objective. The assumption to be tested is that we'll 'make do' with units that aren't allocated to other war objectives. We have the 38th Marine Amphibious Unit preparing for deployment this summer. Our proposal is to send the MAU to Honduras to perform amphibious assault training at La Ceiba. This will be a joint exercise with the Honduran Marine Infantry and could form the basis for future annual exercises in the region."

"To where was the MAU scheduled to deploy before this change?" asked Brzezinski.

"The backbone of the MAU is the USS *Nassau*. They were on a shakedown cruise last year, which got cut short in order to reinforce Guantanamo Bay. They've been back in port since November and weren't scheduled to head out again until next April. We've accelerated their workups given the circumstances of their last abbreviated deployment."

"So, truly a 'make do' situation," said Brzezinski.

"Exactly," said Brown. "Given the 'show the flag' nature of this mission, we're going to issue a press release as soon as we have the details. We want the world to know what we're doing here."

With this last detail presented and agreed upon, the meeting broke up as the various players returned to their offices to write up the specific orders they would present to the President.

Chapter 26

25 March 1980
Shaibah Air Base
Iraq

General Lapunov had moved his headquarters to Shaibah Air Base in order to keep a close eye on the battle as it unfolded. From this location, he could stay in radio contact with his ground forces. He could also monitor the close-air support missions that were being conducted by the Su-7 and Su-20 squadrons stationed here. This was also the location from which the initial helicopter assault would take place. He couldn't be everywhere all the time, but this was as close as he could get.

At 0900 hours, eight Mi-24 attack helicopters lifted off. The Mi-24 combined the armament of a gunship with the ability to carry eight fully armed infantrymen. The men had taken to calling them "Krokodil" because of their toughness and vague resemblance to the reptile. Today's mission would combine both abilities. The Iraqi Army was about to put an end to the cross-border violence emanating from the Iranian side of the Shatt al-Arab River.

Lapunov had positioned two armored divisions in Basra. He needed to get those tanks and BMPs across the river and into Iranian territory. All the vehicles involved in the attack had the ability to cross the river, but the time spent deploying the snorkel would expose them to enemy fire. There was also the likelihood that they would lose tanks to accidents during the crossing. The nightmare of sitting in a disabled tank at the bottom of a river while the snorkel failed and the tank filled with water had kept many tankers awake at night.

The Krokodils' mission was to secure the two large vehicle bridges that crossed the river to the east of Basra and the north of the Iranian city of Khorramshahr. With the bridges secured, the 9th Armoured Division would cross the river and engage the Iranian defenders.

The Krokodils flew over the massed tank formations. At that signal, the tanks started their engines and headed for the bridges. The gamble was that by the time they made it to the bridge, the infantry would have secured it and prevented the enemy from blowing them. If the Krokodils failed, the assault would be slowed by the need to prepare for a river crossing. Either way, the 9th Armoured Division would be in Iran before noon. Men from the tanks waved at their airmobile countrymen. The door gunners waved back as the attack began.

The helicopters split into three groups as they passed the tank formations. Three Mi-24s headed north to secure the larger of the two bridges. Two Mi-24s headed south to secure the smaller bridge, and three in between the two, looking for targets of opportunity. Those three Mi-24s would conduct close-air support (CAS) runs at any Iranian units that looked likely to interfere with the operation. There were additional close-air support missions being launched, but the Mi-24s would be the only units in the area during the critical first minutes of the attack. Soviet satellite imagery had shown where the Iranian 92nd Armoured Division had set up a temporary headquarters. This was the first stop for the CAS group.

To the north, the Krokodils landed on the east bank of the river, just past the bridge, and unloaded their infantry. That assault was textbook. The men rushed out and took up positions on and around the bridge. They checked for explosive charges and found none. Once they knew the bridge wasn't in danger of exploding, they pointed their guns towards the likely enemy approaches and waited for further orders. They knew that the plan was for a massed tank assault. As soon as those tanks had crossed the bridge, their fighting was likely done for the day.

As they were taking up defensive stations, a platoon of Iranian APCs approached from the south and opened fire. The venerable M2 .50-caliber machine guns wouldn't do much damage to the bridge, but they would be more than enough to punish the infantry troops. An enterprising vehicle commander trained and fired a TOW missile, hitting the bridge on the east side. The bridge shook from the explosion, but remained standing. The rocket hadn't done any critical damage, but with more hits like that, it would only be a matter of time before it collapsed, or at least became too weak to support the weight of the T-72 tanks that were about to cross.

The infantry scrambled for cover from the heavy machine-gun fire. The M113s continued to close the distance, and the commander of the Iraqi ground forces called up his RPGs. At this range, they'd be lucky to stop all four of the IFVs, but hopefully they could cause enough damage to turn back the attack. Just before he gave the order to fire on the IFVs, one of the CAS Krokodils screamed overhead and unleashed a volley of rockets.

As the dust cleared, the Iraqis saw dismounted infantry advancing. The helicopter had destroyed or disabled their M113s, but they were still on a mission to blow the bridge. The Iraqis opened fire at five hundred yards. At that range, they weren't proficient enough to reliably hit their targets. They could hope to at least slow them down and buy time for the armor to get across the bridge. Once the tanks were there, the enemy infantry wouldn't stand a chance. One of the enemy IFVs broke out of the smoke, firing its .50-cal and causing the Iraqis to drop for cover once more. An Iraqi with an RPG took out the left tread of the M113, causing the vehicle's left side to dig into the ground and forcing it into a sharp left-hand turn. With the right side exposed, two more Iraqis unleashed RPGs at the wounded vehicle. The first flew over the target and harmlessly into the sky. The second hit squarely at center mass, blowing a hole in the lightly armored side and setting fire to the mortally wounded IFV. As men scrambled out of the burning vehicle, the Iraqis cut them down with AK-74 rifle fire.

At the southern bridge, things were not moving as smoothly. Captain Zaki al-Salek, flying the lead Krokodil, could see enemy units closing on his landing zone (LZ). He flew past his LZ and unleashed his load of rockets on an Iranian M60 tank east of the bridge. The remaining close-air support Krokodils engaged other Iranian targets of opportunity as the battle developed. When Captain Salek brought his helo back over the landing zone, he determined that the LZ was too hot to deploy his troops and ordered his wingman to return to base.

"He *what*?" demanded General Lapunov.

"He's returning to base, General. They could not deploy their troops to secure the southern bridge," replied the liaison for the Mi-24 squadron.

"Get me that jackass on the radio right now!"

****

Captain Zaki al-Salek's heart rate was returning to normal as his Mi-24 clung to the nap of the earth on his way back to Shaibah Air Base. That changed when his radio exploded to life.

"Captain! You will turn your flight around and deploy your troops on the east bank of the river right now! That is not a request, that is an order. If you fail to comply, I will personally shoot you when you get back to base."

The blood drained from Captain Salek's face as he realized that he was being addressed directly by the Soviet "advisor" who had put this plan together. He had no idea what the man was saying, as he didn't speak Russian, but it wasn't long before the liaison explained it to him. Perhaps, deep in his mind, he questioned whether the Soviet general would have the authority or the absolute lack of morality to execute a subordinate. But his conscious brain had no doubt that if he didn't turn back around and complete this mission, he was a dead man. If he faced the Iranians, there was a chance he would die. If he faced General Lapunov after failing to attempt his mission, his death was certain. He turned his helo back for the bridge. His wingman had heard the broadcast and didn't need to be told.

The opening of the plan called for explicit timing. The delay caused by Salek's failure to deploy was now causing downstream effects that he had never considered. As he lowered his Krokodil on the east edge of the bridge, he no longer had the cover of the CAS helos, and the Su-20s hadn't gotten into position to start their attack runs. He was now trying to deploy his troops without covering air support. If he'd thought the LZ was too hot during his last pass, it was on fire this time. Enemy IFVs had advanced to the edge of the bridge, and he was taking fire from the M2s mounted on the vehicles. As he neared the ground, there was a tremendous explosion as the second Mi-24 in his flight pitched over, hit the ground, and exploded.

"Allah protect us!" said Salek as he yanked on the helo's collective and added throttle to get him out of the immediate danger. As he clawed for altitude, he looked around the battlefield, trying to find a place to deploy his men. There was a clearing just downriver from the landing zone, and he made for it as tracer rounds chased him through the sky. As he left the field, he couldn't see the Iranian armor advancing on the bridge unopposed. Without the helicopter soldiers to slow them down, they quickly closed the distance and began shelling the bridge.

The race was on. The Iraqi 9th Armoured Division was committed to getting across the bridge, while the American-built M60 tanks were dedicated to destroying it. Each 105mm shell that slammed into the bridge brought it that much closer to collapse. For the Iraqis crossing the bridge, this meant that at least the Iranians weren't targeting their tanks, while Iraqi tanks on the west bank were able to engage the Iranians directly. As the fourth Iraqi tank made it across the bridge, the Iranian shells finally accomplished their mission. The bridge collapsed as a second four-tank platoon tried to scramble across. As the tanks sank to the bottom of the Shatt al-Arab, their crews desperately tried to escape their dark, sinking tombs.

Between the four T-72s that had crossed the bridge and the tanks firing from the west bank, the Iraqis had destroyed the defenders. Unfortunately, without the bridge, the bulk of the southern prong of the assault force was trapped on the Iraqi side of the river. The units had deployed their snorkels, but this would take time. During that time, they would be out of position to support the continuation of the attack.

****

At the northern bridge, the Iraqis had poured across unopposed. By the time the Iranians had moved into position to counter the Iraqi assault, the Iraqis had made it into Iran in force. Twenty T-72s were on the east side of the river and advancing into Iran. The lead platoon in the assault was Second Platoon of Charlie Company, 1st Battalion of the 9th Armoured Division. Lieutenant Abdul el-Hashmi led his four tanks across the bridge and immediately turned to the east, where the last reports of enemy activity had come from.

In the excitement of the moment, Lieutenant Hashmi had pushed his tanks all-out in a dash to the east. As the tank column exited the bridge, his tanks were the pointy end at the tip of the Iraqi spear. The thought excited him until he recalled his training. If he encountered the enemy in this position, his platoon would likely be wiped out before they had a chance to fully engage. The enemy would concentrate the full weight of their fire on his four tanks. He commanded his driver to slow to half speed to allow the company to form an echelon left formation. This would give them a fearsome frontal assault thrust, while protecting their exposed left flank. The river would protect their right.

It was too late. Before the company could establish their formation, Lieutenant Hashmi located the first of the enemy vehicles approaching. At that moment, Hashmi knew he had caught a break. These were M113s and not the enemy M60s. He ordered his gunner and then the rest of the platoon to open fire at the enemy units. They slaughtered the IFVs. In the opening seconds of what would become the Battle of Khorramshahr, it looked to be a rout. As the Iraqis continued to advance, though, Hashmi identified enemy tanks mixed in with the IFVs. The two forces closed range at a combined thirty miles an hour. Fortunately for Second Platoon, the rest of the company caught up to them as the T-72s hurled 125mm shells at the Iranians, and the M60s fired 105mm shells in return.

Lapunov's plan was to catch the defending Iranians between the two prongs of Iraqi armor. In reality, the southern prong never materialized. As the tank battle raged, it was quickly apparent that the Iraqis would win with sheer numbers and initiative. Hashmi's platoon kept pounding the enemy while the rest of the company advanced. Calls of damage and destruction were coming in through the radio, but as of yet, he hadn't heard any of his own tanks go off-line. He just kept calling targets for his gunner and advancing towards the enemy. To the north of his position, entire platoons were being disabled and destroyed by the Iranian M60s, but every Iraqi tank destroyed had cost the defenders more than one of their own. In less than ten minutes, at 0925 the 1st Armoured Brigade of the Iranian 92nd Armoured Division ceased to exist as a fighting force.

****

At Shaibah Airfield, Lapunov was again furious. His tanks were advancing, and they had defeated the staunch defenders on the outskirts of Khorramshahr. But the cost had been high. Current estimates had the Iraqis losing nearly thirty of their priceless T-72 tanks, while the liaison officers tallied the Iraqi kill totals at ninety enemy tanks. Lapunov knew that this was ridiculous. He made the actual number closer to thirty. Had the southern force been able to link up with the northern, they would have drastically reduced their losses. All because an Iraqi Air Force captain couldn't do his job.

So far, the air campaign had gone in unopposed. Lapunov, in concert with the Iraqi Air Force staff, had agreed to send in massive fighter sweeps along the entire border, but with an emphasis on the skies above the ground invasion. This allowed the Iraqi Su-20 attack aircraft to attack enemy positions with impunity. As a result, the 14th Mechanized Brigade had a clear path to "swim" their BMP-1 IFVs across the river and directly into Khorramshahr. So long as the Iranians couldn't bring attack aircraft into the fight, there was nothing that would stop the Iraqi mechanized infantry from securing the perimeter and beginning block-by-block sweeps to rid the city of any remaining defenders or partisans.

Chapter 27

26 March 1980
Oval Office, White House
Washington, D.C.

President Carter sat in the Oval Office looking out over the South Lawn. He had been thinking about the sin of pride.

"When pride comes, disgrace follows, but with humility comes wisdom," he said to himself.

"What was that?" asked Tim Kraft, Carter's campaign manager.

"Proverbs, chapter eleven, verse two, Tim," said the President. "It's something that I need to remind myself of on days like today, when I feel like I'm growing too comfortable in this chair. It occurred to me just now that for the first time since the inauguration, I have a growing confidence that I'll still be occupying this chair in this office this time next year."

"Well, sir, I think you have excellent reason to believe that," replied Kraft. "Our numbers are strong within the party. Our national polling is the most favorable it has been since just after you took office, and the Republicans will eat each other in this primary race."

"Be that as it may, Tim, we need to stay grounded on this. I feel like we're on the verge of hubris on days like today," replied the President. "Have we heard anything from Ted's camp?"

The night before, Carter had just dominated in the New York primary. After winning every contest outside of Massachusetts, the Carter team was still fending off Ted Kennedy's run. Most pundits agreed Kennedy had put all of his chips into New York. Kennedy was betting the house on coming out on top in a Yankee vs. Dixie showdown. But with the swell of national pride resulting from the rescued hostages and the economic growth born of the stabilizing of energy prices, the Democratic voters were not interested in making a change. With his loss in New York, Tim had expected Kennedy to throw in the towel.

"Yes, Mr. President. Kennedy is ready to make a deal," answered Kraft. "He's willing to suspend his campaign and even go on the trail for you…" Kraft trailed off.

"Spit it out, Tim, what does he want in return?" asked Carter.

"You're not going to like it, Mr. President. He's asking for a straight quid pro quo. He wants you to endorse his run in 1984."

Carter furrowed his brow at that. It was a big ask. After a pause, he replied, "So he wants a clear path next time around… that won't sit well with Fritz." There was no doubt about that. Walter "Fritz" Mondale had looked into a presidential run in '76 but decided against it before things got too serious. His getting named vice president on the Carter ticket was expected to give him the national exposure that would propel him in his own presidential run in 1984. Now Ted Kennedy was asking President Carter to take all of that away from him. "What do you think, Tim?"

"I think it's a bargain. I'd take this deal every day and twice on a Sunday," replied Tim without hesitation. "But I don't have a relationship with Mondale, and I'm not the one who will have to tell him. Unless you want me to tell him?" he added.

"I've never given Mondale a promise on this. It was always an assumption that if he wanted my endorsement, it would be there. And I'm sure there were some general statements of support for a future run… okay, get Steve Smith on the phone, and make the deal." Mondale wouldn't be the first politician asked to bow before the Kennedy royalty, and with things going as they were, he likely wouldn't be the last. "What are your people saying about the Republican race after last night's vote counts?"

"It came out more or less as we'd expected. Mr. Bush took Connecticut, but I really think it's too little too late for him. This win just shows that the GOP does not have a united front right now. Frankly, this is why we still use caucuses. If the party leadership had been making the call, it would have been for Reagan or Connally. Leaving it up to a direct election by the voters has just clouded the field. After the Southern primaries on March eleventh, it should have been clear that Bush was the odd man out."

The March 11 primaries had been a master stroke of John Connally's campaign. Connally's people understood that they didn't have the cash on hand to compete everywhere against the vast field of Republican contenders. Instead, they invested heavily in the South. Connally's surprise victory in South Carolina on March 8 had proven his viability as a candidate. That credibility had paid off three days later, when he'd won Alabama, Florida, and Georgia. This gave him a double-digit lead with only two more contests in March. He had twice as many delegates pledged as Bush and had stunned Reagan, who was counting on those

Southern votes as a knockout punch to convince Bush to drop out. This left Bush in a terrible position.

Coming into the race, the Bush campaign had more or less written off Illinois. His focus had been on the early primaries, where he thought if he could build a substantial lead, he could ride the momentum to victory. However, he didn't think he could compete with Illinois's "Favorite Son," John Anderson, who had mounted a serious campaign. By March 12, Mr. Bush had needed to win Illinois just to stay relevant in a fast-moving race. Unfortunately for the Bush campaign, they were too far behind to make up the distance. Having lost Illinois, they won Connecticut on momentum alone. The groundwork they'd put in over the course of the previous months had paid off. But it just wasn't enough. Everyone following the race was now waiting for Bush to end his campaign and endorse one of the remaining candidates. This could make Bush something of a kingmaker.

"I understand that you think this is the end for Bush, but what does the Bush camp think about all of this? What are you hearing?" asked Carter.

"It's all very quiet right now. I'm not sure if they were actually prepared to win in Connecticut. If I had to guess, I'd say he's waiting right now to see who offers him the best position in a new administration," replied Kraft. "It's possible that one or the other considers him for the VP spot, but at this point I'm not sure he'd take it. It's bad enough being an also-ran, I don't think Bush wants to be labeled as second fiddle to a national loser."

Chapter 28

12 April 1980
Camp Lejeune
Jacksonville, North Carolina

PFC Oliver had just finished his run when Lance Corporal Tim Holmes came over to greet him.

"Hey, Oliver, I just got word that I'm moving over to Second Squad." Holmes had been with the Weapons Squad, but given the casualties in Second Squad, leadership had decided to raid Weapons Squad to help even out the number of replacements for any given squad or team. "I just talked to Staff Sergeant Page, and he told me that I'm on Fire Team Two with you."

"I don't suppose they mentioned who our team leader would be?" asked Oliver as he wiped the sweat from his face.

"Negative. Still no word. Right now it's just the two of us, but from what I'm hearing we'll have replacements by Monday," said Holmes.

"I don't know about you, Holmes, but I don't think I can stand it two more days without a team leader to tell me when to piss," quipped Oliver. Holmes just stood there, not sure what to make of it. He only really knew Oliver by reputation. He hadn't spent any significant time with the Marine. It was clear that Oliver's sense of humor would take a little getting used to.

Before Holmes could break the awkward moment, Sergeant Rodriguez came over to the two of them.

"Good run out there, Oliver," said the sergeant. "How's the arm holding up?" It had been two months since Oliver had been wounded in action, but as advertised, he was back at nearly one hundred percent effectiveness.

"It's always a little stiff, but nothing to worry about. Medical says I'm good to go," replied Oliver.

"What's going on, Holmes? Who let you out of your cage?" asked Rodriguez, turning his attention to the interloper.

"I guess that'd be Staff Sergeant Page," replied Holmes.

"Holmes is now part of Fire Team Two with me, apparently," said Oliver helpfully.

"Well, damn, I wonder if anyone was ever going to tell me?" asked Rodriguez, marveling at the efficiency of Marine Corps leadership. "Welcome aboard, Holmes, I've heard good things about you from Lieutenant Woods and Sergeant Strickland. We can sure use someone like you who's been around the block with Second Platoon."

"Glad to be here, Sergeant. Looks like I just missed PT."

"That you did, Holmes. We're going to shower and shave, then head over to grab some chow. We'll see you over at the chow hall in thirty minutes," said Rodriguez.

As Holmes excused himself, Rodriguez and Oliver headed back towards the gym. On their way over, they ran into Corporal Daryl Evans from First Squad.

"What's the word, Evans?" asked Rodriguez.

"Second Squad's the word today, Sergeant," replied the corporal.

"That's two words, dude," said Oliver.

"Shut the hell up, Private," said Evans.

"Can it, Oliver," said Rodriguez, who stuck his hand out for Evans. "You'll get used to it."

"Anyhow, Mason just sent me over. It looks like I'm coming over to Second Squad as part of the shakeup," reported Evans.

"That's good news, Corporal. I know you did a hell of a job out there with Jimmie, and I'm really light on NCOs right now."

"No place I'd rather be, Sergeant. I can help you out if you're having any discipline problems," said Evans, looking right at Oliver.

"I tell you what, Corporal, I'll take care of Oliver here, and we'll get into introductions after lunch. We're having a squad formation at 1400 at the field house. We'll talk about assignments and go over all the administrative nonsense then. From what I hear, we're going to be getting cherries day after tomorrow, so I'd like to get you regulars sorted out before then."

"Roger that, Sergeant, 1400 at the field house," said Evans. Then to Oliver, "I've got my eye on you, Private."

As they made it to the gym, Rodriguez told Oliver, "You really need to secure that attitude. Mack spoiled you because he thought you were funny and he knew he could count on you. Evans doesn't know anything about you, except that you were acting like a dick, and that's no way to start off with your new team leader."

Oliver swallowed hard. It hadn't occurred to him that Evans would be taking over Fire Team Two. He'd just assumed that he was Cobb's replacement. As he headed for the shower, he thought that this was it. Mack was officially gone and replaced in the big green machine.

Chapter 29

19 April 1980
Arlington, Virginia

Fred Poole passed the Marine Corps Memorial as he cruised north on the George Washington Parkway. Seeing the giant statue of the Marines raising the flag at Iwo Jima reminded him of his recent time in Iran and the firefight that left him with a limp and one hell of a story.

This was Poole's favorite stretch of road in the city. It was hardly ever congested (especially on a Saturday like today), and his little Fiat Spider could zip along the curves as it followed the Potomac River. Off to his right was the exit for the Teddy Roosevelt bridge. He was happy not to be heading into the city today, so he continued north on the GWP. The top was down, and the air was crisp. It was the perfect day for a drive up the Parkway. It was days like today when he wondered why he'd ever left this place. Then he'd remember the summers. And the winters. Oh, and all the self-important jackasses that called this swamp home.

He continued along the river past Teddy Roosevelt Island off to the right, then past Fort Marcy on the left. Finally he came up to the left-hand turn he was looking for, exiting the Parkway and turning onto the access road to the headquarters of the Central Intelligence Agency. He'd returned to the mother ship, where he was hoping to wrap up his current assignment and start working on the next.

He liked to come into the office on Saturdays for the same reasons he liked the midwatch at Sinop. He could get access to anything he needed but wouldn't have to interact with too many people uninvolved with his assignment. This meant he wouldn't be able to gain any political points for climbing the leadership ladder, but he was okay with that. He was a simple man of simple tastes, and he loved his job.

In a place with twenty-four-hour coverage like Langley, there were always people around. Fortunately for Poole, none of them were interested in bothering him as he made his way to the cubicle he called home on the rare occasions he was in town. He sat down at his desk and retrieved the courier package that was waiting for him. The package contained his notes and selected photographs from his assignment in Sinop.

He sat at his beige IBM Selectric typewriter and began plinking out his report. All in all, it was an unsatisfactory report. He had been sent to Sinop to investigate the shifting of massive amounts of JP-4 jet fuel to the sleepy Caspian Sea village of Kaspiysk. At the time, the brass in Langley believed that the fuel was being diverted to Afghanistan for some kind of increased offensive presence in that country.

Having followed up on the tip from his asset, he could conclude that, yes, JP-4 was being diverted from Baku to Kaspiysk. What they were doing with it, though, was still anyone's guess. They could be using it to operate some of the newer ships in the Soviet fleet, but that seemed unlikely. He could quell his superiors' fears that the fuel was being diverted to Afghanistan. It was just sitting there in Kaspiysk. But he couldn't satisfactorily explain exactly what the Soviets were doing with all that jet fuel.

As soon as he completed his report on Kaspiysk, Poole headed to the break room for a cup of coffee before moving on to his next assignment. His friend Carl Miller over in the Latin American office had brought him into a project based on mutual contacts. Dispatches coming out of Havana and Managua referenced a Soviet Spetsnaz general whom Poole had profiled. Carl wanted Fred on the team as the Soviet expert to balance out his team of Latin American experts.

The entire episode had arisen from the CIA's uncovering of a battalion-sized force of Soviet Army personnel in Cuba almost a year ago. In the summer of 1979, the CIA had performed an intelligence audit on Soviet military units in Cuba. During that audit, they had uncovered numerous Soviet tank and infantry units. When word had leaked about the discovery, there was a diplomatic dustup between the US and USSR over the matter. The Soviets contended that the unit had been there for years and it was not a provocation. The Americans contended that it represented a direct threat to the United States and a gross violation of the agreements between the two nations in the aftermath of the Cuban Missile Crisis.

Since that point, the CIA had been trying to untangle the authentic story behind the unit's purpose and the implications it might have for communist movements in Latin America. Miller was an expert on Nicaraguan politics. He had long been resisting pressure in his office to connect direct Soviet involvement to the rise of the Sandinista government, which had taken power in July 1979. That pressure had redoubled since the appointment and confirmation of Dr. Kirkpatrick as the Secretary of State.

Miller still didn't buy the idea that the Soviets had given direct aid to the Sandinistas during their rise. From Miller's point of view, you didn't need the Soviets at all. All you needed was to remove American support for the Somoza regime and collapse was all but guaranteed. It was fairly cut-and-dried. However, even a skeptic like Miller had to admit that there was something going on in the past few months.

Diplomatic traffic between Cuba and Nicaragua was nothing new. The CIA knew that the Sandinista leader, Daniel Ortega, saw Castro's Cuba as a model for what he hoped to accomplish in Nicaragua. What had changed, or at least what was now being noticed, was the similarities in specific dispatches between Moscow, Havana and Managua. The number crunchers at the NSA originally noticed repeating sequences within encoded communications. As the picture unfolded, they linked some of those sequences back to General Stanislav Smotrov. It was all very vague, and Miller needed to put some meat on the bones of that intelligence.

That was where Poole came in. Fred had profiled Smotrov back in 1968. At the time, he had been a colonel leading a tank regiment during the crushing of the Prague Spring. During that brutal campaign, Smotrov's aggressive tactics and disregard for civilian casualties had earned him the nickname "Stanislaughter" among the English speakers and "Smertrov" among the Russian speakers. After the Prague Spring, Smotrov had transferred from the Army to the GRU, the main intelligence unit of the Soviet military machine. From there he had taken a staff position specializing in the suppression of political uprisings and insurrections. Miller needed Poole to see if he could verify the general's presence in Nicaragua, and to get as much information as possible on what activities the general was undertaking there.

The situation in the Middle East was still getting all the headlines. But Secretary Kirkpatrick had made it abundantly clear that the communist regimes in Latin America were a special focus of the administration now. She was an open critic of the Sandinista government in Nicaragua and feared there would be a spillover effect on the surrounding countries. Guatemala and El Salvador had continuing political violence destabilizing their governments. The government in

Honduras was in its infancy, while Costa Rica was the only nation to offer political stability.

Cuba had been a communist thorn in America's side since 1959. Kirkpatrick painted a bleak picture of a world where there was a Cuban problem that spanned from Mexico to Venezuela. For the first time in history, she argued, the United States would be threatened with invasion. It sounded like so much hyperbole. But Kirkpatrick was an academic, not a politician. She didn't deal in hyperbole, and she didn't care what you thought. The weight of that focus of purpose was being felt in every part of the United States' military, intelligence, and diplomatic organizations.

After his coffee, Poole headed back to his desk to crack open the file that Miller had left him. As he did, his thoughts drifted back to Carlos Rodriguez. When he'd mentioned that he might have something for Carlos nearly two months ago, this project hadn't been nearly as hot as it was today. Especially given that Poole would be working outside of his normal area of operations, he really thought he could use someone he could trust with the ability to move around, speak the language, and someone who would kill a bad guy or two. *It's been a while since I've had a real protégé*, he thought.

****

23 April 1980
Northeast of Ramhormoz, Iran

Staff Sergeant Felix Watkins scanned the desert town of Ramhormoz. They'd found exactly what they were expecting. The Iraqis were staging from here. They were building up forces for a major armored thrust on the city of Izeh. Izeh was forty-five miles northeast of Ramhormoz, and intel was certain that it was the next objective of the Iraqi Army.

Watkins and the rest of the 82nd Airborne Division had been given orders to head out to Egypt. Before the ink was dry on those orders, they'd been redeployed to Iran. After spending a week in Tabriz getting the Division situated, they'd started sending out patrols. From what Watkins heard from the brass, the 82nd would be joining the fight in earnest, but for now, they were providing as much support as they could.

“That’s a shitload of armor,” said Specialist Marlon Reeves, one of Watkins’s radiotelephone operators.

“You ain’t kiddin’, Reeves,” replied Watkins. “Let’s see if we can do something about it. Get me Simpson on the line.” Tech Sergeant Wayne Simpson was the Air Force combat controller who was the liaison between Watkins and the nasty surprise the Air Force had flying high above them.

“Hazard One-One, this is Pressure Two-Zero,” said Reeves into his radio.

“Pressure Two-Zero, Hazard, I have you fives.”

“Hazard, we have a massed formation of armor,” Reeves continued, giving the exact position and composition of the target. Once he completed his report, Hazard gave him some advice.

“Pressure Two-Zero, keep your head down but your eyes open. You’re not going to want to miss this.”

“Roger that, Juice. We’ll let you know,” said Reeves, using Simpson’s nickname.

The two Rangers looked at each other. They knew that there would be some close-air support, but they had no idea what made this run special. Within five minutes, they understood. The flight of four aircraft raced in from the northwest on the deck. It took a minute for Watkins to ID them.

“Warthogs,” said the staff sergeant, using the unofficial nickname for the Republic A-10 Thunderbolt IIs. They watched as all four aircraft unleashed six AGM-45 Maverick missiles each. One by one, the tanks exploded. The rapid succession of fireballs was dazzling. They couldn’t be sure, but at least twenty tanks had been damaged or destroyed in the first pass.

Watkins watched as a MANPAD followed one of the Warthogs, exploding behind it. The shrapnel from the warhead didn’t seem to faze the armored menace. Once the flight passed the tank formation, they entered into a wingover maneuver, where they climbed into the sky, then reversed course, heading straight at the enemy.

From their perch in the hills, the Rangers had the perfect view as the A-10s opened up with their GAU-8 Avenger cannons. The 30mm autocannon fired nearly four thousand rounds of depleted uranium a minute at the Iraqis. Even from miles away, the sound of the cannons was impressive.

"It's like fabric ripping," said Reeves.

"I think it sounds like the world's loudest fart," replied Watkins.

"I have no doubt those Iraqis are shitting themselves." After several gun passes, the Warthogs flew to the northeast.

"Pressure Two-Zero, Hazard One-One. How'd you like the show?"

"Totally worth the price of admission," replied Reeves as he and Staff Sergeant Watkins transmitted their battle damage assessment.

****

8 May 1980
Camp Lejeune
Jacksonville, North Carolina

Sergeant Carlos Rodriguez sat in his barracks room and considered the drastic changes in his situation over the past six months. The most obvious was this ridiculous barracks room. He'd moved out of the barracks two years ago, and being back was just a constant reminder of his failure at starting a family—a sign of his defeat. He and Nancy were still fighting over more or less everything. Rodriguez felt that if he could just get this jerk "Duane" out of the picture, they'd be able to work everything out.

But Nancy had made it clear that Duane was there to stay. It crushed Rodriguez whenever he thought about how confusing this must be for his baby girl. For the first year of her life, Jennifer had had one man in it. Now there was Duane. He'd never be her daddy, but with Rodriguez in the Corps, Duane would be around a lot more. As time moved on, Rodriguez could see that he might lose that role in his daughter's life. As much as he hated that thought, he couldn't get past it. Sure, if he and Nancy could work things out, she could help him ensure he was always there. But the way things looked, there was no way that would happen. He wasn't really a husband anymore, and he could see that he was about to lose being a father.

He still had the Corps. That hadn't changed. Except that it had. He'd lost a brother out there in Lionel Mack. While all the casualties were hard enough to bear, Mack's loss was particularly impactful. Rodriguez had never gotten over the idea that his own orders had gotten Mack killed.

Between the obliteration of his family life and combat losses in Iran, Rodriguez was becoming a bitter man.

It had been two months since he'd returned from Iran and nothing had gone right since then. As he considered this, he picked up the card that Fred Poole had left him, turning it over in his hand a few times. It was just a plain white card with his name and a phone number on it. He'd thought about calling that number a few times but had never pulled the trigger. At this point he thought, *What the hell, why not?*

Grabbing a handful of change, he left his room and made his way down the hall to a pay phone. After depositing his initial twenty cents, he dialed the number. An automated voice then told him he needed to deposit another dollar for the first three minutes. He dutifully deposited the required four quarters and waited for the dial tone. The phone rang twice before it was picked up. The number had sent Rodriguez to an answering service. Rodriguez used his $1.20 to leave a quick message letting Fred know that he was calling based on their last conversation in Turkey and that he hoped to hear from him. And that was it. All that buildup, and that was all there was. Rodriguez wondered if the fact that he'd waited until May to call instead of calling in April meant he'd missed his chance.

The next day, Rodriguez and Second Squad were in a classroom working on a review of military operations in urban terrain when a PFC came in and announced that Rodriguez needed to report to the captain ASAP. As he grabbed his cover and headed for the door, he couldn't imagine to what he owed this honor. The quick jog over to the captain's office didn't really give him enough time to come up with a creative solution. As he walked in, Captain Goodwin greeted him.

"Apparently you have a phone call, Sergeant." The captain motioned towards a phone on his desk.

Rodriguez managed a quick "yes, sir" and grabbed the receiver.

"Sergeant Rodriguez."

"Well, damn, Carlos, it took you long enough." It was Fred Poole. "Look, I have something going on that I could really use your help on. I can't go over the details on this line, but I need a Spanish speaker with combat experience. I figured you fit the bill."

At this point, Rodriguez was up for a change of pace. Even without the details, he agreed to meet with Poole the following week in Fort Benning, Georgia. There, they would go over details and see if

Rodriguez would make a long-term commitment to the project. In the meantime, Rodriguez would have to initiate the paperwork for getting his security clearances updated. He'd be able to get mostly up to speed with unclassified information, but they would fast-track his background to get him what he needed. As he hung up the phone, he thought the entire thing happened so fast, he was almost dizzy.

"I don't know what kind of pull you have, Sergeant, but I've never seen the Marine Corps move so fast on anything," said Goodwin as Rodriguez stood there for a second, trying to catch up on what had just happened. "You've got today and tomorrow to get your situation sorted, and you're out of here on Sunday night, heading to Benning. And now thanks to you, I've got another Marine to replace in Second Squad." Rodriguez was taken aback by that. It hadn't occurred to him that as far as Goodwin was concerned, there wasn't much difference between Corporal Cobb getting a medical discharge and Sergeant Rodriguez getting rotated out. They were both useless to the man. And the big green machine kept right on rolling. "But seriously, Rodriguez, you're a great Marine, and we will miss having your leadership here." Goodwin reached out with his right hand, and the two men exchanged a firm handshake before Rodriguez departed.

Chapter 30

3 June 1980
White House
Washington, D.C.

The television broadcast finally confirmed what everyone in the room knew was going to happen. The announcer droned on.

"...with one hundred and twenty delegates from the state of California, Governor Ronald Reagan has secured the nomination of the Republican Party in the 1980 presidential election."

And with that, Tim Kraft turned off the television.

"Gentlemen," said Kraft, "that wraps up the playoffs and now we're moving on to the big game."

Carter wasn't a fan of trivializing the election like this, but everyone was in an excellent mood knowing that this divisive GOP primary had given them a considerable advantage going into the general election. So he gave Tim a pass tonight.

"What does that mean for us, Tim?" asked the President.

"Only that we continue on our course. We have our platform laid out and we know more or less what the Reagan camp will run with. There's still the question of his VP nominee, but there's nothing we can do about that right now. I'd pay good money to be a fly on the wall over at the Connally campaign right now. I bet they have some brilliant ideas on how we can beat ol' Ronnie."

"Careful, Tim," said Hamilton Jordan, Carter's Chief of Staff. "That's the thinking that got Nixon into so much trouble." The men had a laugh in the moment before Jordan moved the conversation along.

"How are we doing with shoring up our own side for the general election?"

"The deal we cut with Kennedy is paying dividends. I doubt we've had this much party unity since Roosevelt." The idea had struck both men. It was one thing to have party support, something that Carter hadn't been sure of even six months ago; having party dominance was another thing altogether. "Right now we're riding a wave of popular support based on our foreign policy achievements. Americans love a winner, and that's what they see when they look at this administration. It won't last forever, but I have to say that the timing is perfect for this election cycle."

"It goes beyond the election cycle," said Jordan. "We should be able to use this to move forward on some of our policy goals within the first year of our second term—"

Carter cut him off. "*If* we get a second term. You know that I don't like it when you take things for granted, Hamilton."

"Of course, Mr. President. If we get a second term. I think we should pick up the ERA. If we can get a mandate out of this election, I believe that we can unify the party behind this amendment as signature legislation. You'll be the President that finally accomplished what your predecessors failed to do."

"And it would be the right thing to do," added the President, mindful that just because others had failed didn't mean that it wasn't a sound decision. "In fact, given our recent surge in the polls, I don't see why we can't make this ERA push a part of our campaign."

Jordan thought about it for a minute, unconvinced.

"I'm not sure I'm following you, sir."

"If we can work with supporters in several of the key states that are on the verge of ratification, we could nudge the votes in favor. You know the polling numbers better than anyone, Ham. There is overall support for it, and the vocal minority is still a minority."

"That's true, Mr. President. However, while you focus on them being a 'minority,' I worry about them being 'vocal.' If we can get one state to ratify the ERA, we'll have made this a campaign issue. It will come up in the debates. You know that Governor Reagan will hammer you with that."

"Let him. We have the benefit of the next four months to be ready for that stage. If we commit to this play, what would be our next move forward?" asked the President.

"We need to identify the best states to focus our efforts. Offhand, I'm confident that Florida and Illinois would be at the top of the list. They have votes scheduled at the end of the summer, and both are too close to call right now."

"We'll still need one more," said Carter. "What about Georgia?" The President's home state was also set to vote on ratification. If he couldn't help push that vote into his corner, maybe this wasn't such a brilliant idea.

"That's a high-risk proposition, Mr. President. If word gets out that we tried to sway the vote in your home state and failed, it would be a disaster."

"In that case, let's not fail. I want a full write-up on a plan to get the ERA ratified this summer, before the debates. I'm reminded of something from my days at the Naval Academy. 'Whoever is first in the field awaits the coming of the enemy.' Let's get there first on the ERA and let the governor come to us."

"Yes, Mr. President," Said Jordan. "We'll want to regroup and reprioritize our agenda for the next term, if there is one. The nation is on a different footing now than it was four years ago. Hell, it's on a different footing than it was six months ago. We will have to deal with Senator Kennedy's national health care legislation. We might push that off until 1984, when he makes his presidential run. It looks like Volcker's interest rate strategy is paying dividends against inflation, so we can take a wait-and-see approach there. I think we will want to bump welfare reform and affirmative action to the top of the list on the domestic side."

"Gentlemen," said Kraft, "I don't want to be the wet blanket here, but we should probably focus on beating Reagan right now." With that, the three men set about preparing to meet the former governor of California on the political battlefield.

Chapter 31

4 July 1980
School of the Americas
Fort Benning, Georgia

Sergeant Carlos Rodriguez had spent Independence Day with "his" class, learning the finer points of conducting an assault patrol with two dozen of his new best friends. The "Hondos" had arrived on site over a month ago and had been getting grilled in the classroom ever since. This accelerated course for junior officers and NCOs was meant to help foster a sense of cohesion within the Honduran military, and to give a shared framework for combined operations with US forces. Carlos wasn't getting a lot of fresh information. He'd learned almost everything they covered at the Marine Corps' Infantry Training School. Sure, there were some variations in the Army's training, but nothing wild.

Carlos wasn't there for the infantry training, though. He was there to gain a better understanding of the strengths and weaknesses of these men. He was there to learn to work with them as a part of their team. Yet he was still separate from them. He would never be in their direct chain of command, but he would operate with and around them. To ensure that he could operate along with other Americans in the hostile areas between Honduras and Nicaragua, he needed to know as much as he could about their tactics and personalities. And so he went to class, and he observed.

He'd spent his first week on base filling out paperwork. Transferring over from the Marine Corps to his new "civilian" job as a "security specialist" for the Southern Air Transport Company took a lot of signatures and a lot of agreements. That was to say nothing of his new security clearance. Once he'd jumped through the hoops, and all the i's were dotted and t's crossed, he was read into the project. The information came at him like water from a firehose. He was picking up background on the governments of Latin America, their relationships with the United States and the Soviet Union as well as the makeup of existing military forces, and the expected improvements being brought in by the Cubans and Soviets.

By the time the Hondos showed up on May 26, Carlos thought he had already maxed out his learning abilities and was thankful for a break. That was when he realized that he would be working in the classroom in addition to his casework, not in place of it. The long and the short of it was that he would travel with the class first to Panama, then to Honduras. While in Honduras he would go on patrols with the Hondos to get the lay of the land. At a future point as yet undetermined, they would introduce him to some members of the "Contrarrevolución," known by the Americans as "Contras."

The Contras would take him across the border and into Nicaragua, where Carlos would be tasked to observe and report on any suspected Soviet activity in the area. This was a terrifying, unfamiliar world for him. Terrifying and exhilarating. He would infiltrate a sovereign nation with the help of a rebel army, and if he got shot out there, he'd be on his own. In order to give him a fighting chance if captured, the Agency had given him a student visa and a school ID from San Diego State. There was little chance this would do him any good if he was captured, and Carlos thought they'd given it to him more to make him feel better than out of any real utility. He hadn't had a haircut in the past six weeks either. His high-and-tight was a lot lower and looser these days.

Carlos and Fred shared a pitcher of beer that night, too tired for any concern with fireworks. "You know, all of this spook business is some real James Bond stuff," said Carlos.

"What are you talking about? I've never seen James Bond dressed in camo, running around the jungle. No, Commander Bond would be in a nice hotel hot tub with some beautiful ladies… exactly where I'll be. No, I think you're more… Captain Willard from *Apocalypse Now*."

"You must be drunk, man. I don't know a lot about much, but there are no five-star hotels where we're going," said Carlos. "In fact, just this afternoon I saw General Paz García and he told me to tell you that you'll be staying in a total mudhole with no running water." Carlos was referring to the current leader of the junta in control of the Honduran government.

"Either way, I don't think Hollywood is going to be knocking on our doors anytime soon," said Fred.

Changing the subject, Carlos said, "There's one thing I don't quite understand." Fred raised an eyebrow but said nothing. "We're training these guys up to fight the commies in Nicaragua. I get that. What I don't get is this: They fought for a total shitbird dictator who flat abused his people. When I talk to the guys, they don't really have a plan for who they'd put in charge if they did manage to beat back the Sandis. They don't really have a love of democracy as far as I can see."

"You're not wrong about Somoza," said Poole. "That family was as corrupt as they come. I'd even go so far as to say that on a personal level, they're much worse than these Sandinistas that we're facing."

"Then what the hell are we doing here?" asked Carlos.

"I can't answer that question for you. At least not satisfactorily. You'll need to answer it for yourself." Carlos narrowed his eyes, suspecting that this was just a BS evasion. "But I can answer the question for me. I'm going down there to oppose a system of government that is far worse than any one junta. I'm going down there because Nicaragua has a history of democratic elections. I believe that if we can strip the communists of power, the outcome of this civil war will be a strong representative democracy. I believe that if we don't go down there, the people of Nicaragua will suffer, and the cancer of Soviet domination will grow. I believe that if we don't do something about the Sandinistas, within ten years we'll have a Stalinist Mexico on our southern border."

"What makes you think that if the Contras win, they'll turn to free elections?" asked Carlos. "I don't think José and the boys can even spell *democracy*."

"They don't have to," said Poole. "They just need to get us in the door. There's a cadre of us who have been watching the history of our attempts to overthrow governments and are convinced that the key to success will be fostering free elections. I don't want to bore you with the details, but there's a push in intelligence and diplomatic circles to move our allies towards greater democracy. I think we'll have some movement soon in Asia, where Taiwan and South Korea could turn the corner soon. Maybe the Philippines too."

"And what if they just elect the socialists that we're fighting?"

"That's the question, isn't it?" said Poole. "That's what happened in Iran during the fifties. We decided we didn't like who the Iranian people elected, so we overthrew the government. I don't think the current administration would sign off on something like that again. I think the key to that would be to ensure that the next round of elections remains free and open. If we're going to give people the freedom to choose, we have to give them the freedom to choose poorly."

Carlos thought about that. It didn't seem too likely that the government would spend this much time and energy fighting the commies just to let them come in through the back door. But then again, this was more Fred's area. He wasn't going to lose much sleep over it.

****

2 August 1980
Eight Miles Southeast of Yamales
Jinotega, Honduras

The jungle was never quiet. There was always something out there creaking or clicking or otherwise letting the world know that it was there. That was the natural state of things in these highlands in South Central Honduras. When that noise abruptly stopped, Carlos knew that the enemy patrol was getting close to the kill zone of his ambush.

He and his squad of Honduran regulars set up camp eight miles south of the main compound at Yamales. From this new camp, they set out to find the most likely transit route for the enemy forces. Once they had a line on where the enemy would be, Carlos watched the Hondos select their ambush site. They chose a section of trail along the mountainous terrain where there was a switchback that nearly perfectly framed the kill zone. With the advantages of elevation and surprise, Carlos thought they'd done well. They had set up the perfect ambush. Now they were just waiting for the shooting to begin.

The first enemy soldier ambled past Carlos's position. This was excellent. Carlos was stationed on the west side of the kill zone to provide security and to prevent the enemy from coming up on his squad's flank. In this position, he was the first person in his unit to see the enemy. This was his least favorite part of grunt work: waiting. He consciously kept himself breathing. His instinct was to hold his breath for fear that the enemy would hear each breath he drew. He saw another soldier creep into view. This second soldier was moving with much more caution than the first. It was almost as if the second soldier knew something was afoot.

Before Carlos could finish his thought, he heard the snapping of a tree branch off his right shoulder. That was the last thing he heard before all hell broke loose. The sounds of rifle fire replaced the eerie quiet that had accompanied the enemy patrol as at least five soldiers burst through the jungle right at Carlos, rifles pointed right at him. That was it—Carlos knew that they'd messed up somehow as an enemy soldier pointed his M16 at Carlos and pulled the trigger.

"Ha-ha! You're dead, Norte," said José Obregón, the leader of the Hondos on the "enemy" squad. José was laughing while Carlos heard the rest of his squad getting overrun. José's squad had countered the perfect ambush and wiped out Carlos's. As the "fighting" subsided and the training exercise ended, both squads met up in the clearing that was supposed to serve as the kill zone. Each side had learned a lot from the exercise. Though Carlos and his unit were on the losing side, the overall mission was a resounding success. Carlos joined the two squad leaders and Staff Sergeant Diego Martinez, US Army Special Forces, for a post-training conference. José was explaining to his counterpart, Oscar Zoido, how the events of the morning had unfolded.

José's squad, with the help of Staff Sergeant Martinez, was tasked with rehearsing combat patrol tactics. They had no notice to expect an ambush, but with the training they had been through to this point, they had always expected the worst and knew to take nothing for granted. With this success, it was clear that with enough training, the lessons would take root and help build the Honduran military into a professional force that could act as the vanguard of US interests in the region.

"This point," said José, pointing at the map, "was one of three we thought were the most likely ambush points along our path. There were too many elements that made this a perfect spot, so we couldn't ignore it. We sent Manuel and Esteban along the path to get your attention and to let you think what you wanted to think, while the rest of the squad climbed up the side of the mountain to push through your flank defense." Carlos winced at the casual reference to his simulated death. The four leaders came to a basic agreement that José's squad had butchered Oscar's squad and taken light casualties in the effort. It had been a valuable lesson for both squads, and each soldier would remember the cat-and-mouse game of ambush along the trails.

In the event of an open conflict with Nicaragua, these types of squad-level actions would be commonplace. The highlands of Honduras would prove impassable by armor and vehicular travel. Instead, the war would be carried out by small infantry units with potential artillery and air support. In a lot of ways, the terrain was a callback to the US experience in Vietnam. Carlos could look out over the hills and valleys and imagine squadrons of UH-1 Iroquois helos flaring to land and drop companies of airmobile infantry on a hilltop or plateau. On the other hand, he could see Soviet-made Mi-24 Hinds circling a hilltop, spraying 12.7 millimeter rounds onto his own position. *That's something we never had to deal with in Vietnam*, thought Carlos. If it came down to a standup fight, Honduras could be every bit the hell that Vietnam was.

They had been working in-country for just over a week. Prior to that, they had spent time in Panama working with the US Army units stationed there. The hope was that the class had received enough basic combat training. Now that they were back in Honduras, they would continue to rehearse with just a single American observer for each squad and, over time, with none at all. From where he was standing, Carlos believed that this process was working. In the morning's exercise, both squads had applied their training well. Carlos had only been there as an observer and a soldier. He had provided no guidance to the Hondos. He assumed that Staff Sergeant Martinez had similarly remained hands-off.

With the amazing successes so far, the American observers wouldn't be needed soon. Once the big shots at HQ decided these little birds were ready to leave the nest, Carlos could move on to the next phase of his operation: the Contras. This was where he would be in an unfamiliar world. Up to this point, he'd been on familiar ground: basic combat training. That was something he could work backwards and forwards in his sleep. Crossing into Nicaragua with a handful of rebels and trying to observe and report on Cuban or Soviet activity was something altogether new. Carlos remembered Poole's foreboding warning:

"If you get caught out there, you'll probably be tortured and slowly killed."

That put everything into a razor-sharp focus. Carlos Rodriguez was on a mission and he would not be stopped.

Chapter 32

17 August 1980
Managua, Nicaragua

General Stanislav Smotrov sat across the table from Daniel Ortega, the chief coordinator of the junta of National Reconstruction and the de facto leader of Nicaragua. Smotrov had little regard for his Latin American host. As far as he was concerned, Ortega was simply the biggest roach in the nest. His sole claim to fame was overrunning the other bugs to take over this backwater. He scoffed at the idea that Ortega and his Sandinista movement had anything to brag about. In the months he had been in-country, he'd seen how undisciplined and uncoordinated their armed forces were. If that was any indication of how poorly their enemies had conducted themselves, Smotrov believed that his single brigade could subdue the entire country in a week's time.

That was what Moscow had given him to work with. The Soviet Army Chief of Staff, Nikolai Ogarkov, had assured Smotrov that they were not expecting him to conquer the Western world with his pathetic banana republic army. Nevertheless, Smotrov resented having to work with such amateurs. Fortunately, thanks to his connections in Moscow, he was getting the support he needed. Additional personnel and equipment had been coming in over the past several months, and on paper, this was looking like a genuine fighting force.

"We are seeing increased activity along the border with Honduras," said Ortega's translator, pulling Smotrov back into the meeting. "My sources have told me that this directly results from Somoza sympathizers preparing an offensive to retake the country." It was clear that Ortega believed not only that the enemy was consolidating forces (which was no doubt true) but also that they could mount a serious offensive to take back what they had lost during the revolution. Smotrov had enough pride in his craft to dismiss the thought. But he knew he must placate the strongman.

"Mr. Ortega, I believe that you are correct. Your enemies are gathering and plotting against you. I don't think any rational person would argue with that. It is our goal to ensure that these oppressors can never return. I assure you that the forces we have in place are more than enough to prevent these counterrevolutionaries from conducting a successful attack on your territory." It was clear from his expression that Ortega wasn't convinced.

"Of course, that says nothing of your Honduran neighbors to the north, nor their American friends," continued Smotrov. "In order to ensure that you can maintain your independence in the face of their naked aggression, I suggest we work with Moscow and Havana to secure naval defenses to ensure that we can defend your coastline against American aggression."

That suggestion was misleading. Smotrov had already been working with Havana and Moscow to secure a small fleet of missile patrol boats. The deal that Smotrov had brokered transferred seven of the venerable Moskit missile boats (referred to in NATO circles as the Osa II), along with crews to operate and train their new owners, to Nicaragua. In exchange, Moscow would send Havana two of their new Vikhr hydrofoils, as well as four Ovod missile corvettes. Everyone came out ahead in this deal. The Nicaraguans would suddenly gain a respectable naval presence in the region, the Cubans would significantly upgrade their capabilities to defend themselves from interference by the United States, and (most importantly to Smotrov) all of these vessels would be pivotal in keeping the United States Navy tangled up in the Caribbean during the coming conflict.

"I don't think you will be able to provide my country with enough naval power to fight the Americans," said Ortega skeptically.

"That's true. Our goal isn't to defeat the entire US Navy. You need to convince them that attacking you will be too costly to bother with." Smotrov knew that reminding Ortega of his overall insignificance on the world stage wouldn't win him any points with the man, but he didn't care. There were realities that they had to deal with, and right now, there was no time for false flattery.

****

Across the desk, Ortega wondered if this was how Castro had felt in 1962 when he had worked with Moscow to have nuclear missiles deployed in Cuba to deter another American invasion attempt. He knew that his position, so far from the US coast, was nowhere near as valuable as Castro's. With time, though, Ortega envisioned a socialist bloc in Latin America. Guatemala was still engulfed in a civil war, but with

Soviet and Nicaraguan help, the loose collection of leftist guerrilla forces could finally turn the tide and liberate the Guatemalan proletariat. With Guatemala secured, El Salvador would be next. The brutal repression of the military junta in charge in San Salvador was already meeting fierce resistance. Once El Salvador was caught in the vise of Guatemala and Nicaragua, they would crack. That would leave Honduras.

The past six months had shaken Ortega's confidence. The United States had shown a renewed interest in the region. The new Secretary of State was pushing for additional support for right-wing governments while paying lip service to the humanitarian reforms for which the socialists were fighting. Ortega knew that for the socialist revolution to take root in Latin America, they had to push now. They couldn't wait to let things play out. Fortunately, the Soviets appeared to agree with this position. Using the Soviet missile boats and the Cuban crews would help push that forward. Moscow had assured him that they could replicate the successes in Asia in America's backyard, and that the revolution would sweep through the Arab world as well. This was a major sea change, and Ortega knew he was an important part of it.

Ortega knew he was getting ahead of himself. He first had to secure his own position, and that meant dealing with these Contras.

"What are we doing to reinforce our defenses along the northern border with Honduras?" Ortega wanted to get back to the point of this meeting.

"In the short term, we are sending a detachment of our helicopter assault unit to look around and assure these counterrevolutionaries that we will not allow any incursions into your territory. In the longer term, we will need to increase the infrastructure in the area." Ortega wrinkled his brow, not sure where this was going as Smotrov continued. "The mountains and jungle make traversing the terrain difficult. We can't effectively fight the enemy with our tanks or armored personnel carriers. There's nothing we can do about that on the whole. However, if we can build a greater network of roads, we can link remote hamlets and newly formed base camps. This will allow us to support small infantry units in the countryside with fire support and logistical hubs. Without improvements to the road system, we will have to do most of our support with helicopters or on foot. We don't have enough of the former, and the latter will drastically slow down our ability to operate."

Ortega considered this. Previously, Smotrov had explained to him that the terrain made traditional "maneuver warfare" unrealistic. If they considered the roads to be more akin to railways, it would be easier to understand. They were fixed transit lines from which there could be no deviation. Just like a railcar. You could transport goods to a point on the network, but once there, it was almost static. As long as you understood these basic rules, you could deploy your forces accordingly. From what Ortega could tell, Smotrov had decided that the existing network was too limited to allow for optimal deployment.

"I see," said Ortega. "We will need additional heavy equipment if we hope to make progress on this. And there will be expense in maintaining these new roads. I will have to speak with the rest of the junta to see if we can commit to this." Ortega knew that Smotrov was aware of what he was doing. He was first asking for a handout: construction equipment for the roads. Then he was threatening to veto the project if he didn't get what he asked for. The only time Ortega mentioned the other members of Nicaraguan leadership was when he didn't want to commit to an action.

"I will speak with my directors in Moscow. It shouldn't be too much to arrange for some heavy equipment. Of course, they'll need your assurances that you will agree to the project before they send anything. In fact, I expect them to ask for more than assurances. I recommend you start work on the new routes as soon as possible as a demonstration of your commitment to security and our partnership."

The two men stood as Ortega put out his hand. They shook on their agreement, and Smotrov left to begin the process of getting some old tractors sent over from Havana.

Chapter 33

20 August 1980
Qom, Iran

Shahab Yazdani crossed the street on his way to meet with one of his primary contacts for executing the war against the Americans and the Iranian government. As he continued on down the narrow lane, he considered the irony of his position. As an atheist, he thought it was peculiar that he was now one leader of a holy war on behalf of a god in whom he did not believe. A dark expression came across his face when he considered that, in fact, he was just as much of a zealot as his coconspirators. But his zealotry was confined to earthly pursuits. The rise of the proletariat and the overthrow of the capitalist slave masters were his calling. The expansion of Marxist-Leninist ideology was his religion.

His father had fought in the Great Patriotic War. That much was true. Kurban Yazdani had been a major in the Red Army, part of an occupying force that had pillaged northern Iran to create a buffer against German invasion through the Caucasus. The rest of Shahab's cover story was taken from his father's war record. The only difference was which side the man was on. The KGB had realized long ago that the best lies held as much truth as possible. The lies came easily for Shahab, as he had a strong emotional attachment to the memories. As he lied, he wasn't manufacturing facts. He was recalling them. It made Shahab a very effective liar, as demonstrated by the wild success he had been having with the Sword of the Revolution.

Of course, they believe you when you tell them what they want to hear, Shahab reminded himself. He remembered the look on Saeed's face when he'd told him they had procured the explosives for the Basra operation. The idiot had been positively gleeful. The "Shia brothers-in-arms" nonsense that Shahab had told Saeed about was actually a collection of KGB assets working with the Soviet Spetsnaz detachment in Baghdad. The Sword of the Revolution had conducted a Soviet attack, using Soviet personnel and Soviet explosives. These jihadist morons were simple and easy to manipulate so far, and he had almost completed his assignment. The real trick, he thought, would be getting out of here when everyone started getting killed.

As he considered his extraction, he entered a bookstore and methodically browsed his way to the back. This gave him the chance to make sure no one was following him without arousing any suspicion. Once he was sure that he wasn't being tailed, he slipped out the back of the store and into the alley behind. From there it was a quick dozen or so steps to the rear entrance of a hotel just down the block. As he came out of the bookstore, he noticed that the alley was empty and he slipped into the hotel. Without stopping at the desk, he made his way to the second floor and then down the corridor to room 205. He knocked on the door in a casual but precise and prearranged pattern and waited for the response.

"Leave me, I'm trying to rest," came the reply from inside the room.

"I know, uncle, but I have brought you your medicine," said Shahab, completing the sequence and gaining access. The door opened, and Shahab entered the compact room.

"Welcome, welcome," said his host. The man was older than Shahab, in his early fifties, with gray in his thick beard and deep wrinkles surrounding his eyes. "I trust you have no surprises for me?" This was an oblique reference to anyone following Shahab. Both men knew that if Shahab had any idea that anyone had followed him, he would have aborted the meeting. But you didn't get to be an old spy by taking things for granted.

"No, there have been no surprises. We have been very fortunate in that."

"It's not good fortune when you do good work. Never take that for granted. You do well because you don't get soft and you don't hope for good fortune," said the old man. "Anyway, this won't take long. You have impressed our friends in Ashgabat with our successes so far. They have even let me know that Moscow has taken notice. Our efforts here have gone a long way to helping Moscow achieve their aims."

"That's good to hear," replied Shahab. "When you are on the street and making these things happen, it's easy to get caught up in the details. In fact, you *have to be* caught up in the details. It is good to know that these details are part of a grander effort."

"And our next part in that effort will be the trickiest. We need to plan an attack on the homeland itself." Shahab was certain that he had heard the words, but they didn't quite register. Attacking a despotic strongman like Saddam was one thing. This… attacking his own country? How had it come to this? Was he being asked to betray his homeland? The old man could see the look of shock on Shahab's normally impassive face.

"I understand your concern. Remember, many people have died for the Greater Bolshevik Revolution. These will not be the first, nor the last. This will be the final piece that brings this operation to a conclusion. Once we have this, we will wind down this operation and move on to our next mission for the Rodina."

"It's not just the people who will die," said Shahab. "This will be difficult to explain to my brothers-in-arms. It was one thing to convince them to attack Saddam. Attacking the Soviets… I don't know if this will be possible."

"I told you this would be the trickiest. But this is what we must do. This attack will be the culmination of our entire effort. We will complete the mission with this attack. We can liquidate the entire operation to see this through."

Shahab winced at the thought. He had just received permission to kill Saeed and Naser if they didn't go along with the plan. *If the KGB is willing to kill everyone involved... does that include me?* he wondered. Then again, if he killed Saeed and Naser, he could continue to run the operation, but he would likely burn any of the contacts he had made through the two men. If nothing else, this let Shahab know just how important Moscow felt this operation was.

"Yes, sir, I understand. I will ensure that this happens, and that the attack is a success." With that acknowledgment, the two men went about the details of how to accomplish the attack on the most powerful military in the world.

Chapter 34

30 August 1980
Bosawás Forest
Nicaragua

The Sandinista patrol moved through the jungle landscape methodically. Humberto Ortega, the leader of the Sandinista People's Army, had sent this patrol to investigate reports of Contrarrevolución activity along the Coco River that separated Honduras and Nicaragua.

The Sandinista People's Militia comprised former Sandinista revolutionary fighters who had returned to their lives after the overthrow of the Somoza regime. They were workers, farmers, tradesmen and teachers. They had fought and won the battle against the Nicaraguan National Guard, who made up the new Contra threat. These two forces had met in battle before. They were destined to meet again.

Clara Gálvez wasn't looking forward to that meeting. She was as brave as the men next to her. She'd proven that on the battlefield in the final year of the Revolution. It wasn't a lack of bravery. It was a weariness. She'd left the regular military service to return to her career as a secondary school teacher in the village of Ayapal. That was where she'd lived when she'd first joined the revolution. She'd returned there once they had banished those despotic bastards, hoping that, by teaching the youth of the nation about the terror of the previous regime, she could help her nation avoid falling back into the same pattern of revolution, empowerment, abuse, revolution that had plagued the entire region for centuries.

"We will stop here for ten minutes to rest up. Then we'll head on," said Arturo, the patrol leader. Clara pulled up to the side of the narrow path and sat down. Her jungle fatigues did what they could to blend into the surroundings. She set her AK-47 rifle next to her and took out her canteen. The militia had recently been outfitted with the Soviet weapons after originally using the American M16 rifles they'd acquired from the National Guard troops they had defeated. Gálvez preferred the American rifle. She'd been told by her compadres that the AK-47 was a superior weapon, but in her brief training, she felt that she was more accurate with the M16. *I suppose it's probably just what I'm used to*, she thought.

After taking a deep drink of water, she wet her hands and ran them through her short black hair. When she'd gone back to teaching, she'd thought she'd grow her hair out again. Once it had become clear that her duties to the militia would keep her in the field on a semiregular basis, though, she'd abandoned the idea. Finding a balance in this life of hers was proving more difficult than she had expected. *And I don't even have a family to try to balance along with everything else*, she thought.

Once upon a time, she'd been engaged. The death of her fiancé, Ángel, had been one of the many events in her life that had led her to the Sandinista movement. At least, she believed that he was dead. One day he'd just disappeared. His only crime was ending up on the nasty side of a well-connected municipal leader. When people disappeared, they never reappeared. Clara hadn't seen a body, but she knew that Ángel was dead. These were the lowest depths of life in a corrupt system.

Being raised in an upper-class family had given her a view of the upper heights of that corrupt system. Her father owned a successful tobacco farm and had connections to several Somoza officials. She'd spent her childhood living in a large plantation house before being sent to the capital city of Managua for secondary school. Her family had enough money to send her to the United States to study biology at Catholic University in Washington, D.C. She knew what was out there for those at the top, but she wasn't so high up that she couldn't see the squalor on the other end of the spectrum. The barrios outside Managua were a constant reminder that the cost of her beautiful life was measured in the misery of thousands of others.

Arturo gave a soft whistle and gestured to everyone that they were moving out. Clara retrieved her rifle and secured her canteen, careful to close the lid tightly. The patrol moved along the path again. Clara looked at Pedro Beldad, who was on point. As he moved through the vegetation, he would dance in and out of her view. As the path twisted, she could catch a glimpse of him when he was at the top of an S and she was at the bottom. She was looking ahead when Arturo put up his hand to signal a halt to the column. Clara took a knee and brought her weapon to the low ready position.

There was a rustling sound off to her left. She had seen no actual movement, but she raised her rifle. Apparently someone further up the line had seen something because the jungle erupted with gunfire. Now she could see muzzle flashes in the distance. She didn't have a solid target to aim at, but she sent a few volleys in the direction of the orange bursts. By this point, the entire patrol was off the path and slowly picking through the branches, vines, and leaves, advancing on the enemy. *If this is an ambush*, she thought, *these idiots did a terrible job*. Her team was now working to the west, closing with the enemy position.

At first it was hard to tell, but as they advanced, it became more apparent that the Contras were pulling back to the north, towards the safety of the river and their home base. Because they were advancing on the enemy, the militia was forced to move slowly. The Contras could double their speed and would leave one soldier behind to fire at the advancing Sandinistas. It wasn't enough to inflict damage, just enough to slow them down and allow the Contras to put more distance between them. Then the rear soldier would sprint ahead (or at least move as quickly as possible in the terrain) and leapfrog the next soldier, who would wait for and fire on the militia.

It didn't take Arturo long to figure out what was happening. He signaled up and down the line for his people to halt their advance. They stopped moving and stopped firing. They held their positions, watched, and listened. After five minutes with no activity, Arturo sent Pedro forward. The rest of the patrol held their ground. Pedro cautiously advanced another fifty yards, looking for any sign of the enemy. There was none, and he returned to the unit. Once they were assembled, they started the long hump back to Ayapal.

"What do you think?" asked Clara.

"It wasn't an ambush, if that's what you're asking," replied Arturo. "I think we just ran into a Contra patrol. I just don't know what they were out here doing."

"I wonder if it has anything to do with our new friends?" Clara asked. There had been a flurry of activity in recent days. Construction crews had cleared extensive areas of land outside of town. A road crew had also paved and widened the road coming into town from the southeast. Most of the workers were Nicaraguan, but some fresh faces were white. She knew they were Russians.

"That's none of our business, Clara," said Arturo. "Our business was to find that patrol. We did that. They couldn't have been operating too far from their base, so I imagine we'll be sent out again soon to find whatever location they're staging from on our side of the river."

Clara wasn't convinced that this wasn't any of her business. She had fought for the Sandinista movement under the promise of a greater sharing of the wealth of Nicaragua, and to destroy the regime that had oppressed the people for so long. Thus far, the government had been living up to the promise of the revolution. She herself was taking part in a literacy program created by the new government. They believed that education was a foundational requirement for improving the quality of life for everyone. As a teacher, Clara believed in this cause and enthusiastically supported these efforts.

In addition to her own classes and her work with the militia, she had been working with younger children from the countryside to establish and improve their basic reading skills. She had hoped that in the next year, they could also begin with math lessons. Her friends in the government had assured her that the economic reforms were underway as well. Large-scale agricultural operations had been broken up and given to the workers who had operated them. As her thoughts drifted from education to the economy, she thought of her parents.

The Gálvez tobacco farm had been one of the "collectivized" operations. With the outcome of the revolution becoming clear, her parents had fled the plantation and run to Honduras. She knew that they had secured the bulk of their wealth in international banks and had built a nice homestead outside of San Miguel in Honduras. She was thankful for that. Many of the plantation owners had been killed in the chaos during the transition.

She liked to believe that her involvement with the Sandinistas and her pleading with her father to leave had saved his life. It was probably true, but she'd never know. What she saw as justice, her family saw as betrayal. She knew she would never hear from her father again. Life was always about balance, and that was a balance she could live with. She'd saved her father's life in exchange for his love. *The world is full of brutal choices*, she thought as she made her way home.

Chapter 35

17 September 1980
Ayapal, Nicaragua

Carlos had been in Nicaragua for a week now. He and his Contra escorts had been working through the jungle the entire time. They were over thirty miles inside the Nicaraguan border and they were finally approaching their goal. Reports had been coming in of increased construction activity in this tiny hamlet in the mountains. There had also been reports of helicopter activity in the area. The assumption by most of the American, Honduran and Contra forces was that the Nicaraguans were building a new military base camp here in the extreme north of the country. Carlos was there to see if there were any signs of Soviet activity.

"Hey, Norte," said Diego, the leader of this Contra recon element. "Look down in the valley. You can see the tractors and bulldozers clearing the sides of the road." Carlos lifted his binoculars and peered into the valley below. Sure enough, he could see what looked like road construction. They were widening the narrow path that led into the village, that was for sure. But Carlos couldn't see anything that would tell him it involved the Soviets, or that there was anything beyond road construction going on. There was a large clearing outside of the town but no new buildings, and no fencing being erected to mark off territory. Just general improvements in the roads. Maybe the Sandinistas were just trying to improve the lot for this tiny village.

"Okay, let's get someone up here to monitor the activity while we find a place to make camp," said Carlos. He wasn't optimistic that they would find anything of interest or value, but they'd made the effort to get out here. They might as well get some rest, collect any intel they could and then get back to Yamales. Diego had Luis, one of his NCOs, take over the watch as Diego and Carlos backed away from the overlook. If Luis saw anything out of the ordinary, he would find them and report back. In all, there were eleven Contras lurking about in the jungle.

"I don't know, Diego, that doesn't look very promising. I think we've wasted a week humping in here. I hope that some of the other units are having better luck."

"*Sí*, I hope they are. But I'm not so sure that this is just innocent construction. Remember, Miguel also reported helicopters in the area."

"Sure, but where are they now? We can only report on what we can see. And Miguel couldn't tell us what type of helicopters there were, just that he could hear helicopters. That could have easily been a part of this construction project for all we know." The two men continued to push through the vegetation until they came upon a level and somewhat clear area that the remaining Contras had selected for their camp. Carlos found a spot out of the way as several of the soldiers went about erecting the green-and-brown lean-tos that they would use for shelter.

He leaned against a tall palm tree and took in the scenery. While getting from point A to point B in the jungle, Carlos took the beauty of this place for granted. It was hard to marvel at the foliage while you were fighting against it with a machete. Trees weren't very grand when their roots were sticking out, trying to trip you up. But at times like this, times when he stopped for just a moment, he was taken in by the beauty of this place. Growing up in Southern California, his world had been full of browns and blues. When he'd first hit North Carolina with the Marine Corps, he had been shocked at how green the forests were. That was nothing compared to the millions of shades of green he was hit with in Honduras and Nicaragua.

He took a drink from his canteen. It wasn't as hot here as he'd thought it would be. The temperature had hovered around the low eighties and hadn't gotten above ninety since he'd been in-country. The humidity was something else, though. He couldn't remember anywhere being so wet when it wasn't actually raining. They'd gotten a good deal of rain as well, which slowed down travel.

With camp set, his squad (minus Luis, who was still on watch at the overlook) sat down for a meal. They didn't have any of the American C rations on hand since they were so far into Nicaraguan territory. In the event that they were captured or killed, there could be no evidence that the Americans were supporting this operation. Instead, Carlos opened a jar of whipped red beans, one of many that had been packed before they'd headed out from Yamales. Though he was definitely getting bored with them, Carlos had to admit that they were far superior to the canned meat from the C ration kits.

They maintained their station, with men rotating watch on the overlook, as well as sentry duty along the perimeter of the camp. It was a dull affair and not at all like the "real James Bond business" Carlos had envisioned during training. Carlos reflected on his combat experience, thinking, *At least nobody is shooting at me.* The hairs on the back of his neck stood up, and he stopped his hand as it was running through his hair. As he honed his senses, he could see several of the other men had frozen in place as well. They could hear it too: the low *thump-thump-thump* of incoming helicopters.

Carlos had been hoping for this. He needed to know what the helo activity in the area was. At the same time, the vision of those Mi-24s circling the hilltop flashed back into his mind. He shivered as a chill ran down his spine. Diego appeared by Carlos's side.

"I guess this is our chance to see what the helicopters are up to, eh, Norte?"

The two men moved slowly to the overlook to check on the town. They didn't want to move too quickly for fear that any movement, even in this dense jungle, would give away their location to someone in the helicopters. When they made it to the crest, Abril de Herrera was peering into the town, watching a large helicopter landing in a clearing just south of the town center. The sun was getting low in the sky as Carlos lifted his binoculars to see what he could see.

Right away, Carlos felt some relief. It was an Mi-8 transport helicopter, not one of the Mi-24 gunships. As he watched the helo touch down, a group of uniformed men darted out from a sizable building and unloaded crates, carrying them back to the building.

"What is that large building off to the left?" asked Carlos.

"That's the local school. The leftists have built schools like that in several of these villages. It's one of the ways they convince the locals to comply," said Diego.

Carlos was sure that he was hearing propaganda from both sides. He doubted that the local peasantry was particularly attached to public education, but he also wasn't convinced that the Sandinistas were just pretending to care about the locals. Either way, the men hustling crates into that building sure as hell weren't teachers, and those crates weren't filled with textbooks. Carlos needed to get in closer to be sure, but those looked like white guys.

"Diego, is there a big *blanco* population around here?"

"Ha! No, Norte, folks out here are far removed from the Peninsulares."

Carlos couldn't swear to it, but he'd bet real money that he was watching Soviet troops unload weapons and store them in the public school at Ayapal. He reached into his pack and retrieved his camera, snapping as many pictures as he thought useful, then packed it back.

"We've got to get back to Yamales. My people will want to see this. I think you've got yourself an infestation of Russkies, Diego. Let's see if we can do something about that."

The unit broke camp, policed up their trash and generally tidied up. They had no idea when they might need this location in the future, so they didn't want to leave any traces of where they'd been. With that, they started the trek back to Yamales. It had taken a week to get down, but they would push hard to shave off a few days if they could. With the Sandinistas stockpiling weapons near the border, there was no telling when they might use them in an offensive.

Chapter 36

21 September 1980
Kremlin
Moscow, Russia

"Comrades," began Soviet General Secretary Leonid Brezhnev. "It has been nine months since we sat in this room and embarked on our current course." He paused and looked around the large mahogany table. None of the members present showed any hint of hesitation or doubt. That was a good sign. "I want to commend everyone in this room for the role you have played in this moment in history. We are about to embark on the most important program in history, and it is only possible because of your efforts."

"Thank you, Comrade General Secretary," said Yuri Andropov, the KGB chief. "I'm sure I speak for the entire Politburo when I tell you that the honor is ours." With that, Andropov was done with pleasantries. "This will be our last opportunity to stop this. If anyone can report that they are unready or unsure in their area of responsibility, we need to know that *now*. Once we begin this operation, we will have no choice but to see it through to its conclusion." It was now Andropov's turn to scan the faces of the members, looking for dissent or regret. There was none.

"Minister Ustinov, can you please brief us on our preparations in Iran?" asked Brezhnev.

"Of course, Comrade General Secretary. The Iraqi invasion of Iran has prompted the US to respond. Now that Iraq has gained the oil-rich territory and refining facilities at the mouth of the Shatt al-Arab River, we will begin preparations for a long defensive holdout. We project that the Iraqis will be able to withstand the Iranian counterattacks for months, even years if need be."

"If they need to withstand them for years, we will all have done something terribly wrong," said Vasili Kosikov, the Minister of the Aviation Industry.

"Indeed, Comrade Minister. Your turn will come. Please continue, Dmitriy," said Andropov.

"The Iraqi military buildup since the last Arab-Israeli war has allowed Saddam to establish overwhelming force while his Iranian foes have been embroiled in internal political upheaval. General Lapunov's battle plan has provided for major Iraqi gains in the south. We see no reason to call off our plans based on what is happening in Iraq."

"Thank you, Comrade Ustinov. What about our efforts in Central America? Comrade Gromyko, where do we stand in Managua?"

"Our man Ortega is not as prepared as that rabid dog in Iraq. He is hesitant to engage with the United States. However, we have units in place that will ensure his commitment in the short term. It will take some coercion to keep them in line once the shooting starts, though."

"The Cubans were similarly difficult to convince. But we managed all the same. Do you believe that his hesitation is sufficient to stop the operation?" asked Andropov.

"No, Comrade Director. Even if the Nicaraguans ended their cooperation tomorrow, we believe that we will have made enough of an impact to meet our goals in the region. If they stay the course, all the better."

"This is excellent news, Andrei Andreyevich. Is it your opinion that we should continue with our operation?"

"Yes, Yuri Vladimirovich. We should go forward without hesitation. Once the Americans are engaged, we will initiate Operation Bogatyr and end this contest once and for all." Bogatyr was a reference to the Slavic knights of Russian folklore. In this case, it was the internal code name for the Soviet plan to overcome the West and bring the revolution to the entire continent of Europe.

The meeting continued. The Minister of Railways and Transport concluded that the pre-positioned supplies were either in place or en route. The Ministers of Industry for Aircraft and Automobile manufacture had reported the shift in production from civilian to military production, and various officers from the Soviet Army and Navy had reported that their men were in position for this stage to move forward. As each man concluded his report, the Soviet Union inched closer to setting the world on course for a Third World War.

Chapter 37

22 September 1980
0600 Hours
USS *Nassau*
Caribbean Sea

The USS *Nassau* was one of the fleet's newest amphibious assault ships. She had been commissioned just over a year ago and was already serving with distinction. During last year's discovery of the Soviet battalion in Cuba, the USS *Nassau* was instrumental in ferrying Marines to Guantanamo Bay to reinforce the garrison there. The ship's crew had been awarded a Meritorious Unit Commendation for that operation.

Today, after a quick nine-month workup period, she was steaming south towards the shore of Honduras. She was carrying the Marine Corps's 38th Marine Amphibious Unit (MAU) with the intent of delivering those Marines to the Honduran coast. To accomplish this, she had an array of helicopters, including ten CH-53 Sea Stallions and twelve of the twin-rotor CH-46 Sea Knights. Between the helicopters and the LCU-1646 landing craft, *Nassau* could move over a thousand Marines and place them anywhere in the world.

Nassau was the flagship of Task Force 120, containing four other amphibious assault ships as well as their defensive escort. The commander of *Nassau*, Captain Jake Holloway, took his position on the bridge. He was joined by his operations officer, Steve Wagner, and the oncoming Officer of the Deck, a young lieutenant named Willie Larson.

"What's the good news, Lieutenant?" asked the captain.

"It's been a quiet night, sir, nothing out of the ordinary to report. We've been making a steady ten knots, weather is clear, and the sea is fair. Oh, the Havana Banana popped up early today. We picked it up just past 0400." Larson was referring to a daily visitor that closely watched their transit through the Florida Straits and into the Caribbean. It was an older Soviet Tu-16 Badger-D maritime patrol aircraft that the Soviets had recently sold to the Cubans to collect as much data on US naval movements as possible.

"I can't imagine what they're after that they haven't already got," said Wagner.

"My best guess is that they're just playing with their new toys," replied Captain Holloway. "That 'Puff Ball' radar of theirs can paint the entire western Caribbean and they don't even have to leave their own airspace."

"That's true enough. You can bet that the second there's a shooting war, that little Banana will be one of the first casualties," said Wagner.

"Be that as it may, there's nothing to do about it now. Maybe we'll send a couple of AV-8As to patrol the international airspace just outside of Cuba." It wasn't unprecedented to use the presence of an enemy support aircraft to practice air intercept missions, but Captain Holloway was focused on the upcoming training in Honduras. Trying to scare the Banana would have some value, but he had bigger fish to fry.

****

0700 Hours
USS *Guam*
Caribbean Sea

Corporal Daryl Evans was well aware that idle hands were the devil's workshop. Keeping his Marines engaged was a fundamental key to ensuring that they didn't get themselves into trouble. It was with this in mind that he had his fire team positioned on the hangar deck at the fantail of the ship. There were two openings that overlooked the Caribbean Sea, and nothing else, for miles. They'd come out here to get Private Riley some trigger time with the M60 machine gun. Earlier in the morning, they'd gone over the teardown and assembly of the "Pig," and now Riley was about to feel some recoil.

"Hey, don't forget, you gotta call out something badass before you unload," said Oliver.

"No, you don't, Riley. Just fire the weapon with short, controlled bursts. Try to get a feel for it. If you're any good with it, maybe we'll ship you off to Fourth Platoon," said Corporal Evans, referring to the company's weapons platoon.

Riley was stuck. He didn't want to disappoint Oliver, but he also didn't want to go against the corporal. He decided to split the difference and gave out an "oorah!" before squeezing the trigger and watching the barrel of the weapon detach and plunge into the sea below. There was a pause as everyone tried to process exactly what had happened. Riley looked over the edge.

"What are you looking for? You think a dolphin is gonna swim up and bring that back?" asked Oliver.

"What the hell?" asked Palmer.

"Shut up, Mouthwash," said Riley, trying to defend himself. "You signed off on my assembly, you dick."

Palmer wasn't happy to be reminded of his new nickname. At the same time, he knew that the new private was right—this was as much his fault as Riley's.

"You idiots," said Evans. "Look, this crap's going to roll uphill. This is my training. I'll go to the LT and let him know what happened. I think you tried to seat the barrel with the barrel latch closed. Then when it wouldn't seat, you just flipped it back and forth and it didn't catch. Dammit. Okay, you guys get back to berthing. I'll deal with the LT and the armory." *Damn, today really sucks*, thought Evans as he took the half of a machine gun and headed back into the ship.

****

0854 Hours
USS *Nassau*
Caribbean Sea

"Hey, Skipper, the ASW bird is reporting something odd," said the Officer of the Deck.

"What is it, Larson?"

"Seven small contacts making about forty knots and heading north in our direction." With that kind of speed, Captain Holloway's first thought was an illegal drug operation. The smugglers would sometimes use speedboats to try and evade the US Coast Guard.

"Hey, Steve!" He motioned to his operations officer. "Are there any known drug routes moving through here?" Holloway was confident that there weren't, but when something made little sense, he liked to think out loud to work through the situation.

"Negative, sir, everything we've been tracking is on the Atlantic coast. The Coasties have the Gulf pretty well locked up," said Commander Wagner.

"Larson, get on Air Operations and send the helo in for a closer look. Let's find out who these clowns are."

The SH-2 Seasprite was conducting an antisubmarine patrol south of the fleet. Flying from the USS *Moosbrugger*, the Seasprite had a wide array of tools for finding submarines. One of those tools was the AN/SPS-59 surface search radar. This was used to pick up any surface disturbances like a periscope wake, or in this case, the seven surface contacts.

The "*Moose*" was one of the three *Spruance*-class destroyers protecting the amphibious units (the others being the USS *Caron* and USS *Briscoe*). Each *Spruance* carried two SH-2s for ASW patrols, which could give the fleet near-constant coverage for a limited area. The three *Spruance*-class destroyers were complemented with a pair of older destroyers. The USS *Sellers* was a *Charles F. Adams*–class ship, commissioned in 1961. Her older Tartar guided-missile fire-control system wasn't as capable as the newer Sea Sparrow in place on the Spruance class, but the Tartar could put up a lot more missiles. The USS *Coontz* was even older than the *Sellers*. Her Terrier air-defense missiles weren't able to provide much support for the anti-air mission, and her lack of a helicopter pad made her a liability in the ASW mission. She was there to lend her support where she could but was outclassed by her sister ships in the defense screen.

The last ship in the ring of defenders that surrounded the big amphibs was the guided missile cruiser USS *Richmond K. Turner*. *Turner* was the fifth of the *Leahy*-class guided-missile cruisers and was commissioned in 1964. Like *Coontz*, *Turner* was saddled with the older Terrier surface-to-air missile system. The chief advantage the *Turner* had over the *Coontz* in the air-defense role was the ability to put up twice as many missiles, thanks to a second Terrier missile launcher located forward of the bridge. While underpowered compared to a carrier battle group, this amphibious group was a good representation of the forces that might be available to secure the Caribbean during the outbreak of World War III.

The Seasprite was about twenty minutes away when they first picked up the contacts. About ten minutes into the transit, the radar operator reported something foreboding. The contacts had maneuvered into two line-ahead columns and created a separation between them. If these boats were trying to look innocent, this was a bad move. This new formation would allow them to attack from two separate bearings. In a fight where missiles were closing on each other at over a thousand miles per hour, every second would count. If an operator or commander hesitated to determine which attack bearing to engage, that hesitation could be the difference between surviving or sinking.

"Skipper, Air Ops is reporting that those boats have formed two line-ahead columns," said Lieutenant Larson.

"Do they have a positive ID on them yet?"

"Negative, sir, they're still about ten minutes out."

"What do you think, Steve?"

The operations officer knew that he needed an answer, even if he had no confidence in it.

"Sir, I have a hard time believing it, but it could be the Cubans out trying to make a point. They know we're out here and they've had days to set this up."

"That makes more sense than the smuggler angle now that they seem to be showing some tactical ability," said Captain Holloway. "Perhaps they want to practice making a run at one of our carrier battle groups. I think we'd make a good stand-in for *Nimitz*, don't you?" Before anyone could answer, Holloway continued, "Get Collier on the horn and have him meet us in the CIC."

Cliff Collier was the ship's intelligence officer. Holloway wanted to get all the brains together in the Combat Information Center to try to work through what was happening. By the time they made it to the CIC, word had come in from the Seasprite that an overflight of the formerly unidentified contacts revealed them to be Osa-class missile boats.

Initially, Holloway glanced at Wagner with approval. Then the surprise came down. "Sir, they're flying Nicaraguan colors," said Radioman Third Class (RM3) Pete Brown. As the men in the room digested this fresh information, Lieutenant Commander Collier entered the room.

"You know anything about a bunch of Nicaraguan missile boats?" asked Wagner.

"Wait, what?" Without context, the question made little sense to Collier. "The Nicaraguans hardly have a navy to speak of. They have a few patrol boats, but nothing capable of firing missiles. Hell, I'm not sure if they even have a torpedo capability."

"It looks like they do now," said the captain.

"What do we have on Cuban Osa-class boats?" asked Wagner.

"The Cubans have a dozen. We believe ten are operational," said Collier off the top of his head. "Can someone tell me what's going on here?"

Wagner and Holloway caught him up on the situation.

"We have reports of Soviet and Cuban cooperation with Nicaragua, but none of that was fleet-related. All the reports we had were to look out for Soviet activity in monitoring our amphibious exercises in Honduras. It sounds like the Army suspects the Soviets and Nicaraguans are up to something in Honduras or El Salvador. If that's true, and I have no reason to believe that it isn't, I'd say the Nicaraguans just came into possession of a nice coastal defense force."

"They're pretty far out to sea for a coastal defense force," replied Wagner.

"That's a good point," said Collier. He looked over to the map board. "They could be operating out of one of these uninhabited islands out here. Essentially, stock it with supplies, then bring the boats out..." He trailed off as he clicked his tongue in thought, then pointed to a spot on the map in between Honduras and Cuba. "We used to have a radio station out here on Swan Island. It's technically Honduran territory, but they don't have a permanent presence there."

"What's the threat level here?" asked Holloway.

"Each Osa has four SS-N-2 'Styx' antiship missiles. Those are pretty old, but they'll punch a hole in your ship just the same. They have a range of around twenty-five miles, so they'll have to get in close to fire them," said Collier.

"I thought the Styx had a longer range than that," said Wagner.

"Newer versions do, but the Cubans, and now Nicaraguans, don't exactly get the pick of the litter. These are older 2A models."

"In that case, we have several Harpoon-equipped ships. They have twice that range," added Wagner.

"That's all good and well, Steve, but it's not like I can just blow the new Nicaraguan Navy out of the water at fifty miles. We're not at war. Hell, we're not even in any degree of hostility with the Nicaraguans, despite whatever Madam Secretary has to say." This last was a remark on Secretary of State Kirkpatrick's emphasis on countering Latin American socialist regimes, which was what had the task force heading to Honduras. “Let’s keep a helo on them and let this play out a while. Thoughts?”

“Sir,” said Collier, “I find it hard to believe that the Nicaraguans are out here looking for a fight. Even in the best of circumstances, none of those ships would survive an engagement. As Commander Wagner mentioned, by the time they’re in close enough to launch an attack, we’ll have enough Harpoons to eliminate every one of them. At that point the Nicaraguans are back to not having a fleet, while the US responds with overwhelming force from Norfolk and San Diego.”

“That points to this being a drill. Those Sandis are out here showing the flag, just like we are,” concluded Wagner, using the newly discovered pejorative term for the “Sandinistas” they were facing.

“I think you’re right. Nevertheless, we will have to monitor the situation, and we won’t blink if they decide to stare us down,” said Captain Holloway. “Someone get some coffee in here. We’re going to be here awhile.”

By 1000 hours, the Osas hadn’t altered course. They were now bracketing the amphibious task force and closing rapidly with four boats in the western line and three on the east. Each minute that passed brought them that much closer to missile range. The Seasprite radioed warning calls to the Osas that they were entering a military operation zone and to alter course. The Osas had replied astutely that they were operating in international waters and the United States Navy had no authority to deny them freedom of navigation. The Nicaraguans had called Holloway’s bluff.

“Let’s go ahead and sound general quarters across the task force,” said Captain Holloway.

“Aye-aye, sir. Should we send the *Caron* out ahead to greet them?” asked Commander Wagner. The USS *Caron* was the *Spruance* destroyer at the front of the defensive ring of escorts protecting the task force.

“Negative. I’ve been thinking about that, but if we do and something goes wrong, we’ll have a big gap in our air-defense coverage.” Holloway knew that the limited Terrier ships couldn’t fill that gap effectively. “Let’s get a couple of Harriers loaded up with some Mk-83s and get them ready for launch. If they want to make a pass at us, the least we could do is return the favor. And make sure the skipper on the *Caron* knows that I want a shot across the bow of the first Osa in range. See if he can get the Osa’s captain to piss himself.”

****

1011 Hours
USS *Guam*
Caribbean Sea

"General quarters, general quarters. All hands, man your battle stations. Set material condition Zebra throughout the ship." The matter-of-fact voice echoed through the armory. Lieutenant Omar Beck and Corporal Daryl Evans both looked at the ceiling, as though the ship itself were talking to them.

"Odd time for a drill," said Evans.

"Odd time's the best time," said Beck.

"Ain't a drill, sir," said the corporal behind the counter, who had been patiently listening to the two grunts explain why they were bringing back half a machine gun. "I'm not sure what's up, but y'all need to get back to the berthing compartment. I'll get this"—he gestured at the barrel-less M60 on the counter—"stored for you, and we'll sort it out once this thing is over."

"Thanks, Corporal," said Beck as he and Evans hustled out the hatch and into the passageway. The two Marines split up as Beck made his way to officer country while Evans headed down to the enlisted Marine berthing. The ship was a mass of activity. Evans turned and started down a ladder well when a rush of sailors came running up.

"Outta the way, cargo!" said one of the sailors.

"Up and forward on the starboard side, asshole," said another.

In the confusion, Evans had forgotten a cardinal rule of life at sea. If he wanted to go down, he needed to cross to the port side of the ship. In order to ensure that men could efficiently move to wherever they were needed, anyone who was moving towards the front of the ship (forward) or moving up would stay on the starboard side. Anyone who needed to move towards the back of the ship (aft) or down would stay on the port side. Thus corrected, Evans made it back to his nest.

"What the hell's going on out there?" asked Riley.

"I don't know, man, but whatever it is, I can promise you it won't be any fun for us," replied Evans.

“There ain’t a damn thing for us to do but wait for all the yelling to die down,” said Oliver, shuffling a deck of cards in his lap.

“Hey, Evans, what happened at the armory?” asked Riley, clearly concerned with how much trouble he was in over losing the M60 barrel.

“LT is pissed. You can expect him to get payback for this mess once we get on the beach. I’m not sure what the armory is going to do about it. We were still figuring it out when they sounded GQ.”

“Hey, you homos playing or what?” asked Oliver, holding up the deck of cards. Just before the alarm sounded, Fire Team Two was about to get a game of spades going. They had nothing better to do. Evans figured it was better than worrying about a crisis about which they knew nothing, so he had no reason to stop them.

****

1033 Hours
USS *Nassau*
Caribbean Sea

Everyone in the CIC was holding their breath. The Osas had closed to within fifteen miles of the *Caron*. This put the task force within range of the twenty-eight SS-N-2 missiles. If anything was going to happen, it would happen soon. The seconds dragged across the clock. The men stared at the monochrome CRT screen of the Naval Tactical Data System (NTDS) display as though, by force of will, they could speed things along. When the tension had built to a bursting point, Petty Officer Brown broke the silence.

“*Caron* reports they have fired across the Osa’s bow to no effect. They’re continuing on a direct course for us.”

“Let’s get those Harriers airborne,” said Captain Holloway. The orders were relayed to the Air Operations team, and the two Marine Corps AV-8A vertical take-off and landing (VTOL) jets initiated flight operations.

The dreaded call came from one of the air-defense operators.

“Vampire! Contact bearing two-zero-nine degrees! Wait! Second contact bearing one-five-one degrees! Multiple contacts at each bearing!”

There was a cool sense of control in the room. Everyone had trained for this, and while nobody had truly expected this to happen today, it *had* happened and they had a job to do. In this moment, the men of the USS *Nassau* focused on their jobs. Any chance they had to reduce the danger lay in their ability to work together as a team to address the threat. The team in the CIC conducted the defense of the ship with the precision of an orchestra. The next few minutes spread out like an eternity. Instead of the agony of waiting, every sailor's brain was now overrun with information. A thousand things seemed to happen at once.

The Osas had coordinated the strike nearly perfectly. Two salvos of SS-N-2 missiles were now speeding towards the Americans. The first missiles out of their tubes were headed for the USS *Caron*. The Soviets had guessed that the ship at the front of the formation would be one of the more capable air-defense platforms in the task force. By engaging *Caron* first, they hoped to knock it out quickly or at least keep it occupied with its own self-preservation long enough for the missiles aimed at the amphibious ships to get past it.

This plan proved successful as *Caron* heeled to the port side and attempted to engage the missiles heading right for it. *Caron* was about as close as possible to the Osas when they fired their missiles. The SS-N-2 needed at least four miles to get out of the tube, acquire a target, and detonate. *Caron* had been just five miles out when the Osas launched.

The first missile closed the distance and struck *Caron* within seconds. The missile exploded just aft of amidships on the starboard side. The ship rocked from the impact and immediately began taking on water. The second SS-N-2 failed to achieve lock and shot past *Caron*. The destroyer defiantly fired off her Harpoon missiles in response, but the Soviet missile hit had damaged a control link for one of the two quad launchers and only four Harpoons left their box.

The other lead ships in the defensive ring were also targeted. *Sellers* was the next one hit. She didn't stand a chance. The Soviet missile blew a massive hole right through the small destroyer. Within a minute of the attack, it was clear that the crew couldn't save her.

The USS *Briscoe* had four missiles targeted at her. A Sea Sparrow air-defense missile took out the first. The ship spent the next few seconds watching in horror as the Super Rapid Bloom Offboard Countermeasures, or SRBOC, fired off chaff bursts. In a matter of seconds, they would know if the incoming missiles would continue tracking the ship or if they would bite on the decoys. The lives of everyone on board hung in the balance. One after another, the missiles detonated in the cloud of aluminum left behind by the SRBOC.

While the escorts were fighting for their lives, the remaining SS-N-2s were on their way to the heart of the task force. On board the USS *Nassau*, Inside the CIC, Captain Holloway knew that his ship was in trouble. It was impossible to tell how many of the incoming missiles would home in on him, but even one would have the potential to sink even a ship as big as *Nassau*.

****

On the bridge, Lieutenant Willie Larson had a front-row seat as the missiles streaked across the sky. As the ship turned to port in an evasive maneuver, Larson moved to the starboard-facing windows. As the SS-N-2s advanced, they separated as each homed in on their designated targets. Chaff bursts clouded aft of the ship. He watched in horror as he listened to the 1MC shipwide communication system announce, “Missiles inbound, starboard side. Brace for impact.” For just a second, Willie Larson could see the missile that had his name on it.

“Dear Lord—”

The SS-N-2 struck *Nassau* just below the giant “4” painted on the island. The one-thousand-pound warhead exploded upon impact, injecting an enormous fireball into the starboard side of the ship. Due to the downward flight path of the missile, the explosion penetrated through the island, under the flight deck, and into the hangar deck below. The explosion rippled through the island and blasted the main access hatch into the main bridge area, instantly killing an ensign unfortunate enough to be standing nearby. Fire followed the hatch into the room and consumed everything in its path. Lieutenant Larson was knocked against the starboard-side window and crumpled to the deck. As he lay on the floor, he could see his shipmates burning and dying as he slowly lost consciousness.

****

The effects inside the crowded hangar deck were catastrophic. Within seconds, flames engulfed the open hangar, which became an absolute hellscape. The blast wave shoved helicopters aside as if they were toys. The heat caused paint to peel and aluminum to melt. The fire suppression system activated and seawater began a race with the fire. Could the system and damage control parties outrun the spread of the fire and prevent the loss of the ship? Before any of the crew could react, one of the CH-46 Sea Knight twin-rotor helicopters exploded, adding its fuel to the inferno.

Seconds after the missile struck *Nassau*, the USS *Fort Snelling* caught a break. The first Styx failed to lock on and sailed past the ship, granting her six hundred souls a few more seconds of life. The tank landing ship, USS *Manitowoc*, was not so fortunate. The first SS-N-2 targeting her hit square amidships, breaking the ship in two. A few crewmen were able to scramble over the sides, but most perished in the waves. Chaff spoofed a second missile targeted on *Fort Snelling*, making her by far the luckiest gator in the task force. The second missile targeting *Manitowoc* failed to lock but found a much more enticing target.

****

"Missiles inbound, port side. All hands brace for impact," called out a calm, nonchalant voice over the 1MC on the USS *Guam*.

"Holy hell," whispered Corporal Evans as he set down the copy of *All's Quiet on the Western Front* he had been reading. The men of Fire Team Two set down their cards and looked at him.

"Ain't nothin' we can do about it," said Oliver.

"Remember the evacuation drills," said Sergeant Klein, Second Squad's new leader. "Remember the route out of here. There's no telling who will be with you and who will get separated. If the worst happens, we should all be able to stick together, but we might get split up. Everyone needs to know how to get to where they need to be." These same orders, or variations on them, were being passed down throughout the fifteen hundred Marines stationed on board. "If we need to evacuate the ship, the thing that will save us is discipline. This is why you didn't join the Army. This is why you're Marines."

The berthing compartment got deathly quiet. Everything that needed to be said had been. Now every Marine was left to his thoughts and prayers. Even PFC Oliver, who always had something to say, found himself unable to formulate the words. The ship shuddered as the Styx struck just above the waterline amidships, instantly killing hundreds of sailors and Marines.

"Jesus Christ!" came a voice from the packed Marines of Second Platoon.

"Shut up and wait for orders!" yelled Staff Sergeant Page. While the sailors on the *Guam* scrambled to assemble damage control parties to fight the fires and prevent the ship from sinking, the men they derisively referred to as "cargo" or "ballast" waited in their watertight compartment, unable to do anything.

****

For the Soviets, the third time was a charm against *Fort Snelling*. As her luck ran out, a missile struck the starboard-side bow. The explosion ripped the entire bow from the ship, causing it to fill with water. The captain immediately counterflooded aft in the hopes of saving the ship. Gunrunner One, an AH-1 Cobra helicopter from Light Attack Helicopter Squadron 269 that had taken off just prior to the missile strike, was passing over *Fort Snelling* at the time of the blast. The pilot could see the front end of the ship vanish. From his perspective, there was no way that ship would survive. He just hoped *Guam* would fare better and he'd have a ship to return to.

While the first of the SS-N-2s were attacking the center of the task force, the slower Harpoon missiles fired from the USS *Caron* engaged the now-fleeing Osa IIs. Having split up in a free-for-all "jailbreak" maneuver, each of the Osas was on their own, heading in a different direction. The intent was to prevent a single missile from being able to acquire more than one ship. This proved prudent as the four Harpoons from *Caron* followed one another into a single fleeing Osa. The ship was obliterated upon the first missile's contact, but the three following slammed into what was left for good measure.

****

On board the USS *Guam*, the Marines of Second Platoon could feel and hear a second hit. They heard the hit announced over the 1MC. "Missile hit, port side." Everyone knew that additional information was running through the 4MC damage control circuit. This second hit was at the waterline, close to the bow, and flooding immediately increased. Having taken two SS-N-2 hits, the crew was struggling to keep *Guam* in the fight. Just north of *Guam*, the USS *Trenton*, the last undamaged gator freighter in the task force, took a hit that caused severe flooding.

The final missile of the twenty-eight-missile salvo was heading for the USS *Nassau*. Less than four minutes from the time of launch, the final missile struck the *Nassau* just below the forward flight deck. This caused additional fires on the hangar deck and devastated crews that had already responded to the initial fire from the missile hit two minutes prior.

The US retaliation was swift. *Caron* had sunk one of the Osas with her Harpoon missiles, and now there were sixteen more missiles heading towards the enemy, as well as two AV-8A Harriers and four AH-1 Cobras. The Cobras might have a hard time sinking the missile boats, being armed with only 70mm unguided rockets. The Harriers were each carrying two Mk-83 one-thousand-pound bombs, each of which could send one of the Osas to the bottom of the Caribbean. The aircraft had a head start, but the missiles were moving faster.

The pair of AV-8As reached the eastern group of Osas first. It wasn't a column at this point, as each Osa was desperately trying to put distance between themselves, the US task force, and each other. But when compared to the speed of the aircraft, the boats were moving in slow motion. They still appeared almost in a line as the Harriers climbed from the deck to their attack altitude of two thousand feet. Flying at such low altitudes and such high speeds meant only having a split second to aim and release their payload. Tiger Five and Tiger Six of Marine Attack Squadron 542 each selected a target from the three Osas below.

Tiger Five lined up for a shallow pass. The Osa spat 30mm rounds at the incoming aircraft, hoping to score a quick hit, or at least to distract the pilot during the critical seconds of the attack. Fortunately for the attackers, they were only facing the anti-aircraft fire from the single boat they were each engaging. The only disadvantage of the Osa's jailbreak maneuver was that it prevented multiple ships from engaging in mutual defense. Whether it was the defensive fire, the pressure of combat, or just dumb luck, Tiger Five missed with both Mk-83s. They hit the sea off the starboard side of the fleeing missile boat.

Tiger Six, flying to the rear and right of Tiger Five, had a brief second longer to react to the incoming fire. With a steady hand, he lined up the Osa and dropped both thousand-pounders. The first plunged into the unarmored deck of the boat, which disappeared in a fireball as the Harrier overflew the wreck. The pilots agreed to extend to the southeast, then turn back to make a guns pass on the remaining two boats on the east column.

As they were coming around, the first of the Harpoon missiles fired by *Briscoe* arrived on the scene. As the radar seekers on the Harpoons came alive, the eight missiles chose between the two remaining ships and obliterated both of them. Each Harpoon carried a four-hundred-and-eighty-eight-pound warhead that punched through the steel hull and detonated inside, destroying the small target and leaving no survivors. The Harriers didn't have any targets for their guns pass. To the west, the same scene was replaying as the eight Harpoons fired from the *Moose* told the same story to the three surviving Osas.

The Americans had made quick work of the attackers, but the price to be paid was still being tallied. They had destroyed all seven of the Nicaraguan missile boats. In exchange, the US Navy had lost two ships, with the survival of four more in the hands of fate and the damage control teams. The US Navy had just suffered their worst losses since the Second World War at the hands of a bottom-tier navy from a backwater banana republic.

Chapter 38

1200 hours
Five Miles Southeast of Yamales
Jinotega, Honduras

The Contra patrol had been pushing hard to get back to base and report the discovery of Soviet activity in Ayapal. From this range, they should be able to make contact with the camp. Carlos thought they'd move ahead another mile or so before taking a break and trying to raise the base. There was a hilltop about four miles from base that they had marked as a communications checkpoint. They'd verified that, in decent conditions, the AN/PRC-77 radio could reach the camp from there. Carlos knew he couldn't give much detail over the open frequency, but he could drop the right code words to get the ball rolling for Poole.

Poole was eleven miles west of the camp in the town of Las Trojes. There was no five-star hotel in town. Contrary to Carlos's assertion, he did, in fact, have running water. All told, he found the town quaint and far from the worst place he'd been stationed. He'd taken up residence in a small house on the top of a hill overlooking the town. From here, he could maintain constant radio contact with the camp at Yamales. With the powerful transmitter hidden on the hill, he could also reach out to Tegucigalpa eighty miles further west. The CIA facilities in the capital city could then reach anywhere on the globe. But the entire operation relied on men with man-portable AN/PRC-77s to get the game of telephone started.

The disadvantage of the hilltop transmission point was that it left them exposed. The same features that made it a perfect transmission point (elevation and being devoid of tall trees) also made it impossible to hide when transmitting. The squad was seven miles inside the border of Honduras, so they weren't too concerned with being detected. Even so, it always made Carlos uncomfortable to be so vulnerable. He wasn't the only one, either. The entire squad stayed back in the tree line while he and Juan Bolivar, the radioman, made the last part of the hike up the hill.

Carlos established contact with the camp's radio operator. In Yamales, they had an old US Army AN/VRC-12 radio that had much better range than the PRC-77s. At this range, contact was a little touch-

and-go until Juan managed to get everything right on his end. Carlos was just about to transmit his coded contact report when the hairs on the back of his neck stood up. He broke off his transmission and quieted Juan, who asked what was going on. From on the hilltop, they could see for miles, and Carlos scanned the skies to the south. His heart stopped when he finally found what he was looking for.

"Go! Go! We've got to get the hell out of here!" said Carlos. Juan jumped at the sudden change in demeanor of the usually calm American. In the immediacy of the moment, Carlos missed the cradle when returning the handset of the radio, and it dangled behind Juan like a tail as he ran for the tree line. As the two men came rumbling down the hill as fast as they could, none of their squad mates had any idea what they were running from. Several of the men raised their rifles, ready to engage whatever monster had chased Juan and Norte off the hill.

"Everyone, get down and don't move, we have incoming helos," said Carlos as he slid into the trees, looking for a place to melt into. The squad dispersed and went prone, trying to look as much like trees as possible. If the helicopters were looking for them, there was little chance they would succeed. In the estimation of both Carlos and Diego, the Contra squad leader, they had a better chance of hiding from the helos than they had of outrunning them.

Carlos lifted his binoculars to his eyes and scanned the sky. He called out to Juan to see if the man could raise Yamales and pass the warning. Juan stopped adjusting the radio long enough to shake his head before going back to trying. A year ago, Carlos would have second-guessed his decision to get off the hilltop before calling in the incoming aircraft. Today he was already past it. Nothing he could do about it now. Instead, he focused on his next steps.

The first priority for his squad was to keep them alive. Next, he needed to get in contact with the camp and let them know what was coming, and third, if possible, he needed to identify the composition of the enemy force. There wasn't anything he could do to help Juan raise the camp, so he instead focused on figuring out what was after them. Fortunately, they were hiking up the south face of the hill on their way north to the camp. This meant they were facing the path of the incoming helos. It took him a minute to acquire them as he looked through the trees and branches, but when he did, his heart sank.

This wasn't a recon mission. He could see four Mi-24 gunships leading two Mi-8 troop transports. He did some quick mental math and put the attacking force at around sixty to eighty troops. Between those troops and the close-air support offered by the Mi-24s, this was about to be a grim day for the Contras and their Honduran allies.

Carlos low-crawled over to Juan, who had managed to get a weak signal through to Yamales. He took the offered handset and called out in his heavily accented Spanish, "Tiburón Base, this is Barracuda Three. We have multiple helicopters inbound to your location. I count four Mike India Twenty-Fours and two Mike India Eights. Total troop estimation eighty, over."

The radioman on the other end replied, "Barracuda Three, message received, out."

As the transmission ended, Carlos could hear the sounds of a siren wailing in the background. At that moment, he knew that the men and women at the camp were scurrying about trying to take cover, prepare defenses and, most importantly, destroy any paperwork or information that could be of intelligence value to the enemy.

The helos passed over the transmission hilltop and continued on towards the garrison at Yamales. There was no hope for the base itself. With only a couple of dozen defenders at the camp, the Nicaraguan (more likely Soviet, Carlos reminded himself) troops would overrun the base. It was only a matter of time.

****

The game of telephone had begun. Carlos called in the strike, and the radio operator immediately relayed the information to Trojes. Fred Poole hadn't been at the radio when the call had come in. José Obregón, his Honduran liaison, had been, and he summoned Poole when the first relay from Barracuda Three came through.

"Damn, this is bigger than anything we'd expected," said Poole.

"*Sí*, but this is war, is it not?" replied José. "They cannot fly in here and deny having come. That's enough to start hostilities. If they attack any of our installations, that will be a de facto declaration of war. I don't give a damn about whether there are any Contras there. They cannot hope to conduct this attack and get away with it."

Poole couldn't argue with the point. It was all true. Six military helicopters, at least four of them armed, entering the sovereign territory of another nation, couldn't be taken back. That was an international incident. The moment those helos fired a rocket or unloaded a troop, it was war. Both sides had been preparing for this possibility, but the Hondurans and their American allies hadn't believed that it would come so quickly.

Poole got on the radio and raised the CIA assets in Tegucigalpa.

"Whaler, this is Albacore. Listen, we've got a situation brewing here. We will need top priority on the network."

"No can do, Albacore. Unless you have an NBC situation, you're number two on the network."

Poole turned red. He was about to report the start of open warfare, and this snot-nosed prick was blowing him off.

"Look here, Whaler, we might be sitting on the start of—"

Whaler cut him off. "Albacore, we're in the middle of a war. I need you off this channel right now."

Poole went cold. Whatever was happening, he wasn't on the leading edge of it. He tuned in to the secondary channel and picked up a different radio operator at Whaler.

"Sorry about the tension, Albacore. There's some kind of Charlie-Foxtrot brewing up in the Caribbean. It looks like the damned Nicaraguans have just FUBARed our amphibious task force."

Chapter 39

1245 Hours
USS *Guam*
Caribbean Sea

At first look, *Guam* appeared to be in a better state than the larger *Nassau*. Both ships had taken two SS-N-2 missile hits. However, with *Guam*, both hits had been below the hangar deck. The *Nassau* had taken both hits higher along the freeboard and into the hangar deck. As a result, the *Guam* had controlled the post-attack fires but was still plagued with flooding. The *Nassau* wasn't dealing with nearly as much flooding but also wasn't able to get control of the fires that were raging beneath her flight deck.

On *Guam*, the captain ordered counterflooding on the port side of the ship. Both Styx missile hits were on the starboard side, and the already ungainly ship was at risk of capsizing as the forward starboard side took on water. Selectively flooding compartments on the port side could stabilize the ship but would also put her much lower in the water. In addition to keeping the ship from capsizing, this would allow the ship to unload as many of the Marines on board as possible. Getting the weight off the ship would help against the flooding, and every Marine that was on a landing craft or helicopter would be one less in the sea if, God forbid, they were forced to abandon ship.

Second Platoon, Kilo Company, 3/6 Marines was assigned to the first wave of the helo assault force. The CH-53s that would carry them to shore were on the flight deck and were being fueled. From within the watertight berthing compartment, Staff Sergeant Page had been manning the sound-powered phone, waiting for orders. When they finally came, it was a relief to everyone in the cramped room. They were moving out. Second Platoon was heading up to the flight deck.

As Corporal Evans followed behind Private Palmer, the last man in Fire Team One, he was a bit awed at how calm and organized everything was. Two hours before, the ship had been in the middle of the largest naval battle in forty years. There had been fire and panic and death. Now, from where he was slowly shuffling along, butt-to-nut with his squad, there was no sense of that chaos. There was still a tension in the air that let you know that the situation was grave, but at the same time, it was calm.

****

On the flight deck, Major Jason “Ripsaw” Thomas was working through his preflight checklist with Captain Philip “Snow” White.

“This has already been one hell of a year, Rip,” said Snow.

“You ain’t kidding, Snow. I’d like to say that we’ll get a nice vacation after this, but I’m pretty sure we’re at war.”

“Living the dream, Major, living the dream. I don’t know about you, but this is why I signed up.” Rip thought about that. He’d joined up during the Vietnam War. He’d had enough combat to last the rest of his life. Of course, he was a Marine, and he’d do his duty to the best of his ability. But he wasn’t out there looking for a fight. He sincerely hoped that in a year from now, Captain White would have lived long enough to get his fill.

They were too far out for the fully loaded CH-53s to make it to their original destination of La Ceiba, so they were evacuating to Banco Chinchorro, an island reef off the coast of Mexico. The helos would drop off a load of Marines, then return to *Guam* for a second load. Between the Sea Stallions and the Sea Knights, they could move all the Marines off the ship in two trips. That was a lot of sustained flight operations for a ship that was also in the midst of damage control, but they would get as many of the Marines off as possible.

At 1345, Bluebeard Five took off from the USS *Guam* en route to Banco Chinchorro. The Sea Stallions were an impressive formation. As they lifted off, the deck crew of *Guam* prepared to get the first batch of Sea Knights ready for the next wave.

“We’ll have about an hour to our destination, so get comfortable back there,” yelled Snow over his shoulder at the Marines in back. “It should be a smooth flight, assuming we don’t get shot down by some Cuban fighters, or some random SAM,” he said, grinning.

****

On board the USS *Nassau*, Captain Holloway remained in the CIC, trying to save his ship and manage his task force.

"Sir," said RM3 Brown, "*Fort Snelling* is ordering all hands to abandon ship."

"Damn. It's still early. This is going to be a long day." His men had been fighting the fire for two hours with no sign of containment. Ever since the massive fire on the USS *Forrestall* in 1967, the US Navy had made firefighting at sea an emphasis of training. In that incident, the fire had started on the flight deck and all the explosive detonations had occurred there. Today, the fires were ravaging *Nassau*'s hangar deck, and the force of each secondary explosion was contained within the ship, causing even more damage. Between the missile attacks and the subsequent fires, they had lost over two hundred men from the nearly one-thousand-man crew.

At 1415, reports came in that the USS *Caron*, the destroyer that had borne the initial missile attacks, had succumbed to her wounds and was being abandoned. Holloway's task force had lost four ships so far. The remaining ships were heading east to close the gap between the task force and Mexico to improve the chances of Mexican SAR assistance. The undamaged ships of the escort force were assisting with the firefighting efforts as best they could while also using their embarked Seasprite helos to drop supplies and equipment to the hundreds of sailors floating in the Caribbean.

Bluebeard Five landed on the uninhabited coast of Banco Chinchorro. Compared to the landing on the Iranian soccer pitch back in February, this was a fairly routine operation. The Marines rumbled down the ramp and set foot on terra firma for the first time in nearly a week. After the morning of patiently waiting to drown in a gray tomb, it was a welcome relief. As the Marines jogged off to ad hoc rally points, the CH-53s lifted back off and headed out over the blue Caribbean Sea.

Life was seemingly normal on *Guam*. Firefighting crews had contained the fires quickly, and the counterflooding had allowed the first wave of helicopters to get off the flight deck. In the hours after the initial attack and the panic that had accompanied it, someone had screwed up. The stress of being under attack wore men down. There was a constant adrenaline rush of knowing that your friends were dead and you could be next. The urgency of getting aircraft up as a matter of life and death pushed the crew, and one of them broke.

A seaman securing equipment in the hangar deck had inadvertently ignited a flare. In his panic at holding a three-foot-long explosive stick, the deck ape had thrown down the flare, which had ignited spilled hydraulic fluid. The small fire had become a big problem as it had spread to one of the AH-1 Cobra attack helicopters that had been prepared to sortie against the Osas that morning. The fire had ignited the unguided 70mm Hydra rockets on the Cobra, causing a secondary explosion and engulfing the hangar in smoke and flames.

Rip and Snow were on their way back to the *Guam* when the radio call came over the net.

"Bluebeard Lead, this is Wasp Nest. Flight operations are terminated. We're unsure when we'll be able to resume. All Bluebeard units are ordered to divert to Banco Chinchorro until further notice."

"What the hell?" asked Snow. "If it's not one thing, it's another. Today is just about as bad as it can get."

"Really, Phil? You know, we could still be sitting on the flight deck for whatever's going on right now. Or even worse, we could be hovering over the ship, running out of gas. Or we could have died in the—"

"Okay, I get it… but still, this sucks."

"Indeed, it does," said Rip as he wheeled the chopper over and headed back to the island.

****

1604 Hours
USS *Nassau*
Caribbean Sea

It was just past 1600 when Captain Holloway made the call. His crew had fought hard to save *Nassau*. But between the fires and secondary explosions that had opened holes in the hull, the damage was too much for them to overcome. The final straw was a failure of the last remaining fire main, which could not be bypassed or repaired.

Holloway took the handset from RM3 Brown and said, "All hands, this is the captain. Stand by to abandon ship. We've done all we can. Repeat, all hands, stand by to abandon ship."

As the day turned to evening, the amphibious task force ceased to exist. Of the amphibious assault ships, only *Guam* had survived, and she had major damage. Once her fires were out, the escort ships committed themselves to retrieving men from the sea. All that remained of the

Marine fighting force were the eight hundred and thirty-eight Marines sitting on an uninhabited island off the coast of Mexico, along with twelve CH-53 Sea Stallions and two M60 Patton tanks that had already been loaded onto landing craft. The 38th MAU was no more, but these Marines would find a way to get back into the fight.

Chapter 40

1300 Hours
Yamales, Honduras

The Contra patrol worked their way through the jungle towards their base camp. Even at just under four miles away, they could hear the sounds of the battle that was raging. They could occasionally see one of the Mi-24 gunships fly overhead after making a pass on the camp, but most of the battle remained outside of visual range. Carlos and Diego had argued about their next step. Carlos had wanted to lie low and report back to Poole when the attack force returned. That would allow the team to pinpoint a line of bearing back to the base from which the attack had launched. Diego refused to hold fast. He would not allow his men to fight and die at Yamales without him.

Carlos relented. He knew that the men were with Diego, and if he stayed on the hill, he would stay alone. So he went with them. He only hoped that once they saw the futility of getting into the fight, they would stop short of a suicide charge into the Soviets. During the trek, he wondered if the enemy would still be there when they arrived. Between the thick vegetation and hiding from the constant threat of helicopters, their pace had slowed to a crawl.

****

In Trojes, Poole could only sit and listen to the sounds of the attack. Not only could he hear the explosions and gunfire from the action eleven miles away, he could also hear the echo through the radio. In an effort to get as much information out as possible, the radioman at Yamales had left the microphone keyed, transmitting the sounds of the slaughter. Being able to hear the fight but impotent to do anything about it left Poole feeling insignificant. During most of his time with the Agency, he'd had a cold detachment from his projects. He wasn't accustomed to hearing men die.

From his balcony, he could see helicopters. Above the camp, two of the Mi-24s circled, looking for anything moving. Once they detected something, they sprayed a steady stream of 12.7mm rounds to ensure that it stopped moving. The other two Mi-24s had made attack runs right through the center of the camp, hitting the tents and huts that housed the camp's barracks and storage areas with dozens of rockets. The explosions rippled through the valleys surrounding the outpost.

Once the rocket attacks were complete, the Mi-24s broke off and flew to the southwest. They would follow Rural Route 125 and hunt down any fleeing vehicles. Once they were a few miles out from the camp, they set down on the road and unloaded their eight-man squads. These men melted into the forest along the side of the road and would wait to ambush any relief efforts that attempted to intervene. When the infantry was deployed, the helos returned to the sky over Yamales and relieved their comrades, circling the camp and engaging any defenders they could find.

Once the gunships had unleashed hell, the troop transport Mi-8 helos overflew the camp, wheeled around and flared to land. Soviet troops poured out of the two helos and fanned out across the area. The Mi-8s dusted off and flew off to the south to hold station for the duration of the raid. On the ground, the Soviets encountered light resistance. Most of the Honduran and Contra forces had evacuated the camp when the report of the raid had first come across the radio. Those that were left behind to sanitize the sensitive material were being systematically hunted down and killed.

The first hint Poole had that the attack was over came when the radio went silent. When there was no follow-on transmission, he knew that the attack had been successful and that the Nicaraguans or the Russians had taken the camp. He had no idea what that meant. Would they occupy the hill and dare the Hondurans to try to take it back? The Americans had used that tactic in Vietnam. He didn't think that was likely, though.

The Nicaraguans didn't have enough of an advantage to hold the hill for long, and they couldn't afford to try to bleed the Hondurans in a war of attrition. The more likely scenario was that this raid was meant to collect intelligence and warn the Contras that they couldn't hide in Honduras any longer.

Poole thought about what Whaler had said: "The damned Nicaraguans FUBARed our task force…" If there was any truth to that, this could be a coordinated attack signaling the start of open hostilities between Nicaragua and Honduras, with the Americans caught in between. But that didn't add up either. There was no way the Nicaraguans would have directly attacked the US Navy. Drawing the US into their war wouldn't make sense. In fact, it could very well lead to their downfall. Then the specter of Vietnam interrupted Poole's analysis. Perhaps the Nicaraguans felt that if the Vietnamese could send the US forces packing, so could they.

****

It had taken the Contra patrol four hours to cover the distance from the transmission hill to the base camp. They had seen the helicopters return to Nicaragua hours ago, and there had been no sounds of fighting since they had left. Whatever had happened, it appeared to be over. They walked into camp and could see fires burning here and there. The jungle was particularly hard to set on fire, so as soon as the tents and huts had burned down, only smoldering ashes remained.

Carlos made his way to the radio shack and found it destroyed. The hut was gutted, the radio spiked, and any paperwork had been removed. Carlos didn't know if the Sandis had taken it or if the Contras had destroyed it. It would take a few days to sort everything out. Hopefully, there would be enough survivors to fill in all the blanks. As he rifled through the remains of the transmitter, he found two of the unit's AN/PRC-77s that looked like they could be repaired. He grabbed them and headed back to his men. It didn't take long to see that there was nothing they could do here. They had about an hour of sunlight left. If they left now, they could make it to the rally point at Capire before night set in. Once they made it to Capire, they could start planning their revenge.

Chapter 41

1105 Hours
Situation Room, White House
Washington, D.C.

"Mr. President, we have another problem here," said Secretary of Defense Harold Brown. The President had been in and out of the Situation Room, going over the current status of the Iraqi invasion of Iran. This war had become the most important thing in the world the moment those Iraqi helicopters had crossed into Iranian territory. That was about to change.

"What is it, Harry? Has the new Turkish government invaded Iran as well?" The President looked up to see Dr. Brown's ghostly pale face.

"No, sir. We've been attacked." The statement hung in the room as everyone stopped what they were doing and stared at the Secretary of Defense.

"We're just now getting reports and we don't have all the information, but there has been a missile attack on our amphibious task force that was en route to Honduras for joint exercises."

"My God, Harry. Have there been any casualties?" asked President Carter.

"The initial reports are catastrophic, Mr. President. I have our people working on an exact number—we'll have a full report on the situation as soon as we get the information compiled. Right now all we know is that missile boats flying the Nicaraguan flag have attacked our task force and sunk at least one American ship."

"Bastards," said Carter. "How could this happen? We let everyone in the world know that we sent that fleet down there. How could we be caught by surprise? Why didn't we have a plan to handle the Nicaraguans?"

"Sir, we were unaware that the Nicaraguans had the capability to launch this kind of attack." In the history of naval warfare, this was not the first time a superior fleet had been dealt a serious blow by a drastically inferior force, nor would it be the last. Yet each time it happened, those who were not in tactical command found it easy to blame the on-site commanders for the failure.

"My God, we've got Pearl Harbor all over again," concluded the President. "Admiral Hayward," Carter said, addressing the Chief of Naval Operations. "I need your people to work on responses to this. I want everything that you can think of, from disproportionate response to overwhelming response. As soon as we have the facts, I want a plan of action. Someone get Ben Civiletti in here too. We'll need to square all of this with the War Powers Act."

As the morning moved towards afternoon, an unbroken channel of information flowed into the White House. It was clear that the world had shifted in the past twelve hours, but it was still too early to know what the new geopolitical situation would look like. One of America's staunchest allies in the Middle East had been invaded. In Latin America, another ally had been directly attacked. And in the middle of it all, American sailors and Marines had died—were still dying. As the number of dead men and sunken ships kept increasing, President Jimmy Carter understood that the United States of America was at war. The Nicaraguans had declared that war when they'd fired on our ships. Now he would have to go to Congress and convince them to do something they hadn't done since 1941.

Even at the height of the conflict in Vietnam, there had never been a congressional declaration of war. Tens of thousands of Americans had died in that campaign without it. Congress had responded with the War Powers Act of 1973. This act was aimed at preventing another undeclared war. Within the boundaries of the act, Carter could initiate a military response. However, he could only commit US military force for sixty days without congressional approval. With the Democrats having a majority in both the House and the Senate, Carter was confident that even absent a declaration of war, he would get statutory authorization to keep the military in action beyond those sixty days.

He was getting ahead of himself, and he knew it. There was no sense in focusing on the military solution before he had actionable military plans available. The process of calling an emergency session of the United Nations Security Council had already been initiated. The ambassadors from various member states had been collected in New York, and the United States Ambassador Donald McHenry had prepared a statement on ending the hostilities in Iran. At this very moment, that speech was being shelved and a new speech condemning the brazen attacks on American and Honduran forces by the Sandinista People's Army was being readied.

Carter knew the importance of this speech. It was the speech of Adlai Stevenson during the Cuban Missile Crisis in 1962 that had galvanized resolve and ensured the popular support for the Kennedy administration, not only among the American people but throughout the West. He was now putting his faith in Donald McHenry. McHenry had proven himself a gifted diplomat during the handling of several Soviet defections. Today he would have to prove himself a gifted orator if the Carter administration was to maximize their support in the international community.

Knowing that they had addressed the present as best they could, the President decided that it was time to work on the future.

"Zbig, Jeane, what does tomorrow look like? What are your recommendations for our response?"

"Mr. President," said Dr. Kirkpatrick, "at the risk of sounding cold, the Sandinistas may have done us a favor." The President fixed her with an icy glare as she continued. "I have been very open in my belief that war in the region was likely. Because they've attacked us now, before they've built up a powerful force in the area, we're completely justified in ripping them out, root and stem."

"You favor all-out war on the Nicaraguans?" asked Carter, looking for clarification.

"I do. The Soviets will perceive anything short of that as weakness. That would be an invitation for further needling along the edges of our sphere of influence."

"Zbig, what are your thoughts on Nicaragua?"

"Mr. President, I have to agree with Secretary Kirkpatrick. Perhaps not total war, but at least significant military action that degrades their ability to make war on their neighbors. Something sufficient to convince not only the Sandinistas but any other leftist regime that attacking the United States will never be worth the costs."

"If I may, Mr. President," said General Jones, the Chairman of the Joint Chiefs of Staff. "The difficulty of following Dr. Brzezinski's recommendation is that the Nicaraguan military is small and concentrated in a limited geographic area. It's hard to imagine striking at that objective without what would amount to the total war scenario that Secretary Kirkpatrick envisions."

"Thank you, General. Jeane, what about containment? Can we expect this to move beyond Nicaragua if we go forward with an invasion?"

"I believe the odds of that are high, Mr. President. By entering the conflict directly, it could unite every leftist uprising in the region under the communists' banner. We could end up with sympathetic governments along the borders in Guatemala and El Salvador. Sort of the Latin American Khmer Rouge if you will."

"That could lead to additional problems, Mr. President," said Dr. Brzezinski. "As part of our human rights campaign, we need to be aware of any government partners with whom we align ourselves."

Secretary Kirkpatrick rolled her eyes. "If ever there was a time to put that on the back burner, Mr. President, this is it," she said. "I don't think I need to remind anyone in this room that had we helped Somoza maintain control in Managua last year, we wouldn't be about to invade Nicaragua today."

There it was. When Brzezinski had first advocated bringing Kirkpatrick into the administration, they had accepted that their failure to support Somoza had allowed the communist Sandinista government to take over the country. At the time, though, Brzezinski hadn't considered that of particular importance. Nicaragua was just another socialist banana republic. It wasn't worth arguing about. As of this morning, that had officially changed.

"That much is true," said Brzezinski, "but we cannot simply write blank checks to despots hoping they use the aid to help us and not repress their own people."

"We will take stock of all aid and support packages as they arise," said Carter, regaining control of the room. "I assure you both that you will have a chance to argue about this again soon. Zbig, what about Iran? How do we get the genie back in the bottle there?"

"The Iraqi invasion changed the calculus there," said Brzezinski. "Before the invasion, I couldn't see any way that we could send a military force into Iran without destabilizing an already delicate situation. With the Iraqi advances and the Soviet presence in Afghanistan, I feel that our hand is being forced. We need to act on this."

"And we can't forget about Moscow," said Kirkpatrick. "This Hussein character is one of theirs and they will likely object to our intervention. Even worse, they may intervene on behalf of the Iraqis. It would be an absolute disaster to have our forces directly engaging the Soviets on behalf of opposite sides in a rivalry that goes back to the start of recorded history."

"Mr. President, if I may," said Vice Admiral Bobby Ray Inman, the Director of the National Security Agency (NSA). "I believe we have a good read on Iraqi intentions. I'm sure Admiral Turner can also shed some light on this. The Iraqis have launched this invasion with the specific goal of capturing the Iranian oil fields and petroleum-processing plants in the southern Khuzestan Province. They're acting under the guise of protecting their own border from terrorist attacks, but we have no doubt that they're after the oil." With that, he looked to Stansfield Turner, the Director of the CIA.

"We have nothing that contradicts this," replied Dr. Turner. "Admittedly, we've run into some trouble with our human intelligence resources on the ground. Saddam Hussein is paranoid and has purged quite a few of our assets since the uptick in attacks this spring."

"It's hardy paranoia if he's purging actual spies, Stan," said Brzezinski with a chuckle.

"Be that as it may," said Turner, "I agree with Bobby Ray—this is an old-fashioned land grab. To General Jones's point, this thing could well be over and done before we can move the 82nd Airborne out of Egypt. I think our best move will be to provide the Iranians with targeting information from our AWACS planes. We have the USS *Eisenhower* and *Midway* out there right now. Between the two of them, we can maintain near-constant surveillance using their E-2 Hawkeye aircraft. Working with the Iranian F-14 squadrons, we should be able to deny the Iraqis access to the airspace over the battlefield."

"We can supplement those with Air Force E-3 Sentries flying out of Egypt or Pakistan," added Air Force Chief of Staff Lew Allen. "It's the same principle, just not reliant on the presence of our aircraft carriers."

"How long will it take to implement this?" asked the President.

"We can start reporting air activity directly to the Iranians immediately," said Admiral Hayward. "We've already got birds in the air. As for the data link to the F-14s, that'll take a day or so."

"It'll take about thirty-six hours to get the E-3s deployed," added General Allen.

"Okay, let's make this happen now. We'll add to it as more information comes out," said the President, thankful to have some action to take.

****

1100 Hours
Managua, Nicaragua

The leader of the Sandinista junta, Daniel Ortega, was having trouble processing exactly what General Smotrov's translator was telling him.

"You have attacked the Americans in the Caribbean?" he asked, seeking clarification.

"No, Señor Ortega. *You* have attacked the Americans in the Caribbean. Those were your missile boats, your missiles. The Americans will come at you like a pack of wild dogs. The good news is that you were very successful. Many of their ships were sunk, and likely thousands of their sailors and Marines have perished in the attack."

"We need to get in touch with the Americans. Let them know that this was some kind of accident. That we didn't—"

Smotrov cut him off. "You will do no such thing." There was a menace in his voice that told Ortega that negotiating with the Americans would cost him his life. "There are things happening that are bigger than you … bigger than Nicaragua. You are a part of the revolution, and sometimes the revolution requires sacrifice. This is one of those times."

"The Americans will come down here and kill us all. We cannot possibly defeat them," said Ortega.

"You need not defeat them, *señor*. You need to fight them. You need to fight the Americans harder than you ever fought the Somoza regime. We have brought you the weapons that you will need. We have trained your men. Your army knows the terrain, and fighting in the jungle is notoriously difficult. Nicaragua itself will defeat much of the Americans' technology, just as the jungles of Vietnam did ten years ago."

"But… how can we fight them if we cannot hope to defeat them?" asked Ortega.

"When the time comes, the Soviet Union will give you more support than you could ever hope for. Together we will conquer not only

Honduras but the entire region, from Colombia to the US border." That got Ortega's attention. "And you, *señor*, will be the man in charge of it all." Smotrov set the hook.

"You must understand, Señor Ortega," continued Smotrov, "yours is not the only uprising of the revolution in the Americas. We have plans in place to help your brethren, and the Americans will not be able to stop them. But to get to the People's Pan-American Union, you need to hold fast now. Fight this war against Honduras. Endure the American attacks. Do this, and we will reward you. If you try to make a deal with the Americans, you will undo the work we have done to liberate this land. We will gladly sacrifice Nicaragua for the greater good of the region if you choose to stand against us."

Smotrov sat back in his chair and gave Ortega a chance to digest everything that was happening. He had now laid out both the carrot and the stick. Ortega didn't really have a choice here, but Smotrov knew that he would perform better if he thought he did. The sooner he took the carrot, the less likely the Soviets would have to use the stick.

"I see, Comrade General," said Ortega. "Do you have any recommendations on how we will conduct this war that we are now waging against the Hondurans and the Americans?" General Smotrov smiled.

"Yes, my friend," said Smotrov, the first time he'd ever used the term. "The military aid that we've provided you thus far can be used to slow down the Americans. We will need to strike quickly if we are going to take advantage of our initiative. Once we have made incursions into Honduras, and when the American Air Force takes over the skies, we will take cover and bleed the Americans. They will pay dearly for every meter of ground they try to take from us."

"General Smotrov, how can we be assured that the CIA won't send an assassin to kill me now and put an end to this adventure?"

"Ahh. Yes, you are a very astute man. If I were in charge of the Americans, I would do exactly that. We know that their CIA is already operating in Honduras. We have an operation in place that will provide incontrovertible proof of that later today. It doesn't take a lot of imagination to believe that they would try to cut the head off the snake. The CIA isn't even the worst of our problems when it comes to keeping you alive. The American Air Force will probably begin attacks on

Managua today. In fact, we can't be sure that American bombers are not already en route to hit Managua as we speak."

Ortega looked at the ceiling as if to see the bombers flying overhead. "Surely we can't stay here! We need to evacuate the city!"

"*Señor*, we need to leave, yes. But let us do it quietly. Causing a panic now will not help the situation. I have dedicated my troops to building a bunker compound outside of Altagracia on Ometepe Island. It is from there that we will conduct the war."

Ometepe was a volcanic island in the center of Lake Nicaragua. The lake provided a natural moat surrounding the new command center for the Sandinista People's Army. In order to reach the island, enemy troops would have to cross at least five miles of water. While this wouldn't protect them from attack from the air, it would slow down any attempts to take out the command structure from the ground. It would offer protection against either a lone CIA assassin or the avenging marauders of the United States Marine Corps.

Chapter 42

1600 Hours
Albrook Air Force Station
Panama

The US response was swift. The nearest forces they could bring to bear consisted of Air Force Corsair IIs belonging to the 24th Tactical Air Support Squadron flying out of Albrook Air Force Station in Panama City, Panama. Within half an hour of the reports that the Marine Amphibious Unit had been attacked, the Golden Jaguars were working through the requirements to strike back. The bigwigs in Washington had determined that a strike at the port facilities on both coasts of Nicaragua would be the most effective use of the Jag's' Corsairs.

The commanders divided the unit into three flights. The first would attack the main east coast port of Bluefields. The second, the smaller port of El Bluff, which lay on the east side of Bluefields Bay. The third and final unit would strike the west coast port of Miramar. Given the relatively small payload of the light attack planes, these attacks were designed to function both tactically and symbolically. These were real targets of military value that could be disrupted and destroyed with the attacking force. Symbolically, they told the Nicaraguans that they lived under the shadow of the United States.

During the preflight briefing, the pilots were told to expect medium anti-aircraft artillery fire in defense of their targets. The Nicaraguans had imported significant numbers of 23mm and 57mm anti-aircraft weapons, including some mobile units. Any of these would be capable of taking out an A-7 if given enough time and a little luck. The plan was to fly up the coast of Costa Rica at altitude and dive to the deck to get below Nicaraguan air-defense radar before popping up just in time to unleash their bombs, then turning around and heading home. The Nicaraguans had no air force to speak of.

One of the pilots quipped, "They didn't have a navy either."

With the mission drawn up and the jets gassed and loaded, the three flights set out just past 1600 hours. The Bluefields attack was the first to enter enemy airspace, crossing over the twelve-mile coastal zone fifteen minutes after they had formed up. As they neared the target, Jaguar Two reported that he was being painted by fire control radar. Within seconds, everyone in the flight could see multiple SAMs being fired from the vicinity of the port. The intelligence hadn't briefed them on the possibility of enemy surface-to-air missiles, so this came as a complete surprise.

The Jaguars of the 24th TASS evaded as the missiles came streaking towards them. The incoming SA-8s destroyed Jaguar Two before he could commence the attack run; however, the rest of the A-7s were able to drop ordnance on the target. Before the bombs had time to fall from the aircraft to the target, more A-7s were taking hits. The SAM launcher destroyed three more of the Corsairs after their launch but before they passed over the target. The fifth and final aircraft managed to overfly the target and extend to the north, where the pilot could see another missile launch over his right shoulder.

The two SA-8 missiles came streaking at him as he tried to put distance between himself and the launcher. The desperate plane dove for the deck, hoping to fool the radar of the incoming missiles by blending in with the ground cover while dumping chaff. The first SA-8 exploded harmlessly in a cloud of aluminum. The second, however, wasn't fooled. It exploded just aft of the Corsair, destroying the engine and sending the plane into an uncontrolled climb. The pilot punched out just north of the town of Bluefields and prayed the Nicaraguans would play by the rules that governed prisoners of war.

The second flight had been flying to the east of the first. They commenced their attack on the port of El Bluff. As with the first flight, just before they were in range of dropping on the target, they saw SAM missiles launched from the Bluefields port facility. Unlike the first flight, only two missiles rose to meet them and they didn't lose a single aircraft to them. They hit the port with a combination of cluster bombs that took out soft targets like the anti-aircraft guns and two-thousand-pound Mk-84 general-purpose bombs that hit the port and storage facilities.

As the flight continued from east to west, they overflew the bay and performed a quick battle damage assessment of the first attack. This was deemed advantageous once the flight leader had determined that the Nicaraguans were out of missiles. The overflight showed significant structural damage to the port, including the destruction of a dock crane and significant damage to the dock itself. There were also fires breaking out in the container storage field, and several burnt-out vehicles that had been caught by the bomblets in the cluster munitions.

As the flight turned to the south to head home, one of the Corsairs was tasked with overflying the airport to the west of the town. Although the flight was Winchester (having run out of mission-applicable ordnance), the flyover looked for military activity for possible follow-on attacks. Unfortunately, the military activity was verified as the quad-mounted 23mm anti-aircraft cannons of a Soviet-made ZSU-23-4 Shilka ripped into the fuselage of the Corsair, making a line from the center point right through the engine. For the second time in the past five minutes, one of the Golden Jaguars hit the silk to float down into the waiting arms of the enemy.

The strike group attacking the west coast had learned from their brethren on the east. With the knowledge of the SAM threat now established, the flight stayed low longer, sacrificing accuracy for greater surprise. The change in approach had the expected effect. As the four planes in the element popped up to let loose their bombs, the waiting SA-8 launcher painted them with its "Land Roll" fire control radar. This time, however, the launcher didn't have time to get a shot off. The area was saturated with hundreds of bomblets that destroyed everything in their path, including the SA-8. The damage to the port wasn't as significant as that on the east coast attacks, but the destruction of the air-defense assets was complete, and the Nicaraguan air defenses weren't able to bring down any of the attackers.

Chapter 43

1715 Hours
United Nations Building
New York City, New York

Every geopolitical crisis in the past thirty-two years had found its way to the floor of the United Nations Security Council. Created by the victorious Allies at the end of the Great Patriotic War, the true power of the UN as a governing body lay in the balancing of power established at the top of this council. While the ten rotating members of the council were there to voice their concerns and participate in the process, what really mattered were the five permanent members: the Soviet Union, the People's Republic of China, France, the United Kingdom, and the United States.

In all matters considered in this body, no action could be taken, no resolution passed without the unanimous consent of these members. If any of the big five said no to a resolution, it was dead. Vetoed. In effect, this meant that the chamber was more deliberative than executive. It provided an arena for the Soviets and the Americans to spar over every detail of international intrigue that bubbled up into the public consciousness.

Soviet Ambassador Oleg Troyanovsky was amused by the whole situation. He had known that this day would come. He and Andropov's people in the KGB had worked on their response. He considered the American position as he entered the immense chamber and sat in his assigned seat. The Americans would come out with bluster and bravado. They would accuse his nation of perpetuating attacks on them and their allies. They would demand concessions. They would demand retribution. And then Oleg Troyanovsky would respond to their petty threats.

American Ambassador Donald McHenry was already in the room. He stood at his section of the semicircular table, reviewing the speech before him. The Security Council met in a large open auditorium. The individual ambassadors sat along a long round table, with four mounted seats behind them to allow room for select members of their delegation. A mural was painted at the closed end of the table. The mural contained several depictions of peace and tranquility above a bleak representation of war and misery. There was gallery seating on the open side of the table. That seating was empty today for security reasons.

It had been just over four months since Troyanovsky and an American diplomat, William vanden Heuvel, had been attacked in this very room by dissident communists. The assailants had been sitting in that gallery. Two dissidents had approached each of the diplomats and proceeded to douse them in red paint. It marked the first time a diplomat had been assaulted within the UN chambers. As the two men had stood, drenched in red paint, Troyanovsky had turned to vanden Heuvel and quipped, "Better red than dead." The memory brought a smile to Oleg's face. He knew that those memories would be all that remained of his happy times at the UN.

The Security Council president, Taieb Slim of Tunisia, called the meeting to order. Oleg wondered if it would have made any difference if this meeting had taken place two weeks from now, when he would have ascended to the monthlong presidency. *Not likely*, he thought. Perhaps he would have felt more in control, but that was all. He would still be bound by the rules and customs to let this play out. On that thought, he waited for his opportunity to address the members.

The first matter for discussion was the Iraqi invasion of Iran. Ambassador McHenry gave an impassioned plea for the cessation of violence and a retreat to the established international borders. By way of concession, McHenry suggested the creation of a Security Council subcommittee on sectarian violence in the region. This was a laughable attempt by the Americans to mollify the world in the face of the aggression of her Iranian allies. Oleg listened to the plea for peace and a return to order, knowing that it was a fruitless quest.

Oleg could have pushed his way to the top of the speakers' list. Most of the assembled diplomats had assumed he would. But he was content to let the rest of the delegations have their say before contributing. Each speaker was outraged by Iraq's disregard for the foundational principles of the United Nations. All agreed that this wanton aggression needed to stop. A few even dared to hint at Soviet involvement in the attack. None provided any evidence of this, but like an attorney arguing to the jury, they left the idea to hang in the air, allowing each individual to fill in the blanks. Finally, it was Oleg's turn to stand and address the assembly.

"Gentlemen, it appears that you have near absolute agreement on the wrongness and criminality of the actions of the nation of Iraq. I would remind each of you that Iraq had been an erstwhile ally of the Soviet Union and has worked closely with my nation to help ensure peace and security in this vital region. I would also remind you all that over the past six months, there have been dozens of attacks against not only the territory of Iraq but also the sovereign territory of the USSR. In the entire history of this body, we have never shown our support for terrorism. I caution everyone at this table against starting such support today."

So far, there was nothing surprising in his speech. That was what he'd wanted. He would give them what they expected in order to accentuate the power of what he said next.

"It is with that in mind that the USSR proposes a joint resolution decrying not only the Iraqi attack on the sovereign territory of Iran but also the Iranian government's role in the growing terrorist threat in the region as a whole. There are no innocents in this war. We will support formal sanctions against all belligerent parties and are prepared to host peace talks in Yerevan, Baku, or even Moscow if the parties agree."

Several of the delegations began whispering amongst themselves at this uncharacteristic show of Soviet cooperation. Oleg continued his speech, laying a heavy amount of the blame for the international incident at the feet of his client state. He made overtures of peace, calling for a cessation of hostilities and for calmer heads to prevail. It was a masterful execution of a well-calculated plan. And the day was just beginning.

The council agreed in principle to a draft resolution calling for a cease-fire and follow-on peace talks. The bulk of the heavy lifting would be worked out with Iran and Iraq through the United States and the Soviet Union. With that plan put into place, the meeting progressed to the next agenda item.

Ambassador McHenry had been impassioned in his defense of Iran. His anger was unbridled in his condemnation of the Sandinistas.

"Distinguished colleagues," said McHenry. "Today marks an alarming first in history. For the first time since the beginning of the modern age established by the founding of this institution, a nation has openly and brazenly attacked a permanent member of the Security Council. These permanent members were assigned the responsibility to maintain peace throughout these United Nations. This was not simply an attack on the United States. It was not simply an attack on the West. This was an attack on the system of the United Nations as a whole, and we cannot allow it to stand.

"Today I come before you as the representative of a nation aggrieved. At ten forty this morning, naval forces of the Republic of Nicaragua conducted an unprovoked and unwarranted attack against ships of the United States Navy. The American task force was sailing in international waters en route to conduct exercises with the military forces of the Republic of Honduras. The Nicaraguan Navy took advantage of the freedom of navigation, a concept debated in these very halls under the Convention on the Law of the Sea, to approach within point-blank range of the American ships before launching their sudden and deliberate attack.

"This attack was not calculated as a warning. This attack was not meant to let the United States know that the Republic of Nicaragua took exception to our defense policy. This attack was meant to kill as many American sailors and Marines as possible. The missiles were fired so near the task force that little could be done to defend. The damage was swift and severe. Men were trapped on ships that were filled with flames. Many of those that did not burn to death drowned as the ships filled with water and sank to the bottom of the Caribbean Sea. Some of those who survived the loss of their ships were torn apart by sharks as they awaited rescue. Those who survived watched their brothers die in the chaos of this morning.

"In response to this treacherous attack, the people of the United States refer to Article 51 of the United Nations Charter. 'Nothing in the present Charter shall impair the inherent right of collective or individual self-defense if an armed attack occurs against a member of the United Nations until the Security Council has taken the measures necessary to maintain international peace and security. Measures taken by members in exercise of this right of self-defense shall be immediately reported to the Security Council and shall not in any way affect the authority and responsibility of the Security Council under the present Charter to take at any time such action as it deems necessary in order to maintain or restore international peace and security.'

"Under Article 51, the United States reserves the right to act in our self-defense against the Republic of Nicaragua. In accordance with this Article, the United States will notify this body of any actions taken in defense once these actions have occurred, and we have determined that there is no military risk of revealing those actions. These actions may consist of military attacks on targets of tactical or strategic value.

"In addition to the attacks on the United States naval vessels, the Republic of Nicaragua conducted attacks against the Republic of Honduras. At the time of these attacks, the United States was engaged in cooperative military exercises with the Republic of Honduras. The attacks on the Yamales region of Honduras were clearly an attempt to disrupt the security relationship of the Republic of Honduras and the United States. As such, the United States again invokes Article 51 to act in our own self-defense, and in the defense of the Republic of Honduras, should they request such assistance."

Ambassador McHenry took his seat. This time Oleg didn't wait to allow other delegations to weigh in on the issue. He stood and addressed the President.

"Mr. President, if I may." He looked to President Slim, who motioned for him to go ahead.

"The people of the Soviet Union stand with the American people in their outrage over these unwarranted attacks. We cannot sit in this chamber and pretend to believe in the cause of peace if we do not join Ambassador McHenry in denouncing the naked aggression of the Nicaraguan government. The sympathy that we feel for the American Navy is equaled only by the regret that we feel in knowing that Soviet weapons were used to conduct this horrific attack. It was our intent to provide the Republic of Nicaragua with sufficient force of arms to secure their territorial claims on the land and the sea. It had never occurred to us that these defensive weapons would be squandered in the suicidal madness that we have witnessed today.

"I have received the full authority of my government to announce that, effective immediately, the USSR suspends all military arms deals with the Republic of Nicaragua. Additionally, our government has been in contact with our allies in Havana and are formally requesting that the Republic of Cuba join us in this arms embargo. Finally, I am authorized to pledge to the government of the United States whatever support we can provide from our intelligence services in the region."

As Oleg returned to his seat, murmurs erupted as delegations digested what had been said. It was an unprecedented concession coming from the Soviet Union. Then again, it was an unprecedented attack against the United States. As the debate on the floor opened up and additional delegations spoke against the Nicaraguan regime, it became clear that the Soviet Union was frightened that this newly hot war in

Latin America could push international tensions to the breaking point. With the United States in Iran, the Soviets in Afghanistan, and now this conflict, the Soviets were doing everything in their power to ensure the greater peace.

Chapter 44

1900 Hours
Camp Lejeune
Jacksonville, North Carolina

The news was never as fast as the rumors on a military base. Nancy had been hearing about the attacks on the Marine Amphibious Unit all day at the bank. She had heard conflicting reports that ran from one extreme to the next. First she heard the Russkies had destroyed every ship in the task force. Next she heard that it was all Cuban propaganda being broadcast as some kind of psychological warfare. Trying to keep up was dizzying when everyone thought they knew something but nobody actually knew anything. After spending the day at work hearing the rumors, she was ready to join Duane on the couch and let the news catch her up.

Nancy and Duane normally tuned into ABC's *World News Tonight* to hear Peter Jennings and Max Robinson deliver the news. Tonight they tuned in to CBS. Nancy had grown up listening to Cronkite during the Vietnam War, and there was something soothing about hearing the man. There was a comfort there that she could only compare to listening to her grandfather. The news bulletins had been coming in during the day, but the military had released no official information until it was time for the evening news. Once the nation's newsmen had prepared the American people, the President would make an address at 6:30 Eastern.

On the screen, "CBS Evening News With Walter Cronkite" appeared in front of the familiar image of Cronkite sitting in his circular "donut" desk. Without additional fanfare, Cronkite launched into his reporting. Facing the camera, he addressed the American people. Above his left shoulder, a map of the Caribbean Sea and the Mexican coast displayed a red "explosion" graphic to show the approximate location of the attack. For the first time, Nancy and the rest of the nation heard the full scope of the attack. The dead numbered in the "hundreds, if not thousands." The attack was "fully unprovoked." The devastation was "unprecedented in a time of peace, if that is indeed what we are living in," reported Cronkite. The most trusted man in America could not put his viewers at ease, but he gave them the baseline understanding of events so that President Carter could address them.

Cronkite finished his recitation of the facts, and without a commercial pause, the camera switched from New York to Washington, D.C., and the Seal of the President of the United States. As the newscast completed the transition from Cronkite to Carter, the familiar image of the President seated at his desk in the Oval Office appeared on the screen. Behind him, the gold curtains were drawn, and he was flanked on his right by the Stars and Stripes. On his left, in the place of the normal Presidential Seal, stood the service flags of the United States Navy and Marine Corps. He spoke the three words that had become the nation's call to attention.

"My fellow Americans. This morning our nation was attacked. Many of our brave servicemen died at the hands of the Sandinista government of Nicaragua. Joint Task Force 120, a collection of United States Navy ships hosting the 38th Marine Amphibious Unit, was attacked without warning. During the attack, the United States Navy suffered the loss of six ships. These are the first ships sunk in combat since the Second World War. While rescue efforts are underway, the result of this attack has been devastating. Thousands of sailors and Marines have perished in the Caribbean Sea.

"Today, as a nation, we have asked ourselves the question: are we at war? The question itself generates uncertainty. Tonight, I want to end that uncertainty. I am calling on the Congress to issue a declaration of war against the Republic of Nicaragua. This need not be a long war. But this will be a total and complete war. Anything less would leave a humanitarian catastrophe. If we learned anything from our actions in Vietnam, let that be the lesson.

"Human rights have been a hallmark of my administration. We have pledged to allow sovereign nations to choose their methods of governance without interference from the United States, and we have asked the world community to join us in that effort. When the Sandinista government overthrew the previous regime through force of arms, the United States patiently waited for the new government to take power and join the international community. We did this in the face of harsh criticism. We were asked, as every administration since the Second World War was asked, to support the existing regime against this communist uprising. We did not. We withdrew our support and allowed events in Nicaragua to play out.

"Today, we learned that in this instance, they rewarded our patience with an unprecedented attack. During this time, as we respond to this aggression, I want to assure the people of the United States, as well as those in the rest of the world, that our fight is not with the Nicaraguan people. We do not believe that the actions of this Marxist regime reflect the wants and desires of the people of Nicaragua. We implore the Nicaraguans to reject this action of their government. We ask that they refuse to take up arms against the United States or our allies. In exchange, I offer my promise that once we remove the Sandinistas from power, we will ensure that we erect a truly representative government in their place. We will ensure the freedom of every Nicaraguan.

"Earlier today, I requested a list of immediate responses from our military leaders. On their recommendation, I authorized selected strikes against Nicaraguan military and infrastructure targets. Our effort to end this war began with those strikes. The mission was successful, but it was not without cost. Several pilots from the 24th Tactical Air Support Squadron were killed during the attack. The cause of freedom is not without sacrifice. Today the men and women of our military bear that sacrifice. I ask that we, the people, do everything that we can to bear that sacrifice with them.

"We need not bear this burden alone. Today, Ambassador Donald McHenry met with the Security Council of the United Nations, and our diplomatic corps has met with the leadership of our key allies. There is near-universal shock and outrage over this brutal action by the Sandinistas. Our allies support our response. The Soviet Union has pledged to assist our efforts to right this wrong. I want to assure everyone who can hear my words: this is not a pretext for a greater war between the East and West. When we act, we will act in the best interests of the United States, but we will act with the support and backing of the United Nations.

"We cannot bring back the men who perished with Task Force 120 and the 24th Tactical Air Support Squadron. We will forever be in debt for their sacrifice. While we can never repay that debt, we can ensure that they did not die in vain. The United States did not ask for this fight, but we have the national resolve to see it through to the end. Please pray for one another as I ask God to bless you all, for God to bless America."

The screen went black for a second before returning to the studio in New York, where Walter Cronkite summarized the President's brief statement to the people. Nancy got up and turned off the TV. They were at war. She hadn't heard from Carlos in weeks. When he had left Camp Lejeune for his temporary assignment, she'd had no idea where he was going. Even if she hadn't been worried about Carlos, there were still a dozen or so Marines in that MAU that she knew and was friends with.

She thought about calling the wives but had second thoughts. That world was in her past. She'd had only intermittent contact with a few of them since she'd left, and she imagined they were dealing with enough right now. She wouldn't really be helping them; she'd be reaching out for her own benefit. Like so many people in the country, she felt helpless. There was nothing she could do, and her proximity to the crisis only magnified that emptiness.

"Everything okay?" asked Duane. "I know this has to be a lot to take in right now, but I want you to know that I'm here for you."

Duane was always good at saying the right thing, but he couldn't understand what was going on in Nancy's mind. She knew she had to say something. Otherwise, Duane would just assume the worst, and everything would get more difficult.

"I'm all right, baby. It's just too much. I know a lot of guys on those ships. It's hard to think about how many of them might have been killed. And what happens with this war? Are you going to have to go fight with them? Will there be another draft?" Nancy had forgotten that Duane's asthma kept him out of Vietnam and would keep him out of this war as well.

"I don't think we have to worry about that, sweetheart. There are a lot of guys they'll take before they get to me."

Nancy wasn't sure how she felt about that. No, she didn't want Duane to have to leave, but at the same time, she wasn't comfortable with how content he was with letting other men fight on his behalf.

Chapter 45

28 September 1980
Ometepe, Nicaragua

General Smotrov's headquarters on the volcanic island in the middle of Lake Managua sounded like it could host a Bond villain. In reality, it was rather mundane. There were radio facilities to help control the battles, but those were set up apart from the main bunker complex and then connected with landlines. The bunkers themselves offered little in the way of hospitality. Smotrov was fond of saying that in battle, survival was the ultimate luxury.

It was within one of these bunkers that one of Smotrov's Nicaraguan aides came to him with a report.

"It is active and moving, Comrade General," said the young corporal. The man had no idea what he was tracking, but he had been ordered to maintain a vigil at a terminal. When the terminal started to issue reports, he was to inform the general without delay.

"Very well, Corporal. I'll take it from here," said Smotrov, walking over to the terminal. After waiting for over a week, his patience was rewarded. He was well aware that his attack on the Contra compound at Yamales hadn't wiped out the entire presence in Honduras. There were so few bodies found on site that they knew the rebels had been tipped off and started an evacuation. Knowing that this was a possibility, the Soviet Spetsnaz troops had quickly modified two of the enemy's man-portable radios and left them in the rubble with the hopes that the Contras would return them to service.

At first, there had been no way to know if the Contras had failed to find the radios, or perhaps they'd thought they were beyond repair. They hadn't been used for days after the attack. But then two days ago, they had come to life. Smotrov's men had been able to triangulate the clandestine signal and pinpoint the location in the village of Capire, southwest of Yamales. Now and again, the radios would transmit a burst. Smotrov had surmised that they were testing the radios to ensure that they worked before sending them back into the field. Today was the first day that they had tracked any movement on those radios.

From the reports that were coming in, a Contra patrol was heading out from Capire, moving southeast. Smotrov and his Nicaraguan staff had determined the most likely objective of this patrol was their growing helicopter base outside of Ayapal. They had begun to put together a plan to ambush this team with the Mi-24 squadron; however, they soon lost all trace of the transmitter. Either the enemy had found it, in which case they'd likely abandoned the radio and their mission, or it had simply malfunctioned and the patrol was still inbound for Ayapal. Smotrov wanted that unit dead. It was clear to him that the Americans were working with them. It was probable that the CIA was involved, and removing any CIA assets from the board would greatly increase his chances of survival.

"We need to locate that patrol," said Smotrov. His Nicaraguan staff looked at him as though he were asking them to sprout wings and fly. As far as they were concerned, once the tracker stopped working, the Contra patrol might as well have vanished into thin air.

"What units do we have on hand that can locate that patrol?" he asked, trying to maintain his composure.

"We could send the helicopters, sir," replied a lieutenant. Smotrov put his hand to his face and ran his fingers across his brow and down his cheek, exasperated.

"We need to locate them without alerting them. If they know that we're after them, they could dig in, or withdraw. No, we need someone to make contact with that patrol and call in their location."

"There's a People's Militia unit in Ayapal," said a sergeant. "They know the terrain, and they've been tracking rebels in the area. I'm sure they could find this patrol for us."

"Thank you, Comrade Lieutenant," replied Smotrov. His use of the wrong rank came as a surprise to everyone at the table. The lieutenant who'd suggested using the helicopters to search for the patrol spoke up.

"Sir, he is a mere sergeant, begging your pardon."

Smotrov looked at the lieutenant with all of the regard he would give a fern.

"That is where you are wrong. He is a lieutenant. Give him your bars, Sergeant." The lieutenant stared at Smotrov as he walked away. Over his shoulder, Smotrov added, "And be quick about this, before I decide to make you a private."

Chapter 46

30 September 1980
Coco River
Honduras-Nicaragua Border

The war was off to a rocky start for the Contras. After the attack on the camp at Yamales, they had regrouped in Capire according to their preestablished plan. That was where they had gotten the news about the decimated task force in the Caribbean. The news was welcome to the Contras. They had practically celebrated when they'd realized that this would bring the full force of the American military onto their side. They thought for sure that they'd be marching in a parade down the streets of Managua by Christmas. It was only after the celebration had begun that they'd noticed that Carlos was oddly quiet.

"I had a lot of friends in that task force," he told them. "I understand why you're happy, and I know that this is going to help our cause in the long run, but right now I can't help but think about the Marines on those ships that died without even getting a chance to fight." Carlos prayed that Second Platoon had made it through. He'd never forgive himself if they had died after he'd left them.

Once the news had been received and everyone had settled down, they were in a holding position for a few days as Poole tried to get new tasking for the new situation. This had proven more difficult than expected. The Americans were bringing in elements of the US Army and Marine Corps to take the fight to the Nicaraguans. While the logistics of that effort were being worked out, they didn't have a lot of time to consider what to do with a rifle platoon attached to a CIA element in the middle of the fight, so they lay low while they could.

That respite had ended two days ago, and the unit was sent back to Ayapal. The Air Force was requesting targets for their 24th Tactical Air Support Squadron out of Panama. Carlos's Contra team was heading down to verify and mark the target for the incoming strike. Given the proximity of the target to the population center, they wanted to be sure of what they were hitting. The fact that the target was itself a school hadn't seemed to bother anyone. Their mission was to get into Ayapal and mark the target for the incoming air strike. This was all part of softening up the central highlands for a future assault. When that assault would occur was anyone's guess, but either way, the Contras were just happy to have a mission to help move the fight forward.

They had just crossed over the Coco River and into Nicaraguan territory and climbed back up out of the valley. They had followed the river as far east as they could before crossing. Now the river bent to the north, while they were heading south. They gave up the relative quick travel along the river for the slow going of the narrow jungle paths. As they pushed on, Carlos considered the past week. The United States was officially at war with Nicaragua. Congress had made that declaration at the request of the President. Poole had managed to pull some strings and find out that Kilo Company 3/6 had survived the attack on the task force, but he didn't have anyone who knew where they were at this point.

They were also short on information about what units were deploying to Honduras. Poole had a man who said with certainty that elements of the 1st Marine Division were coming down from Camp Pendleton, but that was pretty obvious. When asked about what elements of the Old Breed would be deployed, nobody had a clue. The first US Army units to arrive would likely be from the 101st Airborne Division with their new Blackhawk helicopters. For as much as the politicians wanted everyone to know that this "was not another Vietnam," the Army brass knew that the similarities in the terrain were real. Until those units could get into place, the US Air Force would pound the enemy wherever they could find them.

The patrol headed back down into another valley. They were heading for the Par Par River. This tributary of the Coco ran north-south and would take them in the general direction of Ayapal. They had cut across the hills to avoid crossing at the junction of the two rivers, which was a likely ambush spot along their route. They had settled on a path along the river as their pace increased and they moved deeper into enemy territory.

****

Clara Gálvez watched her sector along the Par Par River. She had worked out the location of their recon outposts with Arturo when they'd left Ayapal. The army command had told them that the enemy patrol was moving along the Coco and that they might be preparing to advance on Ayapal. Their mission was to intercept that patrol and track their movements with a radio beacon. This last part had been emphasized by the central command. The mission was to mark the location and movements of the enemy patrol. That had struck Clara as odd. Shouldn't the mission be to engage and destroy the enemy?

She thought about those inconsistencies and was working on a rationalization when movement caught her eye. There was a man moving down the river below. She held her breath for a second, afraid that she would give away her position, trying to will herself to blend into the surrounding vegetation as she watched the lone soldier make his way along the riverbank. If she had been on a normal ambush, she would have had the adrenaline rush of knowing that a firefight was just moments away. With this mission, she was just going to be watching. She gave her Soviet-made radio two quick clicks and waited.

After the point man had almost passed by her field of vision, the main body of the force passed. She counted ten men in the main element, with two more bringing up the rear. From this distance, she couldn't see anything about the patrol that stood out. It appeared to be a simple infantry squad moving in towards her home. *What makes this patrol so special?* she wondered.

Just over a mile downriver, Arturo activated the radio beacon to let the central command know that they had detected the enemy formation. The beacon broadcast a signal that was picked up by a Soviet satellite and relayed back to Smotrov's headquarters in Ometepe.

****

Ometepe Island
Nicaragua

"Sir, we're picking up a signal from one of the patrols," said newly minted lieutenant Javier Encarnación. General Smotrov looked up from the report he was reading.

"Where?"

"They are northwest of Ayapal, just like you predicted."

"Thank you, Lieutenant. Relay the coordinates to the air operations squadron. They are to commence the attack immediately."

Javier hesitated. He wondered why the general hadn't engaged the patrol with conventional forces. The militia patrol that was now tracking them would have been able to turn them back without too much effort. What Javier didn't know was that Smotrov's goal wasn't to win a tactical victory, or to prevent the Contra patrol from accomplishing their mission. His intent was to completely destroy that unit and take whatever American spy assets were in the area off the board. It would be well worth the cost of a Sandinista People's Militia squad to take out the CIA's eyes and ears in the field. It would be trading a pawn for a rook.

"Now, Lieutenant," said Smotrov, noticing Javier's hesitation. The lieutenant complied, lifting his telephone receiver and placing a landline call to the air operations unit.

****

Par Par River
Jinotega, Nicaragua

Detecting the Contra patrol was the easy part of the mission. Tracking them would be vastly more difficult. Clara was at the north end of the surveillance post, and she was to fall in behind the Contras as they passed heading south. The rest of the militia had turned to the south in an effort to stay ahead of the Contras, without giving away their position. It was a mission that would have been challenging for any unit. These citizen-soldiers did not have the training for it. They had managed to keep it together for about twenty minutes before Abram Secada tripped over an exposed root and slid fifteen feet down the side of the hill overlooking the river.

Both patrols froze at the sound. Luis Marqués was the point man for the Contras. He was the first to see Abram as he tried to scramble up the hill. Abram was unmistakably an enemy soldier. His uniform and the distinct shape of his AK-47 left no doubt about that. Without hesitation, Luis raised his M16 and flipped the selector from safe to semi. He lined up the panicked Abram, and immediately he felt the force of a 7.62mm round slam into his side. At that, the entire hillside opened up with incoming fire. As Luis fell dead, several of his squad mates returned fire in the direction of the incoming rounds. Both sides took immediate casualties as the opposing forces scurried for whatever cover they could find.

As the firefight developed, the Sandinistas had the advantage of the high ground, but the Contras had a better disposition. They were close enough to offer mutual support, while the Sandinistas were spread out in a much longer line.

At the north end of that line, Clara could hear the firefight begin but couldn't see anything. She had let the patrol completely pass her before following in order to ensure that she wasn't detected. Now she had to try and move downriver without blundering into an active firefight, and without the Contras detecting her approach.

At the south end of the Sandinista line, Arturo shouted orders to his men. He took two of them and crossed the slow-flowing river in an effort to flank the Contras. They were working their way north to engage from the east bank of the river when the sound of rotors filled the river valley.

****

Carlos heard the incoming helos. He and Juan Bolivar, the radioman, had been bringing up the rear of the patrol when the firing started. Juan was moving recklessly through the jungle to get to the fight while Carlos advanced methodically. The river valley made it impossible to pinpoint the location of the helicopters. Carlos quickly realized that the helos would most likely fly along the river to determine the exact location of their forces. That narrowed his focus as he continued to advance to contact with the enemy.

That focus saved Carlos's life. He caught the image of an Mi-24 Hind over his right shoulder as he checked behind him. He darted off to the right, into the jungle, as the Hind screamed overhead. A fraction of a second after the Hind passed, the valley was ripped with explosions as unguided rockets tore into the earth, trees and water. The attacking helicopters were indiscriminate in their killing. The first two Hinds made passes from the north and south with rockets. They fired in the general area of the firefight. After their first pass, they circled back while a second pair came in.

The sounds of explosions had drowned out the cries of the wounded and dying. As the sound of the explosions faded, Carlos could hear the agonizing sound of his wounded friends. He dashed towards his squad in the hopes that he would be able to pull some to safety. He never made it. His entire world went from green, to orange, to black.

Chapter 47

1 October 1980
White House
Washington, D.C.

The Oval Office was the scene of a constant flow of people and information. The daily briefings that kept the President up-to-date on all issues, foreign and domestic, had taken up more and more of his day. President Carter had insisted on maintaining these meetings in the Oval Office, despite the logistical constraints that presented. His staff had implemented an efficient process for cuing up the various presentations and their presenters, then getting them in the room, having them conduct their business, and getting them back out. They had an assembly line of data parading in front of Carter's desk each day.

"Mr. President," said Secretary of Defense Harold Brown, "we are nearing the force levels the JCS has requested to initiate offensive action in Nicaragua. The 1st Marine Amphibious Brigade is ready to depart from Coronado, and the 2nd MAB has assembled off the coast of Belize. We also have an eight-hundred-man detachment of Marines at the dirt airfield in Puerto Lempira. Those are the survivors from the 38th MAU."

"After that attack, should we consider withdrawing those Marines?" asked the President.

"No, sir. If I had to pick a single unit to send in, it would be those men. They've invested blood in this fight, and they need to be let out of their cage." The President nodded and motioned for Dr. Brown to continue. "We've moved the bulk of the 101st Airborne Division from Fort Campbell to Tegucigalpa and surrounding areas. We've also stationed the Air Force's 9th Tactical Fighter Squadron, 20th Tactical Air Support Squadron and the 91st Tactical Fighter Squadron in Panama. This will give us the air support that we need to conduct offensive operations in theater."

"I see. And we're confident that we don't need any of our heavier divisions in this action?" There had been considerable back-and-forth on the need to include an armored component to the invasion. From a tactical point of view, the terrain and force structure of the Sandinista armed forces meant that there wouldn't be a major role for armored divisions. From a purely political point of view, there was a push to bring out as much force as possible to ensure the American people knew that this wouldn't be "another Vietnam." It didn't help that Governor Reagan had been campaigning for the past two weeks about how the American response to Nicaraguan aggression hadn't been strong enough.

"No, Mr. President. Adding more firepower won't do much to improve our outcome here. Once we make inroads into Nicaragua, it will become apparent. Once the 1st MAB secures the beachhead on the west coast of Nicaragua, the 3rd Marine Tank Battalion will take Managua and the surrounding countryside."

"I understand what you're saying, Harry. I can see now how tempting it must have been for Lyndon Johnson to defer to civilian leadership on military matters. But I promised the Joint Chiefs that I would let them fight this war, and that's what I'm going to do. Where do we stand in Iran?"

"The situation on the ground is stabilizing somewhat. The Iraqis advanced through Khuzestan Province. After a quick pause to rearm and refuel once they had secured Khorramshahr, they made a push north towards Ahvaz. The Iranians gained air superiority, which caused the Iraqis to stop and shore up their defenses. It looks like they've moved considerable mobile SAM assets north to protect their advancing armored divisions."

"What about Soviet involvement?" asked the President.

"So far, we haven't been able to pinpoint any Soviet participation. We have some intelligence collection units tasked to ferret out any Russian transmissions, but so far they haven't come up with anything."

"And our own forces in the area?" asked Carter.

"We've worked out an agreement in principle to stage the 82nd Airborne Division out of Riyadh, Saudi Arabia. Right now they're packing up everything they set up in Cairo. This will put them much closer to the battlefield should the need arise to deploy them to Iran proper. So far the Iranians haven't formally requested our help, and with the battle on the ground slowing down, it doesn't look like they're going to. The Iraqi invasion has solidified the population behind the Bakhtiar government and I don't think they'll do anything to jeopardize that."

"Okay, Harry. Thanks for this. Let's get that offensive going in Nicaragua as soon as we can. The sooner we can get in, the sooner we can get out."

As Dr. Brown collected up his notes and headed out through the door on the right side of the room, Hamilton Jordan came in from the left and took the chair opposite Carter.

"Good morning, Ham. What do we have today?"

"I'm sure you're ahead of me on this, but the Georgia legislature finally held their vote on the ERA."

"Yes," said the President. "It passed one hundred and seven to one hundred and three. I was very pleased with the vote."

"And that's a wrap. We have a Twenty-Seventh Amendment to the Constitution. Congratulations, Mr. President. This is a big win for you, even if it is flying under the radar with the war taking all the headlines."

"Thanks, Ham, I couldn't have done it without you," replied the President.

"Mr. President," said Hamilton as he arranged his notes, "it looks like the lawsuit against the ERA extension will move forward." The court case in question had been filed by several states seeking to declare Congress's extension of the ratification deadline for the ERA unconstitutional. The general argument was that the Constitution had not granted any role in the amendment process to the executive branch. By signing the extension of the ratification deadline, the President had therefore acted contrary to the United States Constitution.

"Hmmm…" The President considered this. "We're winning on the merits, and now they want to use a procedural case to undo the will of the people."

"That's about the long and the short of it," replied Hamilton. "There's not much that we can do with that, but I just wanted you to be aware of it. I've talked to Tim about it, and he has a team working on possible debate responses should this come up."

"Tim has my ear right after you do. I'll be sure to bring it up when he gets here," said the President.

"Next, we have the economic data. It looks like we may have a solution on inflation. Volcker's raising of the prime rate to eighteen percent seems to have slowed inflation considerably. By our latest measures, inflation is sitting at eight percent, which is still too high, but considerably better than the fourteen percent we hit earlier in the year."

"I don't know how much I like an eighteen percent interest rate," said the President. "But at this point I'm just happy that we can report some success on this front. This could be enough to win back the confidence of the people in our economy."

"Inflation wasn't the only good news. There's also a bump in the Dow Jones. We've been on a fairly steady climb since March. That should also go towards adding confidence in the markets. Unemployment is down, and we expect that the surge in military enlistments will push it down further in the next report." Hamilton was referring to the sudden uptick in enlistments that had followed the Nicaraguan attack.

"That's good news all around, Ham. Anything else?"

"That's all we have this morning," said Jordan. "We have a few things working up for the afternoon, but nothing ready just yet."

Jordan took his leave and left the chair open for Tim Kraft, who came in and took his place.

"Good morning, Mr. President. This won't take long," said Kraft. Every member of the administration had gotten this process down to a science. "The polling is still strong on your handling of the Nicaraguans. It looks like going to Congress for a formal declaration of war has given you a lot of credibility with the people. Our success in Iran has also added to that. Support for military action in Nicaragua is polling at ninety-two percent. Unsurprisingly, support for military action in Iran has dropped again to a new low of thirteen percent, so we really need to downplay anything we have going on over there."

"These are solid numbers and, as you said, unsurprising," replied the President.

"We are seeing something regarding the ERA," said Kraft.

"Yes, Ham was just in here talking about that."

Kraft paused for a beat, confused. "Oh, that. No. This is related but different. Ham was talking about the debate prep, right? No, this was a one-off polling question that we put into a few of the questionnaires. We asked about support for a draft should it become necessary in Nicaragua. We returned a twenty-two percent favorable rating on that. When we asked about a gender-neutral draft, support dropped to four percent. Now, the sample size is very small at this point, but I think this is something that we need to be aware of."

"I see," said Carter. "I don't want to start talking about a draft. There's really no reason for that just yet. Things would have to go very wrong in Central America for that to happen."

"Nonetheless, I think this is something that we need to be prepared for. Reagan might even use it in the next debate. You need to be ready to hammer him if he does. That's what Ham was talking about. So far, my team believes that on the issue of the ERA as a whole, you should be fine. As we mentioned when we kicked off this campaign, overall, the people support the amendment. That's not an issue. If Reagan brings up the court filings in Idaho, we need to be aggressive. Let the world know he's using a flimsy legal technicality to get his way. We'd like to figure out how to get a *Dirty Harry* reference in there, since he's so fond of his days in Hollywood." Carter was dubious about the specifics of this tactic but continued to listen.

"If the governor mentions the draft angle of the ERA, we need to come at him for fearmongering. We need to insist that there's no need for a draft, there's no projected need for a draft, and that he's just trying to scare people into voting for him."

"That's easier said than done, Tim," said the President. "You won't be on the stage with that man. He knows how to debate, he's quick on his feet and nimble-witted. We've still got two weeks until the debate, so let's refine the pitch. But I will say I like the direction you're going. There's no reason to play defense right now—we need to take this fight directly to the GOP."

Chapter 48

1 October 1980
Par Par River
Jinotega, Nicaragua

Carlos wasn't sure if he was awake or dreaming. He couldn't see anything, but he could hear the sounds of the jungle. He could smell dirt. He blinked a few times, trying to clear his vision. He figured out that he was blindfolded as his brain woke up and processed the information his senses were delivering. He tried to move but found it difficult. After a brief struggle, he realized that he was tied at the wrists and ankles.

"Oh, you're awake," said a woman in Spanish. It was a voice that he didn't recognize. Before he could spend more than a few seconds trying to process that, he felt a sharp pain in his gut as he heard the sound of thick wood slamming into his belly. He'd been completely unprepared for the blow and immediately doubled over and retched.

"What the hell?" he yelled once he'd regained his voice.

"Shut your mouth if you don't want more of that," said the voice. Carlos was in some serious trouble. He immediately worked through his Survival, Evasion, Resistance, and Escape, or SERE, training. *I've messed up the whole "evasion" bit*, he thought. He hadn't managed to evade, but at least he had somehow survived. Carlos struggled to recall what had happened before he'd found himself here. He could remember the patrol crossing the Coco River. He remembered working their way down the Par Par. There was a firefight. It was a poorly set ambush. He rushed to engage the enemy. He saw the Hinds swoop in over the river… that was it.

"You've already lost the war," said the woman. "Why have you come back? Did you feel lucky because we didn't kill you the first time?"

Carlos was confused. His head was still fuzzy from his unconsciousness. In spite of his training, he blurted out, "I don't know what the hell you're talking about, lady." Then he braced for the next blow to his body. It never came. His eyes were suddenly blinded as his blindfold was ripped from his eyes. He winced at the sudden rush of light and squinted to give his eyes a chance to adjust.

"You're an American," said Clara in English. There was no denying that. His squad mates in the Contras had all given him a hard time over his Californian accent. His brain was catching up to reality at this point. He knew his backstory, and he knew he couldn't admit to being a United States Marine. He looked at his captor for the first time. She was dressed in green fatigues and wore a black beret on top of her shoulder-length black curls. Her black hair and soft features gave her face a girl-next-door look. It occurred to him that she would have been pretty but for the AK-47 she was pointing at him.

"Yes, yes, I'm an American. I'm a student from San Die—" Before he could finish the sentence, she raised the butt of the rifle, ready to slam it into him again. He shut his mouth.

"I don't care if you say you're the dean of the University of California, that's a bunch of BS and you know it. We both know it. I watched you out there, and you are a soldier. You are a part of the Contrarrevolución, and an invader of my country."

Well, that didn't take long, thought Carlos. He looked past her and could see his student visa, along with the rest of his gear, in a pile to the left of the woman. *So, she knew I was an American, but she's playing it close to her vest*, he thought.

"What are you doing here? And don't lie to me. I've lost a lot of friends out here and I want real answers."

She's not messing around, thought Carlos, trying to think of a way out of his predicament.

"Yes, I was a soldier once. I was in the US Army in Germany. When I got out and went back to school—" She raised the rifle. "Wait! Let me finish." She relaxed a bit. "I went back home to San Diego and went back to school. I'm a journalism student." She smashed the rifle butt down on his thigh. "Shit!" With his hands tied, he couldn't grab at his throbbing leg. "I heard about the Contrarrevolución in political science, and I thought I'd come down and do a story on it. I thought I'd be able to get some firsthand experience and write about it for my professors back home."

"And that's why you shot my friends?" she asked. "How stupid do you think I am?" There was no way Carlos would try to answer that question. Not so long as he was tied up, and she had the gun.

"Look, lady, I don't know what to tell you." She raised the rifle. He winced. "You can hit me all day long, but it won't change the truth," he insisted.

"Liar! You're an American and you're here to help the Contras and kill my people," she said with vehemence. "What are you doing here? What were you looking for?"

"Listen, I know what they were looking for," said Carlos. She relaxed again. "They were looking for the Russian helicopters. They thought they were in a village south of here. I don't know the name, it was… Aye something." He feigned enough ignorance to sell his lie.

"Ayapal," she finished for him.

"Yes! That's it. They said that the Russians had attacked them in Honduras and that they needed to find those helicopters. I went with them because I thought that would be an incredible story. With a story like that I could write my ticket for any newspaper in Southern California."

"And they just let you tag along?" she asked.

"I showed them I knew my way around an M16, and they were happy to have another gun." Her eyes narrowed.

"Another gun that you could use to kill my people."

"Oh, damn, lady, I was just trying to stay alive when the shooting started." She ignored his plea.

"It looks like your murderous friends found what they were looking for," she said. Carlos could see an opening.

"What happened? I was just running towards the sound of the fight when I was knocked out."

"Those helicopters came for you and destroyed everything in the valley. Everything except the two of us." Carlos could see her turn the situation over in her mind. Behind her eyes, he could see the conflict that she felt, knowing that her patrol had been deemed expendable. "None of your friends survived," she added.

Carlos considered telling her that they weren't his friends but didn't think it would make any difference. Instead, he thought he'd probe a bit more.

"They killed your entire squad too, didn't they?" he asked.

"What do you care?" she asked, practically spitting the words at him.

"I'm just a reporter. I care as much for your patrol as I did for the Contras. Please don't take offense to this, but your story is much more interesting than theirs was." As soon as the words were out, he wanted to take them back. Had he gone too far? She eyed him with suspicion.

“What is so interesting about a botched mission and a lost patrol?” she asked.

“They betrayed you. Whether or not it was by accident, your own military killed your people.”

“That wasn’t our military!” she snapped, clearly annoyed. Carlos withdrew as best he could before he pretended to have an epiphany.

“Oh, damn. Those were the Russians, weren’t they?” he asked.

Clara was exhausted. The mental, emotional, and physical stress of the past day had worn her down.

“Yes, the Russians,” she confirmed. Carlos remembered watching the Mi-8 unloading supplies in Ayapal. He remembered the white guys that had moved the crates into the school building. This was his first confirmation of what he’d known all along. Those bastards were Russian Special Forces. And now that he had that information, there wasn’t a damn thing he could do with it. Not so long as he was tied up.

“What are we doing?” he asked. “What do you want from me?”

****

Clara eyed the American as she considered it.

“I don’t know,” she admitted. She was out of her depth. Clara was a schoolteacher and a guerrilla soldier. She’d never had a prisoner before, and she didn’t know what to do with him. Moreover, she wasn’t sure she could go back to Ayapal. She wasn’t sure of anything. She’d hoped that the American would answer some of her questions, but instead she found herself just as lost as she had been when she’d found his unconscious body. After a few seconds, she made up her mind.

“I am Clara Gálvez of the Sandinista People’s Militia. You are my prisoner,” she concluded. “If you try to escape, I will shoot you before you get five meters away.”

“Please, you can’t take me to the Russians! They’ll say I’m a spy! They’ll torture me until I’m dead because I have no information to give them!”

“My God, quit whining,” she said with exasperation. “We’re not going back to Ayapal. We’re going to get back on the river. There are a few spots along the bank where we’ve hidden rafts. We’ll take the river for a while. Don’t worry about where we’re going, because you don’t have a choice.”

"Why don't you just let me go? I promise I won't go back to the Contras. As soon as I make it to a town, I'll find a way and get home."

"No way, Hollywood, you wouldn't last two days out there in the jungle. Besides, once I find out what's going on in my country, I want you to tell the story to your people in the United States."

Clara collected her gear and quickly realized that she needed to figure out what to do with Carlos's equipment. She took his M16 and all the magazines she could find for it. She slung the rifle and packed the mags in her backpack. Then she detached the long magazine from her AK and pulled the charging handle to eject the chambered round. Once the rifle was empty, she pushed a button on the rifle behind the bolt. This allowed the top cover of the firing mechanism to pop off. She then removed a long spring from inside the rifle and added it to her already full backpack. Having rendered the gun inoperable, she reassembled it and hung it around Carlos's neck. She then took a strap of his ALICE pack and hung that around his neck as well.

When Carlos protested, she told him, "Either you carry that, or we leave it, and I will not untie you."

"Can you at least pull the strap over one of my shoulders? I can't breathe," he said.

She made the accommodation, and the two started north along the Par Par back to the Coco River. Clara had decided that she would make her way east, to her uncle Pedro in Puerto Cabezas on the Atlantic coast. She needed to connect with someone she could trust. Pedro was a scoundrel, but her father's brother was a loyal scoundrel. He'd survived the revolution, and the Sandinistas generally left him alone. In exchange for a peaceful coexistence, Pedro Gálvez had agreed to retire from his import-export business and give the government his port facilities and his workforce of longshoremen and mariners. If she could get to Pedro, she could figure out what to do next. But could she make it the three hundred miles while escorting her prisoner?

Chapter 49

7 October 1980
Coco River
Nicaragua

The break that Carlos had been praying for never came. He knew that the area along the border was sparsely populated, but he hadn't fully appreciated exactly how few people there were until he was desperate to find one of them. For six days, he and his Sandinista captor traveled along the river. As promised, the pair found a raft along the banks of the Coco. Since then, they'd gone east with the flow of the river.

Carlos racked his brain, trying to remember the geography he had studied back in Georgia. He knew that eventually the Coco would flow into the Atlantic. But he couldn't think of any major cities between here and there. He suspected that there were just small fishing villages along the path. They'd passed one on the first day. His captor simply smiled and waved to a family on shore as the pair drifted by. She'd told him before that if he made any noise, she'd push him off the raft and shoot him in the water. Carlos was brave, but the thought of drowning while bleeding to death was horrifying.

A few days ago, Carlos couldn't remember exactly when, he'd heard the *thump-thump-thump* of helicopters, but he never caught sight of them. Occasionally, he could see the contrails of an airplane flying at high altitude. But that was it. In this quiet river valley, there was no sign that the two nations were at war.

"Listen," said Clara, breaking the hours-long silence. "We're about to get off the river. I need you to understand your position here. You are my prisoner. I will shoot you dead before I let you get away to go back and kill more of my people." Carlos had heard this speech several times before. He wondered if she was trying to convince herself. "I will do all the talking, and you will keep your mouth shut. If someone asks you a question, you don't answer; you look at me and I'll answer it for you. If you can follow these rules, I promise that when we get to where we are going, I'll untie you, and you can start working on your story."

It took Carlos a second to process that last part. Fortunately, he didn't let on. He'd momentarily forgotten that he was posing as a journalism student. That was exactly the kind of slip that could get him killed.

"I understand, thank you" was all he said. She'd made it clear that there wasn't going to be any conversation over the past six days. Every time he would try to establish a rapport with her, she would tell him to shut his mouth. Then she would usually issue some kind of threat.

Using a long pole, Clara guided the raft to the south bank of the river. As they neared the river's edge, she jumped out of the raft and pulled it to shore. Carlos awkwardly scrambled off the raft and made his way ashore while Clara dragged the wooden vessel into the grass. Grabbing her rifle and pack, she made her way into the tree line and found a path that led them away from the river.

"You seem to know your way around," said Carlos. As he expected, his comment was met with silence. He thought about that, though. She knew where to make landing and she knew right where this path was. It was possible, even probable, that every decent landing had a south-leading trail. But there was something about the confidence she showed. There was no hesitation, no looking for the exact spot. *No*, he decided. *She's been here before, and often.*

They followed the trail for about half a mile before the trees opened up to a road with a small collection of houses on it. Clara approached the first house. Before she reached the door, she turned to Carlos.

"You need to stay here. If you run, I will shoot you in the back." Then she turned back to the house and knocked on the door. An older woman answered the door, and the two entered into a hushed conversation that Carlos couldn't hear. After a minute, the old woman pointed down the road along the direction they were already traveling. Clara thanked her and came back to him.

"Let's go," she said, motioning for Carlos to move along the road. He considered his options. On the river, he hadn't had many. He couldn't swim with his hands tied and weighed down with gear. But now, on terra firma, he might stand a better chance of getting into the jungle, then working his way north. He worked his wrists a bit to see if he could loosen the knot. After a few minutes of walking, they came across a gas station.

"Wait here," repeated Clara before walking into the station. He watched as she talked to a man behind the counter. She pointed back at him, and Carlos began to get nervous about his immediate future. Again, he strained at the knot that held his wrists together. He could feel a bit of slack. Or was it his imagination? He kept his eyes on the gas station, where he could see Clara making a phone call. He surmised that this was the only phone in town. Clara exited the station and sat down in the shade with her back against the wall.

"We'll wait here," she said. It was clear from her tone that she felt that was sufficient explanation.

She looks tired, thought Carlos. *That's good. I can use that.*

"What are we waiting for?" he asked.

"All you need to worry about," she replied, "is staying alive long enough to find out."

"That gets right to the point, doesn't it?" he asked.

"Stop talking. I don't care what you have to say."

Carlos wanted to keep a conversation going in order to help mask his attempts to undo his binding, but he didn't want to annoy her so much that she paid closer attention to him either. There didn't seem to be a good way out for him here. They waited in the shade, saying nothing. After the first hour gave way to the second, Clara was nodding off.

Carlos had scoped out the area around the gas station. Based on his travels so far, he estimated that he was only about a mile from the Coco River, and somewhere between twenty to forty miles from the Atlantic coast. His quickest escape route looked like it would be behind the station, then to cut north for the border. Once he got across the river, he could worry about making his way east. With any luck, a friendly village would help him out. He still had his ALICE pack, but he was nearly out of food after the past week in the field. He'd have to figure something out on that front.

He looked over at Clara, who was now completely asleep. During the past five days, he'd never seen her out cold like this. *I suppose she's just out of gas. It's time for you to outlast your opponent, Marine*, he thought as he wiggled the knot at his wrists. He twisted his left hand and finally managed to get his thumb under the loop. Now it was just a matter of—

"What are you thinking about, killer?" came a voice from behind him. Carlos whipped around and saw a man—the man from behind the counter—pointing an old revolver at him.

"Hey, whoa, easy," said Carlos, taking in the depths of his new situation.

"Yes, killer. It would be very easy to shoot you dead right here. But she"—he gestured past Carlos with the gun, in the direction of Clara—"told me to keep you here."

"Going somewhere?" asked Clara. He spun back around towards her.

"No, I… the knot was just tight. I wanted to get the blood moving." Everything went black and it took a second for Carlos to put together that the man behind him had put a sack over his head. He was out of options. Now he just had to wait and see how the situation unfolded.

Carlos couldn't be sure, but he thought it was another half hour before he heard the sounds of an approaching vehicle. The dirt road gave way and the vehicle came to a stop. He heard the door open, then close, followed by another.

"Clara! My dear," said a man in Spanish. "What are you doing here? I thought you were teaching out where the devil lost his poncho."

"Ayapal isn't in the middle of nowhere," replied Clara. "But, yes, it is much more remote than you are used to."

"This place is too remote for me, but when Enrique told me that you were here and needed help, I had to come and see it for myself. I like your fashion sense. *Très chic*. And you really know how to accessorize." Several people laughed at that, and it took Carlos a second to realize that he was Clara's accessory. "Now that I've seen what you're into, let's get you back to civilization."

With that, Carlos was jerked to his feet and led to the car, where he was stuffed inside. Doors closed, and Carlos was pushed against the door as the car made a tight left turn.

A voice came from behind him, "You're in a real situation, kid," said the man who had greeted Clara. "You have run afoul of my niece and she has brought you to me. My name is Pedro Gálvez. I need you to understand something right up front: I am not a man to be trifled with. I do not play games and I will not suffer a fool. When we get to where we are going, we are going to cut through all of the BS and get to the bottom of this."

With that, the man shifted his conversation to Clara. The radio came on, and the sound muffled the conversation in the back seat. As far as he could tell, though, they were talking about family issues and not about him. He wasn't sure if that was a good or a bad sign. *Pedro Gálvez*, thought Carlos. *Why do I know that name?*

After what felt like hours, the trip came to an end. Carlos was hauled out of the car and his hood was removed. The afternoon sun stung his eyes and he had to blink repeatedly as they teared up. He looked around and saw this Pedro Gálvez. He wasn't particularly tall, or fit, but there was a predatory look to the man. Carlos imagined that when he was younger, this man had been a brawler. His attention shifted to the driver, who had retrieved an M16 from the trunk of the car.

"You smell like an ass," said Pedro. "It's going to take a week to get the smell out of my car." He turned to the man standing by the driver's door. "Enrique, show our guest to his cell and let him get cleaned up." Enrique took Carlos's hands and slipped a knife between them, cutting the knot that had kept him bound for so long. The relief of having full use of his arms was cut short by Pedro's admonition.

"Don't get too excited, Mr."—he looked at Carlos's student ID—"Rodriguez. The high walls and the guards will keep you in just as well as they keep the government out." With that, Pedro took Clara by the arm and the two strode away towards a two-story plantation house at the far end of a rectangular reflecting pool.

"Hey, Yankee," called out Enrique, grabbing Carlos's attention. "You're over here." Carlos looked down at the rifle, then to the man's eyes as he nodded in the direction of a separate building. Enrique lifted a handheld radio and spoke into it, but Carlos couldn't quite make out what was being said. He followed Enrique into what looked like a small apartment unit. Enrique stopped in front of a door and jerked his head at it. "You can use this one for now. There's a shower, and some fresh clothes. Don't think about running. Señor Gálvez is right. You are not the first person we've kept here. The only hope you have is cooperating. Your only other option is death."

****

8 October 1980
Puerto Lempira, Honduras

"Just because you say it over and over again don't make it true," said the newly promoted Lance Corporal Oliver.

"You're not even giving him a chance, man," said Palmer.

"Look, Mouthwash," replied Oliver, "I don't have to. Bon Scott was the best front man in all of rock and roll. There's no way this whiney midget is going to take his place." The debate on the beach had been raging for an hour now, but it had really been simmering for the past three months since the release of AC/DC's album *Back in Black.* Most of the Marines could agree that Brian Johnson was an adequate replacement for the dead rocker, but Oliver wasn't one of them. The more they argued, the more he dug in. Oliver knew that the real reason he had no use for *Back in Black* was because he missed his friend Benny Estrada.

Benny and Bon had both left his life in the same month. While Scott had died mysteriously in London, there was no mystery in what had happened to Estrada. His wounding during the Eagle Claw operation had taken him out of 3/6 Marines. The replacements had come in, and Estrada would land somewhere else when he got out of the hospital. But with all the dumb adventures he and Oliver had gone through, Oliver figured it was a sign. He would let AC/DC belong to his past. *Besides, I'm sure these guys will burn out in a few years*, he thought.

"You haven't even listened to the whole album," said Palmer.

"I don't need to. You retards keep playing that 'you shook me' song constantly. I'm done with this conversation." Oliver stood up and shook the sand off his pants. He looked south, along the coastline, wondering when they were going to get orders to get back into the fight. Kilo Company had been sitting on this patch of beach since they'd relocated from Banco Chinchorro, where they had been marooned after the Nicaraguan attack. Since then, it had been the normal "hurry up and wait." Monotonous boredom, punctuated by the threat of imminent action, and broken up by the occasional beach party like tonight.

Oliver made his way over to the cooler and grabbed a Budweiser. He caught himself humming along to "Hell's Bells" and sighed. He wasn't going to get away from this album.

"Hey, Lance Corporal," called out Corporal Evans, Oliver's team leader. "Grab me one, will ya?" Oliver grabbed a beer and handed it over, wondering when Evans was going to lean into him for some infraction or another. "Hey, look. I know that I've given you some shit since I came over to Second Squad. But I wanted you to know that you've really proven yourself through the evacuation and the relocation. I really think our team is the best in the squad, and you have a lot to do with that."

Evans popped the top of his beer and took a pull before continuing. "You still have a terrible attitude and your utter lack of bearing is pathetic. But you're a good Marine, and I know I can count on you. Anyhow, that's all I wanted to say. Now, don't get too drunk. We've got PT in the morning."

"Drunk PT is the best PT, Corporal," replied Oliver with a grin. Evans walked away, shaking his head.

****

8 October 1980
Puerto Cabezas
Nicaragua

Carlos awoke to a pounding on the door. He looked around the room. It was simple and clean. Not exactly a first-class resort, but definitely the nicest jail he'd ever seen. *No, it's clearly not a jail. But what the hell is it?* he wondered.

"Let's go, jackass. The boss wants to see you," said the voice behind the door. Carlos recognized it as Enrique's.

The boss... Pedro Gálvez... why is that name so familiar? he thought.

"I've got it. Just give me a second," said Carlos. He climbed out of the exceptionally comfortable bed and crossed the room to the dresser, where he found a red Hawaiian shirt and some white linen pants to put on. He had also been provided with a pair of huarache sandals to complete the ensemble. *My God, I look like a total dork*, he thought as he headed to the door.

Enrique led him into the courtyard, where he had parted ways with Clara and Pedro the day before. This time, they turned to the right and headed towards what appeared to be the main house on the compound. When they approached the building itself, they saw Pedro sitting on a patio, with Clara sitting next to him and a fantastic spread of food on the table in front of them.

"Ahh, Sergeant Rodriguez! Thank you for coming," said Pedro with a wide smile. Carlos's heart sank.

"Thank you, sir, but nobody calls me Sergeant since I left the Army."

"Tsk. You mean the Marine Corps," replied the Nicaraguan.

As his mind went into panic mode, it suddenly occurred to Carlos. *Oh, dammit. Pedro "El Tiburón" Gálvez is the Nicaraguan shark who moves cocaine from Ecuador into the Caribbean and then on to Florida.* His name had come up in a file of notable people affected by the Sandinista takeover. The rise of the new government had caused the end of his drug-running operations.

Pedro read from a file in front of him, "Sergeant Carlos Miguel Rodriguez, United States Marine Corps. Born February eighth, 1953. Died…" He looked up at Carlos, who had no idea how to react.

"How… I don't… I'm a student from—"

"You are a former Marine who is working for the American government and assisting the Contrarrevolución in their efforts to overthrow the Sandinista National Liberation Front."

Carlos looked at Clara. She stared back with a cold look that made him swallow.

"There's no use in denying any of this. These are facts that we both know to be true. The sooner you accept that, the better off our relationship will be. But, please, have a seat. Eat. I know you've been in the field for a while and I thought you would enjoy breakfast."

Carlos looked at Enrique, but the man simply nodded at his boss, turned and walked away. Carlos uneasily took a seat at the table.

"Tell me, Carlos—do you mind if I call you Carlos?" The Marine nodded his assent. "When you were in Iran, what was that like? We here in Nicaragua heard some of the stories about the raid on the embassy, but I've never actually met anyone who was there."

Carlos knew that this had to be Pedro ensuring that the file he had was detailed and accurate. He swallowed hard and said, "I wasn't actually at the embassy. My unit was responsible for capturing the airfield that we used to extract the hostages." Pedro nodded, and Carlos got the suspicion that he had just passed some kind of test.

"We do not know each other," continued Pedro, "so you will have to take me at my word when I tell you this. The three of us want the same thing." At that, Clara's head whipped towards her uncle. "We want those Russian bastards out of here. I promised the Sandinistas that I would disband my forces and I would go into a nice and quiet retirement. With such a paradise to retreat to, it seemed like an easy plan." He gestured grandly at the surrounding compound. "That deal, however, was rendered null and void when they tried to kill my favorite *pollita* here." He put his hand on Clara's shoulder. "When they did that, they called me out of retirement."

It was finally coming together for Carlos, who looked over to Clara, who returned his look with the same coldness that he'd come to expect.

"I am choosing to forget that just days ago, you were trying to kill her and her unit." Carlos started to protest. "Don't," continued Pedro, raising his right hand. "We need all the cards on the table. You can apologize if you'd like, but I doubt it will do much good. She gets her stubbornness from my brother."

"It wasn't anything personal, Ms. Gálvez. I just had a job to—"

"Don't waste your time, Mr. Rodriguez. It was very personal to me."

"Oh, and it better be personal for you as well, Carlos," said Pedro. "You are neck-deep in a guerrilla war against the Soviet occupation of Nicaragua. You won't last long out here without developing a deep and personal hatred for these bastards." Pedro spat on the ground to emphasize his point. "I have made the calls, and I have begun to gather my boys. They have been restless for these past few months."

Enrique approached the table and said, "Sir, your other guest has arrived."

"Thank you. Please, send him in."

Carlos was expecting one of Pedro's "boys" and was shocked when instead, Fred Poole took the chair next to his.

"You know, Carlos," said Fred, "they don't pay overtime at the Agency."

"What are you doing here?" asked Carlos.

"With the war in full swing, I'd already made contact with Mr. Gálvez—"

"Please, call me Pedro."

"I had already been in contact with Pedro about getting him involved with the fully armed and US-led Contrarrevolución. He told me, if I recall, to 'go fuck a fish.'"

"No, Fred, I told you to go get fucked by a fish. There's a difference."

"Be that as it may, Pedro declined my offer. So imagine my surprise yesterday when I got a call asking if I'd lost one of my spies." Fred stopped explaining and took a long look at Carlos. "What the hell are you wearing?"

"It was either this or my fatigues with two weeks' worth of filth," said Carlos.

"Hey, he looks relaxed. I like it," replied Pedro.

"Long story short, thanks to your recruiting efforts, El Tiburón has had a change of heart, and now we have a war to plan."

"I wasn't really recruiting. It was just dumb luck," said Carlos.

"That's not the way I'm going to write it up in the report. Hell, after the week you've had, you deserve to have things break your way." With that resolved, the four of them began planning out how El Tiburón's forces could most effectively rearm themselves and engage the enemy.

Chapter 50

14 October 1980
Isla del Venado
Nicaragua

Carlos raised the binoculars and again scanned the container yard at the port facility in El Bluff. The uninhabited Isla del Venado sat in Bluefields Bay, in between the town of El Bluff and the town of Bluefields. Within twenty-four hours, the United States Marine Corps was going to assault both towns. Fred Poole's Contra force had been sent to the area to find and destroy the Nicaraguan SA-8s that had given the Air Force a hard time on the first day of the war.

Since that day, the Air Force had conducted several Suppression of Enemy Air Defense, or SEAD, missions. They were unable to locate the mobile missile launchers. It didn't appear that the Nicaraguans were interested in exposing those units. Everyone knew that once an invasion was imminent, those SAM launchers would reappear. It was up to Carlos and the ruthless men of El Tiburón to make sure that as soon as they showed up, they would be destroyed.

"Hey, Hollywood," said Enrique, El Tiburón's right-hand man, using the nickname that Clara had given him. "The team in Bluefields has a lead on something. The locals don't know why, but the government has pushed them out of Gun Boat Creek. That area used to be open for fishing, but government men have shut it down and are patrolling it full-time."

"Roger that, Enrique. Do you think we can slip past their guards?" asked Carlos.

"Hey, man, we're more of a blunt instrument. You and your *blanco* are the sneaky ones," replied Enrique, referring to Fred.

Damn, I really should have put in for Force Recon training when I had the chance, thought Carlos. With that, he walked over to the radio table and keyed the mic.

"Albacore, this is Tiburón Two, over." Carlos was calling Fred Poole, who had set up his operational headquarters at El Tiburón's lavish hacienda.

"Tiburón Two, this is Albacore," replied Fred.

"Albacore, can we get a KENNEN pass over the area?" asked Carlos, referring to the state-of-the-art KH-11 spy satellite.

"Tiburón, Albacore. We can ask, but I can promise you we don't rate a KENNEN pass."

"Understood, Albacore. Do what you can, but I need eyes on"—he consulted his map—"twelve degrees, zero-one minutes, twelve point seven seconds north by eighty-three degrees, forty-six minutes, fifty-four point nine seconds west."

"Don't hold your breath, Tiburón, wait one."

Carlos looked over to Enrique. The man didn't speak a word of English and just raised his eyebrows, questioning.

"We're going to see about getting a satellite to take some pictures of the area, to see what we can see."

The radio came back to life. "Tiburón, this is Albacore. That's a negative on KENNEN or Big Bird," said Fred, referring not only to the KH-11 but the older KH-9 satellite. "The Army has priority tasking, and we're on the outside looking in. I think I can get something just as good. Stand by."

Enrique looked at Carlos inquisitively. Carlos shook his head.

"He thinks we have a chance at something. Now we just wait."

The two men raised their binoculars and went back to scanning the shoreline a mile away. After about fifteen minutes of searching, the radio crackled again.

"Tiburón, this is Albacore."

"Albacore, this is Tiburón. Go ahead," replied Carlos.

"Good news, amigo. The Navy is sending an RF-8 over your patch of land to see what's out there."

"Understood, Albacore, but doesn't that seem risky? I mean, you told them what we're looking for, right?"

"That's affirmative, Tiburón. The Navy deems this to be a top priority. Besides, those Crusaders are so fast, they'll be in and out before those SAM launchers even know it. And if those SA-8s do light up their radars, I'm sure there are some ARMs out there just waiting for the chance to take them out."

"Roger that, Albacore, ETA on that pass?"

"Patience, Tiburón, these things take time. Don't worry, when they make the pass, you won't miss it. They'll have to RTB and unload the film, but we'll know something soon. Now, before we commit to this, are you one hundred percent sure that this is where you want eyes?"

The weight of the question hit Carlos. When this had started, he had just been looking at spending a million dollars of Uncle Sam's money to move a satellite. Now he was asking a man to risk his life getting this information.

"Albacore, yes. This is what we have. It might be a dry hole, but we have to have a look." As soon as the words were out of his mouth, he was at peace with them. He'd had a decision to make based on the information at hand. He'd made that decision, and now it was in the past.

Just over an hour later, while Carlos was again scanning El Bluff, he was shocked as a sonic boom shook the ground. Belatedly, Carlos looked to the west and could see a speck fleeing the scene of the crime. He raised his binoculars and could definitely make out the shape of the fleeing aircraft. He didn't know the American order of battle very well, but he assumed that this was the Crusader that Poole had promised. To his great relief, there were no indications of any SAM response to the overflight.

Two hours later, Poole called it in.

"Tiburón, this is Albacore, over."

"Albacore, this is Tiburón, go ahead."

"Jackpot, Tiburón. The imagery clearly shows Soviet-made armored vehicles, and the Navy believes that you've located an SA-8 nest. Given the terrain, the intel brains think the plan is to deploy those launchers to the peak five hundred and twenty-five meters due west of the location you spotted. They've cleared the peak of timber, and it's a prime spot for air defense. That's the good news."

"Albacore, why do I have the feeling the other shoe is going to drop?"

"Tiburón, because you're going to have to cover that peak tomorrow. You need to be Johnny-on-the-spot to paint those SA-8s with the laser designator."

"Roger, Albacore, understood. Tiburón out."

Carlos walked from the radio table to his pack and retrieved the AN/PAQ-1. He'd never used one before and had only minimal training on the unit in his hands. It looked like a short rifle, but instead of firing a projectile, it fired a high-intensity laser. He would have to get as close as possible to that peak and point this "rifle" at the Soviet hardware. It was the only way to neutralize a threat to his Marine Corps brothers who would assault the beach tomorrow.

"We've got to pack up, Enrique. We're redeploying shoreside." Carlos pointed to the west. "I think we've found what we're looking for."

****

15 October 1980
USS *Mount Whitney*
25 Miles off the East Coast of Nicaragua

Colonel Jermain Hodges stood at the main plot in the CIC of the amphibious command ship USS *Mount Whitney*. The commander of the 6th Marine Regiment watched as his plan unfolded before him.

"Sir," said a Marine at the radio, "India Company has completed the first landings at the FARP. No contact with the enemy." That was a good first sign. The Marines were establishing a forward arming and refueling point, or FARP, in Nicaragua. They were rallying there, then conducting an attack on Bluefields from the north.

The Navy had EA-6B Prowler electronic warfare aircraft flying along both coasts of Nicaragua in an attempt to jam any and all radar in the country. F-14 Tomcats escorted the Prowlers in case the Nicaraguans had any airborne surprises for them. There were also AGM-45-armed A-7 Corsairs, ready to destroy any fire control radars, like those on the SA-8s that had shot down some of the Air Force A-7s on the opening day of the war.

"Any unusual activity in the area surrounding the FARP?" asked the colonel.

After a pause, the radioman replied, "Negative, sir. It's a very remote location."

That's the whole point of putting the FARP there, thought Hodges, but he spared the man his wrath. This was going to be a long day, and everyone needed to work together as a team. Hodges looked at the map and traced a line from the FARP to the airfield at Bluefields. While the FARP was being set up, the USS *Saipan* and the USS *Iwo Jima* were preparing their helicopters. The Marines would hit the airfield from two sides simultaneously. Kilo Company, 3/6 Marines would hit the field from the south, while Lima Company, 3/6 Marines would assault from the west. With the airfield secured, they could rapidly bring in reinforcements from the US.

While this was happening, there would be a simultaneous attack on the port of El Bluff, five miles east of the airfield. The attack on El Bluff was already underway. Marine Recon units stole into the country under the cover of darkness. They remained in hiding while taking hydrographic and beach surveys to prepare for waves of landing craft hitting the shore. When combined with the 1st Marine Division's assault on the west coast, this would be the largest amphibious operation since the Inchon landing in the Korean War.

****

Carlos heard a popping sound off in the distance. He strained his ears, trying to figure out what it was. It was constant and rhythmic. *Pop-pop-pop*—it was like someone lighting off a string of firecrackers.

"Hey, Hollywood," said Enrique, "what is that?"

"I'm not sure, it could be—" Carlos was cut off by a massive explosion in the valley below them. Then another, and another. A seemingly endless string of explosions erupted in the Gun Boat Valley. Carlos looked to his left and saw more explosions bursting around the airfield.

"It's naval gunfire support!" yelled Carlos over the chaos. "They're hitting suspected enemy positions, including our friends in the valley. Even if they don't destroy the SA-8s, they'll definitely drive them out of hiding, so we need to stay sharp." The rounds were dropping a thousand meters away. *This isn't exactly "danger close," but it's close enough*, thought Carlos.

Looking through his binoculars, Carlos focused on the peak to his north. Then he slowly traced a line back to the creek. There was a thick layer of smoke settling in the valley, which made his job more difficult. Even so, with the smoke shifting and billowing, he thought he caught movement.

"Enrique, two o'clock, low in the valley." Carlos kept his eyes on the contact to make sure this was what he was hunting. The smoke shifted again and he watched as an armored behemoth crashed out of the forest and onto the dirt road leading to the hilltop. The large radar dish on top of the vehicle convinced Carlos to drop his binoculars and raise the laser designator.

"Panther Three, this is Tiburón Two."

"Tiburón Two, copy."

"Panther Three, the target is illuminated."

"Copy that, Tiburón, moving to the release point."

High in the skies above Carlos and Enrique, an A-6E from Attack Squadron 35, or VA-35, had been flying offshore, waiting for this call. VA-35 was the first A-6 squadron equipped with the Target Recognition Attack Multisensor, or TRAM. The TRAM could read the laser that Carlos was pointing at the enemy vehicle. It would then transmit that location to the Paveway II five-hundred-pound bomb, which would then "ride" the beam all the way to the target. It was imperative that Carlos keep the laser on the target.

Sweat dripped from his forehead as the tension rose.

"Hollywood! We've got a problem," called Enrique. "There's another one of those things coming this way." Carlos ignored his companion, focusing on painting the target.

"Didn't you hear me?" asked Enrique. "We've got to get the hell out of here."

"I'm staying here until that tank explodes. I don't have a choice," said Carlos. He could feel the ground rumbling, but he couldn't hear the sound of the vehicle's engine over the violence surrounding him.

"Dammit!" said Enrique. "I'll see if I can slow it down."

"To hell with that. Just take cover. Hell, get off this hill. Once our guys find this launcher, they're going to turn this hill into death itself!"

Enrique grabbed a light antitank weapon, or LAW, and ran for the jungle towards the threat.

"Tiburón, Panther Three, weapon released. Hold on tight, this is going to move some earth." The five-hundred-pound bomb was over five times the size of the naval gunfire rounds falling in the area.

"Roger, Panther Three, good hunting today," replied Carlos. He knew it would take about thirty seconds for the bomb to cross the twenty thousand feet between the A-6 and the target. He heard machine-gun fire open up behind him, but he didn't turn. There was an exchange of gunfire, then the whoosh that he assumed was Enrique firing the LAW. The explosion that followed was obscured by the five-hundred-pound Paveway II eliminating the launcher to the north.

Carlos rolled to his left and jumped up just as a burst of rifle fire hit where he had been lying. He darted down the hill, away from the enemy, in order to buy enough time to get his rifle ready. He could still hear firing behind him, and as soon as he was clear, he repositioned to the south and approached the hilltop. As he neared the clearing he had just run away from, he could see the SA-8 launcher. From what he could tell, it looked like Enrique had taken out its left track with the LAW.

Carlos raised his M16 and took aim at one of the crewmen. *This dude's whiter than Fred*, he thought before squeezing the trigger. The man fell over and crawled under the vehicle. Carlos ducked down and moved back towards his previous position. This time when he scanned the battlefield, he was looking for Enrique. The two of them had the crew pinned down, but they were still outnumbered. He found Enrique just in time to see him catch a round to the chest and fall.

"To hell with this," Carlos said to nobody. He pulled an M18 smoke grenade from his vest, pulled the pin and threw it towards the disabled SAM launcher.

"Panther Three, this is Tiburón. I'm marking a target for you, seven hundred meters due south of the original."

"Negative, Tiburón, I'm not receiving any signal," replied the bombardier in the A-6.

Carlos was bolting down the hill through the jungle as he replied, "I'm marking it the old-fashioned way. There's grape smoke on the hill, you can't miss it. I'm fleeing the scene of the crime, out."

"Understood. Stay safe, Tiburón, we'll cover your exit."

Carlos continued to move south until he heard the devastating explosion on the hilltop. He knew he wasn't out of the fire yet. If those were Soviet Spetsnaz, they knew that launcher was as good as dead as soon as the first purple smoke wafted near it. They would likely be regrouping with their unit, and Carlos had no idea where that would be. He could easily run into them on the hill.

"Tiburón Two, this is Albacore, over."

"This is Tiburón Two. Albacore, I'm currently cut off from my unit. I can confirm one KIA, but I don't have any information on the rest of the team."

"Understood, Tiburón—by the way, congratulations. The mission was a success."

“Be sure to tell my daughter all about it at the funeral,” replied Carlos.

“Tiburón, I read you. Try to keep a low profile until the shooting is over, and we’ll get someone out there to extract you.”

“Negative, Albacore. I’m going to make my way down to the airfield. It’s about a mile and a half from my position. I’ll try to hook up with friendly forces there.”

“Roger, Tiburón. How do you know there’ll be friendly forces at the airfield?”

“Albacore,” said Carlos with exasperation, “it’s an airfield. Of course we’re going to capture it to bring in follow-on forces.”

“Roger that, Albacore out.”

Carlos thought he could hear some embarrassment in Poole’s sign-off. Now he just needed to cross a mile and a half of jungle while evading the locals and Soviet special forces, then hope he didn’t get shot by his own people when he made contact.

Chapter 51

20,000 Feet Over Corinto
Western Nicaragua

Samuel "Pharaoh" Bell got an adrenaline rush from the SEAD mission. As a Corsair pilot, you almost had to. The light airframe and relatively low payload meant that carrying a pair of AGM-45 Shrike antiradiation missiles, or ARMs, was a natural fit. During his last combat sortie in Iran, he was carrying a more conventional load-out of cluster bombs. This time, the missiles he carried were specifically designed to home in on enemy radar emissions. If a radar were to energize, the Royal Maces of VA-27 would detect it and engage it with ARMs.

This gave Pharaoh an adrenaline rush because, if the radar was energized, not only could the Maces see the radar, the radar could see the Maces. The enemy that they were hunting was also hunting them. Then it was a race to see who would be the predator and who would be the prey.

Pharaoh panned his head around, taking in the skies. There were no reports of expected enemy air activity. The Air Force had confirmed that the entire air threat had been eliminated. That meant that they had destroyed all four of the antique T-33 Shooting Star jet trainers that made up the Nicaraguan "Air Force." Even so, he needed to keep his head on a swivel. After the shock the Navy had gotten back in August, he wouldn't be surprised if the Russkies had sent over a MiG or two.

But the skies at altitude were nearly empty. Most of the action was going on below them, closer to where the Marines were amassing troops to take the beach. His wingman, Rex "King" Collier, was the only other thing in the skies with him.

His serenity was shattered by his radar warning receiver, alerting Pharaoh that a search radar had gone active on the ground. With all the interference being created by the EA-6B Prowlers, there wasn't much chance that the relatively weak signal would get through, but calculating the odds wasn't Pharaoh's job. Killing that radar was.

"Charger Nine, this is Charger Three," called King. "Stay with me. We're engaging that signal."

"This is Charger Nine, copy that," replied Pharaoh. He followed his wingman in a shallow left turn, heading inland towards the signal.

"Magnum!" said King, indicating that he had fired his Shrike. The missile was barely off the rail before the RBR in Pharaoh's cockpit alerted him to a new signal. A fire control radar had just energized behind them.

"Charger Nine, I'm reversing to engage the new threat," said King. One of the limits of the Shrike was a narrow firing arc, meaning that the Corsairs would have to point the missile at the radar before firing. "Looks like he's on me," said King. Pharaoh could hear the RWR in his wingman's plane warning him of the radar lock. "Engage the target, I'm breaking off to evade." Pharaoh continued his turn, lining up with the enemy radar. "Popping chaff," said King as Pharaoh leveled out.

"Magnum!" said Pharaoh as he launched the weapon.

"I'm hit! Punching out!" shouted King. Pharaoh cranked his neck around, looking for his wingman. The RWR in his cockpit went quiet. He knew that there was no way that the Shrike had time to reach its target. The enemy had turned the radar off, which would render the Shrike harmless. The missile required an active radar signal to ride down. *At least he's not shooting at me*, he thought as he rolled his plane to the right and caught King's parachute in his field of view.

"Mustang, this is Charger Nine," said Pharaoh, calling *Coral Sea*.

"Charger Nine, Mustang, go ahead."

"Mustang, Charger Three is down. I saw a good chute." Pharaoh then transmitted the coordinates to the location just southwest of El Limón, Nicaragua.

"Charger Three, copy. You are ordered to return to base. Your relief is on station."

"Mustang, understood, I'm coming home," replied Pharaoh as he banked his Corsair to the left and headed out to sea.

****

15 October 1980
Puerto Lempira, Honduras

"It's go time, Marines!" shouted Lieutenant Omar Beck. On his signal, the men of Second Platoon, Kilo Company, 3/6 Marines filed out of their formation and broke into a trot towards the awaiting helicopters. Lance Corporal Oliver waited as the platoon fell out by squad. As soon as First Squad cleared the formation, Second Squad followed. Without thinking about it, Oliver moved forward as soon as the Marine in front of him took a step. The Marines had been champing at the bit ever since the battle off Swan Island. It had been a long three weeks, but the Marines of Third Battalion, Sixth Marines were going to get some payback.

Jogging towards the massive CH-53 helicopter, Oliver watched an AH-1 Cobra gunship race ahead of the transports. *That is so badass*, he thought. *Man, I wish I could fly one of those bad boys*. His thoughts were disrupted when he reached his ride and climbed on board.

"Listen up, team!" shouted Sergeant Zach Klein, Oliver's squad leader. "You know the mission. No screwups out there!"

Oliver turned the mission over in his mind. First and Second Platoons of India Company, 3/6 Marines had gone forward to establish a FARP earlier in the day. They had flown one hundred and fifteen miles into Nicaragua, to the Limbaika Natural Reserve. Once there, a security detachment had pushed out around the landing zone and established a defensive perimeter. A second detail of Marines then unloaded enormous fuel bladders and the equipment needed to get the gas from the bladders to the birds.

From this position, the Marines would rearm and refuel the helicopters that were coming to and from the battle for the port city of Bluefields. The CH-53s could make the round trip without stopping, but the CH-46 Sea Knights would have to stop to refuel. The AH-1 Cobras would also use this as a rearming point. This would allow them to reduce their travel time to and from the battlefield significantly.

Oliver's heart jumped as the CH-53 left the tarmac and headed towards the enemy. To his left, he could hear Privates Boone and Palmer belting out AC/DC's "You Shook Me All Night Long." He shook his head. *I gotta put up with these kids*, he thought. He immediately laughed at himself as he recalled himself and Estrada singing their way through the haboob in Iran.

They would rendezvous with the CH-46s near the FARP and continue south. Their objective was the airfield south of town. The AH-1s would sweep ahead of them to rough up any defenders and soften the target. Then the troops would touch down in a clearing near the southwest of the airport. They were coming in a lot closer than they had at Manzariyeh. This time, there was a wooded area that would provide them with cover as they assaulted the objective. In Iran, there had been nothing but desert.

Kilo Company would assemble in the wooded area and assault the airfield from the south. Lima Company would attack from the west, but that was of no consequence to Oliver. Second Squad was tasked with capturing, intact, the Petroleum, Oil, and Lubricant, or POL, facility that was located at the extreme eastern edge of the battlefield. In order to achieve this, they were bringing an M60 team from Fourth Platoon and Doc Watts, the corpsman. They would push farther east than any of the other elements of the attack and would have to hustle to get there before some Sandi got the bright idea to blow the whole thing.

After about an hour of hashing and rehashing the plan, Oliver's heart again jumped as the CH-53 suddenly dropped in altitude. At first, a hint of alarm ran through Oliver's nerves. Then he remembered that this was all in the plan. The helos were dropping to the nap of the earth to avoid enemy detection. He'd overheard some NCOs talking about how the Navy would jam the enemy's radar. Even so, he figured it was better to be safe than sorry.

They knew they were nearing the battlefield when they heard the first explosions from the naval bombardment. The helo made several erratic course changes, and Oliver had to believe that they were dodging anti-aircraft fire. He tried not to think about it. Before he knew it, the lieutenant was yelling, "Heads up everyone, get ready to disperse." The ramp came down and Oliver felt the CH-53 go nose up as it came in for a landing. On the LT's command, he released his safety harness and braced himself for the surge as the Marines scrambled out of the helo in an organized fashion.

As the Marines burst out of the helicopter, Oliver could hear the chatter of rifle fire. As he ran for the cover of the tree line, he glanced left and was horrified to see tracer rounds landing at the rear of one of the other CH-53s. He couldn't tell for sure, but he was confident that 3/6 Marines had just taken their first casualties of the invasion.

The squad was at a sprint, and Oliver followed Corporal Evans when they hit the tree line and advanced into the jungle. They had to slow down once they started to pick through the trees and vines. They quickly formed a line, with Private Brock Banaag at the head. Banaag, a Philippine national, used a bolo knife to hack through the jungle. From the briefing, Oliver knew that they would have to push through about two hundred yards of this growth before it would open up a bit and they could pick up the pace. The sounds of the battle around them urged them onward.

After hacking through the brush, then sprinting across the one hundred and fifty yards of open terrain, the squad came to the last patch of jungle between them and their objective. As they neared the new tree line, Sergeant Klein raised his left fist to halt the group. He pointed to Corporal Evans and motioned for him to take his team to the right, then pointed to Corporal Joseph and motioned for him to take the left flank. Thus divided, Second Squad carefully approached the PLO station.

The area came into view. The thick jungle all but ensured that Second Squad could get to within one hundred yards of the objective undetected. For the Marines, this might as well have been point-blank range. There wasn't a Marine among them who couldn't hit a man-sized target with near-perfect accuracy. On the approach, Oliver noticed a machine-gun nest set up next to the fuel tanks, pointing in his fire team's direction. The three men in the nest were protected by a wall of sandbags that would keep bullets out. Yet each man still had his head exposed. They were staring into the jungle as the sounds of the battle at the airport grew nearer.

Evans ordered everyone to take a knee and each Marine took aim at a target. They then waited for Sergeant Klein to open fire.

The first crack was indistinguishable from the follow-on firing as Second Squad took precise and accurate shots at the enemy soldiers while ensuring that they didn't hit any of the storage tanks. The effect was instant and deadly. Oliver watched as the man in his sights disappeared after he squeezed the trigger of his M16. He was immediately scanning for more targets. A man came out from behind what Oliver thought was a pump house. Oliver fired and another Nicaraguan fell. After a furious minute of shooting, an ominous silence fell on the objective.

Evans rose and worked his way to the right. Oliver fell in with him, as did the rest of Fire Team Two. Sergeant Strickland and his assistant gunner were attached to Fire Team Two, as was Doc Watts. Their mission was to circle past the objective and clear the jungle on the far side. While they did this, the rest of the squad remained hidden, with their rifles trained and scanning for any new threats. The thick jungle that had protected the Marines during the attack was now their biggest issue to overcome in looking for the enemy.

Oliver's head was on a swivel as the patrol neared the eastern edge of the compound. Suddenly, Corporal Evans took a knee and raised a fist to halt the team. Everyone followed suit and they scanned the jungle in every direction. Evans raised his hand and signed to the team that he had visual contact with a force of at least nine enemy soldiers. The team took up firing positions and strained to locate the enemy.

Oliver spotted movement, and slowly, the outline of a man took shape as it moved toward the PLO site. If he had to guess, the plan was to counterattack the Marines, who would now be in possession of the objective. They might even have orders to destroy the site, taking as many Marines as possible with it. Evans opened up with a three-round burst, and the jungle came alive with fire and smoke.

Oliver immediately went with his M203 grenade launcher. He hadn't been able to use it earlier due to the flammable nature of the target, but here in the jungle, he had no such limits. The grenade exploded, and Oliver could see more bodies moving into view. He slid the rack of the M203 forward, ejecting the spent round, and slid another one in. He again took aim and sent another grenade downrange. The enemy was getting too close. He had to switch to his rifle. He heard a Marine call out for Doc Watts.

Oliver was firing burst after burst as the enemy came closer. *How the hell many of these guys are there?* he wondered as he repositioned to his left. As he searched for his next target, he heard a sustained burst from the M60. *Damn, Strickland's gonna melt that barrel if he keeps that up*, he thought. The sound of the M60 was getting closer and Oliver checked over his right shoulder to see what was happening. He could see Strickland moving towards his position. *Where the hell is his A-Gunner?* he thought, referring to the Marine Assistant Machine Gunner that would help haul ammo and keep Strickland ready to rock and roll.

"We're gonna get overrun," said Strickland. "There are a shitload of them out there. I think we ran into a platoon." Oliver didn't like the sound of this and looked around for Corporal Evans, the team leader. "They got Williamson, and it looks bad. Doc's with him, but I don't think he's gonna make it. I need you to lay down some grenades at about forty meters that way"—he pointed to the north—"that'll keep them guessing and cut off any more reinforcements."

Oliver immediately loaded a 40mm grenade and began to methodically pump them out as quickly as he could while Strickland opened up with the machine gun.

The effect of the tactic was immediate. Even in the smoke-choked chaos, Oliver could see the men who were advancing on his position run away from the sustained gunfire of Strickland's M60. At the same time, his own 40mm grenades were driving soldiers farther down the line towards his position. Nicaraguan soldiers were running into each other as they had to choose between the rock and the hard place. It was spectacular to watch, but Oliver was now loading his last grenade. He heard the M60 go quiet as well.

"Fuck you!" yelled Strickland as he threw the now-empty M60 to the ground and drew his M1911 pistol. He ran from his position into the mayhem. Oliver raised his M16 and fired rounds at Nicaraguans as he watched Strickland run up to near-point-blank range and shoot enemy soldiers with his sidearm. For a split second, Oliver considered rushing the enemy as well, but he recognized what was happening. Strickland had lost it. If he survived the engagement, it would be a miracle.

As if on cue, Strickland took a round to his thigh and went down on one knee. He unloaded two more rounds at the nearest Nicaraguan before he took several rounds to the chest and collapsed. Oliver dropped his empty mag and slammed in another as he prepared for what was left of his squad to get overrun. Target after target presented themselves and Oliver fired again and again. Each time, he prayed that this would be the shot that convinced the Nicaraguans that they needed to turn around.

As he fought for his life, Oliver caught movement over his right shoulder. This was it. He was about to die. The enemy had rolled them up. He turned to face the new threat, and his heart soared. It was the rest of Second Squad! They were methodically executing the enemy. Oliver immediately turned back to his right and scanned for targets. Within a matter of minutes, Fire Team Two went from sitting on the defense to efficiently advancing and slaughtering what was left of the Nicaraguan resistance.

Chapter 52

USS *Mount Whitney*
18 Miles off the Nicaraguan Coast

Colonel Hodges looked at the latest map updates. Thus far, the plan was coming together well. By the grace of God, some embedded units had eliminated the SA-8 threat. He was getting reports that on the west coast, the 1st Marine Division had lost some aircraft to the mobile SAM launchers. The two companies he'd assigned to assault the airfield had made short work of it, and he was now preparing to reinforce that beachhead with additional Marines launched from the USS *Saipan* and USS *Iwo Jima*. With the airfield secured, his next phase of the operation was to conduct an amphibious assault on the beaches north of El Bluff. Once that was secured, Hodges would secure the port facilities, and the United States would begin pouring troops and equipment into Nicaragua.

Taking El Bluff would be a much more traditional assault. Hodges would send his task force to within twelve miles of the beach and unleash waves of amphibious landing vehicles, from the tanklike LVPT-7 to the more traditional LCM-8 and LCUs. These craft would depart their parent ships and assault the beaches. Before they got there, the naval gunfire support as well as Marine Corps and naval aviation would pummel the beach and the forests beyond. The spooks in Langley and Fort Meade projected minimal resistance, but after the snafu with the Osa missile boats, there was no way Colonel Hodges was taking any chances.

"Sir, *Saipan* and *Iwo Jima* have begun air operations."

Hodges nodded to the radioman. The amphibious assault ships of his task force were racing towards the "line of departure," an invisible line parallel to the beach at the landing zone. Once they arrived, some of them would disgorge the landing craft they were carrying. The LSTs, however, would continue all the way to the beach, where they would drop their bow ramps and unload their heavy vehicles and equipment.

"Andy," said Hodges, addressing Major Andrew Yates, his brigade intelligence officer, "do the recon teams have anything new on expected enemy resistance?"

"Sir, you'd be the first to know about it if they did," replied Yates.

"Colonel," interrupted the radioman, "the admiral is reporting that the fleet has commenced the naval bombardment."

Hodges checked his watch. "They're early. Dammit." There had been some confusion in the interservice communication between the Navy and the Marines. Even though they coexisted on the ships, they were still two very different organizations with completely separate chains of command. "Get word to the regiment commanders. If the Navy manages to get the duration and intensity right, they'll let up a few minutes early. That's going to increase our exposure as the landing craft race to the beach."

He looked up from the map to the digital Naval Tactical Data System, or NTDS, screen. He was an old-fashioned guy, and he preferred following the main assault plan on the physical map. Nonetheless, he had to admit that there was a lot of value in having a map that was updated in real time as soon as data was received. He watched as the circles that represented his amphibs neared the line of departure.

"Sir, the first load of helos has departed. Saipan is securing from Air Operations and readying the well deck for boat operations."

"Understood," replied the colonel. Unlike the *Iwo Jima*, the *Saipan* carried four of the large LCU landing craft. Each Landing Craft Utility could carry up to four hundred troops, or one hundred and eighty tons of cargo. Right now *Saipan* was flooding her massive well deck, intentionally filling the stern of the ship with water so that the four LCUs could float out of the back as they came about at the line of departure. The USS *Ponce*, USS *Hermitage*, USS *Spiegel Grove* and USS *Nashville* were all going through a similar process.

"Sir, *Iwo Jima* reports the Gunrunners are on deck." The colonel nodded. Besides the transport helicopters, *Iwo Jima* was also carrying a detachment of AH-1 Cobra attack helicopters. These would launch to provide close-air support for the Marines during the assault. Once the boats were out, *Saipan* would add additional punch via a detachment of AV-8A Harriers. The Marines at the airfield had also set up 60mm mortars, which had sufficient range to provide additional support. Between these Marine assets, the naval gunfire support, and a seemingly endless supply of A-6s and A-7s from *Nimitz*, the Marines could call in one hell of a weight of fire.

"Colonel, one of the recon elements taking cover to the north of the objective is reporting that they've located some kind of bunker. It's fresh and well dug in. It was abandoned, but the squad leader believed there were likely more of them out there."

The colonel furrowed his brow. It made sense that the enemy would set defensive positions, but why were they just finding this out now?

"Sir, they also indicate that they've found what looks like a sight for an AT-4 Spigot in the abandoned bunker."

"Get a message out to the regiment commanders. Let them know that there's an increased chance of ATGM activity along the shoreline."

****

El Bluff Beach
Half a Mile North of Puerto El Bluff, Nicaragua

Clara Gálvez was trapped. She and a squad of her uncle's men, affectionately called Las Rémoras, after the fish known to attach themselves to sharks and feed off the detritus left over when the shark was feeding, had been observing the Puerto El Bluff from the north side. This gave them an angle that Carlos's team on Ilsa El Venado couldn't see. Clara couldn't prove it, but she thought that her team had been assigned this spot because it was the place least likely to be hiding the SAM launchers they were hunting. For as tough as El Tiburón might be, Clara knew that he would never put her life in danger unless there were no other options.

They were fairly well hidden, but with all the action going on in Bluefields, there wouldn't be anyone paying attention to this spot of jungle. The morning had been exciting. She couldn't see much of the bombardment, as the forest blocked her view; however, the flat terrain between the city and the beach meant that she could feel the shock waves. And there was no denying the smoke that was rising to the west.

"I'm surprised we haven't seen more activity," said one of the men in the squad.

"I don't want any part of that activity," replied Clara. "I've never been in an artillery barrage, but if it's half as terrifying as the helicopter attack I survived, you can keep it all for yourself." The man didn't have any response to that.

"I'm sorry, Ms. Gálvez, you're absolutely right."

Smart man, she thought. *He knows that pissing me off will piss my uncle off, and that's the last thing this guy wants.* Before she could reply, a five-inch shell exploded on the beach south of them. Everyone instinctively took cover. Round after round pounded the beach and the port to the south.

After the initial shock of the barrage wore off, Clara raised her binoculars and scanned the sea. She could make out the massive Amphibious Assault Ships that were racing towards the shore.

"Raúl, keep an eye on the container yard. If those missile launchers are there, now is the time they'll use them," she said. She intended to keep her eyes on the incoming Americans to make sure that if the time came and they needed to bug out, she'd be ready for it. They had a boat tied up to the beach pier, and they would run west, then north, to get out of harm's way.

Clara watched as helicopters lifted off from the onrushing ships and flew towards El Bluff. She followed them as they flew south and watched as they unleashed rocket attacks on unseen targets. A shudder ran down her spine as she remembered being on the other end of one of those attacks. When she returned her gaze to the ships, several of the larger ships turned to the south, and a series of smaller vessels emerged from within them. It took her a second to understand what was happening.

The Sandinista military didn't have the ability to conduct an amphibious assault. They didn't have any of the big ships, or even any of the landing craft. She had no training in this, but even a novice like her could tell that the big ships couldn't operate in the shallows, and this was how they would get their men and equipment to shore.

The assault was much slower than she'd imagined. It was an onslaught, an irresistible force that was coming to take the harbor. It was a behemoth, about to devour her country. She hated the Soviets, and she'd come to distrust the Sandinistas. But this was still her country, and she felt some heat watching its invasion. She wished that her people could put up more of a fight.

There was a bright flash to her left, down by the port area. It was followed by several more, and something went streaking from the beach towards the approaching landing craft. She watched with mixed emotions as the rockets screamed towards the Americans. Within seconds of the flash, there was the roar of an explosion. She turned to look and could see an aircraft climbing for altitude, leaving a fireball behind it. The fireball erupted at the exact spot from which the rocket had been launched.

She raised her binoculars and trained them on the outgoing rockets. One of them struck one of the smaller craft that looked something like a turtle swimming towards shore. The rocket blew a hole in the front of it. Smoke poured out of the wounded craft and it took on water. Hatches popped open along the top, and Marines scrambled out of the vehicle and into the water.

Another rocket struck one of the larger craft, but the effect wasn't nearly as dramatic. There was an explosion on the front quarter of the boat above the waterline. The open deck was packed with Marines, and she had no doubt that there were casualties from the rocket, yet the vessel pressed on, undaunted.

Every time there was an outbound rocket, there was a nearly instantaneous response from the air. Slender helicopters with nose-mounted cannons and rocket pods would swoop in and tear up anything in the area. She doubted that any of the missile teams out there would get a second shot off. True to her belief, she could see far fewer of the outgoing rockets. After ten minutes, there were no more. The Sandinistas wouldn't stop the invasion. The Marines would land, and then… Clara didn't know what came after that.

****

Northwest of Bluefields Airport
Bluefields, Nicaragua

Carlos appreciated that this was the most danger he'd been in since he'd evaded the Russians on the hilltop. It would be just his luck that he'd have survived this long, only to get iced by his own people right on the verge of the relative safety of friendly lines. Of course, there was still the enemy to worry about as well. Who knew what forces might retreat away from the airfield and head towards him? So he had to be stealthy enough to avoid enemy stragglers while not surprising any friendlies.

With each yard he closed on the airport, he slowed just a bit. He was looking through the jungle, hoping to spot Marines on the perimeter so that he could actually plan how to approach them.

His eyes were straining when suddenly, he heard, "Dallas!"

His heart stopped. The man was just to his left, about ten yards away. He quickly responded with, "Debbie!" completing the countersign that informed the Marine that they were on the same side.

"Holy shit, Sergeant Rodriguez?" asked the Marine.

"I'm sorry, pal, but who are you?"

"It's Corporal Phil Stanley, Lima Company. I thought you quit?"

"You believe all the scuttlebutt you hear?" asked Carlos as he approached. Suddenly, Stanley raised his M16. Carlos stopped and started to raise his own rifle.

"Get down!" shouted Stanley, and Carlos dropped like a lead weight. He could see fire erupt from the rifle as Stanley fired a three-round burst into the forest behind Carlos. Without hesitation, Carlos scrambled for cover so that he could turn and face the threat. From deep in the jungle, he could see the muzzle flashes of at least a dozen rifles. *Damn, these guys were right behind me the whole time*, he thought.

"Pop smoke if you've got it," said Stanley. "We need to fall back closer to the airfield and link up with my platoon. Then we can attack in force." Carlos took his only remaining smoke grenade, pulled the pin and tossed it a few yards in front of him. The smoke billowed out, and with a shift in the wind, his purple mixed and mingled with the green from Stanley's. With a thick haze forming, the two Marines quickly withdrew.

"We need to pick up the pace," said Carlos. "Those bastards know they—"

Boom! An explosion cut through the forest, but Carlos didn't feel a blast wave. He looked over to Stanley.

"Claymore," replied the corporal, referring to the antipersonnel mine that had been the mainstay of the US military since the Vietnam War. "What did you think I was doing out there? Taking a leak?" Carlos grinned and the two headed out of the jungle and towards Lima Company's position, where they would pick up the fight.

Chapter 53

15 October 1980
Bagram Air Base
Bagram, Afghanistan

First Squad, Second Platoon, 9th Company, 345th Independent Guards Airborne Regiment had spent the past seven months settling into a predictable and stable routine. They had brought in replacements for the men they had lost, and with the squad once again whole, they began the drudgery of occupation. They contributed to convoy escorts to move supplies around the Kabul area. Occasionally they would be sent out to investigate reports of bandits in the areas surrounding the capital.

Misha sat in the Second Platoon headquarters, flipping through the pages of the latest *Krasnaya Zvezda* magazine. He had heard reports of some pitched battles in the rural areas when enough goat herders got together to take on a Soviet infantry unit. But those didn't last long. The Afghan rebels weren't able to stand toe to toe with the Red Army. First Squad had seen nothing approaching a proper fight since the Tajbeg Palace months ago. It had gotten to the point that Misha was wondering why they were even there. They'd accomplished the mission as far as he could tell, and now they were just sitting around.

"Comrade Sergeant," said Taras. "Have you noticed something peculiar about 3rd Company?" Misha considered the vague question. He hadn't thought about 3rd Company, and other than Taras asking, he had no reason *to* think about 3rd Company.

"No, Corporal, I have not."

"Have you noticed anything at all about 3rd Company?"

"Please, Taras, I'm in no mood for games. If you have something to say, just get to the point."

Taras was taken aback, but he continued.

"Misha, 3rd Company is gone. They are nowhere to be found."

Misha looked up from the journal he was reading. "That makes no sense, Taras. Check the roster. They're probably just out on patrol."

"Oh, sure. That's true. They are out on patrol and have been for the past three weeks. Not only that, but they've switched patrol assignments twice, but they've never rotated back to Bagram to resupply."

"So now you're an expert on logistics? You are familiar with the concept of helicopters, aren't you?"

"Sure. Maybe. But it doesn't make sense to me. There's more to this, Misha—3rd Company has been reassigned. That's the only conclusion I can draw from this."

"So be it, Taras. It's no concern of ours. Our concern is keeping the squad in fighting shape for our turn at convoy duty."

The two Desantniks slipped into the normal flow of conversation relating to the running of the squad. They were due for vehicle maintenance in two weeks, which would at least give them something to look forward to (such as it was). Then a private ducked his head into the tent and announced that the captain required Misha to report to the company HQ tent immediately.

Captain Sytnikov was sitting at his desk when Misha walked in. Right behind Misha were Sergeants Yuri Aleksenko of Second Squad and Yefim Shishov of Third Squad. Already in attendance was Lieutenant Kadtsyn. Whatever Misha had been summoned for involved the entire platoon.

"Comrades, at long last we finally have orders," said Sytnikov. Misha was relieved to know that there was a change coming. He risked a glance at Aleksenko, who remained fixated on the captain. "All of your assignments on the current duty roster have been reassigned and replaced with a company-wide patrol mission. We will begin processing your BMDs for deployment at warehouse fourteen over by the flight line. Corporal Arafyev will give you additional details on the precise time and order in which you are to arrive at the warehouse. It is imperative that we stick precisely to this timetable. There will be severe consequences for any deviation from this plan. Is that understood?"

"Yes, Captain!" came the unanimous reply as Sytnikov's staff corporal walked over and handed each sergeant and the lieutenant a copy of the company commander's written orders. As he dismissed them, Lieutenant Kadtsyn ordered all the sergeants back to the platoon tent to work on the details. When they entered the tent, there were a few soldiers, including Taras, milling about.

"Get the fuck out of here," said Kadtsyn, clearing the room. When only platoon leadership remained, he continued. "This is no ordinary patrol. We are redeploying to the Carpathian Military District. This entire operation is under the utmost secrecy. That's why we cannot be late or out of order when we prepare to disperse. For everyone outside of the company, it is to be understood that we are on a long-distance patrol to the southern region of the Helmand Province.

"We will be beyond radio range of Bagram, but we will keep limited staff personnel on-site to help maintain the ruse. Our BMD-equipped companies will load into Il-76 aircraft at the warehouse under cover of darkness. We will load each BMD squad while mounted in their vehicles and we will conduct the transport operation while mounted. It will be hot and crowded in there, but this is essential to maintaining the fiction that we are still here in Afghanistan." During a typical operation, only the driver and gunner would remain in the BMD during a drop. Cramming the entire squad in for the duration of the flight was a new wrinkle for them.

We're going to be smashed in there like kashka, thought Misha, referring to Taras's nickname for the meat-and-porridge hash found in their field rations. It was a combination of the words *kasha*, meaning porridge, and *koshka*, meaning cat.

Lieutenant Kadtsyn didn't bother to ask if there were any questions. Frankly, it didn't matter. They had orders; those orders were clear. Now they just needed to execute them. As Misha considered them, he knew that Taras was right: 3rd Company had been secreted away, and 9th Company was about to follow. Misha had no idea where they were going, but he had a foreboding feeling that wherever it was, his life was about to get a lot more dangerous.

Chapter 54

15 October 1980
Baku, Azerbaijan

Saeed Nouzari sat on the bridge of the fifteen-meter fishing boat as they pulled away from the commercial fishing pier on the western edge of the city. This "night fishing" expedition he was on would be the most critical of all the missions to date. In fact, this was the first attack planned and executed by the Sword of the Revolution that required two of the founding members to participate. As a rule, the founders of the movement had agreed that only one of them could be risked in any single action. Tonight was the sole exception to that rule.

The boat chugged out of the harbor in the darkness as Saeed considered the totality of the operation. Azerbaijan hosted the second-highest concentration of his brothers in faith. The repressive Soviet government had subjugated the Shiite population in Azerbaijan since the establishment of the Azerbaijan Soviet Socialist Republic in 1920. It was true that the Muslims in Azerbaijan had more freedom than many other religious practitioners in the Soviet Union and the Communist Bloc of Eastern Europe. But the persecution remained.

This brotherhood had given the Sword of the Revolution access to key areas needed for this operation. For Saeed's part, this meant that he would have access to the port facility at the petroleum terminal on the east side of the Bay of Baku. The harbormaster at the terminal had reached out directly to one of Shahab's contacts through the underground network they had established in the mosques along the Azeri-Iranian border. This contact had initiated the planning that had resulted in this brazen attack on Soviet infrastructure. By the end of the night, the Soviets would lose all access to the oil and gas being produced in the region.

While Saeed was about to destroy the petroleum depot at the dock using a butane/penthrite explosive, Shahab was leading a team of men into the nearby refinery to plant a bomb similar to the one they used at the Iraqi fertilizer plant months before. Between the two attacks, the Soviets would no longer be able to ignore the terrorist threat emanating from Iran. Saeed had been surprised at how well the Iranian Army was holding out against the Iraqi attacks. It was a simple deduction that trying to goad the Soviets into helping depose the Bakhtiar regime would be the necessary next step. Naser had argued that, unlike Iraq, the Russians could wipe the Iranian military out and take over, adding Iran to the Soviet Union and preventing the furtherance of their Islamic Republic. But both Saeed and Shahab had convincingly argued that there was no way the international community would stand by and allow that to happen.

It's too late for regrets, thought Saeed. The current situation was untenable, so they would make a change. Then they would analyze the situation again and decide what to do next. The revolution had taken a winding path to get to this point, and there was no reason to expect that path to straighten out anytime soon.

****

Ten miles away, in an empty railcar, Shahab had one last brief with his men. There were five men on the team in total. Three of the men would head to the south end of the refinery and attack the security forces there. While they were engaged, Shahab and one more soldier would slip into the refinery itself to place and detonate the bomb. It was a risky plan. *What if they lock down the entire facility when the diversion attack starts?* Shahab laughed as he thought about that.

"What is so funny?" asked one of his men.

"It's nothing. I just get nervous at the start of a mission. I'm sure you do too." With that, the five Swordsmen of the Revolution hopped out of the boxcar and started towards their objectives. Shahab held back a few steps as he checked that he had a round chambered and the safety off on his Kalashnikov. Once he had verified that his weapon was hot, he lifted it to his shoulder and began shooting each of his men in the back.

The first to drop was the man who would have accompanied him into the refinery. As the closest threat, Shahab wanted him down and out first. As soon as he was down, Shahab pivoted his aim to the cluster of men heading south. They had been bunched up as they moved, totally unprepared for the attack that cut them down. Shahab laughed again when he thought about the security procedures that had concerned his team. As he went from man to man, ensuring that each was dead, he could hear the massive explosion three miles away. He looked south, towards the sea, and saw an enormous fireball rising over the petroleum depot.

As he marveled at the size of the explosion, a squad of men approached from the east.

“I believe your operation has been a success,” said one of the men, wearing the uniform of a lieutenant in the Coastal Defense Forces of the Soviet Union.

“Yes, Comrade Lieutenant,” said Shahab in Russian. “I believe that we have everything exactly as we need it.” The newcomers bagged up the dead bodies as a truck pulled up for them to be loaded onto. Secondary explosions rang out and the glow from the fires increased. Shahab knew that there had been explosives placed in the fuel storage areas of the depot to ensure that it burned, but he didn’t think they were necessary.

Now the Soviet Union had what it needed. It had the justification to intervene directly in the Iran-Iraq war. Shahab also had what he needed. He was no longer a part of the Sword of the Revolution. As far as anyone would ever know, Shahab Yazdani was martyred tonight. He and his entire team were killed in an attempt to destroy the Soviet oil refinery in Baku, Azerbaijan. He had accomplished his mission and he looked forward to his next assignment.

Chapter 55

16 October 1980
Kaspiysk, Russia

There were three massive warehouses along the coastline of the Caspian Sea, just east of the city of Kaspiysk. These buildings were rather innocuous, especially when viewed from five hundred kilometers away by an American KH-11 satellite. The naval infantrymen of the 810th Guards Naval Infantry Brigade referred to these seaside warehouses as the "Eagles' Nest." Split between the three buildings were four very unusual craft. These unique vessels fell somewhere between ships and aircraft. They could float, like a ship, but they could leave the water and fly at low altitudes, and very high speeds. They were faster than any ship afloat but could carry more cargo than any aircraft of a comparable size.

These were the ekranoplans of the Soviet Naval Infantry. The largest, the KM or "Eagle," had been known as the Caspian Sea Monster. It was a massive frame that could carry over two hundred and fifty fully loaded marines. The KM was originally a prototype used as a proof of concept. The massive unit measured over ninety meters long and could lift over five hundred tons. This made it considerably larger and more capable than the US Air Force's C-5 Galaxy. A large engine mount dominated the front of the KM. The mount carried eight VD-7 turbojet engines, four on each side of the fuselage. The engines had adjustable nozzles that would push the thrust under the main wing of the ship during the take-off process. Once the ship was airborne, the nozzles would direct the thrust directly aft to give the KM additional speed. Two more of the huge engines were mounted on either side of the vertical stabilizer. When cruising, the KM could stay aloft with only the rear-mounted engines.

The three smaller ekranoplans were the derivative offspring of the KM, officially known as the A-90 and affectionately called Eaglets. The A-90s looked more like conventional aircraft than did the KM. The A-90 had two smaller NK-8 turbofan engines concealed in the nose, with a single massive NK-1 turboprop at the top of the tail boom. The wings were set low and just forward of the midpoint of the airframe. Each

Eaglet could carry two BTR amphibious fighting vehicles, and the ten men who would fight each of those vehicles.

The ekranoplans used a principle of physics known as the "ground effect" experienced by all aircraft as they near a fixed surface. As a winged vehicle gets closer to the ground, lift increases and drag decreases. Using a design that maximizes this effect allows an aircraft to move much greater weights at much higher speeds than can be done by a conventional aircraft of equivalent size. As a tradeoff, these vessels could only fly at low altitudes. It hadn't taken Soviet designers long to understand that carrying a lot of cargo over extensive ranges at high speeds, flying below radar coverage, might have military applications.

Tonight was the culmination of months of training and practice. The Soviet high command was going to find out if their investment in this technology and training had any tactical value. During the night, naval infantrymen loaded onto each of the Eaglets. The eight-wheeled BTR-70s loaded up their crews and troops, then backed into the A-90s. Instead of using a traditional ramp, like most transport planes, the entire nose and cockpit section of the A-90 opened on hinges like a giant swinging door. This would allow the vehicles to exit the Eaglet as soon as it hit the beach, without having to "swim."

The KM, as a prototype, lacked any such bells and whistles. Instead, she would need a pier to dock with. With the port-side wing secured to the pier, the two hundred and fifty marines and their equipment would scramble out of the Monster through an access hatch just above the wing. It was an inelegant process and would take much more time than a fully operational vehicle like the A-90. For tonight's live-fire proof-of-concept mission, though, the KM could move the troops needed to secure a beachhead.

Once the marines loaded onto the ekranoplans, each one taxied out into the water and began the take-off process they had been rehearsing for the past several months. Within ten minutes, the three hundred men and six BTRs began the first offensive use of a ground-effect vehicle in combat. It would be a solid two-hour trip. The four ships flew south-southeast toward their target: Chalus.

Chalus was a perfect target for this offensive. It was a fair-sized seaside town close to the capital of Tehran. The only direct access route between Tehran and Chalus was Highway 59, a narrow, winding mountain pass. Any relief effort coming from Tehran would have to travel the gauntlet between the two cities, and the Soviet Air Force had pledged to make that trip impossible. Besides the Su-20s and MiG-27s allocated to the effort, the Soviet Voyenno-Vozdushnye Sily (VVS) were deploying a special detachment of their latest attack aircraft, the Su-25. Within an hour of the attack, the Su-25s would prowl Highway 59, looking for subjects upon which they could test their beautiful new airframes.

Chalus also had the benefit of possessing several commercial piers that could accommodate the KM and allow for the marines to disembark in multiple locations to improve the dispersal. This would allow more troops to cover more territory than could be accomplished in other port towns along the Caspian coastline.

As far as the local commanders were aware, they needed to occupy the city to establish a secure zone inside Iran. This would be the stepping-off point to a pacification operation that would end the constant and increasing terrorist attacks occurring along the border areas. If the Iranians could take positive measures to stop the violence, the Soviets wouldn't need to "pacify" more of the Iranian countryside. If the Iranians wouldn't or couldn't stop the attacks, the Soviets would continue to add troops and consolidate control across the entire northern border from Afghanistan to Turkey.

In reality, the Soviets were making a calculated move to bring in additional US forces. They knew there was no way they could get away with an actual invasion of Iran without eliciting a direct military response from the United States. Instead, they were counting on it. Recent intel had indicated that the Americans had moved a light division into the region, and the Soviets estimated that this action would pull that division into Iranian territory and that the United States would then commit additional troops to the region. The Soviets balanced along the razor's edge of antagonizing the US just enough to bleed their military strength while not going so far as to drive them to initiate direct hostilities.

The ekranoplans closed to within a half hour of their destination. High above them, MiG-25 interceptors and MiG-23 fighters loitered over the borders on either side of the Caspian. If the fighters detected incoming aircraft, they would engage to preserve the surprise of the first wave of the assault. The ground attack aircraft were preparing to take off to join the fray in time for the landings themselves. They would approach at sea level from the north, staying out of sight until the last minute.

Everyone knew that when the first A-90 hit the beach and unloaded the first BTR, all hell would break loose.

Intelligence overflights by MiG-25R reconnaissance planes revealed that the garrison in Chalus had been depleted to counter the Iraqis in the south. The Iranians had no reason to suspect that the town was at risk of attack, other than a possible air raid by the Iraqis. Even that didn't make a lot of sense, given that there was no tactical or strategic value to Chalus regarding the Iran-Iraq war. The entire town was peacefully sleeping when war came to visit them.

The first landing of the three A-90s hit the beach in front of the Noshahr Airport. Within ten minutes of landing, six BTRs were racing to the airport, where the sixty marines would overwhelm the security and police forces. Once subdued, special teams of marines would begin preparing the airport for operations. Within half an hour, troops and equipment would fly in on An-72 and An-12 aircraft. As additional marines arrived at the airport, they would advance, adding control to more territory until they linked up with additional units that had made landings further along the beach.

Three miles to the west of the airport, the KM had docked with the recreational pier at Chalus Beach. The marines on board were piling out of the Sea Monster and scrambling along the wing to the pier, where they would then jog to the beach and form up into squads. Once the marines had gathered together by squads and platoons, they would advance south, securing the major roads that would allow movement throughout the town. The dismounted marines would ensure the security of the area while their heavier equipment was delivered by the A-90s, or from the cargo planes beginning operations at the airport.

At the airport, there was light resistance. None of the security forces there were prepared for actual combat. The police were likewise overwhelmed with little resistance. Sporadic gunfire rang out from the occasional stalwart, but within three hours the marines had secured most of the town. BTRs and the smaller BRDM scout vehicles patrolled the streets, while messages of pacification were being played on loudspeakers. The population didn't need a lot of convincing to stay indoors. The shock and speed of the attack had taken most of them unaware.

In the skies above, Soviet fighters dared the Iranians to come out and play. A pair of F-5 Tigers were on combat air patrol over Tehran when the first calls came in from Noshahr Airport. They sped north to see what aid they could render and were immediately pounced on by waiting Foxbats. Two pairs of R-23 missiles reached out from the MiG-25s and destroyed the Tigers long before the F-5s could get into position to interfere with the landings below. With dozens of Soviet aircraft showing up on ground control radar, the Iranian Air Force refused to commit more aircraft for fear of losing the edge they had in the south against the Iraqis.

This decision saved many planes on both the Soviet and Iranian sides of the conflict. Unfortunately for the Iranians, it also doomed the relief column they had sent from Tehran. The Su-25s of the 200th Independent Attack Squadron detected, engaged, and destroyed the company of M60 Patton tanks that the Iranians had sent to push the Soviets back. The high cliff walls of the mountain pass made detection difficult, but once detected, they gave the Iranians no way to disperse their forces. The Su-25s flew up and down the road, destroying tanks with a mix of five-hundred-pound unguided bombs and Kh-25 air-to-surface missiles. It was a massacre.

On the ground, the Soviet regiment completed their deployment. The Iranians were unwilling to lose more men in the effort to take back the seaside town. By the morning of the seventeenth, the Soviets were in control of a major chunk of the Caspian seashore in Iran.

Chapter 56

18 October 1980
United Nations Building
New York, New York

Oleg Troyanovsky sat in the conference room of the US Mission to the United Nations. Also in attendance were several Soviet attachés and their American counterparts. For the second time in less than a month, Oleg was tasked with easing the anxiety of the Americans. He was aware that much of what he was saying was just political theater, but he honestly didn't know exactly how much. What he did know was the exact parameters of several diplomatic offers that he would make. That was enough for him. Those offers were contained in a manila folder that he shifted in his hands. If none of it was actually true, so be it. If there was a seed of truth in there, all the better.

"Ambassador McHenry," said Oleg, sliding the folder across the table. "I want to start by assuring you we have no desire for a conflict with the United States. The Soviet people want peace in our nation, and in the region. We are here today because we believe that the United States would welcome that outcome." Donald McHenry looked impassively at his Soviet counterpart. Troyanovsky knew how the game was played. McHenry wouldn't tip his hand this early. No, he'd wait for an offer before he said anything.

"The wave of terrorist attacks emanating out of Iran has become untenable. The recent attack that destroyed our port facilities in Baku was the drop that overflowed the cup of our patience. We have been subjected to repeated aggression along our borders with Iran ever since the Ayatollah fell out of power. It was our sincere belief that the invasion of the Iraqi military would likely end these attacks, as the people in Iran would have a common enemy. Clearly, we were mistaken. It was only through the diligent efforts of our internal security forces that the attack on the Baku refineries was stopped before it could disrupt the flow of petroleum."

Troyanovsky knew that much was true. Had the terrorists taken the refinery off-line for any appreciable period, the effects on the Soviet economy could have been devastating.

"Our temporary occupation of the Iranian town of Chalus is our first step in bringing this ongoing conflict to an end. I believe you can appreciate our need to negotiate from a position of power, and having this force in Chalus should establish that. We have no intention of holding this territory, or increasing our military occupation beyond what is necessary to bring the warring factions together." Again, Oleg paused, and again, Donald simply looked him in the eye and waited. Oleg had expected an outburst by now. He believed the American would lecture him on the dangers of destabilizing the region. He thought the US would blast the Soviet aggression against a United States ally. He waited for McHenry to spout off a list of demands. But there were none. Just a quiet, impassive black man waiting for Oleg to continue.

"I cannot overemphasize this point: the Soviet Union does not wish for this crisis in the Middle East to expand beyond the current scope. The Iranians brought us into the conflict by repeated attacks against our territory. Our presence in Iran is simply to help put an end to the violence as a whole. We understand that we cannot do this through force and we cannot do this alone. I am here to formally request the United States' assistance in mediating the conflict between Iran and Iraq, and bringing about the cessation of cross-border terrorist activity. Until yesterday, the Soviet government was content to remain a neutral party in the matters between Iran and Iraq. This policy is no longer viable given the increasing severity of the attacks against our nation."

The first ask was on the table. The Soviets wanted something from the US. McHenry shifted in his chair, giving the appearance that he was about to say something further, but he didn't. He crossed his arms as he leaned back in his chair, again waiting for Oleg.

"The Soviet government proposes the creation of a multilateral peacekeeping force for the Iran-Iraq border. The Soviet Union will commit the military unit currently occupying Chalus, and additional units that are operating in Afghanistan. We invite your government to join us in a resolution before the United Nations Security Council to establish a peacekeeping force made up of these Soviet units as well as American units of your choosing. The mandate of these peacekeepers would be to stop the fighting in Khuzestan, and to bring all sides to the negotiating table. As a show of our peaceful intent and goodwill, the Soviet government will also redeploy some of our frontline divisions out of the German frontier. We will begin removing the 3rd Shock Army, as well as the 79th Guards Tank Division, out of the German Democratic Republic."

Now he had McHenry's full attention. The proposed units were the crack armored forces that would be the spearhead of any Soviet attack on NATO. As the tip of the Soviet spear, removing these units would do a lot to reduce tension along the NATO border with the Warsaw pact.

"Ambassador Troyanovsky, I admire your temerity in suggesting that the Soviet invasion of Iran was anything less than an act of war against an American ally. I'm equally in awe of your confidence that my government would believe that you intend to leave the security of the Warsaw Pact to the goodwill and benevolence of NATO forces." It was Oleg's turn to wait for his adversary to give him something. There was no point stopping McHenry before he made a demand or a concession. "What makes you think we would accept any of what you just said, given the outlandish nature of it all?"

"Donald…" Oleg needed to get the Americans on board. While he enjoyed the normal bluster in these sorts of situations, today he needed to be conciliatory. "We are not leaving ourselves defenseless. We will be turning over these sections of the frontier to our communist brothers from the German, Czech and Polish armies. For example, we have already begun positioning the Polish 20th Armored Division in relief of the 79th Guards. While not an elite division like the Soviet guards unit, they can act as a defensive deterrent during this period of uncertainty. The Red Army General Staff chose the Poles in part because their older tanks and equipment would be a liability in an offensive role, but they would be enough to hold the line if NATO decided to try to take advantage of the situation.

"Regarding our forces in Iran," continued Oleg, "my presence here should assuage some of your concerns. I am asking you to join my government in a diplomatic overture that will prove the truth of my words. If you should choose not to take part, the Soviet government will move forward in our attempts to mediate this crisis without America. You know as well as I do that this will be more effective if you join us, and we can get this settled quickly."

"Let's say we agree to participate in your mediation," said Donald. "What are you looking at as a suitable outcome?"

"I assure you, I honestly have no idea, Donald. That will be between the belligerents. From the Soviet perspective, nothing less than a cessation of hostilities against our people and territory will be acceptable. With Saddam in Iraq, I believe it will come down to money and land. You and I both know that the border between Iran and Iraq is arbitrary."

"Thank you for your candor, Ambassador Troyanovsky. As you can imagine, I'm not prepared to agree to anything at this point, but I can tell you that the United States government is interested in your proposition. I will take what you have presented here"—he gestured to the folder on the table—"to the President and will present you with a formal response in due course."

****

18 October 1980
White House
Washington, D.C.

"What do you think, Donald?" asked President Carter.

"Mr. President, I've only known Oleg Troyanovsky for the past four years, but in those years we've spent a lot of time together. I believe the ambassador is sincere in this offer. I don't dispute that there is probably some ulterior motive for the invasion of Iran, but so far I haven't figured it out. My gut tells me they would use this opportunity to inject a socialist movement into the country, as we've seen in Turkey.

"So far, though, we have seen nothing to suggest that. In fact, if what they're saying is true, they intend to divert some military force they currently have in Afghanistan to shore up the situation in Iran. I think we can use this to push for a withdrawal from Afghanistan. Basically, we can agree to their joint resolution in the Security Council, and in exchange we can ask them to make their withdrawal of force from Afghanistan permanent."

Carter considered that. The Soviet presence in Afghanistan had been a thorn in his side for the past ten months. If he could use this new situation in Iran to address that thorn… yes. that was worth pursuing.

"General Meyer," said the President, addressing Army Chief of Staff Edward Meyer. "What do you think of the proposal of moving an armored division of Soviet Tanks and replacing them with the Poles? Does that have any actual value to us?"

"I believe it does. It signals that the Soviets are willing to take a step back from the brink in order to take care of this crisis. On paper, swapping the divisions doesn't look like much. But in practice, this would make a serious dent in the Soviets' ability to launch offensive operations against NATO."

"How so?" asked the President.

"Sir, we have extensive intelligence on Soviet planning. All of that planning relies on speed in the opening weeks of any conflict. The Russkies know that they need to cover as much ground as possible at the conflict's start. They will have a limited time to engage NATO forces on the Continent before American reinforcements can arrive from North America. That's the reason they keep their sharpest and best-equipped units on the frontier. By withdrawing the 79th Guards, they abandon that plan. The 20th Polish Armored Division may be an excellent division by Polish standards, but they are inferior in every way to the Soviet division they're replacing." President Carter continued to listen without interrupting.

"This is especially true regarding the speed with which the division could be expected to advance in combat. The T-55 tanks of the Polish Army are outdated and inferior to our own M60 Patton tanks. The T-55s are slower, less armored, and have an inferior gun when compared to the M60, or especially the T-72 tanks they're replacing. The Soviets are conceding one of the most important advantages they have."

"I see," said the President. "What would be your best argument against accepting this proposal?" Carter had intentionally put General Meyer on the spot with his question. Meyer considered it for a moment before responding.

"That they're lying," said the general, saying what many in the room were thinking.

"What do we do about that?" asked the President, looking around the room.

"Mr. President, if I may," said Dr. Brzezinski.

"Of course, Zbig."

"We should be able to ask for a verification force on the ground to ensure that they're complying with any agreement we put into place. I imagine a simple transfer of inspectors between the forces would allow for us to monitor the situation. Once we've ensured that the Soviets comply, we can move forward with our participation in this 'peacekeeping' force they're proposing."

"If we can put together an on-site inspection agency for the SALT treaty, we should be able to task some of our people to verify this troop movement," said Carter. "I'm not about to abdicate our role as peacemaker in the Middle East if I can help it. We've done too much of the heavy lifting on this to let the Soviets come in and start dictating terms. Donald, do you believe that they'll go forward with this Security Council Resolution without us?"

"Undoubtedly, sir," said the diplomat with a rare show of certainty.

"Very well. I think that says everything we need to know. Secretary Kirkpatrick, I need you to work with Donald's people and get this down in writing. We want inspectors along the German frontier, and we want a permanent withdrawal of troops from Afghanistan. Once you have that written up, I want you two to agree on the best team to send to New York to hammer this out with the Soviets."

****

20 October 1980
Manzariyeh Air Base
Iran

"Hang on, let me get this straight," said Specialist Marlon Reeves. "The Russkies invaded Iran, a US ally. A nation that we happen to be standing in right now. They fought them with military force. They killed Iranian military and civilian personnel. They are currently in control of an entire city, and surrounding areas… and we're supposed to… what? Thank them for it?"

"That's about the size of it," replied Staff Sergeant Watkins. "We're supposed to work with Ivan and sort this whole thing out. We are now a multinational peacekeeping force along with the Soviet Union.

"You have got to be shitting me," replied Reeves.

"I shit you not," said Watkins. "Anyhow, we're going to go meet up with one of our Russki counterparts to figure this out."

"How's that supposed to work?" asked Reeves. "We don't speak Russian."

"Maybe they speak English," suggested Watkins.

"I didn't think about that," said Reeves.

"I'm screwing with you. We're getting a translator, one of the 97Es from the 313th." Watkins was referencing the human intelligence, or HUMINT, collectors from the 313th Military Intelligence Battalion. These were men trained in foreign languages who could act as interrogators in the event that any Soviet prisoners were taken. "We're taking a Jeep over to their place right now." Reeves grabbed his rifle and helmet and the two headed out of the hangar towards the motor pool.

As they drove south down Highway 71, Reeves asked, "Why the hell are they having us go talk to the Russians? Isn't this way above our pay grade?"

"What?" asked Watkins. "Don't tell me this is your first time negotiating an international crisis on behalf of the United States?"

"You're screwing with me," said Reeves.

"That's right. I am," replied Watkins. "Trust me, there have been a ton of talks at the higher levels. We're just the monkeys that have to do what the bigwigs said we'd do. We're supposed to go on joint patrols with these Russkies. So we're going to get our translator, then go meet some Russian grunts."

"I can't think of anything I'd rather do," said Reeves, still clearly skeptical.

Ten minutes later, they pulled up to Baqerabad. There were a few thousand-meter hills to the west where the intel weenies had set up some listening posts. Fortunately for Watkins and Reeves, their charge wasn't off in the boonies. Within five minutes of their hitting the unit HQ, a sergeant came out from the office behind the counter.

"Sergeant Herman Becker, at your service," said the sergeant.

"Okay, Sergeant," said Watkins, "what do you know about today's mission?"

"Just that you need to have a conversation with Ivan, and I'm here to facilitate that conversation." Watkins looked at Reeves.

"Well, la-de-dah, Mr. Smarty-Pants," said Watkins. Becker looked at him, speechless. "I'm screwin' with you," said Watkins. "Come on, get in the Jeep. We'll work things out on the drive to Tehran."

The ride over to Tehran took an hour and a half. Along the way, Reeves grilled Sergeant Becker about language school, and the job itself.

"You've gotta have an aptitude for languages, kid," said Becker.

"How do I know if I have one?" asked Reeves.

"The Army will let you know," laughed Becker. "They have a weird test that shows how well you'll learn new languages." Reeves appeared interested, so Becker continued. "It's the Defense Language Aptitude Battery, or DLAB. It's kind of crazy. In some sections they add new grammar rules to English, then see if you can remember them and apply them to sentences."

"I don't get it. How does that work?" asked Reeves.

"Okay, so let's say the new rule is that you have to add 'ya' before every verb. So the sentence 'I ran to the building' becomes 'I ya-ran to the building.'" Reeves looked confused. "Then, add another rule. Like you need to have two commas to separate independent clauses." Now Reeves was really confused.

"It helps if you understand English first," laughed Staff Sergeant Watkins.

"That's true," agreed Becker. "After all, the test is in English, even if they are modifying it. Plus, if you haven't been able to figure out English after all these years, what hope will you have of figuring out Chinese?"

When they arrived at Mehrabad International Airport, they were picked up by some MPs, who escorted them to their destination. It was one of the many single-story office buildings on the airport grounds. They were ushered into the building, then into an office where two Soviet naval infantrymen awaited them.

"I am Sergeant Lukyan Dmitrievich Lebedev of the Soviet Naval Infantry. I am pleased to meet you," said the taller of the two in English as he extended his hand.

"Sergeant Felix Watkins," said Watkins as he shook the Russian's hand, then to Becker, "I guess we don't need you after all."

"Oh, the second they start speaking Russian, you're going to want me here."

"You speak Russian?" asked Lebedev in Russian.

"*Da*," said Sergeant Becker with a grin.

"That is good," replied Lebedev. "It should help prevent any suspicion between us." With the communication barrier tackled, Sergeants Wilkins and Lebedev compared notes on the conduct of foot patrols and the areas of responsibility between the Soviet and American infantrymen. The whole scene was surreal to Reeves. *These are the communist supersoldiers that we're supposed to be fighting against? They seem like normal dudes.*

Chapter 57

4 November 1980
Sheraton Washington Hotel
Washington, D.C.

The entire ballroom below had already erupted in celebration long before President Carter took the phone call. Governor Reagan had called him once it was clear that even with his home state of California and the few states in the West that had broken his way, there was no hope that he could pull off the upset. Reagan had been magnanimous in his loss. It had occurred to Carter that the man had had several weeks to prepare himself for this defeat, but even so, it must be a crushing rejection to lose a presidential election in such a landslide.

There was only one hint of regret that the governor allowed himself during that phone call. Reagan had said, "If the nation wasn't at war…I think I'd have given you a run for your money." But even with that, the man was quick to offer his full and unwavering support to the Commander-in-Chief. "Anything you need, anything I can give you, Mr. President, it's yours," he had said. Carter smiled as he recalled the conversation, already reminiscing about an event that was only ten minutes in the past.

"We really should head down there," said his wife, Rosalynn.

"Yes, dear, of course. But first I'd like to watch the governor's speech here in the room before we give ourselves to our supporters." It had been a grueling six months, and the campaign wasn't even the worst of it. While Carter believed that he could let loose tonight, he also wanted to take this moment to savor the victory. It wasn't that he wanted to revel in the humiliation of his vanquished opponent. He wanted to experience a shared human moment, a connection that he wouldn't have with any other man for the rest of his life. The two of them had shared the experience of the presidential election process, and tonight that was coming to an end. It was Carter's final campaign, and he knew that this moment would never come again.

He watched as Ronald Reagan took the stage of the Blossom Ballroom in the Roosevelt Hotel in Hollywood. The governor looked very at home in the hotel that had hosted the first-ever Academy Awards presentation. For the first time in his memory, Carter thought Reagan looked his age. The frustration of his campaign in the closing months had taken its toll. Much to Carter's relief, the governor said all the right things. He urged his supporters to accept the result with grace. He promised any and all support to the new administration, though he wasn't sure what he would be able to lend from his ranch in Santa Barbara. He announced his retirement along with his concession. As the also-ran finished his remarks and excused himself from the crowd, President Jimmy Carter turned off the TV and embraced his wife.

"Thank you for everything, Rosa. You know I never would have made it anywhere in life without you," said the most powerful man in the free world. They shared that embrace and the quiet moment that it contained before parting. Carter laughed at the release of pressure that accompanied the end of the campaign and headed to the ballroom to give his victory speech and enjoy the party. They both knew that there wouldn't be many nights like tonight, so long as the nation was at war.

Chapter 58

15 December 1980
Tehran, Iran

"Look, all I'm saying," said Specialist Marlon Reeves, "is that if you had to buy all of your friends a present on your birthday, instead of having all of your friends buy you a present on the day, you'd find out who your real friends were in a hurry."

"I don't know," replied Staff Sergeant Felix Watkins. "How does that even work? Do you buy them all one big gift that they share? Like a motorcycle?"

"No, Sarge. Look, if you were going to buy me a birthday gift, what would it be?"

"A sack of used condoms," replied Watkins. Reeves sighed and brought his hand to his face in exasperation.

"I'd probably get you a bottle of Jack," said Becker, the Russian translator.

"There you go," said Reeves. "So in my scenario, when it's your birthday, you have to buy all of your friends a bottle of Jack, or something like it."

"Damn," said Watkins, "that's a lot of bread. I don't have that kind of scratch on hand most weeks."

"And that, Sergeant, is my point," said Reeves. "You just have to pick and choose, and you get a lot more picky when it's money out of your pocket."

"No, I still think this is a deeply stupid idea, Reeves. Why are we even talking about this?"

"In Soviet Union," said Sergeant Lukyan Lebedev, "one's day of birth is celebrated with one's family. It is a day dedicated to the loved ones who make your life so rich and wonderful." Reeves raised an eyebrow at that. "I do not understand this obsession with material gifts." The Russian shook his head. "It so… capitalistic."

"Is he shitting us, Becker?" asked Reeves.

"The hell if I know," replied Reeves. "They just taught me the language, man. I didn't follow the culture."

Lebedev looked very serious for a moment. Then he cracked a smile and within seconds he was laughing out loud. It took a few seconds, but everyone joined in. Even the other Russians, who didn't speak English. Once the laughter died down, Lebedev explained his trickery to them, which led to a renewed bout of laughter.

Reeves considered the Russians. He wasn't sure what he expected when he first met the enemy. He'd been training for years to kill these men. But when they met in peacetime, it turned out that they weren't the ten-foot-tall supersoldiers the Army had made them out to be. Instead, they were just soldiers. Grunts doing grunt things.

Tonight was a rare time that the men got a twenty-four-hour pass. Instead of patrolling the streets, breaking up fights and enforcing the curfew, they were relaxing with a couple of cases of Budweiser. *These guys live up to the stereotype of the Russian drinker*, he thought.

"Specialist Reeves," said Lebedev, "do you have a cigarette, *pozhaluysta*?"

"Whaddya got in exchange?" asked Reeves.

"Only the promise of international friendship and goodwill," replied the Russian.

"I guess that's all any of us have out here at this point," said Reeves, offering a smoke to Lebedev, who took it gladly. "Why do you guys love Marlboros so much?" he asked.

"Have you ever smoked a Russian cigarette?" asked Lebedev.

"No," replied the American.

"*Erik, Pachka Belomorkanala est'?*"

"*Da, serzhant*," replied the junior sergeant, producing a square pack from his pocket and offering it to Lebedev.

"*Spasibo*," said Lebedev before turning to Reeves. He pulled a cigarette out and offered it. "Please." Reeves took it and brought it to his lips. He snapped his Zippo open and flicked the striker. The flame licked the end of the cigarette, and Reeves took a deep drag.

He immediately started to cough uncontrollably.

"What the hell is that?" he asked. "It tastes like it's been blended with dried dog shit and left out in a warehouse all summer."

"And that, my friend, is why we covet your American cigarettes." Again there was a bout of laughter.

These guys are all right, thought Reeves.

Chapter 59

30 December 1980
Kremlin
Moscow, USSR

KGB Director Yuri Andropov sat next to General Secretary Brezhnev as the gathered ministers quietly talked amongst themselves. Thus far, he and Brezhnev had orchestrated the greatest modernization of the Soviet military since the start of the Great Patriotic War. In this, they believed that they had truly made a leap beyond the Western powers for the first time since the end of that war. They were in a position to overrun the NATO forces that had prevented the spread of the Revolution. They had been building to this day for over a decade, long before the men in this room had decided on this specific course of action.

"Gentlemen, if you please," said Andropov, who then turned to Brezhnev.

"Comrades," began Brezhnev. "Today is a day of great significance. It has been a year since we gathered and agreed on the path that has led us here. During that time, I have asked much of you. You have not disappointed. I am proud of the work that we have done, and I am proud of the bold operation on which we have embarked. The strength of the people is most apparent in the greatest struggles. The power of the collective will of the Soviet people is being tested, and it will prove to be an unstoppable force."

Towards the back end of the long mahogany table, Pyotr Demichev, the Minister of Culture, tried not to smile as he heard the words of his own ministry coming from the General Secretary. It was very unusual for Brezhnev to give grandiose speeches, but this proved to be the exception to that rule. Demichev had been brought into the room where Andropov, Ustinov and Gromyko had prepared this final push to start the gears of war that couldn't be stopped. Demichev had been just on the outside prior to this, but he had seized his opportunity to show his loyalty to the regime. More importantly, he showed his usefulness. He was a man they could count on.

"I ask," continued Brezhnev, "that you continue to show the strength and perseverance you have demonstrated up to this point. Today, we will issue the orders that will free the workers of the world. In the history of tomorrow, they will remember us for the decision we made today. Comrade Andropov, are we ready to initiate Operation Bogatyr?"

"Comrade General Secretary," said Andropov. "Our campaign to pull the Americans out of position has been a success. Our last reports from the field indicate that the Americans have moved most of their ready response units to Nicaragua, and Iran. I will leave the specifics of enemy disposition to Minister Ustinov, but I am pleased to report that the KGB has achieved complete success in our diversion operations."

"Minister Ustinov, if you please," said Brezhnev.

"Yes, Comrade General Secretary," replied Ustinov. "Our forces are in position. The Polish vanguard is prepared to make the initial thrust, and our own Category A units will be ready to exploit the weakness in the enemy defenses once those units are depleted." The Soviets had pulled their guards units back, but only as far as eastern Czechoslovakia. Once the Polish Armored hit the NATO defenses, they would race to the front to exploit the weakened lines, and drive deep into Germany. This was no "Seven Days to the Rhine," as envisioned by many in the staff. This was a methodical assault that would take time, but it would be thorough.

"NATO forces along the frontier have largely remained intact. There has been some attrition from the war in Nicaragua and the increased presence in the Middle East. Additionally, the withdrawal of Turkey from NATO defense commitments has given us some flexibility in our southern theater. The principal advantage that we have when compared to this time last year is the lessened ability of the Americans to react to our assault. We cannot predict what they will do with their forces in Central America, but it will take longer to extract them than it would to mobilize them from their home bases in the United States. As for their 82nd Airborne Division in Iran, with the help of the Iraqi armored forces, we believe we will be able to remove that unit from combat operations within the first forty-eight hours of the war."

That was a bold pronouncement, but it was still shy of what they had hoped at the onset of the plan. The Soviet General Staff had hoped to convince the United States to commit armor to the peacekeeping efforts in Iran; however, that had never materialized. If they had tied up an armored division to go along with the 82nd and not had to commit any Soviet forces, that would have been an absolute coup. As it was, the Americans had questioned the presence of the Soviet forces that had been committed to the peacekeeping mission. The naval infantry forces were ever present, but the VDV Desantniks were few and far between. Any effort to pin down their location was met with a wall of bureaucratic doublespeak. Given this presumed lack of commitment by the Soviets, the Americans were able to resist any calls for heavier units to the mission.

"Our units are in position across the frontier. Our airborne units are prepared and ready to launch. Support units have their orders and will drive forward as soon as we initiate hostilities. In the Far East, our border units are prepared to defend if the Chinese choose to take advantage of our preoccupation in Europe. The Pacific Ocean fleet stands ready to sortie in support of raiding activity, or open hostilities with US allies should Japan choose to enter the war."

"What of Kim Il-sung in Pyongyang?" asked one of the ministers.

"Obviously, we haven't shared our plans with the DPRK," said Andropov. "That said, we believe that once open warfare begins against the West, North Korea will take advantage of the distraction to attack their neighbor to the south. In fact, we are counting on it. When the time comes, we will ensure that they commit."

"Additionally," said Ustinov, reclaiming the conversation, "the Iraqis have requested a naval presence in the Persian Gulf. We have committed to sending a surface strike group. The heavy cruiser *Kirov* is at the heart of the group, and they have passed into the Atlantic. Once hostilities begin, the *Kirov* group will begin combat operations in the Atlantic. The primary goal will be to divert NATO forces from any convoy duties. The *Kirov*'s mission is simply to survive, but if any targets of opportunity can be engaged, all the better. In short, the Ministry of Defense is ready to initiate Operation Bogatyr."

"How do we know that the Americans aren't already following *Kirov* with one of their submarines?" asked Minister Gromyko.

"Oh, we know that they are following us. The first order of business with the *Kirov* Surface Strike Group will be to destroy whatever assets the Americans or NATO have sent to spy on her. If we can't accomplish that feat, we should reconsider the entire plan," said Ustinov with a smile that indicated his utter confidence that the destruction of those forces was a foregone conclusion as far as he was concerned.

The meeting continued with each minister providing their final report on the readiness of their units and people to initiate the operation.

Not a single minister reported less than one hundred percent readiness and success in their preparations. Andropov knew better than to believe that this was completely accurate. Even so, these men knew that their lives, and the continuation of the Soviet state, hung in the balance of this plan. They had committed themselves. The plan would succeed, or they would all be dead.

"Ministers…," said Brezhnev. "Thank you for your reports. We have worked very hard for this moment, and at last it is here. Initiate Operation Bogatyr."

****

31 December 1980
Bechyně, Czechoslovakia

Sergeant Mikhael "Misha" Kozyrev stamped at the cold. He preferred the cold to the blazing hot temperatures of the Afghan summers, but it still took his body a minute to adjust when moving from the heated company ready room to the courtyard. He'd come out to get some fresh air and to think through the total lack of mission or focus that his unit had received since they were secreted out of Kabul back in July.

Junior Sergeant Taras Knyazev, the squad's driver and mechanic, came out of the company building and lit a cigarette as he walked over to Misha.

"It's always the same. The fools are in a damned hurry to get us somewhere so we can wait for them to decide what to do next. Sometimes I think they are just trying to ensure we have a different view on any given month."

"You give the General Staff too much credit, Taras. Nobody cares about your view."

"That's true. I can't deny it." Taras took a long drag from his cigarette while Misha looked towards the west.

"What do you hear, Taras? You're always my ears in our squad. You must have heard something."

"No, Misha, I haven't. I think I find that more frightening than anything else. It's like with wolves. You don't have to worry about them when they're howling. But once they are silent… watch out."

"How are the men responding to the lull?"

"How do soldiers ever respond to a lull? They are bored and they are going to get into trouble. When we were training every day, at least they were worn out. Since we stopped training last week, they are crawling up the walls. If they have to clean the barracks any more, they're going to wear off the paint."

"We must put something together," said Misha. "Tomorrow we'll take the squad on a run. I think the Air Force has set up a simple obstacle course on the south side of the base. We can take a formation run down there and go through the course a few times, then run back."

"They'll whine about it like children, but it'll do them some good," replied Taras.

As the two considered tomorrow's adventure, Corporal Tisha Dezhnyov opened the door to the company room and called out, "Sergeant Kozyrev, you need to get in here quick!" before ducking back into the room and closing the door behind him. Taras and Misha looked at one another for a brief second before breaking into a trot and getting back into the warm building.

Lieutenant Kadtsyn and Captain Sytnikov, the platoon and company commanders respectively, were standing at the front of the briefing area with a map of the inner-German border between them.

"Good of you two to join us," said the captain. Taras and Misha took their seats in the front row of their platoon's section. Looking around the room, Misha noticed that all the officers and NCOs of the 9th Company were present.

"Men, this is why we exist. Tonight we will take the fight to the capitalist oppressors in Germany." The captain made the statement so matter-of-factly that it took Misha a second to comprehend the gravity of it all. "You need to assemble your men quickly and quietly. We'll board the transports in four hours. The 9th Company is tasked with capturing this airfield here"—he pointed to a spot on the map in the central plain of West Germany—"in Giebelstadt, Germany. Our latest intelligence reports show that we can expect light resistance on the ground from the air-defense company stationed there."

That got Misha's attention. It wasn't what he'd said that was so alarming. It was what he hadn't said. They were airborne troops. How were they going to get on the ground if the base was protected by an air-defense company? The Hawk missiles of the Americans would make quick work of the Il-76 transports carrying his men.

"I have been assured that our friends in the VVS will have destroyed the missile sites before we near the airfield," said the captain. That didn't put Misha's mind at ease. Those bastards in the VVS could fly in and out of the combat zone. If they didn't accomplish the mission, they'd get another one. His men, on the other hand, wouldn't. Taras and Tisha (the squad's driver and gunner, respectively) wouldn't even get a quick death, falling to the earth from altitude while entombed in their BMD infantry fighting vehicle.

"The real challenge," continued Captain Sytnikov, "will be holding that base. We will be the lead division in the assault, and our success will ensure that the rest of the regiment will be able to land at the base. The fascists will want to take that airfield back, and we must not allow that. We must hold it until our mechanized forces link up on their way to Wurzburg.

"You will get additional details for individual squad and platoon assignments once we marshal up for loading and departure. This is it, men. This is war against NATO. Go and prepare your men."

Again, those words. Spoken so dispassionately. When Misha had first joined the VDV, he had dreamt of this moment. Never in all of those dreams had the moment been this mundane.

"Well, this is interesting, isn't it?" asked Taras.

"I almost don't know what just happened there," replied Misha. "I mean, we're going to war. But…"

"I think they are just trying to keep everyone calm during these last few hours. If we get jumpy because we're all about to die, someone will mess up. If not by accident, maybe even on purpose. Better to just push this off as 'business as usual' and try to get us into the airplanes with no one puking."

"Damn, I think *I'm* going to puke."

"That's why they told us first. So you don't puke in front of your men, Comrade Sergeant," said Taras, laughing. "Let's get Tisha and head back to the barracks to let everyone know that we're going to die tonight!"

The lieutenant caught up with them as they headed to the platoon barracks.

"Sergeant Kozyrev, are the men of your squad prepared for tonight's mission?" asked the lieutenant. *What the hell kind of question is that?*

thought Misha. *Even if they weren't, I have no choice but to say that they are.*

"Yes, sir," responded Misha. "We have been training for this for months now. Most of my men have seen combat in Afghanistan. I trust them with my life."

"That's good, Sergeant, because tonight you've bet your life that they are ready!" The lieutenant moved on to catch up with his other squad leaders for a similar pep talk.

"And we're betting that those VVS jackasses won't abandon us to the mercy of those missile batteries," said Taras, always a ray of hope in a bleak world.

At the barracks, the rumors of war had made it back to the platoon before the leaders had. Misha could never quite figure that out. The men were gathering their equipment and milling about nervously. Misha knew that it would be critical to occupy their time between now and boarding.

He collected up his squad and told them what he could. There would be a company airborne assault on an airfield. They expected a moderate defense (he lied), and they would get specific squad assignments en route. Once the mission had been passed down, he quizzed his men on their responsibilities with the vehicle and their responsibilities when dismounted. He asked them about their rifles and about the heavy weapons they might have to man during a defense. He kept them answering questions for as long as he could.

A corporal from the Headquarters Platoon rousted the men, and they formed up outside the barracks. They marched to the motor pool as they had so many times in the past. They began the maintenance and operations checks of the BMD and their weapons. Once they had checked and double-checked everything, Misha shook hands with Taras.

"Good luck tonight, my friend," said Misha. "We'll see you on the ground in Germany."

"Try not to piss yourself on the way down," said Taras with a smile. He pulled Misha in and gave him a great bear hug while pounding his back. When they parted, Taras and Tisha climbed the BMD, while Misha formed up his remaining men and linked with the rest of the dismounted company. Once formed, Company 9 marched to the loading zone on the tarmac. As they had practiced countless times, the formation quickly filed up the ramp of the waiting Il-76 in a double column.

Misha reached his assigned spot along the central column of seats in the plane, where he watched to ensure that his men each clipped their static lines and drop bags to the aircraft. Once he'd ensured that his men were secured, he snapped his own line and took his seat.

He ran through the mission in his mind: The recon and security team would freefall into the drop zone to clear out any defenders. Taras and Tisha would then be dropped with the BMDs and the rest of the heavy equipment. Then it would be his turn. The men would drop in from three hundred meters of altitude. When they hit the ground, Misha would form up the squad and retrieve the search receiver from Private Novikov. Misha would use the receiver to locate Taras and Tisha in the BMD. From there, they would form up with the other assault vehicles in the company and drive north to attack the airfield.

Misha looked at the company of Desantniks heading to meet the enemy. It occurred to him that he was among the first people in the world to know that the Third World War had begun.

From Alex Aaronson

I'm so glad to see that you made it this far. I hope that you found *Advance to Contact: 1980* to be a fun, rollercoaster ride to read because it sure was one to write. If you want to continue the adventure and find out what happens to Carlos, Fred, Nancy, and the rest (as well as meet new characters from across the globe) be sure to check out the next book in the Soviet Endgame Series, *Fire and Maneuver: 1981*, on Amazon.

If you can't wait for the next book to come out, please consider joining my mailing list. This will give you access to additional "Soviet Endgame" content, as well as updates and notices for new books, audiobooks and other projects. To join the mailing list, just click visit: https://frontlinepublishinginc.eo.page/alexaaronson

I love interacting with the readers, so please join me on:

Twitter (@alexaaronson80)

Facebook(https://www.facebook.com/alexander.aaronson.102)

Facebook group (if you don't want to be Facebook friends with a stranger!) https://www.facebook.com/groups/833777043807871

Instagram (https://www.instagram.com/authoralexaaronson/)

Or YouTube (https://www.youtube.com/channel/UCCulp1Ru2EkO3pknPcGkb_Q)

If you have a chance, I would greatly appreciate it if you could stop by Amazon, and/or Goodreads and leave a review of this book. It's a very competitive market out there and ratings and reviews are a tremendous help in bringing in new readers. Unless you thought the book sucked, and you just skipped to the end to find out how to contact me to blow up my accounts with hate posts—in that case, please don't review the book.

Finally, if you enjoyed this book, and you haven't checked out the rest of the Frontline family, please takes some time to do so. I'm partial to the Monroe Doctrine series, since I helped write Volumes IV and V, and the Crisis in the Desert series, since I did a little ghostwriting on those. Check them out on Amazon.

Thank you so much for taking the time to read this. Writing this novel has been a dream come true and I hope you stay with me as we continue the journey together

From James Rosone

I have really enjoyed working with Alex Aaronson over the last two years. It has been exciting to see one of my fellow veterans take wings and fly. He has embodied everything that I had hoped would come true when I started this project to mentor other vets in this writing business.

If you'd like to be added to my personal mailing list, you can do so by clicking on this link. This will help you keep informed of any new releases as well as any upcoming promotional deals.

I enjoy connecting with my readers online. If you'd like to connect, you can find me on:

Facebook (https://www.facebook.com/groups/803443733408830)

Twitter: @jamesrosone

Facebook private reader group (https://www.facebook.com/groups/803443733408830)

Our YouTube page is (https://www.youtube.com/channel/UCCExLcHFoPmwC8IKikNsVvg/videos) if you'd like to listen to some author interviews I've conducted of some fellow writers as well as some of our thoughts on the Ukraine war and the performance of the Russian military and how this plays into China, Taiwan, and other topics.

You may want to see what other books I have written. To find a full list, visit frontlinepublishinginc.com

Abbreviation Key

1MC	The main communications channel on a US warship
4MC	The damage control channel on a US warship
AA	Anti-aircraft
AAV	Amphibious Assault Vehicle
AC/DC	An Australian rock band
ACV	Amphibious Combat Vehicle
ADCAP	Advanced Capability Torpedo
AEGIS	Advanced Electronic Guidance and Instrumentation System
AFB	Air Force Base
AGM	Air-to-Ground Missile
AIM	Air Intercept Missile
AK-74	Standard infantry rifle for Soviet and Soviet-aligned forces
AKS-74	A combat rifle used by Soviet Paratroopers
ALICE	All-purpose Lightweight Individual Carrying Equipment
AMTI	Airborne Moving Target Indicator
AN/PAQ-1	A laser designator used by the US military
AN/PRC-77	A man-portable radio used by the US military
AN/PVS-5	Night Vision Goggles
AN/SPS-59	Surface search radar
AN/VRC-12	A medium-sized radio used by the US military
APC	Armored Personnel Carrier
ARM	Anti-Radiation Missile
ASAP	As Soon As Possible
ASW	Anti-Submarine Warfare
ATGM	Anti-tank Guided Missile
AWACS	Airborne Warning and Control System
BLUF	Bottom Line Up Front
BMD	Russian paradropped infantry fighting vehicle
BMP	Russian infantry fighting vehicle
BOHICA	Bend Over, Here It Comes Again
BTR	Russian armored personnel carrier
C & C	Command and Control
CAS	Close Air Support

CIA	Central Intelligence Agency
CIC	Combat Information Center
CCP	Casualty Collection Point
CIWS	Close-In Weapon Systems
CNO	Chief of Naval Operations
CO	Commanding Officer
COMSEC	Communications Security
CRT	Cathode-ray tube
DLAB	Defense Language Aptitude Battery
DMZ	Demilitarized Zone (area along the border of North Korea and South Korea)
DOD	Department of Defense
DOJ	Department of Justice
DPRK	Democratic People's Republic of Korea (North Korea)
ECM	Electronic Countermeasures
ERA	Equal Rights Amendment
ETA	Estimated Time of Arrival
FARP	Forward Arming and Refueling Point
FBI	Federal Bureau of Investigations
FSO	Foreign Service Officer
FUBAR	F***ed Up Beyond All Recognition
GAU-8	A very large rotary cannon fielded by the A-10 Thunderbolt II
GOP	Grand Ole' Party (the Republican Party in the United States)
GQ	General Quarters (battle stations)
GRU	Soviet military intelligence
HE	High-Explosive
HEAT	High-Explosive Anti-tank
HQ	Headquarters
HUMINT	Human Intelligence
IBM	International Business Machines
ICBM	Intercontinental Ballistic Missile
ID	Infantry Division
IFV	Infantry Fighting Vehicle
IR	Infrared
JP-4	A type of jet fuel

KGB	Soviet intelligence service
KH-11	An American photo reconnaissance satellite
KIA	Killed in Action
KPA	Korean People's Army
LAW	Light Antitank Weapon
LCAC	Landing Craft Air Cushion
Lieutenant JG	Lieutenant Junior Grade
LT	Lieutenant
LZ	Landing Zone
MAC	Military Airlift Command
MANPAD	Man-Portable Air-Defense System
MAB	Marine Amphibious Brigade
MAU	Marine Amphibious Unit
MD	Mechanized Division
MP	Military Police
MRLS	Multiple-Rocket Launch System
NATO	North Atlantic Treaty Organization
NCO	Noncommissioned Officer
NMCA	National Military Command Authority
NSA	National Security Agency
NTDS	Naval Tactical Data System
NVG	Night Vision Goggles
OPEC	Organization of Petroleum Exporting Countries
PA	Public Address
PFC	Private First Class
PI	Philippine Islands
PLA	People's Liberation Army (Chinese Army)
PO2	Petty Officer, Second Class
POL	Petroleum, Oil and Lubricants
PR	Public Relations
PT	Physical Training
PVO	Russian Air Defense Forces
PVV-5A	Soviet explosive compound, similar to C-4
QRF	Quick Reaction Force
R & R	Rest and Recreation
RAF	Royal Air Force
RF	Radio Frequency
RHAW	Radar Homing and Warning

RIM	Radar Intercept Missile
ROE	Rules of Engagement
ROK	Republic of Korea (South Korea)
RM3	Radioman, 3rd Class
RP	Rally Point
RPG	Rocket-Propelled Grenade
RPKS	A Soviet light machine gun used by paratroopers
RSO	Regional Security Officer
RTB	Return to Base
RTO	Radio Telephone Operator
RWR	Radar Warning Receiver
S2	Intelligence Officer
S3	Operations Officer
SACEUR	Supreme Allied Commander, Europe
SAG	Surface Action Group
SALT	Strategic Arms Limitation Treaty
SAM	Surface-to-Air Missile
SAS	Special Air Service (British Army Special Forces)
SEAD	Suppression of Enemy Air Defense
SEAL	Sea-Air-Land (Naval Special Warfare Development Group)
SF	Special Forces
SIGINT	Signals Intelligence
Sitrep	Situation Report
SM	Standard Missile
SRBOC	Super Rapid Bloom Offboard Countermeasures
SSES	Ship's Signals Exploitation Space
TASS	Tactical Air Support Squadron
TOW	Tube-launched, Optically tracked, Wire-guided
TRAM	Target Recognition Attack Multi-sensor
UN	United Nations
USSR	Union of Soviet Socialist Republics
VA-##	Naval Attack Squadron
VADS	Vulcan Air Defense System
VDV	Russian Airborne Infantry Forces
VF-##	Naval Fighter Squadron
VLS	Vertical Launching System
VP	Vice President

VTOL	Vertical Take-Off and Landing
XO	Executive Officer

NATO Equipment

A-6e Intruder	US Navy heavy attack aircraft
A-7e Corsair II	USN/USAF light attack aircraft
AH-1 Cobra	Attack helicopter
Austin-Class	Amphibious transport dock
AV-8A Harrier	VTOL attack aircraft
Blue Ridge-Class	Command ship
C-130 Hercules	Medium transport aircraft
C-141 Starlifter	Heavy transport aircraft
CAR-15	Colt automatic rifle used by US Special Forces
CH-46 Sea Knight	Medium transport helicopter
CH-53 Sea Stallion	Heavy transport helicopter
Charles F Adams	Guided missile destroyer
E2C Hawkeye	USN AWACS aircraft
E-3 Sentry	USAF AWACS aircraft
F-14 Tomcat	USN fleet interceptor
F-4 Phantom	US built multi-role fighter
F-5 Freedom Fighter	US built multi-role fighter
Iwo Jima-Class	Amphibious assault ship
JetRanger	Civilian passenger helicopter
Leahy-Class	Guided missile cruiser
M113	Armored personnel carrier
M16	US military standard combat rifle
M-163	VADS air defense vehicle
M1911	.45 caliber handgun
M2	.50 caliber machine gun
M203	40mm grenade launcher
M60	Squad automatic weapon
M60a1 Patton	Main battle tank
M72 LAW	Single-use light antitank weapon
Midway-Class	Aircraft Carrier
Model 37 Shotgun	Tactical shotgun used by US Special Forces
Nimitz-Class	Nuclear aircraft carrier
RF-8 Crusader	Reconnaissance aircraft
SH-2 Seasprite	ASW helicopter

Spruance-Class	Destroyer
Tarawa-Class	Amphibious assault ship
Thomaston-Class	Dock landing ship
UH-1	Utility helicopter

Warsaw Pact Equipment

A-90 Eaglet	Ground effect vehicle
AKS-74	Compact combat rifle used by Soviet paratroopers
An-12 NATO Codename "Cub"	Medium transport aircraft
An-72 NATO Codename "Condor"	Heavy transport aircraft
BMD	Airlift-capable infantry fighting vehicle
BMP	Infantry fighting vehicle
BRDM	Combat reconnaissance/Patrol vehicle
BTR	Amphibious armored personnel carrier
KM	Prototype ground effect vehicle
Mi-24 NATO Codename "Hind	Attack helicopter
Mi-8 NATO Codename "Hip	Transport helicopter
MiG-23 NATO Codename "Flogger	Multi-role fighter
MiG-25 NATO Codename "Foxbat"	Interceptor/reconnaissance aircraft
MiG-27 NATO Codename "Flogger"	Dedicated attack version of the MiG-23
Osa-Class	Missile patrol boat
RPKS-74	Light machine gun used by Soviet paratroopers
SA-8	Surface-to-air missile
Su-20 NATO Codename "Fitter"	Multi-role Aaircraft
Su-25 NATO Codename "Frogfoot"	Medium attack aircraft
T-72	Main battle tank
Tu-16 NATO Codename "Badger"	Medium bomber

Printed in Great Britain
by Amazon